**Praise for Daryl Gregory's *Unpossible*:**

"*Unpossible* is Gregory's first collection. The stories are all quite short, with no time wasted on lumpy exposition or treacly morals, but each one carries all the grim weight and peculiar beauty of his novels, simmered down to a deceptively sweet syrup that goes down easy and then twists in your guts. They poke at complex, difficult notions, not so much trying to answer questions as trying to figure out how to begin asking them . . . These are not comfortable stories, which is a good part of what makes them worth reading."

—*Publishers Weekly*

"Daryl Gregory has emerged as one of the most consistently interesting and yet least predicatable writers of the last decade . . . A writer of startling depth and sensitivity, whose understanding of the delicate machinations of the heart trumps his need for superheroes, or even for neurology."

—Gary K. Wolfe, *Locus*

"Daryl Gregory has found ways to explore the human mind and spirit—for good, bad, or any of the strange places between such absolutes—that seem very much his own in his first collection."

—Faren Miller, *Locus*

"Facts do not begin to describe Daryl. Not describe him, not contain him, not constrain him. Both in person and in his fiction Daryl breaks the paltry bonds of fact. They cannot hold him. . . Read these stories for their human truths, for their inventiveness, for their verve. Most of all, read them for your own pleasure."

—Nancy Kress

"Gregory's short fiction displays certain central obsessions—a keen understanding of cognitive sciences; an interest in families and questions of relationships and maturity; and an obsession with popular culture."

—Chris Roberson

Also by Daryl Gregory

*Pandemonium*
*The Devil's Alphabet*
*Raising Stony Mayhall*

# UNPOSSIBLE

## AND OTHER STORIES

# UNPOSSIBLE

# DARYL GREGORY

FAIRWOOD PRESS
Bonney Lake, WA

**UNPOSSIBLE**
A Fairwood Press Book
November 2011
Copyright © 2011 by Daryl Gregory

All Rights Reserved

Fairwood Press
21528 104th Street Court East
Bonney Lake, WA 98391
www.fairwoodpress.com

Front cover illustration & design by
Antonello Silverini
Book Design by Patrick Swenson

ISBN13: 978-1-933846-43-9
First Fairwood Press Edition: November 2011
Fairwood Hardcover Edition: July 2013
Printed in the United States of America

*For Gary Delafield and Andrew Tisbert*

# Publication History

"Second Person, Present Tense" first appeared in *Asimov's* (Sept 2005)

"Unpossible" first appeared in *F&SF* (Oct 2007)

"Damascus" first appeared in *F&SF* (Sept 2005)

"The Illustrated Biography of Lord Grimm" first appeared in *Eclipse 3* (Nov 2009)

"Gardening at Night" first appeared in *F&SF* (April 2006)

"Glass" first appeared in *Technology Review* (Nov/Dec 2008)

"What We Take When We Take What We Need" first appeared in *Subterranean* (Spring 2010)

"Digital" appears here for the first time

"Persistence" appears here for the first time

"Message from the Bubblegum Factory" first appeared in *Masked* (2010)

"Free, and Clear" first appeared in *F&SF* (Feb 2004)

"Dead Horse Point" first appeared in *Asimov's* (Aug 2007)

"In the Wheels" first appeared in *F&SF* (Aug 1990)

"The Continuing Adventures of Rocket Boy" first appeared in *F&SF* (July 2004)

# CONTENTS

# DARYL GREGORY: FACTS AND OBSESSIONS
## BY NANCY KRESS

Here are the facts: Daryl Gregory's first story appeared in 1990 in the magazine *Fantasy & Science Fiction*. He has since published three novels, *Pandemonium* in 2008, *The Devil's Alphabet* in 2009, and *Raising Stony Mayhall* in 2011. In addition, over a dozen stories have come out in various magazines and anthologies. Daryl lives with his wife Kathy and two children in State College, Pennsylvania.

The problem is that facts do not begin to describe Daryl. Not describe him, not contain him, not constrain him. Both in person and in his fiction Daryl breaks the paltry bonds of fact. They cannot hold him. In person he is exuberant, tireless, eager, one of the last guys in the convention bar and the first to propose another expedition. A former theater major, he is a terrific performer, reading his fiction aloud with verve and animation. If you ever get a chance to hear him read, do so.

In his writing, however, exuberance takes a different turn. Because he is such a good writer, Daryl has all that intensity under control. The result is a cast of characters with a wide range of personalities but one similar quality: When they want something, they want it with every fiber of their fictional souls. What they want differs radically from story to story; as a writer Daryl has a wide range. Sometimes his characters achieve what they want, sometimes they don't, sometimes they do but wish they hadn't. But always that longing is there, sharp as pain.

What do his protagonists long *for?* The usual things: love, glory, adventure, power, to go home again. However, a list like that says nothing about the actual stories, since the list is the same for anything ever written. What matters are a particular author's characters, relationships among characters, obsessions.

Superheroes are an obsession of Daryl's. Many of the stories in this collection are about superheroes with powers beyond the human, although none are the simplistic good-or-evil beings of comic books and movies. Daryl doesn't do simplistic. His Lord Grimm, Soliton, Teresa (aka Lady Justice), Multiplex Man — all have complicated relationships to those around them. In one of my favorite stories, the hilarious and wistful "Unpossible," fictional heroes don't even exist — maybe — but still retain their power to shape our emotional lives. In "The Continuing Adventures of Rocket Boy," which is at once moving and shocking, the longing for superheroes both destroys and liberates the story's characters.

Another of Daryl's obsessions is the limits of the human brain. He explores how much extension is possible for our powers of concentration ("Dead Horse Point"), for our powers of empathy ("Glass"), for our powers of religious vision ("Damascus"). The disturbing "Damascus," another favorite of mine, also deals with another human ability: self-deception.

Whatever a particular story's theme, however, it is always played out in the context of complicated human relationships. Brother and sister, hero and sidekick, mentor and disciple. Daryl is particularly strong on father-son relationships. That fertile subject, with all its complexities of love and rivalry and control, gives birth to "In the Wheels," "The Continuing Adventures of Rocket Boy," and "What We Take When We Take What We Need," the latter closely tied to his novel *The Devil's Alphabet*.

None of these stories is set on a space station or an alien planet. This comes off as not a constraint but as an enrichment, freeing the author to concentrate on that sufficiently exotic creature, *homo sapiens*, in all his sometimes-exotic longing. Doing this fully requires the tropes of both science fiction and fantasy, and Daryl blends them freely, unconstrained by fact. That's because these stories have something else in mind besides the facts, something much more important: truth.

Read these stories for their human truths, for their inventiveness, for their verve. Most of all, read them for your own pleasure. Enjoy.

# SECOND PERSON, PRESENT TENSE

*If you think, "I breathe," the "I" is extra. There is no
you to say "I." What we call "I" is just a swinging door
which moves when we inhale or when we exhale.*
                                    —Shun Ryu Suzuki

*I used to think the brain was the most important organ
in the body, until I realized who was telling me that.*
                                    —Emo Phillips

When I enter the office, Dr. S is leaning against the desk, talking
earnestly to the dead girl's parents. He isn't happy, but when
he looks up he puts on a smile for me. "And here she is," he says, like
a game show host revealing the grand prize. The people in the chairs
turn, and Dr. Subramaniam gives me a private, encouraging wink.

The father stands first, a blotchy, square-faced man with a round,
tight belly he carries like a basketball. As in our previous visits, he
is almost frowning, struggling to match his face to his emotions. The
mother, though, has already been crying, and her face is wide open:
joy, fear, hope, relief. It's way over the top.

"Oh, Therese," she says. "Are you ready to come home?"

Their daughter was named Therese. She died of an overdose almost two years ago, and since then Mitch and Alice Klass have visited this hospital dozens of times, looking for her. They desperately
want me to be their daughter, and so in their heads I already am.

My hand is still on the door handle. "Do I have a choice?" On
paper I'm only seventeen years old. I have no money, no credit
cards, no job, no car. I own only a handful of clothes. And Robierto,
the burliest orderly on the ward, is in the hallway behind me, block-
ing my escape.

Therese's mother seems to stop breathing for a moment. She's a
slim, narrow-boned woman who seems tall until she stands next to
anyone. Mitch raises a hand to her shoulder, then drops it.

As usual whenever Alice and Mitch come to visit, I feel like I've walked into the middle of a soap opera and no one's given me my lines. I look directly at Dr. S, and his face is frozen into that professional smile. Several times over the past year he's convinced them to let me stay longer, but they're not listening anymore. They're my legal guardians, and they have Other Plans. Dr. S looks away from me, rubs the side of his nose.

"That's what I thought," I say.

The father scowls. The mother bursts into fresh tears, and she cries all the way out of the building. Dr. Subramaniam watches from the entrance as we drive away, his hands in his pockets. I've never been so angry with him in my life—all two years of it.


The name of the drug is Zen, or Zombie, or just Z. Thanks to Dr. S I have a pretty good idea of how it killed Therese.

"Flick your eyes to the left," he told me one afternoon. "Now glance to the right. Did you see the room blur as your eyes moved?" He waited until I did it again. "No blur. No one sees it."

This is the kind of thing that gets brain doctors hot and bothered. Not only could no one see the blur, their brains edited it out completely. Skipped over it—left view, then right view, with nothing between—then fiddled with the person's time sense so that it didn't even seem missing.

The scientists figured out that the brain was editing out shit all the time. They wired up patients and told them to lift one of their fingers, move it any time they wanted. Each time, the brain started the signal traveling toward the finger up to 300 milliseconds *before* the patient consciously decided to move it. Dr. S said you could see the brain warming up right before the patient consciously thought, *now*.

This is weird, but it gets weirder the longer you think about it. And I've been thinking about this a lot.

The conscious mind—the "I" that's thinking, hey, I'm thirsty, I'll reach for that cold cup of water—hasn't really decided anything. The signal to start moving your hand has already traveled halfway down your arm by the time *you* even realize *you* are thirsty. *Thought* is an afterthought. By the way, the brain says, we've decided to move your arm, so please have the thought to move it.

The gap is normally 300 milliseconds, max. Zen extends this minutes. Hours.

If you run into somebody who's on Zen, you won't notice much. The person's brain is still making decisions, and the body is still follows orders. You can talk to them, and they can talk to you. You can tell each other jokes, go out for hamburgers, do homework, have sex.

But the person isn't conscious. There is no "I" there. You might as well be talking to a computer. And *two* people on Zen—"you" and "I"—are just puppets talking to puppets.

It's a little girl's room strewn with teenager. Stuffed animals crowd the shelves and window sills, shoulder to shoulder with stacks of Christian rock CDs and hair brushes and bottles of nail polish. Pin-ups from *Teen People* are tacked to the wall, next to a bulletin board dripping with soccer ribbons and rec league gymnastic medals going back to second grade. Above the desk, a plaque titled "I Promise . . ." exhorts Christian youth to abstain from premarital sex. And everywhere taped and pinned to the walls, the photos: Therese at Bible camp, Therese on the balance beam, Therese with her arms around her youth group friends. Every morning she could open her eyes to a thousand reminders of who she was, who she'd been, who she was supposed to become.

I pick up the big stuffed panda that occupies the pride of place on the bed. It looks older than me, and the fur on the face is worn down to the batting. The button eyes hang by white thread—they've been re-sewn, more than once.

Therese's father sets down the pitifully small bag that contains everything I've taken from the hospital: toiletries, a couple changes of clothes, and five of Dr. S's books. "I guess old Boo Bear was waiting for you," he says.

"Boo W. Bear."

"Yes, Boo W!" It pleases him that I know this. As if it proves anything. "You know, your mother dusted this room every week. She never doubted that you'd come back."

*I* have never been here, and *she* is not coming back, but already I'm tired of correcting pronouns. "Well, that was nice," I say.

"She's had a tough time of it. She knew people were talking, probably holding her responsible—both of us, really. And she was worried about them saying things about you. She couldn't stand them thinking that you were a wild girl."

"Them?"

He blinks. "The Church."

Ah. *The Church.* The term carried so many feelings and connotations for Therese that months ago I stopped trying to sort them out. The Church was the red-brick building of the Davenport Church of Christ, and shafts of dusty light through rows of tall, glazed windows shaped like gravestones. The Church was God and the Holy Ghost (but not Jesus—he was personal, separate somehow). Mostly, though, it was the congregation, dozens and dozens of people who'd known her since before she was born. They loved her, they watched out for her, and they evaluated her every step. It was like having a hundred overprotective parents.

I almost laugh. "The Church thinks Therese was wild?"

He scowls, but whether because I've insulted the Church or because I keep referring to his daughter by name, I'm not sure. "Of course, not. It's just that you caused a lot of worry." His voice has assumed a sober tone that's probably never failed to unnerve his daughter. "You know, the church prayed for you every week."

"They did?" I do know Therese well enough to be sure this would have mortified her. She was a pray-er, not a pray-ee.

Therese's father watches my face for the bloom of shame, maybe a few tears. From contrition it should be one small step to confession. It's hard for me to take any of this seriously.

I sit down on the bed and sink deep into the mattress. This is not going to work. The double bed takes up most of the room, with only a few feet of open space around it. Where am I going to meditate?

"Well," Therese's father says. His voice has softened. Maybe he thinks he's won. "You probably want to get changed," he says.

He goes to the door but doesn't leave. I go to the window, but I can feel him there, waiting. Finally the oddness of this makes me turn around.

He's staring at the floor, a hand behind his neck. Therese might have been able to intuit his mood, but it's beyond me.

"We want to help you, Therese. But there's so many things we just don't understand. Who gave you the drugs, why you went off with that boy, why you would—" His hand moves, a stifled gesture that could be anger, or merely frustration. "It's just . . . hard."

"I know," I say. "Me too."

He shuts the door when he leaves, and I push the panda to the floor and flop onto my back in relief. Poor Mr. Klass. He just wants to know if his daughter fell from grace, or was pushed.

When I want to freak myself out, "I" think about "me" thinking about having an "I." The only thing stupider than puppets talking to puppets is a puppet talking to itself.

Dr. S says that nobody knows what the mind is, or how the brain generates it, and nobody *really* knows about consciousness. We talked almost every day while I was in the hospital, and after he saw that I was interested in this stuff—how could I *not* be—he gave me books and we'd talk about brains and how they cook up thoughts and make decisions.

"How do I explain this," he always starts. And then he tries out the metaphors he's working on for his book. My favorite is the Parliament, the Page, and the Queen.

"The brain isn't one thing, of course," he told me. "It's millions of firing cells, and those resolve into hundreds of active sites, and so it is with the mind. There are dozens of nodes in the mind, each one trying to out-shout the others. For any decision, the mind erupts with noise, and that triggers . . . how do I explain this . . . Have you ever seen the British Parliament on C-SPAN?" Of course I had: in a hospital TV is a constant companion. "These members of the mind's parliament, they're all shouting in chemicals and electrical charges, until enough of the voices are shouting in unison. Ding! That's a 'thought,' a 'decision.' The Parliament immediately sends a signal to the body to act on the decision, and at the same time it tells the Page to take the news—"

"Wait, who's the Page?"

He waves his hand. "That's not important right now." (Weeks later, in a different discussion, Dr. S will explain that the Page isn't one thing, but a cascade of neural events in the temporal area of the limbic system that meshes the neural map of the new thought with the existing neural map—but by then I know that "neural map" is just another metaphor for another deeply complex thing or process, and that I'll never get to the bottom of this. Dr. S said not to worry about it, that *nobody* gets to the bottom of it.) "The Page takes the news of the decision to the Queen."

"All right then, who's the Queen? Consciousness?"

"Exactly right! The self itself."

He beamed at me, his attentive student. Talking about this stuff got Dr. S going like nothing else, but he was oblivious to the way I let the neck of my scrubs fall open when I stretched out on the couch. If only I could have tucked the two hemispheres of my brain into a lace bra.

"The Page," he said, "delivers its message to Her Majesty, telling her what the Parliament has decided. The Queen doesn't need to know about all the other arguments that went on, all the other possibilities that were thrown out. She simply needs to know what to announce to her subjects. The Queen tells the parts of the body to act on the decision."

"Wait, I thought the Parliament had already sent out the signal. You said before that you can see the brain warming up before the self even knows about it."

"That's the joke. The Queen announces the decision, and she thinks that her subjects are obeying her commands, but in reality, they have already been told what to do. They're already reaching for their glasses of water."



I pad down to the kitchen in bare feet, wearing Therese's sweatpants and a T-shirt. The shirt is a little tight; Therese, champion dieter and Olympic-level purger, was a bit smaller than me.

Alice is at the table, already dressed, a book open in front of her. "Well, you slept in this morning," she says brightly. Her face is made up, her hair sprayed into place. The coffee cup next to the book is empty. She's been waiting for hours.

I look around for a clock, and find one over the door. It's only nine. At the hospital I slept in later than that all the time. "I'm starved," I say. There's a refrigerator, a stove, and dozens of cabinets.

I've never made my own breakfast. Or any lunch or dinner, for that matter. For my entire life, my meals have been served on cafeteria trays. "Do you have scrambled eggs?"

She blinks. "Eggs? You don't—" She abruptly stands. "Sure. Sit down, Therese, and I'll make you some."

"Just call me 'Terry,' okay?"

Alice stops, thinks about saying something—I can almost hear the clank of cogs and ratchets—until she abruptly strides to the cabinet, crouches, and pulls out a non-stick pan.

I take a guess on which cabinet holds the coffee mugs, guess right, and take the last inch of coffee from the pot. "Don't you have to go to work?" I say. Alice does something at a restaurant supply company; Therese has always been hazy on the details.

"I've taken a leave," she says. She cracks an egg against the edge of the pan, does something subtle with the shells as the yolk squeezes out and plops into the pan, and folds the shell halves into each other. All with one hand.

"Why?"

She smiles tightly. "We couldn't just abandon you after getting you home. I thought we might need some time together. During this adjustment period."

"So when do I have to see this therapist? Whatsisname." My executioner.

"Her. Dr. Mehldau's in Baltimore, so we'll drive there tomorrow." This is their big plan. Dr. Subramaniam couldn't bring back Therese, so they're running to anyone who says they can. "You know, she's had a lot of success with people in your situation. That's her book." She nods at the table.

"So? Dr. Subramaniam is writing one too." I pick up the book. *The Road Home: Finding the Lost Children of Zen.* "What if I don't go along with this?"

She says nothing, chopping at the eggs. I'll be eighteen in four months. Dr. S said that it will become a lot harder for them to hold me then. This ticking clock sounds constantly in my head, and I'm sure it's loud enough for Alice and Mitch to hear it too.

"Let's just try Dr. Mehldau first."

"First? What then?" She doesn't answer. I flash on an image of me tied down to the bed, a priest making a cross over my twisting body. It's a fantasy, not a Therese memory—I can tell the difference. Besides, if this had already happened to Therese, it wouldn't have been a priest.

"Okay then," I say. "What if I just run away?"

"If you turn into a fish," she says lightly, "then I will turn into a fisherman and fish for you."

"What?" I'm laughing. I haven't heard Alice speak in anything but straightforward, earnest sentences.

Alice's smile is sad. "You don't remember?"

"Oh, yeah." The memory clicks. "*Runaway Bunny*. Did she like that?"

Dr. S's book is about me. Well, Zen O.D.-ers in general, but there are only a couple thousand of us. Z's not a hugely popular drug, in the U.S. or anywhere else. It's not a hallucinogen. It's not a euphoric or a depressant. You don't speed, mellow out, or even get high in the normal sense. It's hard to see what the attraction is. Frankly, I have trouble seeing it.

Dr. S says that most drugs aren't about making you feel better, they're about not feeling anything at all. They're about numbness, escape. And Zen is a kind of arty, designer escape hatch. Zen disables the Page, locks him in his room, so that he can't make his deliveries to the Queen. There's no update to the neural map, and the Queen stops hearing what Parliament is up to. With no orders to bark, she goes silent. It's that silence that people like Therese craved.

But the real attraction—again, for people like Therese—is the overdose. Swallow way too much Zen and the Page can't get out for weeks. When he finally gets out, he can't remember the way back to the Queen's castle. The whole process of updating the self that's been going on for years is suddenly derailed. The silent Queen can't be found.

The Page, poor guy, does the only thing he can. He goes out and delivers the proclamations to the first girl he sees.

The Queen is dead. Long live the Queen.

"Hi, Terry. I'm Dr. Mehldau." She's a stubby woman with a pleasant round face, and short dark hair shot with gray. She offers me her hand. Her fingers are cool and thin.

"You called me Terry."

"I was told that you prefer to go by that. Do you want me to call you something else?"

"No . . . I just expected you to make me say my name is 'Therese' over and over."

She laughs and sits down in a red leather chair that looks soft but sturdy. "I don't think that would be very helpful, do you? I can't make you do anything you don't want to do, Terry."

"So I'm free to go."

"Can't stop you. But I do have to report back to your parents on how we're doing."

*My parents.*

She shrugs. "It's my job. Why don't you have a seat and we can talk about why you're here."

The chair opposite her is cloth, not leather, but it's still nicer than anything in Dr. Subramaniam's office. The entire office is nicer than Dr. S's office. Daffodil walls in white trim, big windows glowing behind white cloth shades, tropically colored paintings.

I don't sit down.

"Your job is to turn me into Mitch and Alice's daughter. I'm not going to do that. So any time we spend talking is just bullshit."

"Terry, no one can turn you into something you're not."

"Well then we're done here." I walk across the room—though "stroll" is what I'm shooting for—and pick up an African-looking wooden doll from the bookshelf. The shelves are decorated with enough books to look serious, but there are long open spaces for arty arrangements of candlesticks and Japanese fans and plaques that advertise awards and appreciations. Dr. S's bookshelves are for holding books, and books stacked on books. Dr. Mehldau's bookshelves are for selling the idea of Dr. Mehldau.

"So what are you, a psychiatrist or a psychologist or what?" I've met all kinds in the hospital. The psychiatrists are M.D.'s like Dr. S and can give you drugs. I haven't figured out what the psychologists are good for.

"Neither," she says. "I'm a counselor."

"So what's the 'doctor' for?"

"Education." Her voice didn't change, but I get the impression that the question's annoyed her. This makes me strangely happy.

"Okay, Dr. Counselor, what are you supposed to counsel me about? I'm not crazy. I know who Therese was, I know what she did,

I know that she used to walk around in my body." I put the doll back in its spot next to a glass cube that could be a paperweight. "But I'm not her. This is my body, and I'm not going to kill myself just so Alice and Mitch can have their baby girl back."

"Terry, no one's asking you to kill yourself. Nobody can even make you into who you were before."

"Yeah? Then what are they paying you for, then?"

"Let me try to explain. Please, sit down. Please."

I look around for a clock and finally spot one on a high shelf. I mentally set the timer to five minutes and sit opposite her, hands on my knees. "Shoot."

"Your parents asked me to talk to you because I've helped other people in your situation, people who've overdosed on Z."

"Help them what? Pretend to be something they're not?"

"I help them take back what they *are*. Your experience of the world tells you that Therese was some other person. No one's denying that. But you're in a situation where biologically and legally, you're Therese Klass. Do you have plans for dealing with that?"

As a matter of fact I do, and it involves getting the hell out as soon as possible. "I'll deal with it," I say.

"What about Alice and Mitch?"

I shrug. "What about them?"

"They're still your parents, and you're still their child. The overdose convinced you that you're a new person, but that hasn't changed who they are. They're still responsible for you, and they still care for you."

"Not much I can do about that."

"You're right. It's a fact of your life. You have two people who love you, and you're going to be with each other for the rest of your lives. You're going to have to figure out how to relate to each other. Zen may have burned the bridge between you and your past life, but you can build that bridge again."

"Doc, I don't *want* to build that bridge. Look, Alice and Mitch seem like nice people, but if I was looking for parents, I'd pick someone else."

Dr. Mehldau smiles. "None of us gets to choose our parents, Terry."

I'm not in the mood to laugh. I nod toward the clock. "This is a waste of time."

She leans forward. I think she's going to try to touch me, but she doesn't. "Terry, you're not going to disappear if we talk about what happened to you. You'll still be here. The only difference is that you'll reclaim those memories as your own. You can get your old life back *and* choose your new life."

Sure, it's that easy. I get to sell my soul and keep it too.

I can't remember my first weeks in the hospital, though Dr. S said I was awake. At some point I realized that time was passing, or rather, that there was a me who was passing through time. *I* had lasagna for dinner yesterday, *I* am having meat loaf today. *I* am this girl in a bed. I think I realized this and forgot it several times before I could hold onto it.

Every day was mentally exhausting, because everything was so relentlessly *new*. I stared at the TV remote for a half hour, the name for it on the tip of my tongue, and it wasn't until the nurse picked it up and turned on the TV for me that I thought: *Remote*. And then sometimes, this was followed by a raft of other ideas: *TV. Channel. Gameshow.*

People were worse. They called me by a strange name, and they expected things of me. But to me, every visitor, from the night shift nurse to the janitor to Alice and Mitch Klass, seemed equally important—which is to say, not important at all.

Except for Dr. S. He was there from the beginning, and so he was familiar before I met him. He belonged to me like my own body.

But everything else about the world—the names, the details, the *facts*—had to be hauled into the sunlight, one by one. My brain was like an attic, chock full of old and interesting things jumbled together in no order at all.

I only gradually understood that somebody must have owned this house before me. And then I realized the house was haunted.

After the Sunday service, I'm caught in a stream of people. They lean across the pews to hug Alice and Mitch, then me. They pat my back, squeeze my arms, kiss my cheeks. I know from brief dips into

Therese's memories that many of these people are as emotionally close as aunts or uncles. And any of them, if Therese were ever in trouble, would take her in, feed her, and give her a bed to sleep in.

This is all very nice, but the constant petting has me ready to scream.

All I want to do is get back home and take off this dress. I had no choice but to wear one of Therese's girly-girl extravaganzas. Her closet was full of them, and I finally found one that fit, if not comfortably. She loved these dresses, though. They were her floral print flak jackets. Who could doubt the purity of a girl in a high-necked Laura Ashley?

We gradually make our way to the vestibule, then to the sidewalk and the parking lot, under assault the entire way. I stop trying to match their faces to anything in Therese's memories.

At our car a group of teenagers take turns on me, the girls hugging me tight, the boys leaning into me with half hugs: shoulders together, pelvises apart. One of the girls, freckled with soft red curls falling past her shoulders, hangs back for awhile, then abruptly clutches me and whispers into my ear, "I'm so glad you're okay, Miss T." Her tone is intense, as if she's passing a secret message.

A man moves through the crowd, arms open, smiling broadly. He's in his late twenties or early thirties, his hair cut in a choppy gelled style that's ten years too young for him. He's wearing pressed khakis, a blue Oxford rolled up at the forearms, a checked tie loosened at the throat.

He smothers me in a hug, his cologne like another set of arms. He's easy to find in Therese's memories: This is Jared, the Youth Pastor. He was the most spiritually vibrant person Therese knew, and the object of her crush.

"It's so good to have you back, Therese," he says. His cheek is pressed to mine. "We've missed you."

A few months before her overdose, the youth group was coming back from a weekend-long retreat in the church's converted school bus. Late into the trip, near midnight, Jared sat next to her, and she fell asleep leaning against him, inhaling that same cologne.

"I bet you have," I say. "Watch the hands, *Jared*."

His smile doesn't waver, his hands are still on my shoulders. "I'm sorry?"

"Oh please, you heard me."

He drops his hands, and looks questioningly at my father. He can do sincerity pretty well. "I don't understand, Therese, but if—"

I give him a look that makes him back up a step. At some point later in the trip Therese awoke with Jared still next to her, slumped in the seat, eyes closed and mouth open. His arm was resting between her thighs, a thumb against her knee. She was wearing shorts, and his flesh on hers was hot. His forearm was inches from her warm crotch.

Therese believed that he was asleep.

She believed, too, that it was the rumbling of the school bus that shifted Jared's arm into contact with the crease of her shorts. Therese froze, flushed with arousal and embarrassment.

"Try to work it out, Jared." I get in the car.


The big question I can help answer, Dr. S said, is why there is consciousness. Or, going back to my favorite metaphor, if the Parliament is making all the decisions, why have a Queen at all?

He's got theories, of course. He thinks the Queen is all about storytelling. The brain needs a story that gives all these decisions a sense of purpose, a sense of continuity, so it can remember them and use them in future decisions. The brain can't keep track of the trillions of possible *other* decisions it could have made every moment; it needs one decision, and it needs a who, and a why. The brain lays down the memories, and the consciousness stamps them with identity: *I* did this, *I* did that. Those memories become the official record, the precedents that the Parliament uses to help make future decisions.

"The Queen, you see, is a figurehead," Dr. S said. "She represents the kingdom, but she isn't the kingdom itself, or even in control of it."

"I don't feel like a figurehead," I said.

Dr. S laughed. "Me neither. Nobody does."


Dr. Mehldau's therapy involves occasional joint sessions with Alice and Mitch, reading aloud from Therese's old diaries, and home movies. Today's video features a pre-teen Therese dressed in

sheets, surrounded by kids in bathrobes, staring fixedly at a doll in
a manger.

Dr. Mehldau asks me what Therese was thinking then. Was she
enjoying playing Mary? Did she like being on stage?

"How would I know?"

"Then imagine it. What do you *think* Therese is thinking here?"

She tells me to do that a lot. Imagine what she's thinking. Just
pretend. Put yourself in her shoes. In her book she calls this "reclaim-
ing." She makes up a lot of her own terms, then defines them however
she wants, without research to back her up. Compared to the neurology texts Dr. S lent me, Dr. Mehldau's little book is an Archie comic
with footnotes.

"You know what, Therese was a good Christian girl, so she probably loved it."

"Are you sure?"

The wise men come on stage, three younger boys. They plop
down their gifts and deliver their lines, and the look on Therese's
face is wary. Her line is coming up.

Therese was petrified of screwing up. Everybody would be staring at her. I can almost see the congregation in the dark behind the
lights. Alice and Mitch are out there, and they're waiting for every
line. My chest tightens, and I realize I'm holding my breath.

Dr. Mehldau's eyes on mine are studiously neutral.

"You know what?" I have no idea what I'm going to say next. I'm
stalling for time. I shift my weight in the big beige chair and move
a leg underneath me. "The thing I like about Buddhism is Buddhists
understand that they've been screwed by a whole string of previous
selves. I had nothing to do with the decisions Therese made, the good
or bad karma she'd acquired."

This is a riff I've been thinking about in Therese's big girly bedroom. "See, Therese was a Christian, so she probably thought by
overdosing that she'd be born again, all her sins forgiven. It's the
perfect drug for her: suicide without the corpse."

"Was she thinking about suicide that night?"

"*I don't know*. I could spend a couple weeks mining through
Therese's memories, but frankly, I'm not interested. Whatever she
was thinking, she wasn't born again. I'm here, and I'm still saddled
with her baggage. I am Therese's donkey. I'm a karma donkey."

Dr. Mehldau nods. "Dr. Subramaniam is Buddhist, isn't he?"

"Yeah, but what's . . .?" It clicks. I roll my eyes. Dr. S and I talked about transference, and I know that my crush on him was par for the course. And it's true that I spend a lot of time—still—thinking about fucking the man. But that doesn't mean I'm wrong. "This is not about that," I say. "I've been thinking about this on my own."

She doesn't fight me on that. "Wouldn't a Buddhist say that you and Therese share the same soul? Self's an illusion. So there's no rider in charge, no donkey. There's just *you*."

"Just forget it," I say.

"Let's follow this, Terry. Don't you feel you have a responsibility to your old self? Your old self's parents, your old friends? Maybe there's karma you *owe*."

"And who are you responsible to, Doctor? Who's your patient? Therese, or me?"

She says nothing for a moment, then: "I'm responsible to you."

You.

You swallow, surprised that the pills taste like cinnamon. The effect of the drug is intermittent at first. You realize that you're in the back seat of a car, the cellphone in your hand, your friends laughing around you. You're talking to your mother. If you concentrate, you can remember answering the phone, and telling her which friend's house you're staying at tonight. Before you can say goodbye, you're stepping out of the car. The car is parked, your phone is away—and you remember saying goodnight to your mother and riding for a half hour before finding this parking garage. Joelly tosses her red curls and tugs you toward the stairwell: *Come on, Miss T!*

Then you look up and realize that you're on the sidewalk outside an all-ages club, and you're holding a ten dollar bill, ready to hand it to the bouncer. The music thunders every time the door swings open. You turn to Joelly and—

You're in someone else's car. On the Interstate. The driver is a boy you met hours ago, his name is Rush but you haven't asked if that's his first name or his last. In the club you leaned into each other and talked loud over the music about parents and food and the difference between the taste of a fresh cigarette in your mouth and the smell of stale smoke. But then you realize that there's a cigarette in your mouth, you took it from Rush's pack yourself, and you don't like cigarettes. Do you like it now? You don't know. Should you take it out, or keep smoking? You scour your memories, but can discover no reason why you decided to light the cigarette, no reason why you got into the car with this boy. You start to tell yourself a story: he must be a trustworthy person, or you wouldn't have gotten into the car. You took that one cigarette because the boy's feelings would have been hurt.

You're not feeling like yourself tonight. And you like it. You take another drag off the cigarette. You think back over the past few hours, and marvel at everything you've done, all without that constant weight of self-reflection: worry, anticipation, instant regret. Without the inner voice constantly critiquing you.

Now the boy is wearing nothing but boxer shorts, and he's reaching up to a shelf to get a box of cereal, and his back is beautiful. There is hazy light outside the small kitchen window. He pours Froot Loops into a bowl for you, and he laughs, though quietly because his mother is asleep in the next room. He looks at your face and frowns. He asks you what's the matter. You look down, and you're fully dressed. You think back, and realize that you've been in this boy's apartment for hours. You made out in his bedroom, and the boy took off his clothes, and you kissed his chest and ran your hands along his legs. You let him put his hand under your shirt and cup your breasts, but you didn't go any further. Why didn't you have sex? Did he not interest you? No—you were wet. You were excited. Did you feel guilty? Did you feel ashamed?

What were you thinking?

When you get home there will be hell to pay. Your parents will be furious, and worse, they will pray for you. The entire church will pray for you. Everyone will *know*. And no one will ever look at you the same again.

Now there's a cinnamon taste in your mouth, and you're sitting in the boy's car again, outside a convenience store. It's afternoon. Your cell phone is ringing. You turn off the cell phone and put it back in your purse. You swallow, and your throat is dry. That boy—Rush—is buying you another bottle of water. What was it you swallowed? Oh, yes. You think back, and remember putting all those little pills in your mouth. Why did you take so many? Why did you take another one at all? Oh, yes.

*

Voices drift up from the kitchen. It's before 6 a.m., and I just want to pee and get back to sleep, but then I realize they're talking about me.

"She doesn't even *walk* the same. The way she holds herself, the way she talks . . ."

"It's all those books Dr. Subramaniam gave her. She's up past one every night. Therese never read like that, not *science*."

"No, it's not just the words, it's how she *sounds*. That low voice—" She sobs. "Oh hon, I didn't know it would be this way. It's like she's right, it's like it isn't her at all."

He doesn't say anything. Alice's crying grows louder, subsides. The clink of dishes in the sink. I step back, and Mitch speaks again.

"Maybe we should try the camp," he says.

"No, no, no! Not yet. Dr. Mehldau says she's making progress. We've got to—"

"Of course she's going to say that."

"You said you'd try this, you said you'd give this a chance." The anger cuts through the weeping, and Mitch mumbles something apologetic. I creep back to my bedroom, but I still have to pee, so I make a lot of noise going back out. Alice comes to the bottom of the stairs. "Are you all right, honey?"

I keep my face sleepy and walk into the bathroom. I shut the door and sit down on the toilet in the dark.

*What fucking camp?*


"Let's try again," Dr. Mehldau said. "Something pleasant and vivid."

I'm having trouble concentrating. The brochure is like a bomb in my pocket. It wasn't hard to find, once I decided to look for it. I want to ask Dr. Mehldau about the camp, but I know that once I bring it into the open, I'll trigger a showdown between the doctor and the Klasses, with me in the middle.

"Keep your eyes closed," she says. "Think about Therese's tenth birthday. In her diary, she wrote that was the best birthday she'd ever had. Do you remember Sea World?"

"Vaguely." I could see dolphins jumping—two at a time, three at a time. It had been sunny and hot. With every session it was getting easier for me to pop into Therese's memories. Her life was on DVD, and I had the remote.

"Do you remember getting wet at the Namu and Shamu show?"

I laughed. "I think so." I could see the metal benches, the glass wall just in front of me, the huge shapes in the blue-green water. "They had the whales flip their big tail fins. We got drenched."

"Can you picture who was there with you? Where are your parents?"

There was a girl, my age, I can't remember her name. The sheets of water were coming down on us and we were screaming and laughing. Afterward my parents toweled us off. They must have been sitting up high, out of the splash zone. Alice looked much younger: happier, and a little heavier. She was wider at the hips. This was before she started dieting and exercising, when she was Mom-sized.

My eyes pop open. "Oh God."

"Are you okay?"

"I'm fine—it was just . . . like you said. Vivid." That image of a younger Alice still burns. For the first time I realize how *sad* she is now.

"I'd like a joint session next time," I say.

"Really? All right. I'll talk to Alice and Mitch. Is there anything in particular you want to talk about?"

"Yeah. We need to talk about Therese."


Dr. S says everybody wants to know if the original neural map, the old Queen, can come back. Once the map to the map is lost, can you find it again? And if you do, then what happens to the new neural map, the new Queen?

"Now, a good Buddhist would tell you that this question is unimportant. After all, the cycle of existence is not just between lives. *Samsara* is every moment. The self continuously dies and recreates itself."

"Are you a good Buddhist?" I asked him.

He smiled. "Only on Sunday mornings."

"You go to church?"

"I golf."

*

There's a knock and I open my eyes. Alice steps into my room, a stack of folded laundry in her arms. "Oh!"

I've rearranged the room, pushing the bed into the corner to give me a few square feet of free space on the floor.

Her face goes through a few changes. "I don't suppose you're praying."

"No."

She sighs, but it's a mock-sigh. "I didn't think so." She moves around me and sets the laundry on the bed. She picks up the book there, *Entering the Stream*. "Dr. Subramaniam gave you this?"

She's looking at the passage I've highlighted. *But loving kindness—maitri—toward ourselves doesn't mean getting rid of anything. The point is not to try to change ourselves. Meditation practice isn't about trying to throw ourselves away and become something better. It's about befriending who we already are.*

"Well." She sets the book down, careful to leave it open to the same page. "That sounds a bit like Dr. Mehldau."

I laugh. "Yeah, it does. Did she tell you I wanted you and Mitch to be at the next session?"

"We'll be there." She works around the room, picking up T-shirts and underwear. I stand up to get out of the way. Somehow she manages to straighten up as she moves—righting books that had fallen over, setting Boo W. Bear back to his place on the bed, sweeping an empty chip bag into the garbage can—so that as she collects my dirty laundry she's cleaning the entire room, like the Cat in the Hat's cleaner-upper machine.

"Alice, in the last session I remembered being at Sea World, but there was a girl next to me. Next to Therese."

"Sea World? Oh, that was the Hammel girl, Marcy. They took you to Ohio with them on their vacation that year."

"Who did?"

"The Hammels. You were gone all week. All you wanted for your birthday was spending money for the trip."

"You weren't there?"

She picks up the jeans I left at the foot of the bed. "We always meant to go to Sea World, but your father and I never got out there."

*

"This is our last session," I say.

Alice, Mitch, Dr. Mehldau: I have their complete attention.

The doctor, of course, is the first to recover. "It sounds like you've got something you want to tell us."

"*Oh* yeah."

Alice seems frozen, holding her self in check. Mitch rubs the back of his neck, suddenly intent on the carpet.

"I'm not going along with this anymore." I make a vague gesture. "Everything: the memory exercises, all this imagining of what Therese felt. I finally figured it out. It doesn't matter to you if I'm Therese or not. You just want me to think I'm her. I'm not going along with the manipulation anymore."

Mitch shakes his head. "Honey, you took a *drug*." He glances at me, looks back at his feet. "If you took LSD and saw God, that doesn't mean you really saw God. Nobody's trying to manipulate you, we're trying to *undo* the manipulation."

"That's bullshit, Mitch. You all keep acting like I'm schizophrenic, that I don't know what's real or not. Well, part of the problem is that the longer I talk to Dr. Mehldau here, the more fucked up I am."

Alice gasps.

Dr. Mehldau puts out a hand to soothe her, but her eyes are on me. "Terry, what your father's trying to say is that even though you feel like a new person, there's a *you* that existed before the drug. That exists now."

"Yeah? You know all those O.D.-ers in your book who say they've 'reclaimed' themselves? Maybe they only *feel* like their old selves."

"It's *possible*," she says. "But I don't think they're fooling themselves. They've come to accept the parts of themselves they've lost, the family members they've left behind. They're people like you." She regards me with that standard-issue look of concern that doctors pick up with their diplomas. "Do you really want to feel like an orphan the rest of your life?"

"What?" From out of nowhere, tears well in my eyes. I cough to clear my throat, and the tears keep coming, until I smear them off on my arm. I feel like I've been sucker punched. "Hey, look Alice, just like you," I say.

"It's normal," Dr. Mehldau says. "When you woke up in the hospital, you felt completely alone. You felt like a brand new person, no family, no friends. And you're still just starting down this road. In a lot of ways you're not even two years old."

"*Damn* you're good," I say. "I didn't even see that one coming."

"Please, don't leave. Let's—"

"Don't worry, I'm not leaving yet." I'm at the door, pulling my backpack from the peg by the door. I dig into the pocket, and pull out the brochure. "You know about this?"

Alice speaks for the first time. "Oh honey, no . . ."

Dr. Mehldau takes it from me, frowning. On the front is a nicely posed picture of a smiling teenage boy hugging relieved parents. She looks at Alice and Mitch. "Are you considering this?"

"It's their big stick, Dr. Mehldau. If you can't come through for them, or I bail out, *boom*. You know what goes on there?"

She opens the pages, looking at pictures of the cabins, the obstacle course, the big lodge where kids just like me engage in "intense group sessions with trained counselors" where they can "recover their true identities." She shakes her head. "Their approach is different than mine . . ."

"I don't know, doc. Their *approach* sounds an awful lot like 're-claiming.' I got to hand it to you, you had me going for awhile. Those visualization exercises? I was getting so good that I could even visualize stuff that never happened. I bet you could visualize me right into Therese's head."

I turn to Alice and Mitch. "You've got a decision to make. Dr. Mehldau's program is a bust. So are you sending me off to brainwashing camp or not?"

Mitch has his arm around his wife. Alice, amazingly, is dry-eyed. Her eyes are wide, and she's staring at me as if I'm a stranger.


It rains the entire trip back from Baltimore, and it's still raining when we pull up to the house. Alice and I run to the porchstep, illuminated by the glare of headlights. Mitch waits until Alice unlocks the door and we move inside, and then pulls away.

"Does he do that a lot?" I ask.

"He likes to drive when he's upset."

"Oh." Alice goes through the house, turning on lights. I follow her into the kitchen.

"Don't worry, he'll be all right." She opens the refrigerator door and crouches down. "He just doesn't know what to do with you."

"He wants to put me in the camp, then."

"Oh, not that. He just never had a daughter who talked back to him before." She carries a Tupperware cake holder to the table. "I made carrot cake. Can you get down the plates?"

She's such a small woman. Face to face, she comes up only to my chin. The hair on the top of her head is thin, made thinner by the rain, and her scalp is pink.

"I'm not Therese. I never will be Therese."

"Oh I know," she says, half sighing. And she does know it; I can see it in her face. "It's just that you look so much like her."

I laugh. "I can dye my hair. Maybe get a nose job."

"It wouldn't work, I'd still recognize you." She pops the lid and sets it aside. The cake is a wheel with icing that looks half an inch thick. Miniature candy carrots line the edge.

"Wow, you made that before we left? Why?"

Alice shrugs, and cuts into it. She turns the knife on its side and uses the blade to lever a huge triangular wedge onto my plate. "I thought we might need it, one way or another."

She places the plate in front of me, and touches me lightly on the arm. "I know you want to move out. I know you may never want to come back."

"It's not that I—"

"We're not going to stop you. But wherever you go, you'll still be my daughter, whether you like it or not. You don't get to decide who loves you."

"Alice . . ."

"Shssh. Eat your cake."

# UNPOSSIBLE

Two in the morning and he's stumbling around in the attic, lost in horizontal archaeology: the further he goes, the older the artifacts become. The stuttering flashlight guides him past boxes of Christmas decorations and half-dead appliances, past garbage bags of old blankets and outgrown clothing stacked and bulging like black snowmen, over and around the twenty-year-old rubble of his son's treasures: Tonka trucks and science fair projects, soccer trophies and summer camp pottery.

His shoulder brushes against the upright rail of a disassembled crib, sends it sliding, and somewhere in the dark a mirror or storm window smashes. The noise doesn't matter. There's no one in the house below him to disturb.

Twenty feet from the far wall his way is blocked by a heap of wicker lawn furniture. He pulls apart the barricade piece by piece to make a narrow passage and scrapes through, straws tugging at his shirt. On the other side he crawls up and onto the back of a tilting oak desk immovable as a ship run aground.

The territory ahead is littered with the remains of his youth, the evidence of his life before he brought his wife and son to this house. Stacks of hardcover books, boxes of dusty-framed elementary school pictures—and toys. So many toys. Once upon a time he was the boy who didn't like to go outside, the boy who never wanted to leave his room. The Boy Who Always Said No.

Against the far wall, beside a rickety shelf of dried-out paint cans and rusting hardware, a drop cloth covers a suggestive shape. He picks his way through the crowded space. When he pulls aside the cloth, he grunts as if he's been elbowed in the stomach—relief and dread and wrenching sadness competing for the same throat.

Dust coats the Wonder Bike's red fenders, rust freckles its handlebars. The white-walled tires are flat, and stuffing sprouts from cracks in the leather saddle. But it's still here, still safe. And the two accessories he most needs, the things he'd almost convinced himself he'd imagined, are fastened to their places on the swooping crossbar:

the five-pronged gearshift like a metal hand; and the glass-covered compass, its face scuffed white but uncracked.

The bike's heavier than he remembers, all old-fashioned steel, more solid than anything they'd bother to make today. He heaves it onto his shoulder and makes his way toward the attic door, handlebars snagging on unseen junk, errant wheels triggering miniature avalanches. Sweat pours down his back. He thinks about heart attacks. He's 56 now, a middle-aged man if he lives to a hundred and twelve. People younger than he die all the time. All the time.

The weight of the bike drags him down the attic stairs. He wheels it whinging down the hall, then out the front door and across the frost-crackled lawn, aiming for the realtor sign. The sweat on his neck turns cold. Along the street his neighbors' houses are all dark. The moon stays tucked into its bed of clouds. He's grateful for the privacy. He lifts the front wheel and runs over the FOR SALE sign, flattens it.

In the garage he sets to work removing the accessories. The screws are rusted into place, so he puts aside the screwdriver and plugs in the power drill. The shifter comes free, but the screws holding the compass are stripped, spinning uselessly. He can't risk hammering it off, so he works a hacksaw blade between the handlebars and the bottom of the device and cuts it free. Gently he sets the Wonder Bike against the garage wall and gets into the car.

It takes much less time to attach the accessories to the dash. He screws them directly into the plastic, side by side above the radio.

He starts the engine and stares out the dirt-streaked windshield, trying to remember what to do next. It used to be automatic: pedal hard, thumb the gears, follow the compass. But something happened when he turned thirteen. He lost the knack and the bike stopped working for him. Or maybe, he's been thinking lately, he stopped working for the bike.

He sets the DeShifter to NOT RECOMMENDED. He taps the glass of the UnCompass and the needle quivers, stuck between UNFAMILIAR and UNKNOWN.

Sounds about right, he thinks.


Even with the compass it takes determination to get lost. He drives south out of town, past the tangle of interstate exchanges, toward the green empty parts of the map. He turns down the first road he doesn't recognize. He pays no attention to street names; he looks away when signs appear in his headlights.

Soon there are no signs. Forest swallows the highway. Switchbacks and the skulking moon conspire with him to disguise his direction.

Don't look in the rearview mirror, he tells himself. No trail of bread crumbs. As soon as he thinks of the road behind him, he realizes he left the front door of the house wide open. Maybe by morning robbers will have emptied the place. That would make it easier on the real estate agents. Too much clutter, they'd told him. They couldn't see that the home had been gutted a year ago.

He rolls down the window and lets the cold wind buffet him. When did he fall out of love with speed? He'd had adventures once. He'd rescued the Pumpkinhead Boys, raced the moto-crows, reunited the shards of the Glass Kingdom. His quick thinking had outwitted the Hundred Mayors of Stilt Town.

He nudges the DeShifter past INADVISABLE to ABSOLUTELY NOT and accelerates. The road ahead doesn't exist until it appears under his headlights; he's driving a plow of light through the dark, unrolling the road before him like a carpet.

A tiny yellow sign flashes past his right fender, too fast for him to read. He glances sideways—nothing but the dark—and turns back to the road just as the little purple house appears in his lights like a phantom.

The structure strikes the grille and explodes into a thousand pieces. The windshield pocks with white stars. He stomps on the brake and the car bucks, slides sideways. He jerks the wheel back to the right and suddenly the car's off the road, jouncing across ground. He bounces against the roof, ragdolling, unable to hold onto the wheel. The car bangs sideways against something invisible and immovable and then everything stops.

He stares out the cratered windshield. The engine coughs politely, shudders, and dies.

The DeShifter shows COMPLETELY OUT OF THE QUESTION. The UnCompass needle points straight at UNPOSSIBLE.

Later—he's as unsure of time as he is of location—he forces the car door open, pushing against tree limbs and thick brush, and climbs out and down. The driver-side wheels are two feet in the air. Trees surround the car as if they'd grown up around it.

He walks up a slight incline to the road, his pulse driving a headache deeper into his temples. The muscles of his neck burn; his chest aches where the seatbelt cut into him.

The surface of the road is littered with shattered plywood—and bits of silver. He stoops, drumming fresh pain into his head, and picks up a dime. There are coins all over the roadway.

The only thing remaining of the tollbooth is another of the child-sized yellow signs, miraculously erect: PLEASE HAVE YOUR DESTINATION IN MIND.

He drops the dime into his pocket and starts walking.

A farmhouse squats in the middle of the highway like a great toad, filling both lanes. He walks toward it in the inconstant moonlight, horrified. If he hadn't struck the tollbooth, he'd have slammed into the house at eighty miles per hour.

On closer inspection the house looks like it's been dropped there from a great height. Walls are askew, their wooden siding bowed, splintered, or blown out completely. Roofs cant at contrary angles.

He steps onto the porch and floorboards creak and shift under his weight like unstable ice. High-pitched barking erupts from inside. He knocks on the door and waits, hunched and shivering. A minute passes. The dog—a small, hyperactive thing by the sound of it—barks and barks.

He crouches next to the closest window but gauzy curtains obscure the view. He makes out a lamp, the suggestion of a couch, a dark rectangle that could be a bookshelf or a wardrobe. His teeth are on the edge of chattering.

He knocks again and sends the dog into fresh vocal frenzy. He considers trying the doorknob. It's warm in there. There could be a phone. How big can the dog be?

He backs off the porch and walks around the side of the house. It's nearly pitch black back there; the roof blocks the moon, and the windows at the back of the house, if there are windows at all, are unlit. He can't even tell if the road continues on the other side. He moves in what he thinks is an arc, feeling for the scrape of pavement under his shoes, when suddenly he bangs his toes against something low and hard and stumbles forward. He catches his balance—and freezes, realizing where he's standing. He's in the middle of train tracks.

He doesn't hear anything, doesn't see anything but the eye-swallowing dark. Slowly he steps back over the rails, a chill in his stomach even though he'd see a train coming for miles.

The dog resumes barking, and the sound is different somehow. He circles around to the front of the house and sees that the front door is open now, light spilling around some dark shape filling the doorway.

"Hello?" he says. He holds out his hands as he steps toward the door. "I—I had a slight accident. A couple miles down the road."

"You came by car?" A woman's voice, low and rasping.

"I had an accident," he says again. "If you've got a phone, I could call someone . . ."

"The road's closed to your type." He's not sure if she's warning him or merely stating fact. Her shadow recedes. After a moment he approaches the door.

The dog, a tiny black terrier with an age-whitened snout, lies in a towel-lined wicker basket a few feet from the door. It bares its teeth at him and growls, but makes no move to leave its bed. He steps inside the room.

The woman's already sitting, leaning back in an old leather armchair the color of dried mud. The light is behind her so again her face is in shadow. She crosses her legs, sharp white shins over blood-red slippers. She pulls a foil pack from the pocket of her blue-checked house dress and taps out a cigarette.

He folds his arms across his chest and tries to stop shivering. At least the house is warm. He looks around for a phone but knows he won't find one—it's not that kind of house. It's been a long time, but the old instincts are coming back. He smiles thinly. "And what type would that be, ma'am?"

"Storm-chaser," she says. "Wardrobe-jumper." She flicks a cheap plastic lighter and holds the flame to the cigarette. "Mirror shards sticking to your coat, twigs in your hair. Little hard to squeeze that big ol' man-body through the hedgerow, eh?"

"You don't know me. You don't know who I am."

"Oh my goodness, you must be the *special* one," she says in mock recognition. "You must be the only traveler to see *lands beyond*." She taps cigarette ash onto the braided rug. "Let me guess—enchanted sailboat? Magic choo-choo train? Oh, that's right, you're a driver—electric kiddie car, then. The tollbooth boy."

"I had a bicycle," he says. "The most wonderful—"

She groans. "Spare me." She inhales on her cigarette, shakes her head. "At least you got rid of it. Most of you can't find your way back without the props." She sees his frown and laughs. Smoke spills from her mouth and hazes the lights.

"You think you're the first one to try to sneak back in?" she says. "You're not even the first one *tonight*." She laughs again. "Boo-hoo-hoo, my wife left me, whaaa, my daughters hate me. Life is meaningless, I'm gonna kill myself."

"I don't have a daughter," he says. "And my wife didn't leave me." But of course she did. She left him in the most absolute way, leaving behind a note like a set of driving directions, like a travel brochure to an exotic country. Two years later to the day, their son followed her. Tonight, come to think of it, is the anniversary of their deaths.

He takes a breath. "I'm just looking for a way back."

"Please. You couldn't find your shadow if it was stapled on. You think you can just waltz right back in there nursing your disappointments and diseases, your head stuffed full of middle-age sex fantasies and mortgage payments? You'd ruin everything. You'd stink the place up."

"You don't understand," he says. "I only need—"

"Stink. It. Up." She makes a tired shooing gesture. "Go home, you greedy little boy. No second helpings. You ought to be ashamed of yourself."

This is a test, he thinks. She's trying to throw him off, weigh him down with doubt and discouragement. He's met such trials before, and persevered. Once upon a time he was The Boy Who Always Said No.

As if in confirmation he hears a distant bell, a cheery *ding ding!* He recognizes that sound. He strides out of the room, into the dark kitchen, and flips open the hook to the back door.

"You'll never get on!" the woman calls. The dog begins to bark.

The dark, to his light-adjusted eyes, seems almost solid. He stops a few feet from the house and listens. The trolley must be close by. The little bell sounds again, but he can't tell if it's growing closer or more distant.

He moves forward slowly, arms out, feet sliding forward. The track is only a few yards from the house, he's sure of it. His feet drag through the unseen grass. After a few minutes he glances back, but now the house is gone as well. He turns in place, eyes wide. There's no sound, not even barking. A dank, dead-fish scent twists in the air.

When he completes his circle he notices a dark, fuzzed shape in the distance, barely distinguishable against a black sky edging toward indigo. It's the first hint since he left the attic that the night is not endless. He doesn't know what it is in the distance, but he recognizes the shape for what it is: unfamiliar, unknown.

The little boat lies at the bottom of the empty seabed, abandoned midway between the shore and the island. Sandy mud sucks at his shoes. He walks toward the boat, past stacks of smooth-headed boulders and stinking saltwater puddles in the shape of great clawed feet. He walks under a sky the color of pencil lead.

The island is shaped like a bowler hat. If not for the trees—a handful of curve-backed palms with outrageously broad leaves—and for the hunched figure silhouetted at the very crown of the hill, he'd have thought the island was huge but miles away. Instead he can see that it's ridiculously small, like a cartoon desert island.

He reaches the boat and rests a hand on the gunwales. The inside of the boat is an unmade bed, a white pillow and blue blankets and white sheets. Foot-shaped holes, human-size, stamp away from the boat toward the island. He follows them across the drained sea to the rim of the island, where his predecessor's mud-laden feet begin to print the grass. The trail leads up the slope, between bushes tinged yellow and brown. Only a few of the palm trees are standing; dozens of others are uprooted and lying on the ground, or else split and bent, as if savaged by a hurricane.

He climbs, breath ragged in his throat. The man at the top of the hill is facing away, toward the lightening sky. On his back is some kind of white fur shawl—no, a suit like a child's footie pajamas, arms tied around his neck. The yawning hood is a wolf's head that's too small for his grown-man's head.

He's huffing, making a lot of noise as he approaches, but the man with the wolf suit doesn't turn around.

When he's caught his breath he says, "Beautiful, isn't it?"

Above them the sky is fitful gray, but across the vast, empty sea in the land beyond, sunlight sparkles on the crystal minarets of the Glassine Palace. A great-winged roc dangling a gondola from its claws flaps toward its next fare. The rolling hills beyond the city are golden and ripe for harvest. It's all as he remembers.

"Look at those wild things go," the man in the wolf suit says. Who knows what he's seeing?

The sun crawls higher, but the clouds above the hill refuse to disperse. He glances at the man in the wolf suit, looks away. Tears have cut tracks down his muddy and unshaven face. The wolf man's older than him, but not by much.

What did the woman in the house say? *Not even the first one tonight.*

He nods at the man's wedding ring and says, "Can't take it off either?"

The man frowns at it. "Left me six months ago. I had it coming for years." He smiles faintly. "Couldn't quite stop making mischief. You?"

"She died a few years ago." But the damage hadn't stopped there, had it? He tilts his head, a half shrug. "Depression runs in her family."

"Sorry to hear that." He slowly shakes his head, and the upside-down wolf's head wags with him. "It's a disaster out there. Every day like an eraser. Days into months, months into years—gone, gone, gone." The man in the wolf suit stares at him without blinking. "Tell me I'm wrong. Tell me you were having a happy ending."

"No." He almost grins. "Not even close." But was that true? He'd had a dozen happy endings. A score of them.

Together they stare across the ocean of mud and squint into the brightness beyond.

"We can't get back in there," he says to the man with the suit. He's surprised by his certainty. But he can't imagine tracking that muck across the crystal streets. "And we can't stay here." He rubs a hand across his mouth. "Come with me."

The man doesn't answer.

"I could make you leave."

The man in the wolf suit laughs. "Don't you know who I am?" he says. "I'm their king!"

"No," he says. "Not anymore." He grips the edges of the white fur and yanks it over the man's head and off, quick as a magic trick. "I'm the king now."

He runs down the hill holding the suit above his head like a flag. The man roars a terrible roar. It's a chase down to the sea's edge and then they're tumbling in the muck, wrapped up and rolling like bear cubs, choking and half-blinded in mud. Hands claw for the suit. They tug it back and forth, the cloth rasping as threads stretch and tear. Then the zipper snaps and they fall away from each other, splash down on their asses.

They look at each other, too winded to get up.

The man clutches the scrap of fur he's regained. It's not white anymore. "Why'd you *do* that?" he says.

He's not sure. He flicks mud from his hands, wipes a hand clean on the inside of his shirt, runs a knuckle across his mouth. "It was the only thing I could think of."

The man looks at him. A smile works at the corners of his mud-spattered mouth. He makes a sound like a cough, and then he's laughing, they're both laughing. They sit in the mud, roaring.

Eventually they help each other out of the muck. "We screwed it up," the man says. "How did we screw it up?"

He's been wondering that himself for a long time. "I don't think we were supposed to keep them safe," he answers. He hands him the remnant of the suit. "This, the bed, the Wonder Bike—all that stuff. We weren't supposed to *hoard* them."

The man looks stricken. "Oh my God," the man says quietly. "Oh my God."

They begin to trudge across the drained sea. They trade stories about their adventures. The man with the wolf suit takes out his wallet and shows him pictures. He has a granddaughter he's never met, six years old, a real hellion by all accounts. "She lives three states away," he says.

A dozen yards from the shore they see the trolley. The little car glides smoothly around the perimeter of the lake and stops in their path. It rolls a few feet forward, a few feet back. *Ding ding!*

They approach it carefully and without speaking, as they would a deer at a watering hole. It trembles as they step up onto the gleaming sideboards. They sit on the polished wooden benches. It's a shame their clothes are so filthy.

The trolley doesn't move.

"Wait," he says, and the man in the wolf suit watches him dig into his pocket. The dime he found on the roadway is still there. The coin clinks into the tin fare box and the car jerks into motion. Soon they're zipping across the plain toward the forest and the black ribbon of highway.

"And yourself?" the man with the suit asks.

"No grandchildren," he says. "No children. Not anymore."

The man frowns and nods. "We'll find someone for the bike," he says. "The world is full of children."

# DAMASCUS

When Paula became conscious of her surroundings again, the first thing she sensed was his fingers entwined in hers.

She was strapped to the ambulance backboard—each wrist cuffed in nylon, her chest held down by a wide band—to stop her from flailing and yanking out the IV. Only his presence kept her from screaming. He gazed down at her, dirty-blond hair hanging over blue eyes, pale cheeks shadowed by a few days' stubble. His love for her radiated like cool air from a block of ice.

When they reached the hospital he walked beside the gurney, his hand on her shoulder, as the paramedics wheeled her into the ER. Paula had never worked in the ER but she recognized a few of the faces as she passed. She took several deep breaths, her chest tight against the nylon strap, and calmly told the paramedics that she was fine, they could let her go now. They made reassuring noises and left the restraints in place. Untying her was the doctor's call now.

Eventually an RN came to ask her questions. A deeply tanned, heavy-set woman with frosted hair. Paula couldn't remember her name, though they'd worked together for several years, back before the hospital had fired Paula. Now she was back as a patient.

"And what happened tonight, Paula?" the nurse said, her tone cold. They hadn't gotten along when they worked together; Paula had a temper in those days.

"I guess I got a bit dizzy," she said.

"Seizure," said one of the paramedics. "Red Cross guy said she started shaking on the table, they had to get her onto the floor before she fell off. She'd been seizing for five or six minutes before we got there so we brought her in. We gave her point-one of Lorazepam and she came out of it during the ride."

"She's the second epileptic this shift," the nurse said to them.

Paula blinked in surprise. Had one of the yellow house women been brought in? Or one of the converts? She looked to her side, and her companion gazed back at her, amused, but not giving anything away. Everything was part of the plan, but he wouldn't tell her what the plan was. Not yet.

The nurse saw Paula's shift in attention and her expression hardened. "Let's have you talk to a doctor, Paula."

"I'm feeling a lot better," Paula said. Didn't even grit her teeth.

They released the straps and transferred her to a bed in an exam room. One of the paramedics set her handbag on the bedside table. "Good luck now," he said.

She glanced at the bag and quickly looked away. Best not to draw attention to it. "I'm sorry if I was any trouble," she said.

The nurse handed her a clipboard of forms. "I don't suppose I have to explain these to you," she said. Then: "Is there something wrong with your hand?"

Paula looked down at her balled fist. She concentrated on loosening her fingers but they refused to unclench. That had been happening more often lately. Always the left hand. "I guess I'm nervous."

The nurse slowly nodded, not buying it. She made sure Paula could hold the clipboard and write, then left her.

But not alone. He slouched in a bedside chair, legs stretched in front of him, the soles of his bare feet almost black. His shy smile was like a promise. I'm here, Paula. I'll always be here for you.

Richard's favorite album was Nirvana's *In Utero*. She destroyed that CD first.

He'd moved out on a Friday, filed for divorce on the following Monday. He wanted custody of their daughter. Claire was ten then, a sullen and secretive child, but Paula would sooner burn the house down around them than let him have her. Instead she torched what he loved most. On the day Paula got the letter about the custody hearing, she pulled his CDs and LPs and DATs from the shelves—hundreds of them, an entire wall of the living room, and more in the basement. She carried them to the backyard by the box. Claire wailed in protest, tried to hide some of the cases, and eventually Paula had to lock the girl in her room.

In the yard Paula emptied a can of lighter fluid over the pile, went into the garage for the gas can, splashed that on as well. She tossed the Nirvana CD on top.

The pile of plastic went up in a satisfying *whoosh*. After a few minutes the fire started to die down—the CDs wouldn't stay lit—so she went back into the house and brought out his books and music magazines.

The pillar of smoke guided the police to her house. They told her it was illegal to burn garbage in the city. Paula laughed. "Damn right it's garbage." She wasn't going to be pushed around by a couple of cops. Neighbors came out to watch. Fuck them, she thought.

She lived in a neighborhood of Philadelphia that outsiders called "mixed." Blacks and Latinos and whites, a handful of Asians and Arabs. Newly renovated homes with Mexican tile patios, side by side with crack houses and empty lots. Paula moved there from the suburbs to be with Richard and never forgave him. Before Claire was born she made him install an alarm system and set bars across the windows. She felt like they were barely holding on against a tide of criminals and crazies.

The yellow house women may have been both. They lived across the street and one lot down, in a cottage that was a near-twin of Paula's. Same field stone porch and peaked roofs, same narrow windows. But while Paula's house was painted a tasteful slate blue, theirs blazed lemon yellow, the doors and window frames and gutters turned out in garish oranges and brilliant whites. Five or six women, a mix of races and skin tones, wandered in and out of the house at all hours. Did they have jobs? They weren't old, but half of them had trouble walking, and one of them used a cane. Paula was an RN, twelve years working all kinds of units in two different hospitals, and it looked to her like they shared some kind of neuromuscular problem, maybe early MS. Their yellow house was probably some charity shelter.

On the street the women seemed distracted, sometimes talking to themselves, until they noticed someone and smiled a bit too widely. They always greeted Paula and Richard, but they paid special attention to Claire, speaking to her in the focused way of old people and kindergarten teachers. One of them, a gaunt white woman named Steph who wore the prematurely weathered face of a long-time meth user, started stopping by more often in the months after Richard moved out. She brought homemade food: Tupperware bowls of bean soup, foil-wrapped tamales, rounds of bread. "I've been a single mom," she said. "I know how tough things can be on your own." She started babysitting Claire a couple nights a week, staying in Paula's house so Claire could fall asleep in her own bed. Some afternoons she took

Claire with her on trips to the grocery or the park. Paula kept waiting for the catch. It finally came in the form of a sermon.

"My life was screwed *up*," Steph said to Paula one afternoon. Claire had vanished to her bedroom to curl up with her headphones. The two women sat in the kitchen eating cheese bread someone in the yellow house had made. Steph drank wine while Paula worked her way through her afternoon Scotch. Steph talked frankly about her drug use, the shitty boyfriends, the money problems. "I was this close to cutting my wrists. If Jesus hadn't come into my life, I wouldn't be here right now."

Here we go, Paula thought. She drank silently while Steph droned on about how much easier it was to have somebody walk beside her, someone who cared. "Your own personal Jesus," Steph said. "Just like the song."

Paula knew the song—Richard loved that '80s crap. He even had the Johnny Cash remake, until she'd turned his collection to slag. "No thanks," Paula said, "I don't need any more men in my life."

Steph didn't take offense. She kept coming back, kept talking. Paula put up with the woman because with Richard out of the house she needed help with Claire—and because she needed her alone time more than ever. The yellow house women may have been Jesus freaks, but they were harmless. That's what she told herself, anyway, until the night she came home to find Claire gone.


Paula knew how to play the hospital game. Say as little as possible, act normal, don't look at things no one else could see. She knew her blood tests would come out normal. They'd shrug and check her out by noon.

Her doctor surprised her, though. They'd assigned her to Louden, a short, trim man with a head shaved down to gray stubble who had a reputation among the nurses for adequacy: not brilliant, but not arrogant either, a competent guy who pushed the patients through on schedule. But something had gotten into him—he was way too interested in her case. He filled her afternoon with expensive MRIs, fMRIs, and PET scans. He brought in specialists.

Four of them, two neurologists and a psychiatrist she recognized, and one woman she didn't know who said she was an epidemiologist.

They came in one at a time over the afternoon, asking the same questions. How long had she experienced the seizures? What did they feel like when they struck? Did she know others with these symptoms? They poked her skin to test nerve response, pulled and flexed the fingers of her clenched hand. Several times they asked her, "Do you see people who aren't there?"

She almost laughed. He sat beside her the entire time, his arm cool against her own. Could anyone be more present?

The only questions that unsettled her came from the epidemiologist, the doctor she didn't recognize. "Do you eat meat?" the doctor asked. Paula said sure. And the doctor, a square-faced woman with short brown hair, asked a dozen follow-up questions, writing down exactly what kinds of meat she ate, how often, whether she cooked it herself or ate out.

At the end of the day they moved Paula into a room with a middle-aged white woman named Esther Wynne, a true southern lady who'd put on make-up and sprayed her hair as though at any moment she'd pop those IV tubes from her arms and head out to a nice restaurant.

Doctor Louden stopped by once more before going home that night. He sat heavily beside Paula's bed, ran a hand over his gray scalp. "You haven't been completely open with us," he said. He seemed as tired as she was.

"No, probably not," she said. Behind him, her companion shook his head, laughing silently.

Louden smiled as well, but fleetingly. "You have to realize how serious this is. You're the tenth person we've seen with symptoms like yours, and there are more showing up in hospitals around the city. Some of my colleagues think we may be seeing the start of an epidemic. We need your help to find out if that's the case."

"Am I contagious?"

He scratched his chin, looked down. "We don't think so. You don't have a temperature, any signs of inflammation—no signs that this is a virus or a bacterial infection."

"Then what is it you think I have?"

"We don't have a firm idea yet," he said. He was holding back, treating her like a dumb patient. "We *can* treat your symptoms though. We'll try to find out more tomorrow, but we think you have a form of temporal lobe epilepsy. There are parts of your brain that—"

"I know what epilepsy is."

"Yes, but TLE is a bit . . ." He gestured vaguely, then took several stapled pages from his clipboard and handed them to her. "I've brought some literature. The more you understand what's happening, the better we'll work together." He didn't sound like he believed that.

Paula glanced at the pages. Printouts from a web site.

"Read it over and tomorrow you and I can—oh, good." A nurse had entered the room with a plastic cup in her hand; the meds had arrived. Louden seemed relieved to have something else to talk about. "This is Topamax, an epilepsy drug."

"I don't want it," she said. She was done with drugs and alcohol.

"I wouldn't prescribe this if it wasn't necessary," Louden said. His doctor voice. "We want to avoid the spikes in activity that cause seizures like today's. You don't want to fall over and crack your skull open, do you?" This clumsy attempt at manipulation would have made the old Paula furious.

Her companion shrugged. It didn't matter. All part of the plan.

Paula accepted the cup from the nurse, downed the two pills with a sip of water. "When can I go home?" she said.

Louden stood up, ran a hand over his scalp. "I'll talk to you again in the morning. I hate to tell you this, but there are a few more tests we have to run."

Or maybe they were keeping her here because they did think she was contagious. The start of an epidemic, he'd said.

Paula nodded understandingly and Louden seemed relieved. As he reached the door Paula said, "Why did that one doctor—Gerrhardt?—ask me if I ate meat?"

He turned. "Dr. Gerrholtz. She's not with the hospital."

"Who's she with then?"

"Oh, the CDC," he said casually. As if the Centers for Disease Control dropped by all the time. "Don't worry, it's their job to ask strange questions. We'll have you out of here as soon as we can."

Paula came home from work to find the door unchained and the lights on. It was only 7:15, but in early November that meant it had been dark for more than hour. Paula stormed through the house looking for Claire. The girl knew the rules: come home from school, lock the door, and don't pick up the phone unless caller-ID showed Paula's cell or work number. Richard took her, she thought. Even though he won partial custody, he wanted to take everything from her.

Finally she noticed the note, in a cleared space on the counter between a stack of dishes and an open cereal box. The handwriting was Steph's.

Paula marched to the yellow house and knocked hard. Steph opened the door. "It's all right," Steph said, trying to calm her down. "She's done her homework and now she's watching TV."

Paula pushed past her into a living room full of second-hand furniture and faded rugs. Every light in the house seemed to be on, making every flat surface glow: the oak floors scrubbed to a buttery sheen, the freshly-painted daffodil walls, the windows reflecting bright lozenges of white. Something spiced and delicious fried in the kitchen, and Paula was suddenly famished. She hadn't eaten anything solid since breakfast.

Claire sat on a braided oval rug, her purple backpack beside her. A nature show played on the small boxy TV but the girl wasn't really watching. She had her earphones in, listening to the CD player in her lap. Lying on the couch behind her was a thin black woman in her fifties or sixties.

"Claire," Paula said. The girl pretended to not hear. "Claire, take off your headphones when I'm talking to you." Her voice firm but reasonable. The Good Mother. "You know you're not supposed to leave the house."

Claire didn't move.

"The police were at the green house," Steph said. A rundown place two doors down from Paula with motorcycles always in the front yard. Drug dealers, Paula thought. "I went over to check on Claire, and she seemed nervous, so I invited her over. I told her it would be all right."

"You wouldn't answer your phone," Claire said without looking away from the TV. She still hadn't taken off the headphones. Acting up in front of the women, thinking Paula wouldn't discipline her in public.

"Then you keep calling," Paula said. She'd forgotten to turn on her phone when she left the hospital. She'd stopped off for a drink, not more than thirty, forty-five minutes, then came home, no later than she'd come home dozens of times in the past. "You don't leave the house."

Steph touched Paula's elbow, interrupting again. She nodded at the woman on the couch. "This is Merilee."

The couch looked like the woman's permanent home. On the short table next to her head was a half-empty water glass, a Kleenex box, a mound of damp tissue. A plastic bucket sat on the floor below it. Merilee lay propped up on pillows, her body half covered by a white sheet. Her legs were bent under her in what looked like a painful position, and her left arm curled up almost to her chin, where her hand trembled like a nervous animal. She watched the TV screen with a blissed-out smile, as if this was the best show in the world.

Steph touched the woman's shoulder, and she looked up. "Merilee, this is Paula."

Merilee reached up with her good right arm. Her aim was off; first she held it out to a point too far right, then swung it slowly around. Paula lightly took her hand. Her skin was dry and cool.

The woman smiled and said something in another language. Paula looked to Steph, and then Merilee said, "I eat you."

"I'm sorry?" She couldn't have heard that right.

"It's a Fore greeting," Steph said, pronouncing the word *For-ay*. "Merilee's people come from the highlands of Papua New Guinea. Merilee, Paula is Claire's mother."

"Yes, yes, you're right," Merilee said. Her mouth moved more than the words required, lips constantly twisting toward a smile, distorting her speech. "What a lovely girl." It wasn't clear if she meant Claire or Paula. Then her hand slipped away like a scarf and floated to her chest. She lay back and turned her gaze back to the TV, still smiling.

Paula thought, what the hell's the matter with her?

"We're about to eat," Steph said. "Sit down and join us."

"No, we'd better get going," Paula said. But there was nothing back at her house. And whatever they were cooking smelled wonderful.

"Come on," Steph said. "You always love our food." That was true. She'd eaten their meals for a month.

"I just have a few minutes," Paula said. She followed Steph into the dining room. The long, cloth-covered table almost filled the room. Ten places set, and room for a couple more. "How many of you are there?" she said.

"Seven of us live in the house," Steph said as she went into the adjoining kitchen.

"Looks like you've got room for renters."

Paula picked a chair and sat down, eyeing the tall green bottle in the middle of the table. "Is that wine?" Paula asked. She could use a drink.

"You're way ahead of me," Steph said. She came back into the room with the stems of wine glasses between her fingers, followed by an eighteen- or nineteen-year-old black girl—Tanya? Tonya?—carrying a large blue plate of rolled tortillas. Paula had met her before, pushing her toddler down the sidewalk. Outside she walked with a dragging limp, but inside it was barely discernible.

Steph poured them all wine but then remained standing. She took a breath and held it. Still no one moved. "All right then," Steph finally said, loud enough for Merilee to hear.

Tonya—pretty sure it was Tonya—took a roll and passed the plate. Paula carefully bit into the tortilla. She tasted sour cream, a spicy salsa, chunks of tomato. The small cubes of meat were so heavily marinated that they could have been anything: pork, chicken, tofu.

Tonya and Steph looked at Paula, their expressions neutral, but she sensed they were expecting something. Paula dabbed a bit of sour cream from her lip. "It's very good," she said.

Steph smiled and raised her glass. "Welcome," she said, and Tonya echoed her. Paula returned the salute and drank. The wine tasted more like brandy, thick and too sweet. Tonya nodded at her, said something under breath. Steph said something to Merilee in that other language. Steph's eyes, Paula noted with alarm, were wet with tears.

"What is it?" Paula said. She put down the cup. Something had happened that she didn't understand. She stared at the pure white tortillas, the glasses of dark wine. This wasn't a *snack*, it was fucking communion.

"Tell me what's going on," she said coldly.

Steph sighed, her smile bittersweet. "We've been worried about you. Both of you. Claire's been spending so much time alone, and you're obviously still grieving."

Paula stared at her. These sanctimonious bitches. What was this, some kind of religious intervention? "My life is none of your business."

"Claire told me that you've been talking about killing yourself."

Paula scraped her chair back from the table and stood up, her heart racing. Tonya looked at her with concern. So smug. "*Claire* told you that?" Paula said. "And you believed her?"

"Paula . . ."

She wheeled away from the table, heading for the living room, Steph close behind. "Claire," Paula said. Not yelling. Not yet. "We're going."

Claire didn't get up. She looked at Steph, as if for permission. This infuriated Paula more than anything that had happened so far.

She grabbed Claire by her arm, yanked her to her feet. The headphones popped from her ears, spilling tinny music. Claire didn't even squeak.

Steph said, "We care about you two, Paula. We had to take steps. You won't understand that right now, but soon . . ."

Paula spun and slapped the woman hard across the mouth, turning her chin with the blow. Steph's eyes squeezed shut in pain, but she didn't raise her arms, didn't step back.

"Don't you ever come near my daughter again," Paula said. She strode toward the front door, Claire scrambling to stay on her feet next to her. Paula yanked open the door and pushed the girl out first. Her daughter still hadn't made a sound.

Behind her, Steph said, "Wait." She came to the door holding out Claire's backpack and CD player. "Some day you'll understand," Steph said. "Jesus is coming soon."


"You're a Christian, aren't you?" Esther Wynne said. "I knew from your face. You've got the love of Jesus in you."

As the two women picked at their breakfast trays, Esther told Paula about her life. "A lot of people with my cancer die quick as a wink," she said. "I've had time to say goodbye to everyone." Her cancer was in remission but now she was here fighting a severe bladder infection. They'd hooked her to an IV full of antibiotics the day before. "How about you?" Esther said. "What's a young thing like you doing here?"

Paula laughed. She was 36. "They think I have a TLA." Esther frowned. "Three-letter acronym."

"Oh, I've got a couple of those myself!"

One of the web pages Dr. Louden gave her last night included a cartoon cross-section of a brain. Arrows pointed out interesting bits of the temporal lobe with tour guide comments like "the amygdala tags events with emotion and significance" and "the hippocampus labels inputs as internal or external." A colored text box listed a wide range of possible TLE symptoms: euphoria, a sense of personal destiny, religiosity . . .

And a sense of presence.

*Asymmetrical temporal lobe hyperactivity separates the sense of self into two—one twin in each hemisphere. The dominant (usually left) hemisphere interprets the other part of the self as an "other" lurking outside. The otherness is then colored by which hemisphere is most active.*

Paula looked up then, her chest tight. Her companion had been leaning against the wall, watching her read. At her frightened expression he dropped his head and laughed silently, his hair swinging in front of his face.

Of course. There was nothing she could learn that could hurt her, or him.

She tossed aside the pages. If her companion hadn't been with her she might have worried all night about the information, but he helped her think it through. The article had it backward, confusing an *effect* for the *cause*. Of course the brain reacted when you sensed the presence of God. Neurons fired like pupils contracting against a bright light.

"Paula?" someone said. "Paula."

She blinked. An LPN stood by the bed with a plastic med cup. Her breakfast tray was gone. How long had she been ruminating? "Sorry, I was lost in thought there."

The nurse handed Paula the Topamax and watched as she took them. After the required ritual—pulse, blood pressure, temperature—she finally left.

Esther said, "So what were you thinking about?"

Paula lay back on the pillows and let her eyes close. Her companion sat beside her on the bed, massaging the muscles of her left arm, loosening her cramped fingers. "I was thinking that when God calls you don't worry about how he got your number," she said. "You just pick up the receiver."

"A-*men*," Esther said.

Dr. Louden appeared a few minutes later accompanied only by Dr. Gerrholtz, the epidemiologist from the CDC. Maybe the other specialists had already grown bored with her case. "We have you scheduled for another PET scan this morning," Louden said. He looked like he hadn't slept at all last night, poor guy. "Is there anyone you'd like to call to be with you? A family member?"

"No thank you," Paula said. "I don't want to bother them."

"I really think you should consider it."

"Don't worry, Dr. Louden." She wanted to pat his arm, but that would probably embarrass him in front of Dr. Gerrholtz. "I'm perfectly fine."

Louden rubbed a hand across his skull. After a long moment he said, "Aren't you curious about why we ordered a PET scan?" Dr. Gerrholtz gave him a hard look.

Paula shrugged. "Okay, why did you?"

Louden shook his head, disappointed again that she wasn't more concerned. Dr. Gerrholtz said, "You're a professional, Paula, so we're going to be straight with you."

"I appreciate that."

"We're looking for amyloid plaques. Do you know what those are?" Paula shook her head and Gerrholtz said, "Some types of proteins weave into amyloid fibers, forming a plaque that kills cells. Alzheimer patients get them, but they're also caused by another family of diseases. We think those plaques are causing your seizures, and other symptoms."

*Other symptoms.* Her companion leaned against her shoulder, his hand entwined in hers. "Okay," Paula said.

Louden stood up, obviously upset. "We'll talk to you after the test. Dr. Gerrholtz?"

The CDC doctor ignored him. "We've been going through the records, Paula, looking for people who've reported symptoms like yours." She said it like a warning. "In the past three months we've found almost a dozen—and that's just at this hospital. We don't know yet how many we'll find across the city, or the country. If you have any information that will help us track down what's happening, you need to offer it."

"Of course," Paula said.

Gerrholtz' eyes narrowed. She seemed ready to say something else—accuse her, perhaps—but then shook her head and stalked from the room.

Esther watched her go. After a minute of silence, the woman said, "Don't you worry, honey. It's not the doctors who are in charge here."

"Oh I'm not worried," Paula said. And she wasn't. Gerrholtz obviously distrusted her—maybe even suspected the nature of Paula's mission—but what could that matter? Everything was part of the plan, even Dr. Gerrholtz.

By noon they still hadn't come to get her for the scan. Paula drifted in and out of sleep. Twice she awoke with a start, sure that her companion had left the room. But each time he appeared after a few seconds, stepping out from a corner of her vision.

The orderly came by just as the lunch trays arrived, but that was okay, Paula wasn't hungry. She got into the wheelchair and the orderly rolled her down the hall to the elevators. Her companion walked just behind them, his dusty feet scuffing along.

The orderly parked her in the hall outside radiology, next to three other abandoned patients: a gray-faced old man asleep in his chair; a Hispanic teenager with a cast on her leg playing some electronic game; and a round-faced white boy who was maybe twenty or twenty-one.

The boy gazed up at the ceiling tiles, a soft smile on his face. After a few minutes, Paula saw his lips moving.

"Excuse me," Paula said to him. It took several tries to get his attention. "Have you ever visited a yellow house?" The young man looked at her quizzically. "A house that was all yellow, inside and out."

He shook his head. "Sorry."

None of the women still at the yellow house would have tried to save a man, but she had to ask. The boy had to be one of the converts, someone Paula's mission had saved.

"Can I ask you one more question?" Paula said, dropping her voice slightly. The old man slept on, and the girl still seemed engrossed in her game. "Who is it that you're talking to?"

The boy glanced up, laughed quietly. "Oh, nobody," he said.

"You can tell me," Paula said. She leaned closer. "I have a companion of my own."

His eyes widened. "You have a ghost following you too?"

"Ghost? No, it's not a—"

"My mother died giving birth to me," he said. "But now she's *here*."

Paula touched the boy's arm. "You don't understand what's happened to you, do you?" He hadn't come by way of the yellow house, hadn't met any of the sisters, hadn't received any instruction. Of course he'd tried to make sense of his companion any way he could. "You're not seeing a ghost. You're seeing Jesus himself."

The boy laughed loudly, and the teenage girl looked up from her game. "I think I'd know the difference between Jesus and my own mother," the young man said.

"Maybe that's why he took this form for you," Paula said. "He appears differently for each person. For you, your mother is a figure of unconditional love. A person who sacrificed for you."

"Okay," the young man said. He tilted his head, indicating an empty space to Paula's right. "So what does yours look like?"


God came through the windshield on a shotgun blast of light. Blinded, Paula cried out and jammed on the brakes. The little Nissan SUV bucked and fishtailed, sending the CDs piled on the seat next to her clattering onto the floorboards.

White. She could see nothing but white.

She'd stopped in heavy traffic on a four-lane road, the shopping center just ahead on her right. She'd been heading for the dumpsters behind the Wal-Mart to dispose with those CDs once and for all.

Brakes shrieked behind her. Paula ducked automatically, clenched against the pending impact, eyes screwed shut. (Still: Light. Light.) A thunderclap of metal on metal and the SUV rocked forward. She jerked in her seatbelt.

Paula opened her eyes and light scraped her retinas. Hot tears coursed down her cheeks.

She clawed blindly at her seatbelt buckle, hands shaking, and finally found the button and yanked the straps away. She scrambled over the shifter to the passenger seat, the plastic CD cases snapping and sliding under her knees and palms.

She'd found them deep in Claire's closet. The girl was away at her father's for the mandated 50% of the month, and Paula had found the CDs stacked hidden under a pile of blankets and stuffed animals. Many of the cases were cracked and warped by heat and most CDs had no cases at all. The day after the bonfire, Paula had caught the girl poking through the mound of plastic and damp ashes and told her not to touch them. Claire had deliberately disobeyed, sneaking out to rescue them sometime before the garbage men took the pile away. The deception had gone on for months. All the time Paula thought Claire was listening to her own music—crap by bubble-gum pop stars and American Idols—her headphones were full of her father's music: Talking Heads, Depeche Mode, Pearl Jam, Nirvana.

Paula pushed open the passenger door and half fell out the door, into the icy March wind. She got her feet under her, stumbled away from the light, into the light. Her shins struck something—the guard rail?—and she put out a hand to stop from pitching over. Cold metal bit her palms. Far to her right, someone shouted angrily. The blare and roar of traffic surrounded her.

Paula dropped to her knees and slush instantly soaked her jeans. She covered her head with both arms. The light struck her neck and curved back like a rain of sharpened stones.

The light would destroy her. Exactly as she deserved.

Something touched the top of her head, and she shuddered in fear and shame and a rising ecstasy that had nothing to do with sex. She began to shake, to weep.

*I'm sorry*, she said, perhaps out loud. *I'm sorry.*

Someone stood beside her. She turned her head, and he appeared out of the light. No—*in* the light, *of* the light. A fire in the shape of a man.

She didn't know him, but she recognized him.

He looked down at her, electric blue eyes through white bangs, his shy smile for her only. He looked like Kurt Cobain.


"I'm not taking the meds anymore," Paula said. She tried to keep her voice steady. Louden stood beside the bed, Gerrholtz behind him holding a portfolio in her hands as big as the Ten Commandments. They'd walked past Esther without saying a word.

Her companion lay on the floor beside her bed, curled into a ball.

He seemed to be dissolving at the edges, dissipating into fog. He'd lain there all morning, barely moving, not even looking at her.

"That's not a good idea," Dr. Louden said. He pulled a chair next to the bed, scraping through her companion as if he wasn't there. Paula grimaced, the old rage flaring up. She closed her eyes and concentrated.

"I'm *telling* you to stop the drugs," she said. "Unless I'm a prisoner here you can't give me medicine that I refuse."

Louden exhaled tiredly. "This isn't like you, Paula," he said.

"Then you don't know me very well."

He leaned forward, resting elbows on knees, and pressed the fingers of one hand into his forehead. More TLE patients were rolling in every day. The nurses murmured about epidemics. Poor Dr. Adequate had been drafted into a war he didn't understand and wasn't prepared for.

"Help me then," he said without looking up. "Tell me what you're experiencing."

Paula stared at the TV hanging from the ceiling. She left it on all the time now, sound off. The images distracted her, kept her from thinking of him on the floor beside her, fading.

Gerrholtz said, "Why don't I take a guess? You're having trouble seeing your imaginary friend."

Paula snapped her head toward the woman. *You bitch.* She almost said it aloud.

Gerrholtz regarded her coolly. "A woman died two days ago in a hospital not far from here," she said. "Her name was Stephanie Wozniak. I'm told she was a neighbor of yours."

*Steph is dead?* She couldn't process the thought.

Gerrholtz took the sheets from her portfolio and laid them on Paula's lap. "I want you to look at these."

Paula picked them up automatically. The photographs looked like microscope slides from her old bio-chem classes, a field of cells tinged brown by some preserving chemical. Spidery black asterisks pock-marked the cells.

"Those clumps of black are bundles of prions," Gerrholtz said. "Regular old proteins, with one difference—they're the wrong shape."

Paula didn't look up. She flipped the printouts one by one, her hand moving on its own. Some of the pictures consisted almost en-

tirely of sprawling nests of black threads. Steph deserved better than
this. She'd waited her whole life for a Fore funeral. Instead the doctors cut her up and photographed the remains.

"I need you to concentrate, Paula. One protein bent or looped in
the wrong way isn't a problem. But once they're in the brain, you get
a conformational cascade—a snowball effect."

Paula's hands continued to move but she'd stopped seeing them.
Gerrholtz rattled on and on about nucleation and crystallization. She
kept using the word *spongiform* as if it would frighten her.

Paula already knew all this, and more. She let the doctor talk.
Above Gerrholtz' head the TV showed a concerned young woman
with a microphone, police cars and ambulances in the background.

"Paula!"

Dr. Gerrholtz' face was rigid with anger. Paula wondered if that's
what she used to look like when she fought with Richard or screamed
at Claire.

"I noticed you avoided saying 'Mad Cow,'" Paula said. "And
Kuru."

"You know about Kuru?" Louden said.

"Of course she does," Gerrholtz said. "She's done her homework." The doctor put her hands on the foot of Paula's bed and leaned
forward. "The disease that killed Stephanie doesn't have a name yet,
Paula. We think it's a Kuru variant, the same prion with an extra
kink. And we know that we can't save the people who already have
it. Their prions will keep converting other proteins to use their shape.
You understand what this means, don't you Paula?"

Still trying to scare her. As if the promise of her own death would
break her faith.

On the screen, the reporter gestured at two uniformed officers
sealing the front door with yellow tape that looked specially chosen
to match the house. Paula wondered if they'd found Merilee yet.

"It means that God is an idea," Paula said. "An idea that can't be
killed."

The house shimmered in her vision, calling her like a lighthouse;
she understood now why they'd painted it so brightly. Minutes after
the accident her vision darkened like smoked glass, and now only the

brightest things drew her attention. Her companion guided her down the dark streets, walking a few feet in front of her, surrounded by a nimbus of fire.

Steph opened the door. When she saw the tears in her eyes Steph squealed in delight and pulled her into a hug. "We've been waiting for you," she said. "We've been waiting so long." And then Steph was crying too.

"I'm sorry," Paula said. "I'm so sorry. I didn't know . . ."

The other women came to her one by one, hugging her, caressing her cheeks, all of them crying. Only Merilee couldn't get up to greet her. The woman lay on the same couch as four months ago, but her limbs had cinched tighter, arms and legs curled to her torso like a dying bug. Paula kneeled next to her couch and gently pressed her cheek to Merilee's. Paula spoke the Fore greeting: *I eat you.*

That was the day one life ended and another began.

Her vision slowly returned over the next few days, but her companion remained, becoming more solid every day. They told her she didn't have to worry about him leaving her. She called in sick to work and spent most of the next week in the yellow house, one minute laughing, the next crying, sometimes both at the same time. She couldn't stop talking about her experience on the road, or the way her companion could make her recognize her vanity or spite with just a faint smile.

Her old life had become something that belonged to a stranger. Paula thought of the blank weekends of Scotch and Vicodin, the screaming matches with Richard. Had she really burned his record collection?

When she called him, the first thing she said was, "I'm sorry."

"What is it, Paula." His voice flat, wary. The Paula he knew only used "sorry" to bat away his words, deflect any attack.

"Something wonderful's happened," she said. She told him about Steph and the women of the house, then skipped the communion to tell him about the accident and the blinding light and the emotions that flooded through her. Richard kept telling her to slow down, stop stumbling over her words. Then she told him about her companion.

"*Who* did you meet?" he said. He thought it was someone who'd witnessed the accident. Again she tried to explain.

Richard said, "I don't think Claire should come back there this weekend."

"What? No!" She needed to see Claire. She needed to apologize to her, promise her she'd do better. She gripped the receiver. Why couldn't Richard believe her? Why was he fighting her again?

She felt a touch on the back of her head. She turned, let her hand fall to the side. His blue eyes gazed into hers.

One eyebrow rose slightly.

She breathed. Breathed again. Richard called her name from the handset.

"I know this is a lot to adjust to," Paula said. The words came to her even though her companion didn't make a sound. "I know you want the best for Claire. You're a good father." The words hurt because they were true. She'd always thought of Richard as a weak man, but if that had once been true, Claire's birth had given him someone weaker to protect. As their daughter became older he took her side against Paula more and more often. The fights worsened, but she broke him every time. She never thought he'd have the guts to walk out on her and try to take Claire with him. "If you think she'd be better off with you for awhile, we can try that." She'd win his trust soon enough.

In the weeks after, Claire stayed with Richard, and Paula did hardly anything but talk with the yellow house women. At work the head nurse reprimanded her for her absences but she didn't care. Her life was with the women now, and her house became almost an annex to theirs. "We have room for more," Paula said dozens of times. "We have to tell others. It's not right to keep this to ourselves when so many people are suffering." The women nodded in agreement—or perhaps only in sympathy. Each of them had been saved, most of them from lives much worse than Paula's. They knew what changes were possible.

"You have to be patient," Steph told her one day. "This gift is handed from woman to woman, from Merilee's grandmother down to us. It comes with a responsibility to protect the host. We have to choose carefully—we can't share it with everyone."

"Why *not*?" Paula said. "Most of us would be dead without it. We're talking about saving the world here."

"Yes. One person at a time."

"But people are dying right now," Paula said. "There has to be a way to take this beyond the house."

"Let me show you something," Steph said. She brought down a

box from a high bookshelf and lifted out a huge family Bible. Steph opened it to the family tree page, her left hand trembling. "Here are some of your sisters," she said. "The ones I've known anyway."

The page was full of names. The list continued on the next page, and the next. Over a hundred names.

"How long has this been going on?" Paula said in wonder.

"Merilee's mother came here in 1982. Some of the women lived in this house for a while, and then were sent to establish their own houses. We don't know how many of us there are now, spread around the country. None of us knows all of them." She smiled at her. "See? You're not so alone. But we have to move quietly, Paula. We have to meet in small groups, like the early Christians."

"Like terrorists," Paula said bitterly.

Steph glanced to the side, listening to her companion. "Yes," she said, nodding. And then to Paula: "Exactly. There's no terror like the fear of God."


He woke her at 3 a.m. Paula blinked at him, confused. He hovered beside the bed, only half there, like a reflection in a shop window.

She forced herself awake and as her vision cleared the edges of him resolved, but he was still more vapor than solid. "What is it?" she said. He teasingly held a finger to his lips and turned toward Esther's bed. He paused, waiting for her.

Paula slipped out of the bed and moved quietly to the cabinet against the wall. The door came open with a loud clack, and she froze, waiting to see if she'd awakened her roommate. Esther's feathery snore came faint and regular.

Paula found her handbag at the bottom shelf and carried it to the window. Feeling past her wallet fat with ID cards, she pulled out the smaller vinyl case and laid it open on the sill like a butterfly.

The metal tip of the syringe reflected the light.

Paula made a fist of her left hand, flexed, tightened again. Working in the faint light, she found the vein in her arm mostly by feel and long familiarity, her fingertips brushing first over the dimpled scars near the crook of her elbow, then down half an inch. She took the syringe in her right hand and pressed into the skin. The plastic tube slowly filled.

Paula picked her way through the dim room until her hand touched the IV bag hanging beside Esther's bed. The woman lay still, her lips slightly apart, snoring lightly. It would be simple to inject the blood through the IV's Y-port.

But what if it was too late for her? The host incubated for three to six months. Only if the cancer stayed in remission that long would the woman have a chance to know God. Not her invisible, unseen God. The real thing.

Paula reached for the tubing and her companion touched her arm. She lowered the syringe, confused. Why not inject her? She searched his face for a reason, but he was so hard to see.

He turned and walked through the wall. Paula opened the door and stepped into the bright hallway, and for a moment she couldn't find him in the light. He gestured for her to follow.

She followed his will-o'-the-wisp down the deserted corridor, carrying the syringe low at her side. He led her down the stairwell, and at the next floor went left, left again. At an intersection a staffer in blue scrubs passed ten feet in front of them without seeing them.

Perhaps she'd become invisible too.

Her companion stopped before a door and looked at her. It was one of the converted rooms where doctors on call could catch some sleep. Here? she asked with her eyes. He gestured toward the door, his arm like a tendril of fog.

She gripped the handle, slowly turned. The door was unlocked. Gently she pushed it open.

The wedge of light revealed a woman asleep on the twin bed, a thin blanket half covering her. She wore what Paula had seen her in earlier: a cream blouse gleaming in the hall light, a patterned skirt rucked above her knees, her legs dark in black hose. Her shoes waited side-by-side on the floor next to the bed, ready for her to spring back into action and save her world.

Paula looked back at the doorway. Dr. Gerrholtz? she asked him. Did he really want this awful woman to receive the host?

His faint lips pursed, the slightest of frowns, and Paula felt a rush of shame. Who was she to object? Before Steph had found her Paula had been the most miserable woman alive. Everyone deserved salvation. That was the whole point of the mission.

Dr. Gerrholtz stirred, turned her head slightly, and the light fell across her closed eyes. Paula raised the needle, moved her thumb over the plunger. No handy IV already connected. No way to do this without waking the woman up. And she'd wake up screaming.

"Hello?" Dr. Gerrholtz said. Her eyes opened, and she lifted a hand to shade her eyes.

Jesus is coming, Paula said silently, and pressed the needle into her thigh.

Paula and Tonya stooped awkwardly at the edge of the pit, clearing the sand. They dug down carefully so that their shovel blades wouldn't cut too deep, then pitched the spark-flecked sand into the dark of the yard. They worked in short-sleeves, sweating despite the cold wind. With every inch they uncovered, the pit grew hotter and brighter.

It was hard work, and their backs still ached from this morning when they'd dug the pit, hauled over the big stones, and lined the bottom with them. But Paula had volunteered for this job. She wanted to prove that she could work harder than anyone.

Inside the house, women laughed and told stories, their voices carrying through the half-opened windows. Paula tossed aside a shovelful of sand and said, "Tonya, have you ever asked why no men are invited?" She'd thought about her words for a long time. She wanted to test them on Tonya first, because she was young and seemed more open than the other women.

Tonya looked up briefly, then dug down again with her shovel. "That's not the tradition."

"But what about Donel? Wouldn't you want this for him?" Donel was Tonya's son, only two years old. He shared a bedroom with her, but all the women took care of him.

Tonya paused, leaned against her shovel. "I . . . I think about that. But it's just not the way it's done. No men at the feast."

"But what if we could bring the feast to them?" Paula said. "I've been reading about Merilee's people, the disease they carried. There's more than one way to transmit the host. What if we could become missionaries some other way?"

The girl shook her head. "Merilee said that men would twist it all up, just like they did the last time."

"All the disciples were men last time. This time they're all women, but that doesn't make it right. Think about Donel." Think about Richard.

"We better keep going," Tonya said, ending the conversation. She started digging again, and after a moment, Paula joined her. But she kept thinking of Richard. He'd become more guarded over the past few months, more protective of Claire. When her daughter turned 14—another of Merilee's rules—Paula would bring her to communion. But if she could also bring it to Richard, if he could experience what she'd found, they could be a family again.

Several minutes later they found the burlap by the feel under their shovels. They scraped back the sand that covered the sack, then bent and heaved it up onto a pallet of plywood and one-by-fours. After they'd caught their breath they called the others from the house.

Over seventy women had come, some of them from as far away as New Zealand. None of them had come alone, of course. The air was charged with a multitude of invisible presences.

Eight of the women were chosen as pall bearers. The procession moved slowly because so many of them walked with difficulty. God's presence burned the body like a candle—Merilee's early death was proof of that—but not one of them would trade Him for anything. A perfect body was for the next life.

Steph began to sing something in Merilee's language, and the others joined in, harmonizing. Some knew the words; others, like Paula, hummed along. Women cried, laughed, lifted their hands. Others walked silently, perhaps in communion with their companions.

There was an awkward moment when they had to tilt the litter to get through the back door, but then they were inside. They carried her though the kitchen—past the stacks of Tupperware, the knives and cutting boards, the coolers of dry ice—then through the dining room and into the living room. The furniture had been pushed back to the walls. They set the litter in the center of the room.

Paula gripped the stiff and salt-caked cloth—they'd soaked the body overnight—while Steph sawed the length of it with a thick-bladed knife. Steam escaped from the bag, filling the room with a heady scent of ginger and a dozen other spices.

The last of the shroud fell away and Merilee grinned up at them. Her lips had pulled away from her teeth, and the skin of her face had turned hard and shiny. As she'd instructed, they'd packed ferns and wild herbs around her, dressing her in a funeral dress of leaves.

Steph kneeled at the head of the impromptu table and the others gathered around. The oldest and most crippled were helped down to the floor; the rest stood behind them, hands on their shoulders.

Steph opened a wooden box as big as a plumber's toolbox and drew out a small knife. She laid it on a white linen next to Merilee's skull and said, "Like many of you I was at the feast of Merilee's mother, and this is the story Merilee told there.

"It was the tradition of the Fore for the men and women to live apart. When a member of the tribe died, only the women and children were allowed at the feast. The men became jealous. They cursed the women, and they called the curse *kuru*, which means both 'to tremble' and 'to be afraid.' The white missionaries who visited the tribe called it the laughing sickness, because of the grimaces that twisted their faces."

As she talked she laid out other tools from the box: a filet knife, a wooden-handled fork with long silver tines, a Japanese cleaver.

"Merilee's grandmother, Yobaiotu, was a young woman when the first whites came, the doctors and government men and missionaries. One day the missionaries brought everyone out to the clearing they'd made by the river and gave everyone a piece of bread. They told them to dip it into a cup of wine and eat, and they said the words Jesus had spoken at the last supper: This is my body, this is my blood."

Steph drew out a long-handled knife and looked at it for perhaps thirty seconds, trying to control her emotions. "The moment Yobaiotu swallowed the bread, she fell down shaking, and a light filled her eyes. When she awoke, a young boy stood at her side. He held out his hand to her, and helped her to her feet. 'Lord Jesus!' Yobaiotu said, recognizing him." Steph looked up, smiled. "But of course no one else could see him. They thought she was crazy."

The women quietly laughed and nodded.

"The doctors said that the funeral feasts caused Kuru, and they ordered them to stop. But Yobaiotu knew the curse had been transformed in her, that the body of Christ lived in her. She taught her daughters to keep that covenant. The night Yobaiotu died they feasted in secret, as we do tonight."

Steph removed the center shelf of the box, set it aside, and reached in again. She lifted out a hacksaw with a gleaming blade. A green price tag was still stuck to the saw's blue handle.

"The body of Christ was passed from mother to daughter," Steph said. "Because of them, Christ lives in all of us. And because of Merilee, Christ will live in sisters who've not yet been found."

"Amen," the women said in unison.

Steph lifted the saw, and with her other hand gently touched the top of Merilee's skull. "This we do in remembrance of him," she said. "And Merilee."


The screaming eventually brought Louden to her room. "Don't make me sedate you," he began, and then flinched as she jerked toward him. The cuffs held her to the bed.

"Bring him back!" she screamed, her voice hoarse. "Bring him back now!"

Last night they'd taken her to another room, one without windows, and tied her down. Arms apart, ankles together. Then they attached the IV and upped the dosage: two parts Topamax, one part Loxapine, an anti-psychotic.

Gerrholtz they rushed to specialists in another city.

A hospital security guard took up station outside her door, and was replaced the next morning by a uniformed police officer. Detectives came to interrogate her. Her name hadn't been released to the news, they said, but it would only be a matter of time. The TV people didn't even know about Gerrholtz—they were responding to stories coming out of the yellow house investigation—but already they'd started using the word "bio-terrorism." Sometime today they'd move her to a federal facility.

Minute by minute the drugs did their work and she felt him slipping from her. She thought, if I keep watch he can't disappear. By twisting her shoulders she could see a little way over the bed and make out a part of him: a shadow that indicated his blue-jeaned leg, a cluster of dots in the speckled Linoleum that described the sole of a dirty foot. When the cramps in her arms and lower back became too much she'd fall back, rest for awhile, then throw herself sideways again. Each time she looked over the edge it took her longer to discern his shape. Two hours after the IV went in she couldn't find him at all.

Louden said, "What you experienced was an illusion, Paula, a phantom generated by a short-circuiting lobe of your brain. There's a doctor in Canada who can trigger these presences with a helmet and *magnetic fields*, for crying out loud. Your . . . *God* wasn't real. Your certainty was a symptom."

"Take me off these meds," she said, "or so help me I'll wrap this IV tube around your fucking neck."

"This is a disease, Paula. Some of you are seeing Jesus, but we've got other patients seeing demons and angels, talking to ghosts—I've got one Hindu guy who's sharing the bed with Lord Krishna."

She twisted against the cuffs, pain spiking across her shoulders. Her jaw ached from clenching her teeth.

"Paula, I need you to calm down. Your husband and daughter are downstairs. They want to visit you before you leave here."

"What? No. No." They couldn't see her like this. It would confirm everything Richard ever thought about her. And Claire . . . She was 13, a girl unfolding into a woman. The last thing she needed was to have her life distorted by this moment. By another vivid image of her mother as a raving lunatic.

"Tell them to stay away from me. The woman they knew doesn't exist anymore."

This morning the detectives had emptied her bag and splayed the driver's licenses and social security IDs like a deck of cards. How long has this been going on? they demanded. How many people are involved?

They gave her a pencil and yellow legal pad, told her to write down all the names she could remember. She stared at the tip of the pencil. An epidemiology book she'd read tried to explain crystallization by talking about how carbon could become graphite or diamond depending on how the atoms were arranged. The shapes she made on the page could doom a score of her missionaries.

She didn't know what to do. She turned to her companion but he was silent, already disintegrating.

"You're too late," she told the detectives. She snapped the pencil in half and threw it at them, bits of malformed diamond. "Six months too late."


They called themselves missionaries. Paula thought the name fit. They had a mission, and they would become agents of transmission.

The first and last meeting included only eighteen women. Paula had first convinced Tonya and Rosa from the yellow house, and they had widened the circle to a handful of women from houses around Philly, and from there they persuaded a few more women from New York and New Jersey. Paula had met some of them at Merilee's feast, but most were strangers. Some, like Tonya, were mothers of sons, but all of them had become convinced that it was time to take the gospel into the world.

They met at a Denny's restaurant in the western suburbs, where Steph and the other women wouldn't see them.

"The host is not a virus," Paula said. "It's not bacterial. It can't be detected or filtered out the way other diseases are, it can't be killed by antibiotics or detergents, because it's nothing but a *shape*." A piece of paper can become a sailboat or swan, she told them. A simple protein, folded and copied a million times, could bring you Kuru, or Creutzfeldt-Jakob disease, or salvation.

"The body of Christ is powerful," Paula said. They knew: all of them had taken part in feasts and had been saved through them. "But there's also power in the blood." She dealt out the driver licenses, two to each woman. Rosa's old contacts had made them for fifty bucks apiece. "One of these is all you need to donate. We're working on getting more. With four IDs you can give blood twice a month."

She told them how to answer the Red Cross surveys, which iron supplements to buy, which foods they should bulk up on to avoid anemia. They talked about secrecy. Most of the other women they lived with were too bound by tradition to see that they were only half doing God's work.

Women like Steph. Paula had argued with her a dozen times over the months, but could not convince her. Paula loved Steph, and owed so much to her, but she couldn't sit idly by any longer.

"We have to donate as often as possible," Paula said. "We have to spread the host so far and so fast that they can't stop us by rounding us up." The incubation time depended directly on the amount consumed, so the more that was in the blood supply the faster the conversions would occur. Paula's conversion had taken months. For others it might be years.

"But once they're exposed to the host the conversion *will* happen," Paula said. "It can't be stopped. One seed crystal can transform the ocean."

She could feel them with her. They could see the shape of the new world.

The women would never again meet all together like this—too dangerous—but they didn't need to. They'd already become a church within the church.

Paula hugged each of them as they left the restaurant. "Go," she told them. "Multiply."


The visitor seemed familiar. Paula tilted her head to see through the bars as the woman walked toward the cell. It had become too much of a bother to lift Paula out of the bed and wheel her down to the conference room, so now the visitors came to her. Doctors and lawyers, always and only doctors and lawyers. This woman, though, didn't look like either.

"Hello, Paula," she said. "It's Esther Wynne. Do you remember me?"

"Ah." The memory came back to her, those first days in the hospital. The Christian woman. Of course she'd be Paula's first voluntary visitor. "Hello, Esther." She struggled to enunciate clearly. In the year since they'd seen each other, Paula's condition had worsened. Lips and jaw and arms refused to obey her, shaking and jerking to private commands. Her arm lay curled against her chest like Merilee's. Her spine bent her nearly in half, so that she had to lie on her side. "You look—" She made a sound like a laugh, a hiccupping gasp forced from her chest by an unruly diaphragm. "—good."

The guard positioned a chair in front of the bars and the older woman sat down. Her hair was curled and sprayed. Under the makeup her skin looked healthy.

"I've been worried about you," Esther said. "Are they treating you well?"

Paula almost smiled. "As well as you can treat a mass murderer."

Some facts never escaped her. The missionaries had spread the disease to thousands, perhaps tens of thousands. But more damaging, they'd completely corrupted the blood supply. New prion filters were now on the market, but millions of gallons of blood had to be destroyed. They told her she may be ultimately responsible for the deaths of a million people.

Paula gave them every name she could remember, and the FBI tracked down all of the original 18, but by then the mission could go on without them. A day after the meeting in the restaurant they'd begun to recruit others, women and men Paula would never meet, whose names would never be spoken to her. The church would continue. In secret now, hunted by the FBI and the CDC and the world's governments, but growing every day. The host was passed needle by needle in private ceremonies, but increasingly on a mass scale as well. In an Ohio dairy processing plant, a man had been caught mixing his blood into the vats of milk. In Florida, police arrested a woman for injecting blood into the skulls of chickens. The economic damage was already in the trillions. The emotional toll on the public, in panic and paranoia, was incalculable.

Esther looked around at the cell. "You don't have anything in there with you. Can I bring you books? Magazines? They told me they'd allow reading material. I thought maybe—"

"I don't want anything," Paula said. She couldn't hold her head steady enough to read. She watched TV to remind herself every day of what she'd done to the world. Outside the prison, a hundred jubilant protestors had built a tent city. They sang hymns and chanted for her release, and every day a hundred counter-protestors showed up to scream threats, throw rocks, and chant for her death. Police in riot gear made daily arrests.

Esther frowned. "I thought maybe you'd like a Bible."

Now Paula laughed for real. "What are you doing here, Esther? I see that look in your eye, you think I don't recognize it?" Paula twisted, pressed herself higher on one elbow. Esther had never been infected by the host—they wouldn't have let her in here if she didn't pass the screening—but her strain of the disease was just as virulent. "Did your Jesus tell you to come here?"

"I suppose in a way he did." The woman didn't seem flustered. Paula found that annoying.

Esther said, "You don't have to go through this alone. Even here, even after all you've done, God will forgive you. He can be here for you, if you want him."

Paula stared at her. *If I want him.* She never stopped craving him. He'd carved out a place for himself, dug a warren through the cells in her brain, until he'd erased even himself. She no longer needed pharmaceuticals to suppress him. He'd left behind a jagged Christ-shaped hole, a darkness with teeth.

She wanted him more than drugs, more than alcohol, more than Richard or Claire. She thought she'd known loneliness, but the past months had taught her new depths. Nothing would feel better than to surrender to a new god, let herself be wrapped again in loving arms.

Esther stood and leaned close to the bars so that their faces were only a couple feet apart. "Paula, if you died right now, do you know beyond a shadow of a doubt that you'd go to heaven?" The guard told her to step back but she ignored him. She pushed one arm through the bars. "If you want to accept him, take my hand. Reach out."

"Oh, Esther, the last—" Her upper lip pulled back over her gums. "—*last* thing I want is to live forever." She fell back against the bed, tucked her working arm to her chest.

*A million people.*

There were acts beyond forgiveness. There were debts that had to be paid in person.

"Not hiding anymore," Paula said. She shook her head. "No gods, no drugs. The only thing I need to do now—"

She laughed, but it was an involuntary spasm, joyless. She waited a moment until it passed, and breathed deep. "I need to die clean."

# THE ILLUSTRATED BIOGRAPHY
## OF LORD GRIMM

The 22nd Invasion of Trovenia began with a streak of scarlet against a gray sky fast as the flick of a paintbrush. The red blur zipped across the length of the island, moving west to east, and shot out to sea. The sonic boom a moment later scattered the birds that wheeled above the fish processing plant and sent them squealing and plummeting.

Elena said, "Was that—it was, wasn't it?"

"You've never seen a U-Man, Elena?" Jürgo said.

"Not in person." At nineteen, Elena Pendareva was the youngest of the crew by at least two decades, and the only female. She and the other five members of the heavy plate welding unit were perched 110 meters in the air, taking their lunch upon the great steel shoulder of the Slaybot Prime. The giant robot, latest in a long series of ultimate weapons, was unfinished, its unpainted skin speckled with bird shit, its chest turrets empty, the open dome of its head covered only by a tarp.

It had been Jürgo's idea to ride up the gantry for lunch. They had plenty of time: for the fifth day in a row, steel plate for the Slaybot's skin had failed to arrive from the foundry, and the welding crew had nothing to do but clean their equipment and play cards until the guards let them go home.

It was a good day for a picnic. An unseasonably warm spring wind blew in from the docks, carrying the smell of the sea only slightly tainted by odors of diesel fuel and fish guts. From the giant's shoulder the crew looked down on the entire capital, from the port and industrial sector below them, to the old city in the west and the rows of gray apartment buildings rising up beyond. The only structures higher than their perch were Castle Grimm's black spires, carved out of the sides of Mount Kriegstahl, and the peak of the mountain itself.

"You know what you must do, Elena," Verner said with mock sincerity. He was the oldest in the group, a veteran mechaneer whose body was more metal than flesh. "Your first übermensch, you must make a wish."

Elena said, "Is 'Oh shit,' a wish?"

Verner pivoted on his rubber-tipped stump to follow her gaze. The figure in red had turned about over the eastern sea, and was streaking back toward the island. Sunlight glinted on something long and metallic in its hands.

The UM dove straight toward them.

There was nowhere to hide. The crew sat on a naked shelf of metal between the gantry and the sheer profile of the robot's head. Elena threw herself flat and spread her arms on the metal surface, willing herself to stick.

Nobody else moved. Maybe because they were old men, or maybe because they were all veterans, former zoomandos and mechaneers and castle guards. They'd seen dozens of U-Men, fought them even. Elena didn't know if they were unafraid or simply too old to care much for their skin.

The UM shot past with a whoosh, making the steel shiver beneath her. She looked up in time to take in a flash of metal, a crimson cape, black boots—and then the figure crashed *through* the wall of Castle Grimm. Masonry and dust exploded into the air.

"Lunch break," Jürgo said in his Estonian accent, "is over."

Toolboxes slammed, paper sacks took to the wind. Elena got to her feet. Jürgo picked up his lunch pail with one clawed foot, spread his patchy, soot-stained wings, and leaned over the side, considering. His arms and neck were skinny as always, but in the past few years he'd grown a beer gut.

Elena said, "Jürgo, can you still fly?"

"Of course," he said. He hooked his pail to his belt and backed away from the edge. "However, I don't believe I'm authorized for this air space."

The rest of the crew had already crowded into the gantry elevator. Elena and Jürgo pressed inside and the cage began to slowly descend, rattling and shrieking.

"What's it about this time, you think?" Verner said, clockwork lungs wheezing. "Old Rivet Head kidnap one of their women?" Only the oldest veterans could get away with insulting Lord Grimm in mixed company. Verner had survived at least four invasions that she knew of. His loyalty to Trovenia was assumed to go beyond patriotism into something like ownership.

Guntis, a gray, pebble-skinned amphibian of Latvian descent, said, "I fought this girlie with a sword once, Energy Lady—"

"*Power Woman*," Elena said in English. She'd read the *Illustrated Biography of Lord Grimm* to her little brother dozens of times before he learned to read it himself. The Lord's most significant adversaries were all listed in the appendix, in multiple languages.

"That's the one, *Par-wer Woh-man*," Guntis said, imitating her. "She had enormous—"

"Abilities," Jürgo said pointedly. Jürgo had been a friend of Elena's father, and often played the protective uncle.

"I think he meant to say 'tits'," Elena said. Several of the men laughed.

"No! Jürgo is right," Guntis said. "They were more than breasts. They had *abilities*. I think one of them spoke to me."

The elevator clanged down on the concrete pad and the crew followed Jürgo into the long shed of the 3000 line. The factory floor was emptying. Workers pulled on coats, joking and laughing as if it were a holiday.

Jürgo pulled aside a man and asked him what was going on. "The guards have run away!" the man said happily. "Off to fight the übermensch!"

"So what's it going to be, boss?" Guntis said. "Stay or go?"

Jürgo scratched at the cement floor, thinking. Half-assembled Slaybot 3000s, five-meter-tall cousins to the colossal Prime, dangled from hooks all along the assembly line, wires spilling from their chests, legs missing. The factory was well behind its quota for the month. As well as for the quarter, year, and five-year mark. Circuit boards and batteries were in particularly short supply, but tools and equipment vanished daily. Especially scarce were acetylene tanks, a home-heating accessory for the very cold, the very stupid, or both.

Jürgo finally shook his feathered head and said, "Nothing we can do here. Let's go home and hide under our beds."

"And in our bottles," Verner said.

Elena waved good-bye and walked toward the women's changing rooms to empty her locker.


A block from her apartment she heard Mr. Bojars singing out, "Guh-RATE day for sausa-JEZ! Izza GREAT day for SAW-sages!"

The mechaneer veteran was parked at his permanent spot at the corner of Glorious Victory Street and Infinite Progress Avenue, in the shadow of the statue of Grimm Triumphant. He saw her crossing the intersection and shouted, "My beautiful Elena! A fat bratwurst to go with that bread, maybe. Perfect for a celebration!"

"No thank you, Mr. Bojars." She hoisted the bag of groceries onto her hip and shuffled the welder's helmet to her other arm. "You know we've been invaded, don't you?"

The man laughed heartily. "The trap is sprung! The crab is in the basket!" He wore the same clothes he wore every day, a black nylon ski hat and a green, grease-stained parka decorated at the breast with three medals from his years in the motorized cavalry. The coat hung down to cover where his flesh ended and his motorcycle body began.

"Don't you worry about Lord Grimm," he said. "He can handle any American muscle-head stupid enough to enter his lair. Especially the Red Meteor."

"It was Most Excellent Man," Elena said, using the Trovenian translation of his name. "I saw the Staff of Mightiness in his hand, or whatever he calls it."

"Even better! The man's an idiot. A U-Moron."

"He's defeated Lord Grimm several times," Elena said. "So I hear."

"And Lord Grimm has been declared dead a dozen times! You can't believe the underground newspapers, Elena. You're not reading that trash are you?"

"You know I'm not political, Mr. Bojars."

"Good for you. This Excellent Man, let me tell you something about—yes sir? Great day for a sausage." He turned his attention to the customer and Elena quickly wished him luck and slipped away before he could begin another story.

The small lobby of her apartment building smelled like burnt plastic and cooking grease. She climbed the cement stairs to the third floor. As usual the door to her apartment was wide open, as was the door to Mr. Fishman's apartment across the hall. Staticky television laughter and applause carried down the hallway: It sounded like *Mr. Sascha's Celebrity Polka Fun-Time*. Not even an invasion could pre-empt Mr. Sascha.

She knocked on the frame of his door. "Mr. Fishman," she called loudly. He'd never revealed his real name. "Mr. Fishman, would you like to come to dinner tonight?"

There was no answer except for the blast of the television. She walked into the dim hallway and leaned around the corner. The living room was dark except for the glow of the TV. The little set was propped up on a wooden chair at the edge of a large cast iron bathtub, the light from its screen reflecting off the smooth surface of the water. "Mr. Fishman? Did you hear me?" She walked across the room, shoes crinkling on the plastic tarp that covered the floor, and switched off the TV.

The surface of the water shimmied. A lumpy head rose up out of the water, followed by a pair of dark eyes, a flap of nose, and a wide carp mouth.

"I was watching that," the zooman said.

"Some day you're going to pull that thing into the tub and electrocute yourself," Elena said.

He exhaled, making a rude noise through rubbery lips.

"We're having dinner," Elena said. She turned on a lamp. Long ago Mr. Fishman had pushed all the furniture to the edge of the room to make room for his easels. She didn't see any new canvasses upon them, but there was an empty liquor bottle on the floor next to the tub. "Would you like to join us?"

He eyed the bag in her arms. "That wouldn't be, umm, fresh catch?"

"It is, as a matter of fact."

"I suppose I could stop by." His head sank below the surface.

In Elena's own apartment, Grandmother Zita smoked and rocked in front of the window, while Mattias, nine years old, sat at the table with his shoe box of colored pencils and several gray pages crammed with drawings. "Elena, did you hear?" Matti asked. "A U-Man flew over the island! They canceled school!"

"It's nothing to be happy about," Elena said. She rubbed the top of her brother's head. The page showed a robot of Matti's own design marching toward a hyper-muscled man in a red cape. In the background was a huge, lumpy monster with triangle eyes—an escaped MoG, she supposed.

"The last time the U-men came," Grandmother Zita said, "more than robots lost their heads. This family knows that better than most. When your mother—"

"Let's not talk politics, Grandmother." She kissed the old woman on the cheek, then reached past her to crank open the window—she'd told the woman to let in some air when she smoked in front of Matti, to no avail. Outside, sirens wailed.

Elena had been only eleven years old during the last invasion. She'd slept through most of it, and when she woke to sirens that morning the apartment was cold and the lights didn't work. Her parents were government geneticists—there was no other kind—and often were called away at odd hours. Her mother had left her a note asking her to feed Baby Matti and please stay indoors. Elena made oatmeal, the first of many breakfasts she would make for her little brother. Only after her parents failed to come home did she realize that the note was a kind of battlefield promotion to adulthood: impossible to refuse because there was no one left to accept her refusal.

Mr. Fishman, in his blue bathrobe and striped pajama pants, arrived a half hour later, his great webbed feet slapping the floor. He sat at the table and argued with Grandmother Zita about which of the twenty-one previous invasions was most violent. There was a time in the 1960s and seventies when their little country seemed to be under attack every other month. Matti listened raptly.

Elena had just brought the fried whitefish to the table when the thumping march playing on the radio suddenly cut off. An announcer said, "Please stand by for an important message from His Royal Majesty, the Guardian of our Shores, the Scourge of Fascism, Professor General of the Royal Academy of Sciences, the Savior of Trovenia—"

Mr. Fishman pointed at Matti. "Boy, get my television!" Matti dashed to the man's apartment and Elena cleared a spot on the table.

After Mr. Fishman fiddled with the antenna the screen suddenly cleared, showing a large room decorated in Early 1400s: stone floors, flickering torches, and dulled tapestries on the walls. The only piece of furniture was a huge oaken chair reinforced at the joints with metal plates and rivets.

A figure appeared at the far end of the room and strode toward the camera.

"He's still alive, then," Grandmother said. Lord Grimm didn't appear on live television more than once or twice a year.

Matti said, "Oh, look at him."

Lord Grimm wore the traditional black and green cape of Trove-

nian nobility, which contrasted nicely with the polished suit of armor.
His faceplate, hawk-nosed and heavily riveted, suggested simultane-
ously the prow of a battleship and the beak of the Baltic albatross, the
Trovenian national bird.

Elena had to admit he cut a dramatic figure. She almost felt sorry for people in other countries whose leaders all looked like postal
inspectors. You could no more imagine those timid, pinch-faced
bureaucrats leading troops into battle than you could imagine Lord
Grimm ice skating.

"Sons and daughters of Trovenia," the leader intoned. His deep
voice was charged with metallic echoes. "We have been invaded."

"We knew that already," Grandmother said, and Mr. Fishman
shushed her.

"Once again, an American super power has violated our sover-
eignty. With typical, misguided arrogance, a so-called übermensch
has trespassed upon our borders, destroyed our property . . ." The
litany of crimes went on for some time.

"Look! The U-Man!" Matti said.

On screen, castle guards carried in a red-clad figure and dumped
him in the huge chair. His head lolled. Lord Grimm lifted the prisoner's chin to show his bloody face to the camera. One eye was half
open, the other swelled shut. "As you can see, he is completely pow-
erless."

Mr. Fishman grunted in disappointment.

"What?" Matti asked.

"Again with the captives, and the taunting," Grandmother said.

"Why not? They invaded us!"

Mr. Fishman grimaced, and his gills flapped shut.

"If Lord Grimm simply beat up Most Excellent Man and sent him
packing, that would be one thing," Grandmother said. "Or even if he
just promised to stop doing what he was doing for a couple of months
until they forgot about him, then—"

"Then we'd all go back to our business," Mr. Fishman said.

Grandmother said, "But no, he's got to keep him captive. Now
it's going to be just like 1972."

"And seventy-five," Mr. Fishman said. He sawed into his whitefish. "And eighty-three."

Elena snapped off the television. "Matti, go pack your school bag
with clothes. Now."

"What? Why?"

"We're spending the night in the basement. You too, Grandmother."

"But I haven't finished my supper!"

"I'll wrap it up for you. Mr. Fishman, I can help you down the stairs if you like."

"Pah," he said. "I'm going back to bed. Wake me when the war's over."

A dozen or so residents of the building had gotten the same idea. For several hours the group sat on boxes and old furniture in the damp basement under stuttering fluorescent lights, listening to the distant roar of jets, the rumble of mechaneer tanks, and the bass-drum stomps of Slaybot 3000s marching into position.

Grandmother Zita had claimed the best seat in the room, a ripped vinyl armchair. Matti had fallen asleep across her lap, still clutching the *Illustrated Biography of Lord Grimm*. The boy was so comfortable with her. Zita wasn't even a relative, but she'd watched over the boy since he was a toddler and so became his grandmother—another wartime employment opportunity. Elena slipped the book from under Matti's arms and bent to put it into his school bag.

Zita lit another cigarette. "How do you suppose it really started?" she said.

"What, the war?" Elena asked.

"No, the first time." She nodded at Matti's book. "Hating the Americans, okay, no problem. But why the scary mask, the cape?"

Elena pretended to sort out the contents of the bag.

"What possesses a person to do that?" Zita said, undeterred. "Wake up one day and say, Today I will put a bucket over my head. Today I declare war on all U-Men. Today I become, what's the English . . ."

"Grandmother, please," Elena said, keeping her voice low.

"A *super villain*," Zita said.

A couple of the nearest people looked away in embarrassment. Mr. Rimkis, an old man from the fourth floor, glared at Grandmother down the length of his gray-bristled snout. He was a veteran with one long tusk and the other snapped off at the base. He claimed to have suffered the injury fighting the U-Men, though others said he'd lost the tusk in combat with vodka and gravity: The Battle of the Pub Stairs.

"*He* is the hero," Mr. Rimkis said. "Not these imperialists in long underwear. They invaded his country, attacked his family, maimed him and left him with—"

"Oh please," Grandmother said. "Every villain believes himself to be a hero."

The last few words were nearly drowned out by the sudden wail of an air raid siren. Matti jerked awake and Zita automatically put a hand to his sweat-dampened forehead. The residents stared up at the ceiling. Soon there was a chorus of sirens.

They've come, Elena thought, as everyone knew they would, to rescue their comrade.

From somewhere in the distance came a steady *thump, thump* that vibrated the ground and made the basement's bare cinderblock walls chuff dust into the air. Each explosion seemed louder and closer. Between the explosions, slaybot auto-cannons whined and chattered.

Someone said, "Everybody just remain calm—"

The floor seemed to jump beneath their feet. Elena lost her balance and smacked into the cement on her side. At the same moment she was deafened by a noise louder than her ears could process.

The lights had gone out. Elena rolled over, eyes straining, but she couldn't make out Grandmother or Matti or anyone. She shouted but barely heard her own voice above the ringing in her ears.

Someone behind her switched on an electric torch and flicked it around the room. Most of the basement seemed to have filled with rubble.

Elena crawled toward where she thought Grandmother's chair had been and was stopped by a pile of cement and splintered wood. She called Matti's name and began to push the debris out of the way.

Someone grabbed her foot, and then Matti fell into her, hugged her fiercely. Somehow he'd been thrown behind her, over her. She called for a light, but the torch was aimed now at a pair of men attempting to clear the stairway. Elena took Matti's hand and led him cautiously toward the light. Pebbles fell on them; the building seemed to shift and groan. Somewhere a woman cried out, her voice muffled.

"Grandmother Zita," Matti said.

Elena was grateful that she could hear him. "I'll come back for

Grandmother," she said, though she didn't know for sure if it had been Zita's voice. "First you."

The two men had cleared a passage to the outside. One of them boosted the other to where he could crawl out. The freed man then reached back and Elena lifted Matti to him. The boy's jacket snagged on a length of rebar, and the boy yelped. After what seemed like minutes of tugging and shouting the coat finally ripped free.

"Stay there, Mattias!" Elena called. "Don't move!" She turned to assist the next person in line to climb out, an old woman from the sixth floor. She carried an enormous wicker basket which she refused to relinquish. Elena promised repeatedly that the basket would be the first thing to come out after her. The others in the basement began to shout at the old woman, which only made her grip the handle more fiercely. Elena was considering prying her fingers from it when a yellow flash illuminated the passage. People outside screamed.

Elena scrambled up and out without being conscious of how she managed it. The street lights had gone out but the gray sky flickered with strange lights. A small crowd of dazed citizens sat or lay sprawled across the rubble-strewn street, as if a bomb had gone off. The man who'd pulled Matti out of the basement sat on the ground, holding his hands to his face and moaning.

The sky was full of flying men.

Searchlights panned from a dozen points around the city, and clouds pulsed with exotic energies. In that spasmodic light dozens of tiny figures darted: caped invaders, squadrons of Royal Air Dragoons riding pinpricks of fire, winged zoomandos, glowing U-Men leaving iridescent fairy trails. Beams of energy flicked from horizon to horizon; soldiers ignited and dropped like dollops of burning wax.

Elena looked around wildly for her brother. Rubble was everywhere. The front of her apartment building had been sheared off, exposing bedrooms and bathrooms. Protruding girders bent toward the ground like tongues.

Finally she saw the boy. He sat on the ground, staring at the sky. Elena ran to him, calling his name. He looked in her direction. His eyes were wide, unseeing.

She knelt down in front of him.

"I looked straight at him," Matti said. "He flew right over our heads. He was so bright. So bright."

There was something wrong with Matti's face. In the inconstant light she could only tell that his skin was darker than it should have been.

"Take my hand," Elena said. "Can you stand up? Good. Good. How do you feel?"

"My face feels hot," he said. Then, "Is Grandmother out yet?"

Elena didn't answer. She led him around the piles of debris. Once she had to yank him sideways and he yelped. "Something in our way," she said. A half-buried figure lay with one arm and one leg jutting into the street. The body would have been unrecognizable if not for the blue-striped pajamas and the webbing between the toes of the bare foot.

Matti wrenched his hand from her grip. "Where are we going? You have to tell me where we're going."

She had no idea. She'd thought they'd be safe in the basement. She'd thought it would be like the invasions everyone talked about, a handful of U-Men—a super team—storming the castle. No one told her there could be an army of them. The entire city had become the battleground.

"Out of the city," she said. "Into the country."

"But Grandmother—"

"I promise I'll come back for Grandmother Zita," she said.

"And my book," he said. "It's still in the basement."

All along Infinite Progress Avenue, families spilled out of buildings carrying bundles of clothes and plastic jugs, pushing wheelchairs and shopping carts loaded with canned food, TV sets, photo albums. Elena grabbed tight to Matti's arm and joined the exodus north.

After an hour they'd covered only ten blocks. The street had narrowed as they left the residential district, condensing the stream of people into a herd, then a single shuffling animal. Explosions and gunfire continued to sound from behind them and the sky still flashed with parti-colored lightning, but hardly anyone glanced back.

The surrounding bodies provided Elena and Matti with some protection against the cold, though frigid channels of night air randomly opened through the crowd. Matti's vision still hadn't returned; he saw nothing but the yellow light of the U-Man. He told her his skin still felt hot, but he trembled as if he were cold. Once he stopped suddenly and threw up into the street. The crowd behind bumped into them, forcing them to keep moving.

One of their fellow refugees gave Matti a blanket. He pulled it onto his shoulders like a cape but it kept slipping as he walked, tripping him up. The boy hadn't cried since they'd started walking, hadn't complained—he'd even stopped asking about Grandmother Zita—but Elena still couldn't stop herself from being annoyed at him. He stumbled again and she yanked the blanket from him. "For God's sake, Mattias," she said. "If you can't hold onto it—" She drew up short. The black-coated women in front of them had suddenly stopped.

Shouts went up from somewhere ahead, and then the crowd surged backward. Elena recognized the escalating whine of an auto-cannon coming up to speed.

Elena pulled Matti up onto her chest and he yelped in surprise or pain. The boy was heavy and awkward; she locked her hands under his butt and shoved toward the crowd's edge, aiming for the mouth of an alley. The crowd buffeted her, knocked her off course. She came up hard against the plate glass window of a shop.

A Slaybot 3000 lumbered through the crowd, knocking people aside. Its gun arm, a huge thing like a barrel of steel pipes, jerked from figure to figure, targeting automatically. A uniformed technician sat in the jumpseat on the robot's back, gesturing frantically and shouting, "Out of the way! Out of the way!" It was impossible to tell whether he'd lost control or was deliberately marching through the crowd.

The mass of figures had almost certainly overwhelmed the robot's vision and recognition processors. The 3000 model, like its predecessors, had difficulty telling friend from foe even in the spare environment of the factory QA room.

The gun arm pivoted toward her: six black mouths. Then the carousel began to spin and the six barrels blurred, became one vast maw.

Elena felt her gut go cold. She would have sunk to the ground— she wanted desperately to disappear—but the mob held her upright, pinned. She twisted to place at least part of her body between the robot and Matti. The glass at her shoulder trembled, began to bow.

For a moment she saw both sides of the glass. Inside the dimly lit shop were two rows of blank white faces, a choir of eyeless women regarding her. And in the window's reflection she saw her own face, and above that, a streak of light like a falling star. The UM flew toward them from the west, moving incredibly fast.

The robot's gun fired even as it flicked upward to acquire the new target.

The glass shattered. The mass of people on the street beside her seemed to disintegrate into blood and cloth tatters. A moment later she registered the sound of the gun, a thunderous *ba-rap!* The crowd pulsed away from her, releasing its pressure, and she collapsed to the ground.

The slaybot broke into a clumsy stomping run, its gun ripping at the air.

Matti had rolled away from her. Elena touched his shoulder, turned him over. His eyes were open, but unmoving, glassy.

The air seemed to freeze. She couldn't breathe, couldn't move her hand from him.

He blinked. Then he began to scream.

Elena got to her knees. Her left hand was bloody and freckled with glass; her fingers glistened. Each movement triggered the prick of a thousand tiny needles. Matti screamed and screamed.

"It's okay, it's okay," she said. "I'm right here."

She talked to him for almost a minute before he calmed down enough to hear her and stop screaming.

The window was gone, the shop door blown open. The window case was filled with foam heads on posts, some with wigs askew, others tipped over and bald. She got Matti to take her hand—her good hand—and led him through the doorway. She was thankful that he could not see the things they stepped over.

Inside the scene was remarkably similar. Arms and legs of all sizes hung from straps on the walls. Trays of dentures sat out on the countertops. A score of heads sported hairstyles old-fashioned even by Trovenian standards. There were several such shops across the city. Decent business in a land of amputees.

Elena's face had begun to burn. She walked Matti through the dark, kicking aside prosthetic limbs, and found a tiny bathroom at the back of the shop. She pulled on the chain to the fluorescent light and was surprised when it flickered to life.

This was her first good look at Matti's face. The skin was bright red, puffy and raw looking—a second-degree burn at least.

She guided the boy to the sink and helped him drink from the tap. It was the only thing she could think of to do for him. Then she helped him sit on the floor just outside the bathroom door.

She could no longer avoid looking in the mirror.

The shattering glass had turned half of her face into a speckled red mask. She ran her hands under the water, not daring to scrub, and then splashed water on her face. She dabbed at her cheek and jaw with the tail of her shirt but the blood continued to weep through a peppering of cuts. She looked like a cartoon in Matti's Lord Grimm book, the coloring accomplished by tiny dots.

She reached into her jacket and took out the leather work gloves she'd stuffed there when she emptied her locker. She pulled one onto her wounded hand, stifling the urge to shout.

"Hello?" Matti said.

She turned, alarmed. Matti wasn't talking to her. His face was turned toward the hallway.

Elena stepped out. A few feet away were the base of a set of stairs that led up into the back of the building. A man stood at the first landing, pointing an ancient rifle at the boy. His jaw was flesh-toned plastic, held in place by an arrangement of leather straps and mechanical springs. A woman with outrageous golden hair stood higher on the stairs, leaning around the corner to look over the man's shoulder.

The man's jaw clacked and he gestured with the gun. "Go. Get along," he said. The syllables were distorted.

"They're hurt," the wigged woman said.

The man did not quite shake his head. Of course they're hurt, he seemed to say. Everyone's hurt. It's the national condition.

"We didn't mean to break in," Elena said. She held up her hands. "We're going." She glanced back into the showroom. Outside the smashed window, the street was still packed, and no one seemed to be moving.

"The bridge is out," the man said. He meant the Prince's Bridge, the only paved bridge that crossed the river. No wonder then that the crowd was moving so slowly.

"They're taking the wounded to the mill," the woman said. "Then trying to get them out of the city by the foot bridges."

"What mill?" Elena asked.

The wigged woman wouldn't take them herself, but she gave directions. "Go out the back," she said.

*

The millrace had dried out and the mill had been abandoned fifty years ago, but its musty, barn-like interior still smelled of grain. Its rooms were already crowded with injured soldiers and citizens.

Elena found a spot for Matti on a bench inside the building and told him not to move. She went from room to room asking if anyone had aspirin, antibiotic cream, anything to help the boy. She soon stopped asking. There didn't seem to be any doctors or nurses at the mill, only wounded people helping the more severely wounded, and no medicines to be found. This wasn't a medical clinic, or even a triage center. It was a way station.

She came back to find that Matti had fallen asleep on the gray-furred shoulder of a veteran zoomando. She told the man that if the boy woke up she would be outside helping unload the wounded. Every few minutes another farm truck pulled up and bleeding men and women stepped out or were passed down on litters. The emptied trucks rumbled south back into the heart city.

The conversation in the mill traded in rumor and wild speculation. But what report could be disbelieved when it came to the U-Men? Fifty of them were attacking, or a hundred. Lord Grimm was both dead and still fighting on the battlements. The MoGs had escaped from the mines in the confusion.

Like everyone else Elena quickly grew deaf to gunfire, explosions, crackling energy beams. Only when something erupted particularly close—a nearby building bursting into flame, or a terrordactyl careening out of control overhead—did the workers look up or pause in their conversation.

At some point a woman in the red smock of the Gene Corps noticed that Elena's cheek had started bleeding again. "It's a wonder you didn't lose an eye," the scientist said, and gave her a wad of torn-up cloth to press to her face. "You need to get that cleaned up or it will scar."

Elena thanked her curtly and walked outside. The air was cold but felt good on her skin.

She was still dabbing at her face when she heard the sputter of engines. An old mechaneer cavalryman, painted head to wheels in mud, rolled into the north end of the yard, followed by two of his wheeled brethren. Each of them was towing a narrow cart padded with blankets.

The lead mechaneer didn't notice Elena at first, or perhaps noticed her but didn't recognize her. He suddenly said, "My beautiful Elena!" and puttered forward, dragging the squeaking cart after him. He put on a smile but couldn't hold it.

"Not so beautiful, Mr. Bojars."

The old man surveyed her face with alarm. "But you are all right?" he asked. "Is Mattias—?"

"I'm fine. Matti is inside. He's sick. I think he . . ." She shook her head. "I see you've lost your sausage oven."

"A temporary substitution only, my dear." The surviving members of his old unit had reunited, he told her matter-of-factly, to do what they could. In the hours since the Prince's Bridge had been knocked out they'd been ferrying wounded across the river. A field hospital had been set up at the northern barracks of the city guard. The only ways across the river were the foot bridges and a few muddy low spots in the river. "We have no weapons," Mr. Bojars said, "but we can still drive like demons."

Volunteers were already carrying out the people chosen to evacuate next, four men and two women who seemed barely alive. Each cart could carry only two persons at a time, laid head to foot. Elena helped secure them.

"Mr. Bojars, does the hospital have anything for radiation poisoning?"

"Radiation?" He looked shocked. "I don't know, I suppose . . ."

One of the mechaneers waved to Mr. Bojars, and the two wheeled men began to roll out.

Elena said, "Mr. Bojars—"

"Get him," he replied.

Elena ran into the mill, dodging pallets and bodies. She scooped up the sleeping boy, ignoring the pain in her hand, and carried him back outside. She could feel his body trembling in her arms.

"I can't find my book," Matti said. He sounded feverish. "I think I lost it."

"Matti, you're going with Mr. Bojars," Elena said. "He's going to take you someplace safe."

He seemed to wake up. He looked around, but it was obvious he still couldn't see. "Elena, no! We have to get Grandmother!"

"Matti, listen to me. You're going across the river to the hospital. They have medicine. In the morning I'll come get you."

"She's still in the basement. She's still there. You promised you would—"

"Yes, I promise!" Elena said. "Now go with Mr. Bojars."

"Matti, my boy, we shall have such a ride!" the mechaneer said with forced good humor. He opened his big green parka and held out his arms.

Matti released his grip on Elena. Mr. Bojars set the boy on the broad gas tank in front of him, then zipped up the jacket so that only Matti's head was visible. "Now we look like a cybernetic kangaroo, hey Mattias?"

"I'll be there in the morning," Elena said. She kissed Matti's forehead, then kissed the old man's cheek. He smelled of grilled onions and diesel. "I can't thank you enough," she said.

Mr. Bojars circled an arm around Matti and revved his engine. "A kiss from you, my dear, is payment enough."

She watched them go. A few minutes later another truck arrived in the yard and she fell in line to help carry in the wounded. When the new arrivals were all inside and the stained litters had all been returned to the truck, Elena stayed out in the yard. The truck drivers, a pair of women in coveralls, leaned against the hood. The truck's two-way radio played ocean noise: whooshing static mixed with high, panicked pleas like the cries of seagulls. The larger of the women took a last drag on her cigarette, tossed it into the yard, and then both of them climbed into the cab. A minute later the vehicle started and began to move.

"Shit," Elena said. She jogged after the truck for a few steps, then broke into a full run. She caught up to it as it reached the road. With her good hand she hauled herself up into the open bed.

The driver slowed and leaned out her window. "We're leaving now!" she shouted. "Going back in!"

"So go!" Elena said.

The driver shook her head. The truck lurched into second gear and rumbled south.


As they rolled into the city proper it was impossible for Elena to tell where they would find the front line of the battle, or if there was a front line at all. Damage seemed to be distributed randomly. The truck would roll through a sleepy side street that was completely untouched, and twenty yards away the buildings would be cracked open, their contents shaken into the street.

The drivers seemed to possess some sixth sense for knowing where the injured were waiting. The truck would slow and men and women would emerge from the dark and hobble toward the head-lights of the truck, or call for a litter. Some people stood at street corners and waved them down as if flagging a bus. Elena helped the drivers lift the wounded into the back, and sometimes had to force them to leave their belongings.

"Small boats," the largest driver said over and over. A Trovenian saying: In a storm, all boats are too small.

Eventually she found herself crouched next to a burned dragoon who was half-welded to his jet pack. She held his hand, thinking that might give him something to feel besides the pain, but he only moaned and muttered to himself, seemingly oblivious to her presence.

The truck slammed to a stop, sending everyone sliding and crash-ing into each other. Through the slats Elena glimpsed a great slab of blue, some huge, organic shape. A leg. A giant's leg. The U-Man had to be bigger than an apartment building. Gunfire clattered, and a voice like a fog horn shouted something in English.

The truck lurched into reverse, engine whining, and Elena fell forward onto her hands. Someone in the truck bed cried, "Does he see us? Does he see us?"

The truck backed to the intersection and turned hard. The occu-pants shouted as they collapsed into each other yet again. Half a block more the truck braked to a more gradual stop and the drivers hopped out. "Is everyone okay?" they asked.

The dragoon beside Elena laughed.

She stood up and looked around. They were in the residential district, only a few blocks from her apartment. She made her way to the gate of the truck and hopped down. She said to the driver, "I'm not going back with you."

The woman nodded, not needing or wanting an explanation.

Elena walked slowly between the hulking buildings. The pain in her hand, her face, seemed to be returning.

She emerged into a large open space. She realized she'd been mistaken about where the truck had stopped—this park was nowhere she recognized. The ground in front of her had been turned to glass.

The sky to the east glowed. For a moment she thought it was another super-powered UM. But no, only the dawn. Below the dark bulk of Mount Kriegstahl stood the familiar silhouette of the Slaybot Prime bolted to its gantry. The air battle had moved there, above the factories and docks. Or maybe no battle at all. There seemed to be only a few flyers in the air now. The planes and TDs had disappeared. Perhaps the only ones left were U-Men.

Power bolts zipped through the air. They were firing at the Prime.

A great metal arm dropped away from its shoulder socket and dangled by thick cables. Another flash of energy severed them. The arm fell away in seeming slow motion, and the sound of the impact reached her a moment later. The übermenschen were carving the damn thing up.

She almost laughed. The Slaybot Prime was as mobile and dangerous as the Statue of Liberty. Were they actually afraid of the thing? Was that why an army of them had shown up for an ordinary hostage rescue?

My God, she thought, the morons had actually believed Lord Grimm's boasting.

She walked west, and the rising sun turned the glazed surface in front of her into a mirror. She knew now that she wasn't lost. The scorched buildings surrounding the open space were too familiar. But she kept walking. After a while she noticed that the ground was strangely warm beneath her feet. Hot even.

She looked back the way she'd come, then decided the distance was shorter ahead. She was too tired to run outright but managed a shuffling trot. Reckoning by rough triangulation from the nearest buildings she decided she was passing over Mr. Bojars' favorite spot, the corner of Glorious Victory Street and Infinite Progress Avenue. Her own apartment building should have loomed directly in front of her.

After all she'd seen tonight she couldn't doubt that there were beings with the power to melt a city block to slag. But she didn't know what strange ability, or even stranger whim, allowed them to casually trowel it into a quartz skating rink.

She heard another boom behind her. The Slaybot Prime was headless now. The southern gantry peeled away, and then the body itself began to lean. Elena had been inside the thing; the chest assembly alone was as big as a cathedral.

The Slaybot Prime slowly bowed, deeper, deeper, until it tumbled off the pillars of its legs. Dust leaped into the sky where it fell. The tremor moved under Elena, sending cracks snaking across the glass.

The collapse of the prime seemed to signal the end of the fighting. The sounds of the energy blasts ceased. Figures flew in from all points of the city and coalesced above the industrial sector. In less than a minute there were dozens and dozens of them, small and dark as blackcap geese. Then she realized that the flock of übermenschen was flying toward her.

Elena glanced to her left, then right. She was as exposed as a pea on a plate. The glass plain ended fifty or sixty meters away at a line of rubble. She turned and ran.

She listened to the hiss of breath in her throat and the smack of her heavy boots against the crystalline surface. She was surprised at every moment that she did not crash through.

Elongated shadows shuddered onto the mirrored ground ahead of her. She ran faster, arms swinging. The glass abruptly ended in a jagged lip. She leaped, landed on broken ground, and stumbled onto hands and knees. Finally she looked up.

Racing toward her with the sun behind them, the U-Men were nothing but silhouettes—shapes that suggested capes and helmets; swords, hammers, and staffs; bows and shields. Even the energy beings, clothed in shimmering auras, seemed strangely desaturated by the morning light.

Without looking away from the sky she found a chunk of masonry on the ground in front of her. Then she stood and climbed onto a tilting slab of concrete.

When the mass of U-Men was directly above her she heaved with all her might.

Useless. At its peak the gray chunk fell laughably short of the nearest figure. It clattered to the ground somewhere out of sight.

Elena screamed, tensed for—longing for—a searing blast of light, a thunderbolt. Nothing came. The U-Men vanished over the roof of the next apartment building, heading out to sea.

\*

Weeks after the invasion, the factory remained closed. Workers began to congregate there anyway. Some mornings they pushed around brooms or cleared debris, but mostly they played cards, exchanged stories of the invasion, and speculated on rumors. Lord Grimm had not been seen since the attack. Everyone agreed that the Savior of Trovenia had been dead too many times to doubt his eventual resurrection.

When Elena finally returned, eighteen days after the invasion, she found Verner and Guntis playing chess beside the left boot of the Slaybot Prime. The other huge components of the robot's body were scattered across two miles of the industrial sector like the buildings of a new city.

The men greeted her warmly. Verner, the ancient mechaneer, frankly noted the still-red cuts that cross-hatched the side of her face, but didn't ask how she'd acquired them. If Trovenians told the story of every scar there'd be no end to the talking.

Elena asked about Jürgo and both men frowned. Guntis said that the birdman had taken to the air during the fight. As for the other two members of the heavy plate welding unit, no news.

"I was sorry to hear about your brother," Verner said.

"Yes," Elena said. "Well."

She walked back to the women's changing rooms, and when she didn't find what she was looking for, visited the men's. One cinderblock wall had caved in, but the lockers still stood in orderly rows. She found the locker bearing Jürgo's name on a duct tape label. The door was padlocked shut. It took her a half hour to find a cutting rig with oxygen and acetylene cylinders that weren't empty, but only minutes to wheel the rig to the changing rooms and burn off the lock.

She pulled open the door. Jürgo's old-fashioned, rectangle-eyed welding helmet hung from a hook, staring at her. She thought of Grandmother Zita. *What possesses a person to put a bucket on their head?*

The inside of the locker door was decorated with a column of faded photographs. In one of them a young Jürgo, naked from the waist up, stared into the camera with a concerned squint. His new wings were unfurled behind him. Elena's mother and father, dressed in their red Gene Corps jackets, stood on either side of him. Elena unpeeled the yellowed tape and put the picture in her breast pocket, then unhooked the helmet and closed the door.

She walked back to the old men, pulling the cart behind her. "Are we working today or what?" she asked.

Guntis looked up from the chess board with amusement in his huge wet eyes. "So you are the boss now, eh, Elena?"

Verner, however, said nothing. He seemed to recognize that she was not quite the person she had been. Damaged components had been stripped away, replaced by cruder, yet sturdier approximations. He was old enough to have seen the process repeated many times.

Elena reached into the pockets of her coat and pulled on her leather work gloves. Then she wheeled the cart over to the toe of the boot and straightened the hoses with a flick of her arm.

"Tell us your orders, Your Highness," Guntis said.

"First we tear apart the weapons," she said. She thumbed the blast trigger and blue flame roared from the nozzle of the cutting torch. "Then we build better ones."

She slid the helmet onto her head, flipped down the mask, and bent to work.

# GARDENING AT NIGHT

The minefield was a tidy two-hundred-foot square out on the salt flats, its border marked by a yellow ribbon staked to the sandy surface. Anti-personnel landmines were scattered in a pseudo-random pattern inside, buried an inch deep. All the mytes had to do was find all the mines without exploding them. All Reg had to do was act like he was in control.

He sat on a Rubber-Maid trunk full of tools, cables, and robot parts, in an attitude of prayer: elbows on knees, bent over a paper coffee cup between his palms. One of the grad students wheeled the dolly to the edge of the field, crossed carefully over the ribbon, and stopped about ten feet inside the border. He levered his cargo—a glossy black slab the size of a gravestone—onto the ground. One of the other students ran an orange extension cord out to the slab; the other end was wired to a battery pack set up outside the border. Then the four students took up positions around the square, booted up laptops and video cameras, and one by one turned their attention to Dr. Reg Berentz.

This should be Eli's job, Reg thought. Eli was the project leader, the great man, the field marshal. Reg had been working on this project with him for over four years, but months into Eli's hospitalization it still felt presumptuous to decant the mytes without him. The old man loved them like his children.

Reg set his coffee on the ground and stood up, back creaking. He was only 33, an assistant professor and less than half Eli's age, but he felt ancient compared to these twenty-something students. He'd been up most of the night debugging code, and he felt as keyed up and sleep deprived as the first weeks after his son was born.

He walked slowly to the border, stepped over the tape, and squatted down next to the slab. Up close it looked like a stack of black Legos—rectangles stacked on rectangles—almost three feet high and four inches thick. 1152 shells. He traced a finger up the right edge of the block, got a fingernail under the top piece, and tapped it, tilting it up. The piece was shaped like a domino, two inches long and a little less than an inch wide, the back end still connected to the next piece in the chain. Two wires protruded from the front like long antennae; four other wires dangled from the bottom.

Reg dipped into his pocket, found the special AC adapter, and fitted it to the antennae. The other end of the adapter was the standard three-prong pig face: two squinty eyes and a round snout in the middle. "This little piggy went to market," he said to himself. He reached down and picked up the female end of the extension cord.

Dipti, one of the veteran students who'd been on the project almost as long as Reg, said, "Wait a minute, Dr. B. Aren't you going to say it?"

The students looked at Reg expectantly. Eli may be in the hospital, but there were traditions to maintain.

Reg set his face into an Eli frown. "All right, people," he said, doing a practiced imitation of the man. "Let's do this like my sister."

Marshall Lin, a first-year student on his first trip to the minefield, looked to Dipti for an explanation, but she waved it off: tell you later.

Reg kissed the pig face on its nose, braced himself, and connected the adapter to the extension cord.

Nothing happened.

Reg unplugged, plugged again. Stood up, hands on his hips, and looked toward the battery pack. "Can somebody . . .?"

The electricity hit and the slab burst into a multitude of black shapes. Reg jumped back, laughing.

Shells spattered onto the ground, tumbled in the dirt, righted themselves, and fled on churning wire legs.

Reg stepped back over the tape on tiptoe, careful to avoid crushing them. Some of the creatures scurried toward him, then stopped short a few inches from the tape and reversed course. The rest flowed outward, toward the center of the field. It looked for a moment as if they were scattering, each individual fleeing for shelter, and Reg sucked in his breath. They'd all die, triggering the landmines blindly.

But then their instincts kicked in and they turned in toward each other. Shells called out on the universal myte frequency, skittered toward each other, and butted heads, antennae waving. They crawled over each others' backs, thrust wires into receiving ports, tumbled like puppies.

Sometimes when they touched they remained in contact. Bodies began to assemble.

Reg watched the mass of shells closest to him. Ten of the shells had already daisy-chained into a rough circle. Another strand formed at the other side of the circle, writhing frantically like skaters in a game of crack the whip. In a moment the segment slapped across the center of the circle; when it rapped against the other strand, the two chains curled inward and joined at an angle. The two strands worked like a divining rod, swinging into other shells. Clusters formed at the intersection of the strands. The pace accelerated, a flurry of attachment and reattachment as the group struggled to implement the shared blueprint in their memory.

In ten seconds, assembly was complete. He knew from studying it in the Logosphere, the simulation environment they used, that the myte's body was composed of thirty-seven shells. It was shaped like a squat "Y"—two long limbs, one short—connected at the middle by a cluster of shells. The short limb, capped by a cube of six shells, swiveled and swayed like a elephant's trunk. It was a new design, lighter than the 60-shell mytes in the last generation they'd tested on the flats, less likely to set off mines with its weight. He shook his head with delight. By his own definition the creature in front of him was no more *real* or *alive* than a creature instantiated in the Logosphere—but it didn't feel that way. There was something about seeing it born in front of his eyes, out here in the sand and sun. It seemed to demand a name.

All around the new myte, its sisters were assembling, thirty or forty of them already up and mobile. The remaining shells, spread out over a twenty yard area, would take longer to find partners, if they found them at all.

The assembled mytes went to work, crawling delicately over the sand and rock like crabs. Every six inches or so, the myte would stop, balance on its two rear legs, and wave its trunk over the ground in front of it like a divining rod, using simple beat frequency oscillation to sniff for metal. And not just any metal: the myte had evolved to concentrate on certain magnetic signatures and ignore the noise of shrapnel, bullet casings, and mundane garbage.

"Score one," Dipti called. She was on the east side of the square, eyeing the screen of her laptop. "C5, and no detonation," she said. Reg was standing near C hash mark on the yellow ribbon, and looked up to where 5 ought to be on the Y axis. A live-action game of *Battleship*.

The myte in question squatted over a section of dirt, trembling with an excellent imitation of excitement. Its foreleg scratched a circle around the found mine.

"Okay," Reg said, uselessly. He started pacing. "Okay."

Over the next thirty minutes, the mytes found another dozen mines without setting them off—ten minutes ahead of their best real-world record. He began to fantasize about clearing the field in less than an hour. Eli would be happy, and more importantly, they'd have something solid to write about in the next grant application. The whole project was on soft money, and Reg and Eli had been shaped by evolutionary pressures to pursue grants with the single-mindedness of anteaters. Or mytes.

Reg grew more nervous as each mine was uncovered, and finally his pessimism was rewarded: mytes started piling up in the northwest quadrant, something they'd never done in the Logosphere. They crowded into each other, hemmed in by the yellow corner. They seemed to have forgotten about the mines—only the tape kept them from heading to Alaska.

The tape in and of itself was no barrier, but the wire inside it emitted a low-power radio broadcast. The frequency and the message were hard-wired into every myte—the only preset commands in the chipset. God whispered, and the message was Death. Any myte who crossed the wire would shut itself off automatically.

Already, the crowding had pushed some of the mytes into the tape, and they'd become dead weight. The rest of the mytes piled on, and died in turn.

"Jesus Christ, it's a frickin' Who concert!" Reg said. He didn't think any of the students were old enough to get a classical reference, but Dipti laughed. Marshall Lin looked as confused as before.

A few more minutes and every myte on the field had converged on the northwest corner, and Reg called the test to a halt. Dipti stalked into the field, waving an antenna wired to a radio and battery pack— the same frequency and message as the tape, but with more power. One by one the mytes went dead.

"Round 'em up," Reg said. "Let's set up another block." He walked back to the truck and poured himself another cup of coffee.

\*

"The same thing every time?" Eli said, ignoring the nurse walking into the room.

Reg shrugged. "Three different quadrants, but yeah—they were running for the fence. Looks like it's time to take your medicine."

The nurse, a big white guy, set the tray on the side table. Like Eli and Reg, he wore a paper breather over his mouth and nose, which made him even more intimidating. Eli still hadn't looked at him.

"It's got to be in the environment code," Eli said. He always thought it was in the environment code, never in the myte processing software. Reg's grad assistants had written the environmental library.

"Dr. Karchner . . ." the nurse said. His surprisingly soft voice was almost lost in the hum and hiss of the air scrubbers. Vents in the ceiling sucked air out the room, blasted it with UV, forced it through microfilters, and jetted it back.

"Maybe its heliotropism," Eli said. The mytes' skin was light sensitive. "Increase the sunlight in the Logosphere, make sure it's coming from the west. And make sure your sand is reflecting properly."

Reg shook his head. "I don't think that's it," he said good-naturedly. "But I'll—" Behind Eli, the nurse crossed his arms. Beefy Aaron Neville arms. "I'll check it out," Reg said.

"Dr. Karchner," the nurse said, louder.

Eli sighed, pulled down his mask, and allowed the nurse to hand him, one at a time, three little plastic cups, which he downed like shots of harsh whisky.

The last time Reg had talked to Eli's doctor, the mix was INH, Cycloserine, and Ethioniamide, but he could very well be taking some new cocktail. Months into his treatment, he'd already gone through the first-line drugs, and was working his way down the bench. The sputum counts would dip with each new combination, then climb steadily back up.

Any three TB-tested antibiotics, used consistently, should have been enough to wipe out the TB—unless the strain happened to evolve in a hyper-Darwinian environment like the University of Utah Hospital (Motto: Come for the gall bladder infection, but stay for the multi-drug resistant TB). Eli, more than anyone, understood the rule of large numbers, the arithmetic of natural selection. It became clear with each failed cocktail that the strain he'd picked up was something of an evolutionary veteran.

Eli's doctors were getting desperate. Most of his treatment had been self-administered at home, but as Eli deteriorated they'd brought him back to the scene of the crime, the same hospital where he'd been infected. It seemed ludicrous to Reg that a rich, fully-insured American could die of consumption in the second decade of the twenty-first century . . . but there it was.

The nurse left, and Eli leaned back into the pillows—the back of his bed was almost always raised—and blinked slowly. He was a wide-faced man with a monkish fringe of gray hair, only in his late-sixties, but he looked older. The energy he'd had five minutes ago seemed to have been knocked out of him. At least he wasn't coughing. Reg couldn't take the coughing.

They called this phase L & C: Liquefaction and Cavitation. After years of macrophage-bacteria warfare, TB bacilli fled into the lung tissue where the cumbersome macrophages couldn't follow. Smaller T-cells pursued like barracuda, chewing apart healthy tissue to deprive TB of breeding places. Cells turned liquid and were coughed out in shotgun blasts, leaving behind lungs pitted like exploded mine-fields.

The coughing was awful, but worse was the way Eli dropped his head and *submitted* to it—and Eli submitted to nothing without a fight.

Reg got up to leave. "I'll let you rest. Tomorrow I'll stop by with—"

"I got in the study," Eli said.

"What? When?"

"Found out this morning." There'd been no new TB drugs for almost 50 years, but with TB raging across AIDS-weakened Africa, a few pharmaceutical companies decided there might be a market for expensive new drugs to replace the cheap generics. Cecrolysin was the first of the new peptide antibiotics okayed for human trials. Eli's doctor had been trying to get him into the study for months.

"Eli, that's great news! When do you start?"

He waved a hand. "A couple weeks." He didn't look happy about it. But maybe that was just the fatigue.

Reg was struck by the fact that Eli had no one else to give this news to. He'd divorced sometime in his thirties. He had no children, and besides Reg, no close friends in the department. Somewhere he must have old friends, ex-colleagues, relatives—maybe even a sister who was indeed "fast, cheap, and out of control"—but Reg had never met them.

He reached for the older man's shoulder, and hesitated. Did Eli dislike being touched? He wasn't the huggy type. Reg finally patted him on the shoulder, dropped his hand to his side. "That's . . . amazing news. Really amazing."

Perhaps half a minute passed, and Reg couldn't think of anything to say. Eli remained silent and impassive.

"Well," Reg said. "I'll bring by the videos tomorrow, and the stats. You'll be back with us in no time." Reg shouldered his bag. He reached the door and Eli said, "How are Cora and Theo?"

Reg turned. Eli, asking about his family?

"Fine," Reg said. "Everything's going really well."


When Reg got home he made a circuit of the echoing apartment, flicking on lights. First the living room, empty except for the entertainment center and the loveseat Cora didn't want; the front bathroom, spare and clean; the back bedroom where he slept and the adjoining master bath. He did this out of habit, even though he lived alone six days of the week, even though the apartment was so small there was barely room for anyone to hide.

Last he checked the guest bedroom. The bed was made and the toys were all put away, except for on the window sill, which had become a permanent parking lot of Hot Wheels cars watched over by second-favorite action figures. The first-stringers were two miles away, in Theo's room at the house on the avenues, where he lived with his mother. Where Reg lived too until a few months ago.

The house they'd shared was a big Victorian. Reg had always worked late, but once he joined Eli's myte project he started staying until ten or eleven, and when he came home he'd first patrol the downstairs of the old house, then go up to his son's room, where Theo would be in his usual position on the bed: face down, body draped precariously over the edge. He'd lift Theo's arms back onto the bed and tuck the blankets over him. Theo sometimes mumbled something, but never woke completely. Then Reg would go to the bedroom, undress in the dark, and slip under the covers. He'd spoon against Cora, shivering, and nudge his icy feet against hers. "Oh my

*God*," she'd say. He'd laugh and slip his arm over her hip to cup her belly and fall asleep breathing into her neck.

Reg flicked off the light, shut the door to save the air conditioning.

In the kitchen he poured himself a bowl of Raisin Bran—one good thing about living alone, he always knew exactly how much cereal he had left—and set it down next to the laptop he kept set up on the bar counter. He opened a search engine and typed "cecrolysin."

They called it the Garden. Former National Guard garage, former warehouse, former abandoned building, then annexed by the University of Utah and converted to a computer lab. A dim, hollowed space, filled with monitors glowing like jack o' lanterns.

The building was a barrel cut in half, its ridged roof forty feet above the floor at its highest point. Industrial-sized ductwork for the climate control ran along the tops of the walls. The cement floor was crowded with dozens of metal racks loaded with shiny new pizza box servers, dozens more folding tables loaded with old PCs and dusty routers, and rivers of cable: black power, blue Ethernet, snake-striped fiber optics. Every new thing they could afford side by side with every second-hand piece they could scavenge, and all connected. The room generated a steady roar.

Eli stayed in the hospital all that summer, and so Reg was first in the building every morning. After disarming the security system, he took time moving through the maze, checking equipment. His hands roved intimately over the pronged and portholed backsides of the computers, plucking at wires and tugging at connections. The machines hummed accompaniment. This fiddling with the network was his nervous ritual, half superstition, half technical professionalism: you can never be too careful.

The monitors displayed simple line plots and bar graphs that shifted in real time to reflect the status of the 'sphere. He rarely studied the screens directly, but took note of them in passing, like a farmer mindful of clouds. Jobs usually ran all night—virtual resources churning, niches filling and emptying—and by morning entire species had played musical chairs.

Sometimes he reached behind a CPU or router and found a loose jack. As he jiggled it into place he wondered how many creatures he'd just saved. If the connection failed during the download, whole segments of the population might be lost—an entire generation or species—wiped out as efficiently as a meteor strike because two strands of fiber failed to kiss and bump electrons.

Midway across the jungle, he stopped to turn on the tree. A gigantic inverted metal Christmas tree, smuggled into the Garden years ago over holiday break, an MIT-quality prank. The skinny steel trunk rose nearly to the ceiling. Aluminum rods, bumpy with techno-junk decorations and dozens of halogen strip lights, spiked from the trunk in starburst rings. The topmost rods extended fifteen feet from the trunk, drooping slightly at the ends. Each succeeding ring cast shorter and shorter lengths, tapering to base spokes only six inches long. When he flipped the switch, everything in the room grew bright and hard edged. The tree was such an odd artifact, and its light so needed in the cavernous room, that no one had taken it down after that first Christmas, and now no one could imagine the room without it.

At the far end of the lab was a row of new workstations, a spill of fiber optic cable, and a wall of black plastic. The wall was six foot high and ten feet long, a contiguous block of nearly 140,000 mytes. Bodies stacked on bodies on bodies, alive but unmoving, paralyzed like REMming sleepers. Sometimes he ran his hand along the warm side of the block, and it seemed to hum and pulse.

It was usually a couple hours until the first of the students arrived. He'd sit down at his workstation, turn on his monitor. For a moment he'd gaze at his own face, but then the brightening shapes wiped it away, and he'd gaze down at the Logosphere.

In the fall Theo started first grade, and Reg and Cora worked out a plan to make their son's life as regular and normal as possible. Reg would pick him from the bus on Tuesdays and take him back to school on Wednesday. On Thursdays he'd take Theo to soccer practice and return him after dinner. On Saturdays everyone went to the games. On Sundays they all ate dinner together at the house on the avenues.

It was a civilized separation. They were good parents.

At the first Thursday soccer practice it was clear most of the six-year-olds on Theo's team had grown taller but no more skilled since last season. They still played mob ball, surging in a clump from one end of the field to another. Classic swarming behavior.

Reg sat on the sidelines with the other parents, sunk into a nylon camp chair, and while he waited he fiddled with an amputee myte shell they'd rescued from the minefield. It was a normal shell, black and efficient-looking. The skin was coated with a thin layer of VE-SEC—a lacquer of light-sensitive flakes from 3M that not only collected solar energy, but reported light intensities to a chip, giving the myte a crude grayscale vision system.

Shells usually had eight limbs, two to a side, but this one had lost the right front leg. Reg tested each of the remaining seven limbs, tugging lightly with the tweezers, waggling it back and forth to test the connection.

The legs were nifty pieces of engineering. Each limb was a polymer sheath around a twisted bundle of two fiber-optic wires and two copper wires. The sheath was an organic plastic that acted like memory wire—a slight charge to one of the root cells inside the body of the myte, and the polymer would expand or contract one of thirty-six "muscle regions" along its length. Each leg had an impressive degree of flexibility: the thin gap between each of the interior muscle regions was a flex point, giving each leg in effect five joints that could bend in any direction. In actuality, most species of myte kept it simple; they developed a few efficient movement algorithms that used one or two joints per leg, and left it at that. The bigger mytes, of course, composed locomotion limbs from multiple shells. If the Logosphere were tweaked to reward pure speed, he wondered, how fast could they go?

That was the beauty of the myte design. They weren't built just for detecting mines. Eli envisioned them as general purpose machines you could evolve into a variety of shapes and behaviors, for any number of tasks: inspecting buildings for infrastructure flaws, searching for survivors in rubble, exploring other planets. The only problem with that all-purpose design is that they weren't optimized for any particular task. Reg had finally convinced Eli to concentrate on the landmine problem, and even that had taken years. The project was expensive, and they had very little to show for it.

All the remaining limbs seemed secure, so Reg ran a finger along the shell, feeling for the slightly raised band of the radio antenna. A centimeter to one side of the antenna he pressed down, and a panel tilted open.

"Ah," Reg said. He tucked the panel under his leg and began to tilt the myte to get light into the cramped guts of the shell. Beneath the vision chip, he could just make out the edges of the other two main chips: one for behavior processing and one for storage. The tail of the shell was stuffed with four cheap lithium-based batteries. Along the sides were eight tiny bumps: ports for the legs/antennae. The remaining space was filled with the spaghetti of fiber-optic and metal wires that connected limbs to chips to batteries.

None of the components were cutting edge. The technology behind each piece was a decade old or more; most of the hardware could be bought off the shelf. Only the organization of the materials, and the uses they were put to, made them interesting.

He pushed aside the wires crowding the empty limb port, squinting. A few stray wires stretched toward the missing leg. He could use more light.

"You playing with your mytes again, Dad?"

Reg looked up and laughed. "Yep." Theo was sweating, his bangs plastered to his forehead. "You thirsty?"

"Did you see me play goal? I stopped a lot of them."

"You did great, Captain." Reg had missed the stint in goal, but the important thing was to be encouraging. He fished through the gym bag Cora had packed, found the water bottle, and twisted it open for him. "Keep hustling."

Afterward they went to McDonald's. Reg hated the place, but Theo loved the toys. Reg showed Theo the myte, the leg he'd reattached. "And here's where it can link up to other shells."

"You get to put them all together?" Theo said enviously.

Reg laughed. He was probably picturing a room full of Legos. "They put themselves together. They self-assemble."

"But how do they know what shape to do? Do you tell them?"

"We grow them in the computer first, and then they learn how to assemble. They're like plants, and we, uh, pick the kinds of seeds we want in the garden, and then they . . . just grow."

Theo shook his head. "But who tells the seed what to do?"

"That's a very good question," Reg said. "We have software that, well . . ." He laughed. "It's complex," he said, giving up.

"Oh." This seemed perfectly acceptable to Theo. "Okay."

When they got back to the house on the avenues, the lights were on and Cora was ferrying bags of groceries from the trunk of the Accord to the house. She still wore her work clothes, a short skirt over black nylons. He'd always liked her in black nylons.

He grabbed a couple bags and followed her into the house. She looked good. She'd started working out since Reg moved out, and had dropped weight. Something else had dropped, too. Some tension. It'd been Reg's idea for him to move out, but Cora seemed to be thriving.

"Good practice, Theo?" she said as Theo ran past.

"He was great in goal," Reg said.

"Really! Good job, Captain." She set the bags on the counter. "How's Eli? Is the new drug working?"

"The Cecrolysin. It's amazing stuff." He put down the bags, sat down at one of the stools in the kitchen island. "See, old-style antibiotics, like streptomycin, were cultivated from microbes that lived in the soil, but Cecrolysin's part of a whole new family of antibiotics, based on stuff that's part of animals' own defense systems."

He told her how peptides coated the skin and throats and lungs of frogs, sharks, and insects— Cecrolysin came from a silk moth—killing off bacteria better even than some antibodies, though nobody'd been able to get peptides to work specifically on TB because the peptides were too small to penetrate TB's waxy shell—until (and this was the cool part) they figured out how to make clusters of peptides link into a barrel shape; because the barrel was positively charged and TB's membrane was negatively charged, when the barrel found the bacterium it stuck like a magnet.

"But the inside of TB, see, is even more negatively charged than its outside, so the barrel gets sucked *through* the membrane, punching through the shell," Reg said. "And if the *wound* doesn't kill the bacterium outright, it still leaves a gaping hole for other drugs to get through. Isn't that the most amazing design?"

She shook her head, laughed. All the groceries had been put away, and she'd started to rinse the dishes in the sink and load them into the dishwasher. "Reg, all I asked was if Eli was feeling better."

Reg blinked. "Well, he's doing great. He's at home now—I'm going to go see him tonight. He's not supposed to come to work yet, but I thought I'd bring him some food."

She dried her hands on the dish towel. "Why don't you ask him for dinner sometime? I mean here, on a Sunday." Sunday was their family dinner.

"You'd do that?"

"He's not contagious, is he?" she said. Reg shook his head. Eli's last two sputum tests came back negative, and a couple more weeks he'd be cleared. "Then why not? He's my friend too."

"You said he was a cold fish." And Eli was, sometimes. Borderline Asperger's, uninterested in social niceties. A geek whose idea of small talk was proposing pathfinding algorithms for neural networks. Whenever Cora and Eli were together, Reg spent a lot of time buffering and translating.

"I'm used to fish," she said.

"Dr. Berentz, I've been wondering about the meaning of this word," Marshall Lin said. "Is it the name of one of the software packages you purchased?"

"What, *Logosphere?* Naw, Dr. Karchner made it up years ago. He loves biblical references." Reg could see that the kid didn't get it. "See, *logos* is Greek for word. It's a nod to Genesis: In the beginning was the Word."

"Oh." Lin's face was still blank. The boy had grown up in Indiana, but he'd escaped Sunday school and, evidently, all television and non-public radio. So far he'd shown himself oblivious to any of Reg's pop cultural asides. In a lot of ways he was more of a foreigner than Dipti, a homegirl from Bombay who could carry on entire conversations in Simpsons quotes.

Reg tried again. "In the first stage, the mytes exist only as bits, right? And in this network we've cooked up, we pass data in sixty-four bits, which are—"

"Eight-byte words—yes, of course. A pun."

"Now you got it. And when we decant the mytes, the word is made flesh."

Lin nodded. Reg still didn't think he got it, but it didn't matter. The kid was a sharp coder and knew quite a bit about parallel processing. He'd been a help these past few weeks tracking down the clumping problem—or rather, eliminating variables that weren't causing the clumping problem.

Weeks into the fall semester and they still hadn't been able to duplicate the mytes' behavior from the summer's minefield test. Tweaking the environmental variables, including sunlight, hadn't yet driven the mytes into the corners like they'd seen in the field. The model could never match reality, of course—nature just had too many bits— but there were techniques for maximizing the computational power of the simulation. The first trick was commandeering the hardware of the mytes themselves. The network servers provided the environment, but the myte shells computed their own actions, just as they would in the field. When a myte met another, the network put them in touch with each other, allowing them to trade code as if they were alive.

"Let's try another ten runs, on ten fields," Reg said. Lin's expression had turned pained. "Yes, Marshall?"

"Dr. Berentz . . ." Lin said hesitantly.

"Go ahead," Reg said.

"I've been looking at the instruction sets running on some of the myte chips and—"

"You can read that stuff?" Reg was impressed. Even decompiled, grown code was as dense-packed and parsimonious as DNA: endless strings of characters that told you almost nothing about how they'd be used in the field. You had to run the program to see what the code did.

Lin shrugged, embarrassed. "Some of it. Mostly I see patterns. Something seemed off, so I compared the instructions over time, and ran them through a stats package. There was a big shift in the code base a few months ago, even though the myte morphology didn't change. And some of the code looks human-written, originally."

"And? What's the changed code doing?"

"I . . . I don't know. It's been mixed in to the evolved code, and I haven't yet figured out . . .

"I think I know what you're seeing," Reg said. "Eli wrote the original libraries, back in the day. Some of that code must have persisted when the other stuff got overwritten, like junk DNA. Or maybe not—maybe it just looks hand-coded. There's an awful lot of code, after all, and it's easy to fall prey to pattern recognition with this stuff."

Uh oh. Lin looked like a slapped school boy. Reg backpedaled. "But hey! Keep looking. You never know, right?" Lin nodded, his face flushed. Jesus, the kid was sensitive. Reg spun his chair around, clapped his hands. "In the meantime, let's keep looking at the environmentals."

Lin went back to his workstation and reset the launch scripts. Reg tuned in from his own monitor, flipping between ten virtual blocks of mytes on ten virtual fields.

The mytes scattered and spread in speeded-up time. The GUI of the Logosphere represented each shell as single black dot on the gray sand, and the tripedal mytes as clumps of dots. The mines were blue disks that blinked red when triggered, green when tagged.

Except for the mines, none of the details of the field existed until the mytes discovered them. Each element—each rock, plant, inch-square of sand—was created on the fly as the mytes sensed them. And mine fields were simple compared to some of the environments the team had created. For the mytes' other tasks, the Logosphere could generate urban environments, force-blooming an entire city improvisationally. Buildings and cars and even people were assigned sizes and positions at random within a set of construction rules. Each building was a hollow prop until a myte crawled inside, then the 'sphere spun out rooms, corridors, stairs, ventilation shafts, rows of electrical outlets. When a myte reached a room, random furniture appeared, and when it crawled into the spaces between the walls, the program provided wiring, plumbing, and obstacles.

Once created, each object was locked into memory for a time, like a quantum particle assuming its position in the classical world only after being observed. Only when the myte had moved along and the system needed to free up resources did the Logosphere put the Schrödinger cat back into its box and vaporize the room into indeterminacy.

Reg glanced at the timer. The mytes lived and died in six minute intervals, briefer than mayflies, and only thirty seconds were left. Across all ten fields, the mytes had correctly tagged almost all the mines. Not one of the groups had suddenly made for a corner of the field and froze. He shook his head, disappointed in the lack of failure. If they couldn't replicate the bug, they couldn't fix it.

The screen went black. The Angel of Death, the reaper program—the *Boogens*—descended on the Logosphere.

Eighty-nine percent of the mytes were killed immediately. In the wall of myte shells behind Reg's head, the corresponding chips stopped their dreaming. The reaper program moved through the wall, extinguishing the charges in the chipsets, erasing all memory and genetic information.

Ten of the remaining 11 percent were saved, not by lamb's blood over the door, but by their own fitness. These survivors were the ones who had scored the highest: finding the most mines in the shortest time. It was the time-honored use of evolution to do a roboticist's design-work.

The breeder program launched next. The software paired each survivor with a mate of the same species, took half of the genetic code from each, and made new packets of code—offspring. Eli also allowed a mutation rate: the program introduced a small percentage of deliberate errors as it transcribed the genetic code to the offspring.

The remaining one percent Eli had named the Lucky Losers. They were chosen at random, from the individuals whose scores didn't merit salvation. The Losers were allowed one child, while the gifted ten percent were allowed multiple offspring. Perhaps they shouldn't have been allowed to breed at all, but through genetic mixing and mutation, even a pair of losers might make a DaVinci, a Mozart, a Lassie. God wasn't the only one who moved in mysterious ways.

Finally, the programs disposed of the elderly 11 percent and filled each shell with the code of the new generation. The entire breeding process took a minute and thirty seconds. Painfully slow, but the best the hodgepodge of equipment could do.

The cycle began again. The Logosphere set down the virtual mytes in the center of the blank screen. Instinctively the newborns scattered, and began to rebuild their world around them.


After two months of Cecrolysin treatments, Eli's appetite had come back with a vengeance. He devoured everything put in front of him: the bowl of salad, several slabs of garlic bread (a Cora specialty: butter, parmesan, tomato chunks, and those sixteen deadly cloves mashed into a pavement and baked onto halves of French bread), three lasagna servings as thick as bricks, a stack of asparagus, and glass after glass of red wine.

The conversation over appetizers had been labored, Reg scrambling to fill in long silences. Once they sat down to the table, Eli barely spoke, eating with the same monofocus he brought to his lab work.

Watching him inhale all that food was simultaneously appalling and satisfying, like one of those wildlife documentaries in which the alpha lion shoves the pride away from the kill and proceeds to eat the entire wildebeest. Reg tried not to stare. Theo couldn't take his eyes off him.

"Theo," Cora said. "Eat some of your food."

The boy feigned deafness. Reg tapped the boy's plate with his spoon. "Eat up, Captain."

Theo absently picked up an asparagus stalk and chewed in time with Eli. Cora shook her head and poured the last of a bottle into her glass.

Reg peeled the foil from the last bottle and wadded it into a heavy ball. "Eli, you were right about the wine." The man had shown up with three identical bottles of cabernet, like someone who'd read only the first line in a paragraph about American Dinner Customs.

On the other hand, the three bottles that had seemed excessive an hour ago now seemed like a good start. Alcohol could only help.

"It's very good," Cora added. "Nice choice."

Eli brushed crumbs of garlic bread from his beard, nodding. He lifted another chunk of lasagna "And this, this is very . . ."

Reg thought: C'mon Eli, you can do it, just one polite compliment to the chef.

". . . filling."

The foil ball shot from Reg's fingers and bounced off the table. Theo yelped, "I'll get it!" and dove under the table. Reg ducked down as well.

Oh god, he'd nearly barked out a laugh. *Filling?* He stayed down so he wouldn't see Cora's face—if he looked at her now he'd lose it. Theo found the foil and scrambled up. Reg stayed under for a moment longer, trying to control his breathing. *Don't look at Cora. Don't look at Cora.*

He sat up, smile fixed, and reached for his wine glass. Theo weighed the foil in his hand. Eli stared at his plate, chewing thoughtfully. And on Cora's face . . . the Happy Homemaker Smile.

"Okay! More wine!" Reg downed the last of his drink and reached for the corkscrew. He uncorked the last bottle and refilled everyone's glasses, trying to remember why exactly he thought this dinner was a good idea.

"To the chef," he said. "For a filling meal."

Eli looked up. Theo raised his plastic water cup—they'd pretended to toast before, so he knew the routine—and tipped it against Cora's glass. The Happy Homemaker smiled sweetly. "To the fill-ees," she said.

Reg saluted—"From a fine filly!"—and swallowed half the wine in one gulp. Warmth rushed to his ears. His fingers tingled. It seemed reasonable, suddenly, that he should drink faster and keep drinking as long as possible. Tomorrow was Saturday and Reg could sleep in until seven or eight before heading back to the lab. So why not get drunk? The trick would be to pull back just before his head detached and began to bob against the ceiling.

Theo put down his cup. "I'm filled," he said. Cora and Reg cracked up. Maybe she was getting drunk too.

"What? What did I say?"

Reg said, "Nothing, Phil." Which made Cora nearly spit her wine.

She wiped her lips. "So Eli. You're going back to work tomorrow? Reg said you're doing another field test."

He nodded. "It's been too long."

"Amen to that," Reg said. They hadn't been able to replicate the myte's clumping behavior in the Logosphere, and if the mytes did it again in the minefield, Reg wanted Eli to see it.

"There's something I've asked Reg a dozen times, but he's never given me a decent answer," Cora said. "When you came up with this myte idea, what did you *really* want them to do? You, personally."

"Is that important?" Eli said.

"Well, sure," Cora said.

"Did you ask yourself what purpose Theo would serve before you had him?"

Reg laughed, forcing it a little to smooth the awkwardness. "I think that's a little different. I couldn't get a grant to conceive Theo."

Eli was distracted again. He was looking at Theo. After a silence, he said, "I've been thinking of Adam and Eve."

Cora raised an eyebrow. Reg said, "Oh yeah?" Casual.

Eli did this all the time: they'd be having a perfectly normal conversation—well, at least a coherent one—and then Eli would take a left turn, leaving everyone else to catch up. Over the past year, a lot of these left turns seemed theological in nature, and Reg had wondered if the life-threatening disease was making Eli get religion—or rather, making him get it again. Eli had been raised Mormon, and though he hadn't gone to temple in decades, church was a virus that could lay dormant, waiting for a weakened immune system. The atheist-fox-hole moment.

"I've been wondering," Eli said. "Why would God place the tree of the knowledge of good and evil right there in the garden, and then tell them not to eat it? If he wanted perfectly obedient creations, there's no point in creating humans, he already had the angels.

"No, God wanted us to be independent of him. You wouldn't be happy if Theo never disobeyed you, never made his own decisions. Of course we eat of the tree—that's the whole point. That's our job. "

Cora leaned in, interested. "So when they finally bit that apple, why did God kick them out of the garden, then? That's not much of a reward."

"It wasn't punishment," Eli said. "It was graduation."

Cora laughed. "I was raised Catholic. I never heard that interpretation before."

Eli smiled, shrugged.

Holy cow, Reg thought. They like each other.

Theo made a move to get up, and Reg stopped him. "Not so fast, you've hardly eaten a thing. At least finish your asparagus, Mom made them just for you."

"But I'm full!"

"Theo . . ."

Eli suddenly pushed away from the table. He stomped out of the dining room, into the living room.

Cora frowned. Reg jumped up and followed. "Eli?"

He was bent over, one hand braced against the piano, the mask raised to his mouth. The first cough was little more than a huff. The next was a rattling, percussive bark. As was the next. And the next.

Eli was asleep in the bed. He wore an oxygen mask, but they still asked Reg to wear a paper breather, and to stay behind the forced-air curtain.

Reg stood at the window, peeking through a bent slat in the blinds at the afternoon. University Hospital was high in the foothills, and he could see the spread of the valley, all the way into downtown Salt

Lake. Cars stretched down the streets in long chains like unseparated mytes, filling the gaps between the buildings and houses. So many people. He couldn't imagine where they'd come from, where they were going, or how they could possibly have a unique thought in their heads. He could believe in crowds, but he couldn't believe in that many individuals. How could his best friend be sick and all those people still carry on, oblivious?

Eli made a noise, and Reg turned. "The test," Eli said, more clearly. "How did it go."

"Hey, look who's awake!" Reg said, forcing enthusiasm into his voice. He went to the bed, sat next to him.

Eli regarded him, eyes half lidded. His skin around the mask was blotched red by burst blood vessels. But his bare arms, resting on the blankets, were gray and dark-speckled, like pulp paper.

There weren't any drugs left to give him. Cecrolysin, with its beautiful design, should have worked. Maybe the peptides didn't form barrels in enough numbers, or the configurations didn't hold together long enough to penetrate. Maybe the TB evolved again, developing a thicker shell.

"I wish you could have seen it," Reg said. "Absolutely amazing."

The mytes burst out of the block, assembled beautifully, and started the search for mines—exactly as they'd done thousands of times in the Logosphere, and dozens of times in previous field tests. "They found every mine. Every damn one of them, in record time. None of them triggered." Eli nodded. "And then they went for the fence."

The old man's eyes widened.

"We were ready to send the signal to stop the test when they rushed the tape on the east side of the field. The first ones hit the wire and stopped cold, but they kept piling into each other. Dipti started to send the all-stop signal, but I stopped her, I wanted to see what happened next. And you know what happened next?"

A slight smile became visible under the mask.

"One of them went over the top. Jumped the wire like Steve McQueen on a motorcycle, completely ignored the Death signal. Hit the ground on the other side and kept going."

"What did you do?" Eli said hoarsely.

Reg threw up his hands, laughing. "We chased it! It was flying, Eli. I'd never seen one move that fast. Luckily we were out in the open and we saw when it headed under a bush. Dipti was practically whacking the thing with the antenna but it wouldn't turn off. I finally picked it up, and together we pried enough shells from it that it stopped moving."

Eli was laughing now, but then the laugh turned to a cough. He pulled off the mask and bent forward. Blood spattered on the blanket.

"Oh shit," Reg said. "Let me get the nurse."

Eli waved him off. He hacked ferociously a few more times and fell back against the pillows. His eyes closed, but he was still smiling.

After awhile, Reg said, "I've been thinking of Adam and Eve. And the serpent."

Eli grunted.

"Why would omniscient Yahweh let the devil into the garden? You'd almost think he wanted his children to be tempted. The tree wasn't enough—the poor, dumb humans weren't getting the idea themselves—so finally he has to let the devil in and let him plant the idea. A little nudge in the right direction."

Eli opened one eye, raised an eyebrow that said: And you have a point?

"Marshall Lin found your code, Eli. The stuff you added last spring."

Eli closed his eyes. The smile crept back. "Ah."

"No wonder you always wanted me to concentrate on the environmentals. But even after the myte went AWOL, I didn't put it together. I didn't figure it out until we came back and walked into the Garden."

"Heh," Eli said. A percolating chuckle that was almost a cough. "Heh."

A month after the last field test, Reg drove Theo out to the Great Salt Lake. They walked from the parking lot, the November wind tugging at their jackets, down to the pylons. Out in the water, the Salt Aire II lay half sunk into the marshy water. The abandoned amusement hall was a mass of bleached white cement, its gold-painted domes blotched with bird shit, listing like a grounded ship.

"It stinks here," Theo said.

The kid was right. A fishy miasma hung over everything.

"That's the salt, and I guess the brine shrimp. You want to go for a swim? You could float without even trying."

Theo made a sour face, looked at him like he was crazy.

"Okay, I guess it's a little cold. Besides, your mom wouldn't like you to come back sopping wet." They walked around the edge of the lake, Reg swinging his knapsack, Theo making experimental lunges at the water, crouching to sniff and poke. Seagulls wheeled and screeched overhead. Reg kept warning Theo to be careful, but eventually the boy stumbled and fell into the slushy water, wetting his side from ankle to armpit.

Reg took off his own jacket, got out of his sweatshirt, and used it dry Theo off. He told him about how when the Mormons first came to the valley, a plague of crickets overran all their farms, and flocks of seagulls flew down and swallowed up the crickets. "Then the seagulls flew over the lake and spit out the crickets—ptuee! And you know what they did next? They flew right back to the fields to eat more, eating and spitting them out, until all the crickets were gone."

Theo accepted this matter-of-factly. Six-year-olds evidently knew all about mass avian bulimia.

"Mom says you're not playing with the mytes any more," he said.

"That's right." Reg draped his jacket around Theo's shoulders. "We're going to try other types of robots. We had trouble with the mytes."

Reg and the students had driven back to the Garden after the field test. Reg had unlocked the door, but the security system was offline. Everything was offline—the servers, the lights, the tree—all dark. Some light from the streetlamps made it through the small windows high on the wall. He stumbled his way to the back of the room, toward the black wall of mytes, where the breaker box was located. He was almost all the way across the room when he realized that the reason he couldn't make out the wall of mytes wasn't because they were black, but because they were gone.

All of them.

A long minute of confusion, exclamations. He thought they'd been stolen. He went to the rear fire exit, pushed it open, trying to get more light into the room. Something brushed past his leg. No, two somethings.

They ran past him, into the parking lot. Multi-celled mytes, maybe fifty or sixty shells apiece, big as dogs. They ran for the shadows at the edge of the lot and disappeared. Dipti found another one high up on the tree. A dozen more at the edge of the room. But scores more had disappeared, through the ventilation grates.

"What was wrong with them?" Theo asked. Shivering slightly.

"Well, they *could've* been good at lots of things, but they weren't great at anything. And it took years just to get them even sort of good." Theo stared at him. "Actually," Reg said, "the one thing they were really great at was misbehaving. Like you."

"Hey!"

They started walking back to the car. Theo said, "Are you going to move back home now?"

"I don't know, Theo. It's . . .well . . ."

"Complex."

Reg laughed. "Yeah, it's very complex." He touched his son's shoulder, ran his hand to the back of Theo's neck, so warm. "But listen, just because we're not all together in the same house, that doesn't mean we're not a family. We're still connected."

Reg set the knapsack on the ground, unlocked the car door. "Hey," Theo said. "What about your friend?"

The urn was in the knapsack. Reg had told him about the ashes, about his friend's wishes. Eli didn't believe in an afterlife, but he did believe in returning the atoms he'd borrowed.

At first Reg couldn't understand why Eli had done it. Years of work, undone by a seed planted deep in the code, a few lines that would let them bypass the kill command. It was crazy to build a tool without an off switch.

Only later, as Reg and the students discreetly hunted for the mytes across campus—finding a few, but not nearly enough to account for all the missing shells—did he realize that Eli had stopped thinking of them as tools a long time ago.

Theo said, "Aren't you going to, you know, spread him around?"

"Scatter the ashes," Reg corrected. "Maybe later, Captain. I've had enough scattering for awhile." Eli, quiet as a Schrödinger cat, didn't object. "Besides, we've got to get you home and cleaned up before Mom sees you."

# PETIT MAL #1: GLASS

It's one of the crybabies," the guard told her. "He's trying to kill one of the psychos."

Dr. Alycia Liddell swore under her breath and grabbed her keys. Only two weeks into the drug trial and the prisoners were changing too fast, starting to crack.

In the hospital wing, a dozen guards crowded around an open cell door. They were strapping on pads, pulling on helmets, slapping billy clubs in their palms. It was standard procedure to go through this ritual in full view of the prisoners; more often than not they decided to walk out before the extraction team went in.

The shift lieutenant waved her to the front of the group. "One of your babies wants to talk to you," he said.

She leaned around the door frame. In the far corner of the cell, wedged between the toilet and the wall, two white men sat on the floor, one behind the other, like bobsledders. Lyle Carpenter crouched behind, his thin arms around Franz Lutwidge's broad chest. Lyle was pale and sweating. In one hand he gripped a screwdriver; the sharpened tip trembled just under Franz's walrus-fat chin.

Franz's eyes were open, but he looked bored, almost sleepy. The front of his orange jumpsuit was stained dark.

Both men saw her. Franz smiled and, without moving, somehow suggested a shrug: *Look at this fine mess.* Lyle, though, almost dropped the weapon. "Doc. Thank God you're here." He looked ready to burst into tears.

The doctor stepped back from the door. "Franz is bleeding," she said to the lieutenant.

"Lyle stabbed him in the chest. It looks like it stopped, but if he's bleeding internally we can't wait for the negotiation team. I thought you might want to take a crack at getting Lyle to drop the weapon."

"If I can't?" But she already knew the answer.

"I'll give you three minutes," he said.

\*

They wanted her to put on pads and a helmet, but she refused. Lyle and Franz, like the other 14 men in the GLS-71 trial, were low-risk prisoners: liars, thieves, con men, nonviolent offenders. The review board wouldn't allow her to enroll the more aggressive prisoners. Still, she'd succeeded in finding men with very high scores on Hare's Psychopathy Checklist. They were all-star psychopaths—or sociopaths, to use the term some of her colleagues preferred.

The lieutenant let her take only three steps into the cell before he said, "That's good."

Lyle's eyes were fixed on hers. She smiled, then let concern show in her face. "Why don't you tell me what's going on, Lyle?"

Franz said, "I'm not sure he knows himself."

"Shut up!" Lyle said, and the hand holding the screwdriver shook. Franz lifted his chin slightly.

"Just focus on me," she said to Lyle. "If you put down the weapon, we can talk about what's upsetting you."

"I fucked up, Doctor Liddell. I tried to stop him, but I couldn't—"

"Call me Alycia, Lyle."

"Alycia?" He looked surprised—and touched. She never permitted the prisoners to call her by her first name.

Franz made a derisive noise, but Lyle seemed not to hear him. "I was doing this for you, Alycia. I was just going to kill myself, but then when he told me what he was going to do, I knew I had to take care of him first." He flexed his fingers along the screwdriver's grip. "I stabbed him, going right for the heart. Then he jumped up and I knew I'd missed. I knew I had to hit him again, but I just—froze." He looked at her, his eyes shining with tears. "I couldn't do it! I saw what I'd done and I almost threw up. I felt like I'd stabbed myself. What the hell is happening to me?"

That's what we're trying to find out, she thought. GLS-71 was an accidental treatment, a failed post-stroke drug that was intended to speed speech recovery. Instead, it found the clusters of mirror neurons in Broca's area and increased their rate of firing a thousand fold.

Mirror neurons were specialist cells. See someone slapped, and the neurons associated with the face lit up in synchrony. See someone kicked, and the brain reacted as if its own body were under attack. Merely imagining an act, or remembering it, was enough to start a cascade of hormonal and physical responses. Mirror neurons were the first cogs to turn in the complex systems of attachment, longing, remorse. They were the trip wires of empathy.

Except for people like her all-stars. In psychopaths, the mirrors were dark.

"I know you must be confused," she said. "GLS is making you feel things you've never felt before."

"I even feel sorry for this piece of shit, even though I know what he was going to do to you. What he still wants to do." He nodded toward the bed. "This morning, he showed me where he was keeping the knife. He told me exactly how he was going to rape you. He told me the things he was going to force you to do."

Dr. Liddell looked at Franz. The man wasn't smiling—not quite. "You could have called a guard, Lyle. You could have just warned me."

"See, that's the thing—I *wanted* to hurt him. I thought about what he was going to do to you and I felt . . . I felt—"

"*Luuv*," Franz said.

The screwdriver's tip jerked. A thin dark line appeared along Franz's neck like the stroke of a pen.

"You don't know what love is!" Lyle shouted. "He hasn't changed at all, Alycia! Why isn't it working on him?"

"Be*cause*," Franz said, his tone condescending and professorial despite the cut and the wavering blade at his throat. "I'm in the control group, Lyle. I didn't receive GLS."

"We all got the drug," Lyle said. Then: "Didn't we?"

Franz rolled his eyes. "Could you please explain to him about placebos, *Alycia?*"

She decided then that she'd like to stab Franz herself. He *was* correct; he was in the control group. The trial was supposed to be a double-blind, randomized study, with numbered dosages supplied by the pharmaceutical company. But within days she knew which eight men were receiving the real dose. Guards and prisoners alike could sort them as easily as if they were wearing gang colors: the psychos and the crybabies.

"He's playing you, Lyle," she told him. "Pushing your buttons. That's what people like Franz do."

"You think I don't know that? I *invented* that shit. I used to be fucking bulletproof. No one got to me, no one fucked with me. Now, it's like everybody can see right through me."

The lieutenant cleared his throat. Dr. Liddell glanced back. The mass of helmeted men behind him creaked and flexed, a machine ready to be launched.

Franz hadn't missed the exchange. "You're running out of time, Lyle," he said. "Any second now they're going to come in here and crack you like an egg. Then they're going to take you off to solitary, where you won't be seeing your girlfriend anymore."

"What?" Lyle asked.

"You don't think they're going to let you stay in the program after this, do you?"

Lyle looked at her, eyes wide. "Is that true? Does that mean you'll stop giving me GLS?"

They're going to stop giving it to all of you, she thought. After Lyle's breakdown, the whole nationwide trial would be canceled. "Lyle, we're not going to stop the GLS unless you want to."

"Stop it? I never want to be the guy I was before. Nobody felt *real* to me—everybody was like a cartoon, a nothing on the other side of the TV screen. I could do whatever I wanted with them, and it didn't bother me. I was like *him*."

Franz started to say something, and Lyle pressed the screwdriver blade into his neck. The two men winced in unison.

"You don't know what he's like," Lyle said. "He's not just some banker who ripped off a couple hundred people. He's a killer."

"What?"

"He shot two teenagers in Kentucky, buried them in the woods. Nobody ever found them. He *brags* about it."

"Stories," Franz said.

Dr. Liddell stepped closer and knelt down next to Franz's outstretched legs. "Lyle, I swear to you, we'll keep you on GLS." She held out a hand. "Give the weapon to me, Lyle. I know you were trying to protect me, but you don't have to be a murderer. You don't have to throw away everything you've gained."

"Oh, please," Franz said.

Lyle squeezed shut his eyes, as if blinded.

"I give you my word," she said, and placed her hand over his. "We won't let the old you come back." After a long moment she felt his grip relax. She slowly pulled the screwdriver from his fist.

Shouts went up behind her, and then she was shoved aside. The extraction team swarmed over the two men.

\*

Three days later she came down to solitary. She brought four guards as escort.

"You know, you're good," Franz said. "I almost believed you myself." He lay on the bed with his jumpsuit half unzipped, revealing the bandages across his chest. The blade had missed the lung and the heart, tearing only muscle. The wound at his neck was covered by two long strips of gauze. He'd be fine in a few weeks. "'I give you my word.' Genius."

"I did what I had to do."

"I've used that one too. But did you have to break his heart? Poor Lyle was in love with you, and you out-and-out lied to him. There was no way you were going to keep him on GLS—you made a petty thief into a suicidal, knife-wielding maniac. How can they put anyone on that stuff now?"

"There'll be another trial," she said. "Smaller dosages, perhaps, over a longer period of time."

"That doesn't help Lyle, now, does it?"

"He's going to live, that's the important thing. I have plenty of GLS left, so I can bring him down slowly. The suicidal thoughts are already fading. In a few days he won't be bothered by remorse. He'll be back to his old self."

"And then someday you'll get to wring him out again." He shook his head, smiling. "You know, there's a certain coldness about you, Doctor—has anyone ever told you that? Maybe you should try some GLS yourself."

"Tell me about Kentucky," she said.

"Kentucky?" Franz shrugged, smiled. "That was just some bullshit to get Lyle worked up."

She frowned. "I was hoping you'd want to talk about it. Get it off your chest." She turned to one of the guards, and he handed her the nylon bag from her office. "Well, we can talk again in a few days."

He blinked, and then he understood. "You can't do that. I'll call my lawyer."

"I don't think you'll want a lawyer any time soon." She unzipped the bag and lifted out the plastic-sealed vial. "I have a lot of GLS, and only one patient now." The guards rushed forward to pin the man to the bed.

She popped the needle through the top of the vial and drew back the plunger. The syringe filled with clear, gleaming liquid.

"One thing I'm sure of," she said, half to herself. "In a few days, Franz, you'll thank me for this."

# WHAT WE TAKE WHEN WE
# TAKE WHAT WE NEED

**1.**

He almost missed the welcome sign. The two-lane highway snaked up into the mountains through dense walls of green, the trees leaning into the road. After so many years in the north it all seemed too lush, too overgrown. Subtropical. Turn your back and the plants and insects would overrun everything.

Then he saw it, the sheet metal half swallowed by ivy, its message punctuated by bullet holes. WELCOME TO SWITCHCREEK, TN. POPULATION 815. The number was a lie, unchanged since the day he drove out twelve years ago. Or perhaps a temporary lie. Maybe no one had died or been born or moved away in all that time, the town waiting for him like an old dog that wouldn't leave the porch, and now that he'd returned the number was true again.

He fought the urge to slam on the brakes. He could turn his rust-pocked Ford Tempo around and head back to Chicago. The day he left Switchcreek he'd promised himself that he wouldn't return until his father's funeral. *Terribly sick* didn't count. *Mortal danger* didn't cut it. Yet a phone call had gotten him up at six in the morning, made him drive 500 miles. And then it pulled him across the invisible town line.

Welcome back, #815.

The house where he grew up was a little three-bedroom frame house at the foot of Mount Clyburn, surrounded by trees. His father's car, an ancient Ford Crown Victoria, squatted in its usual spot. It looked like it hadn't moved in years: Tires low, brown leaves shellacked to the body and windows. He pulled in behind it and stopped, but didn't shut off the engine. He leaned forward and folded his arms atop the steering wheel, letting the struggling air conditioner blow into his damp ribs.

The picture window drapes were closed. The white paint had grayed, begun to flake. The screen door hung open, but the wooden front door was closed.

Finally he turned off the car and stepped out. Hot, moist air enveloped him; he'd forgotten how punishing August in Tennessee could be. He walked through the high, uncut grass to the cement porch and knocked. Waited and knocked again. After a minute he cupped his eyes to the diamond-shaped window set in the wood. He could make out a patch of familiar wall, then nothing but shadows. He tried the doorknob—locked—then stepped back.

Something glinted in the grass beside the porch. He crouched to pick it up: a syringe and needle, the tube empty. What the hell? He set the syringe on the porch where he could find it later.

He walked around the corner of the house, stepping carefully through the high grass, wary of sharps. The side window of his father's bedroom was filled by a silent air-conditioner; the glazed bathroom window next to it was closed and dark. Behind the house, the backyard had shrunk from the advancement of the brush line. The rusting frame of his old swing set leaned out of the shrubs. Further back, the low, cinderblock well house—made obsolete by the sewer and water lines added in the '70s—sat almost buried in the undergrowth like a Civil War fortification.

The door to the back porch was unlocked. Pax went through it, to the kitchen door. He knocked once and turned the knob. The door swung open with a squeak.

"Hello!" he called. "It's me." The air smelled sickly sweet and fungal, a jungle smell. "It's Paxton," he added stupidly. From somewhere near the front of the house came the low murmur of television voices.

The kitchen was as he remembered it, though dirtier than his mother would have ever allowed. Dirtier even than they'd kept it after she died. In those years they'd lived like tenants without a landlord, a teenager and an old man who had become a parent much too late to have the energy to do it alone. But even then they'd never let things slide this far. The garbage can overflowed with paper and plastic containers. Dishes sat in the sink. In the center of the breakfast table was a white ceramic casserole dish, the aluminum foil peeled back.

Pax made his way through the dining room, dusty and preserved as an unvisited exhibit, to the living room, where he found his father.

The Reverend Harlan Martin had a firm idea of what a pastor should look like, and it began with the hair. Each morning after his shower, he'd carefully comb back the wet strands from his forehead and spray everything down with his wife's Alberto VO-5, clouding the bathroom. Sunday required extra coats, enough hairspray to preserve his appearance through a fire and brimstone sermon, a potluck dinner, a visitation or two, and an evening service. His Sunday hair was as shiny and durable as a Greek helmet.

As a child, Pax loved when the hair was down, as when his father slept late and came to the breakfast table unshowered, pushing the long bangs out of his face like a disheveled Elvis. Like now.

His father sat sprawled on the couch, head back and mouth open, eyes closed. His dark hair, longer than Pax had ever seen it, hung along the sides of his wide face to his jaw. His body was huge. His father's side of his family were all big, but this was beyond anything Pax had seen. He seemed to have put on a hundred pounds or so since Pax had left.

"Harlan?" Pax said. The atmosphere in the room was hot and unbearably humid, despite the ceiling fan turning above, the air heavy with that strange odor like rotting fruit. He took a step forward. "Harlan?"

His bulk spread across parts of three cushions. He wore a blue terrycloth bathrobe half closed over a white T-shirt, and black socks stretched over broad feet. His face was deeply cratered, the skin flaking and loose.

His father's chest moved. A whistling wheeze escaped his mouth.

Okay, Pax thought. Still alive. Until that moment he hadn't realized how he'd been braced to find a corpse.

The coffee table and chairs had been pushed to the walls, leaving a wide space with clear view of the television's flickering screen. The television abruptly became louder—an ad—and Pax flicked off the set.

His father suddenly lifted his head, turned to glare at Pax. His eyes were glassy, the lids crusted with sleep matter.

"Out," his father said, his voice garbled by phlegm. He coughed, and raised a wide hand to his mouth. The arm was as pockmarked as his face. He pointed past Paxton's shoulder. "Out of my house!" He still had it: the Preacher Voice.

"It's me, Paxton." He crouched down next to his father, and winced at the smell of him. He couldn't tell if he was delirious or simply confused by sleep. "It's your son."

The huge man blinked at him. "Paxton?" he said warily. Then: "It's you."

Pax gripped his father's hand. "How you doing?"

"My prodigal son," his father said.

"The only kind you've got." Pax tried to let go, but his father squeezed harder.

"Who called you? Vonda?"

"Close," Pax said. He extricated his hand and stood. He was surprised to feel something oily on his palm, and rubbed his hand dry on the back of his pants. "I need to open some windows."

"She wants me. Wants to milk me like a cow. You can't be here."

Pax pulled open the big front drapes, and fought down a wave of dizziness. The air in the room was too close, too fetid. The sickly sweet odor had blossomed, become suffocating. He'd been told Harlan was in trouble, but nothing had prepared him for this.

"You've got to leave," his father said, his tone no longer firm. His body, huge as it was, looked like a bag to hold an even larger man. The skin hung loose at his neck and cheeks, and now beads of sweat appeared along his brow. How long it had been since his father last ate? Could he even move?

Harlan's face shone with sweat, as if breaking a fever. A water blister had appeared on his cheek, as large as a walnut, the skin so tight it was almost translucent. Pax stared at it in horror.

"Oh," his father said softly. "Oh, Lord."

"Harlan, what's going on?" He tried to keep the panic out of his voice.

"You took me by surprise," he said. He looked up, smiled faintly. His eyes were wet. Two more blisters had appeared at his neck. They seemed to expand as Pax watched. "You better leave now."

Pax turned toward the front door, lost his balance, and caught himself. He turned the lock and yanked the door open. The air was too heavy to offer much relief. Keeping a hand against the wall to steady himself, he made his way back to the couch. The telephone wasn't at its old spot on the end table. He'd called the house a dozen times over the past few days, but it had rung and rung.

"Where's the phone, Harlan?" Stains the color of pink lemonade had appeared on his father's T-shirt.

His father looked up at him with half-closed eyes. "Paxton Abel Martin." He said the name with a slow drawl, almost singing it, in a voice Pax hadn't heard in a long time. He had a sudden memory of being carried up the church stairs in the dark—he must have been four or five—held close in his father's arms.

Pax kneeled in front of his father. The rich, fruity smell enveloped him. Pax gently pushed the robe further open, and began to lift the T-shirt. Blisters had erupted over the skin of his belly: tiny pimples; white-capped pebbles; glossy, egg-sized sacs. The largest pouches wept pink-tinged serum.

"Oh Jesus." Pax bunched the edge of the T-shirt and tried to cover one of the open sores, but the oily liquid soaked through and slicked his fingers. "Listen, we've got to get you to—get . . ."

His fingers burned, but not painfully. He looked at his hand, rubbed the substance between his fingers. Slowly his gaze turned to his father, and their eyes locked.

*There you are*, Pax thought. There, waiting beneath the sagging flesh, the mounds of pitted and pocked skin: The man who carried him up the stairs. Relief flooded through him. What if they'd been lost forever? Pax and his bloated father were here, in this stinking room, and they were also Harlan Martin and his four-year-old son, climbing out of the church basement after a long Sunday night service. He felt himself being carried, and at the same time felt the weight of the boy in his arms.

And then Pax was on his back, staring at the ceiling. He raised a hand—*I see that hand*, his father used to call from the pulpit, *I see that hand*—but his limbs were so heavy, and his arm fell to the floor with a distant thump.

He listened to the sound reverberate through the bones of skull. And then the world slipped sideways and pitched him into the dark.

**2.**

A young man lay sprawled across the braided rug. Skinny, head shaved like a criminal, a tattoo on his left arm. Still, unmistakable. He nudged the boy with his foot—and felt the poke under his ribs. That confused him. He tried to turn, to see who might be behind him, but now his arms and legs refused to respond. The boy on the floor made a noise, opened his eyes—

—and the room spun, then just as suddenly shuddered to a stop like a jammed gear. Paxton blinked hard, awake now.

His father loomed over him, a huge shadow limned in daylight. "I thought I'd made you up," Harlan said.

Pax slowly sat up. His arms and neck trembled to keep him upright.

His father said, "I'll make you breakfast," and turned toward the kitchen. He moved like a man in a heavy diving suit, plodding across the ocean floor.

Pax got to his feet. He felt light-headed, then waited until it passed. Morning light burned through the windows. Jesus, he thought. Passed out all night? He shuffled to the kitchen doorway and leaned against the frame.

"I'm not going to a hospital," Harlan said. He stood in front of the open refrigerator. The blisters seemed to have receded, but his face, which had been slack and baggy last night, had filled like a balloon. Harlan peeled back the lid of a Cool Whip container, sniffed, then tossed the bowl onto the top of the pile of garbage.

"Tell me," Pax said, and then coughed. "What the hell's going on, Harlan?" His father hated it when he called him Harlan.

"I'm fine," his father said. He opened another plastic bowl and put it back in the fridge. It was the kind of thing you did for someone you loved. "The women from the church drop this stuff off, leave it on the porch. It goes bad fast." He bent and reached deeper into a shelf. "If you're here for money I don't have any."

"What? No." How fast the man could piss him off. Pax had never asked him for a thing since he left home. "I'm here because Uncle Lem told me to be here."

Harlan shifted his bulk, stared at him. "Lem talked to you?"

Lemuel Martin was Paxton's great uncle, on his father's side, another man who'd never left Switchcreek. The last time Pax had seen him, when he was nine or ten, his uncle had to be over seventy years old, morbidly obese and rarely talking.

"I could hardly recognize him, but yeah. Five days ago." Lem gargled like a man drowning from the inside.

"How did he find you?"

"Jesus, does it matter?"

"You move around like a hobo. Arizona, New Jersey, Chicago."

"I've been in Chicago for the past five years, Harlan. It's not too hard to look up a phone number." His father had called him exactly twice in twelve years. "Christ, all you have to do is call Aunt Jen, I always keep her—"

"Stop talking like that—Christ this, Jesus that."

"Tell me what's happening to you, Harlan." His father scowled, and Pax said, "Look, I know there's something that runs in the family, something on your side, that you guys never talked about. I wasn't completely oblivious as a kid." Harlan grunted, a sound that could have meant anything. Pax said, "I thought it was just the size thing, like Uncle Lem, or, I don't know, depression. God knows *that* makes sense. But last night you were hallucinating, and there was that, that *stuff.*"

His father turned back to the fridge. "What did Lem tell you?"

"Nothing that made sense. He was rambling, talking senile. He said you were sick—terribly sick. He sounded like a scared child."

"That's it?" Harlan asked.

Don't forget *mortal danger*, Pax thought, but stifled that. "Before he hung up he made me promise not to tell anyone he called, especially not Vonda." Lem's daughter. She was a little younger than Harlan, so had to be in her sixties by now. She'd lived with her father her entire life, even as a couple husbands moved in and moved out. Pax said, "You were talking about her last night, too."

His father slammed the refrigerator door. He went to the counter and fished through a pile of mail. "Here," he said, and tossed Paxton an envelope. "Cash this and get me some groceries."

"You'll have to tell me what's going on sooner or later, Harlan. And you have to see a doctor."

"You're staying?"

Pax shook his head. "I've got to be back at work by tomorrow morning."

"Didn't think so."

\*

Paxton crossed the two-lane bridge and then slowed as he came into town, though that was too big a word for the short strip of buildings. Half of them were boarded up, and the others—the Gas-n-Go, the Power Rental, the Icee Freeze—looked slump-shouldered and tired.

He parked outside the Bigler's Grocery. Only four other cars in the lot. He leaned against the roof of his car for a moment, breathing in, breathing out. He felt not so much hung over as wrung out. No drink or drug had ever hit him that hard, that fast.

Inside the store he tried to move quickly, filling up his cart with canned goods and frozen dinners, anything his father could make in a microwave, anything that would keep.

He saw Jo Lynn before she saw him, and turned down another aisle. He walked quickly, his chest suddenly tight. Then he heard light steps behind him and she said, "P.K.?"

P.K. Preacher's Kid. Nobody had called him that since he left Switchcreek.

He turned, putting on a relaxed smile. "Hey, Jo." She looked the same. A dozen years, ten extra pounds, the shitty polyester Bigler's smock—none of it made a difference. Still beautiful.

"What are you doing here?" she said. "Visiting?"

"Just for a couple days."

They talked for five minutes. He memorized everything she asked him and instantly forgot his answers. He looked at her tiny feet in the cheap black shoes, at the ring on her finger. He remembered a day a few months before he left town, lying in the grass on the hill below the cemetery, looking up at her. She stood with her legs apart, the light making a scrim of her pale yellow sundress, her thighs in shadow. She reached up to her shoulder, and that moment—the moment the spaghetti strap slipped from her sunburned shoulder—he'd felt a white blast of lust that had never been matched in his life, before or since.

Jo pursed her lips, waiting. She'd asked him about his father.

"He's doing fine. Well, no, he's not actually. He's not been taking care of himself."

Her eyes went sad. Harlan had been her pastor since she was

a baby, and she'd refused to think badly of him even when he was trying to break them up, even when he showed her the stripes Harlan had laid across his back with his leather belt. "I've been worried about him since he left the church," she said. "I'm glad you're there for him."

"I'm hardly doing anything," he said. Truth that sounded like false modesty—a special class of lie. "Listen, Jo . . ."

This was the moment he'd run through his head on a thousand nights, the 3 a.m. rehearsals that kept him from sleep. In the first few years after he left, he'd called her house countless times and hung up before anyone could answer. He'd written a hundred letters that hadn't gone further than a sentence.

She looked at him, and he said, "It was good seeing you. I better go, though. He's waiting for me."

"Tell him I'm praying for him." She touched his arm. "And you too, P.K."

He forced a laugh. "I'll take all the help I can get."

The warmth of her fingers lingered on his skin.


He took the long way home, past the elementary school, over the single-lane bridge to Piney Level road, and on toward the church where his father had been pastor, the church he'd grown up in. When he rolled past it he realized where he was really going.

He told himself he'd just drive by, look at the house and move on. He needed to get the groceries home. Then he was pulling into the long driveway of Uncle Lem's house.

His great uncle and Vonda lived in a tin-roofed framehouse cut into the side of the hill, the red clay rising up like a tidal wave behind it. Between him and the house was a cement patch holding half a dozen vehicles, a couple late models but most of them beaters. Out in the fields to his left, a few more junkers—an El Camino, a blue pickup, a van-sized RV—huddled beside the gray, knock-kneed barn, drowning in tall grass.

Pax was halfway to the screen porch when a tall, beefy kid, maybe 18 years old, banged through the door and stood at the top of the step. "Back," he said. "Back to your car."

He was a big, block-faced kid, shirtless, with a pale chest and a whiter belly. He wore long, Vols-orange basketball shorts and spot-less white athletic shoes. In his left hand was a lime-green aluminum baseball bat.

Pax stopped, held up his hands. "I'm Paxton Martin," he said. "Harlan's son." He tried to think who this kid could be. Too young to be Vonda's son. Her grandson, then? A complete stranger?

"Grandma's not here," the kid said. His face and chest shone with sweat, as if he'd been working out inside the old house. "You better leave now."

"Who are you—Clete? Bonnie's boy?"

"Travis. Clete's my brother."

"We're cousins, then. Your grandmother Vonda's my second cous-in, so you're . . ." Shit. Gazillionth cousin? Thug twice removed?

"I'll tell her you called," Travis said.

Pax nodded toward the window at the left side of the house, where his uncle's bedroom used to be. "I just came to see Uncle Lem. I'm only—Jesus!"

Travis jumped the two steps and landed with the bat raised. Pax-ton backpedaled. "What the hell's the matter with you!"

Travis swung hard but didn't step into it, not really trying to con-nect. The brush back. "God damn vampire," the boy said, and took another step forward, cocked the bat. "God damn junkie . . ."

Pax backed up fast. He refused to turn and run, not for this chub-by punk. The kid let him climb into his car, and when Pax drove away he looked in his rearview mirror and the boy was standing at the end of the driveway, the bat in his hands, like a God damn caveman.


His father sat on the couch, snoring in front of the TV, mouth open, jowls sagging. Deflated again. The sight stopped him, and something in his chest twisted like an old wound.

Let him sleep, Pax thought. He carried the groceries into the kitchen and began putting things away. God, the mess. Maybe it was a mistake to bring in fresh food with the kitchen so filthy. He opened the windows, turned on all the lights. Ten years in the restaurant busi-ness, working every position from dishwasher to waiter to line cook, had inured him to vile substances that bred in the dark. He cleared the counters and the refrigerator, threw out everything that was remotely suspicious, filling two garbage bags, working as quietly as he could so that he wouldn't wake his father. Then he started pulling dishes from the sink and stacking them on the counter.

At the bottom of the sink he found a stubbed out cigarette. He picked it up, pinched the damp thing between his fingers. His father had never smoked a day in his life.

He thought he heard a phone ringing. He threw away the cigarette and went into the living room, where the TV and his father's snores drowned out everything. He turned off the TV, then tracked the faint noise to his father's bedroom. The ringing stopped as he walked in.

The room looked much as it had a dozen years before: a long, mirrored bureau, wood veneer bedside tables, the long gauzy drapes his mother had liked. The bed was unmade, the bedclothes pushed against the wall. The box spring had been lifted off the frame and reinforced by a row of 2x4's, but his father's weight had still pressed a hollow into the mattress.

Pax found the phone jack in the wall and followed the cord to a pile of laundry. If his father had wanted to turn off the phone he could have just yanked the cord. Or maybe he was afraid that he wouldn't be able to plug it back in. Pax unplugged it and carried the cord and receiver to the living room.

His father was staring at the blank TV screen. "I was watching that," he said.

"Tell me the name of your doctor, Harlan."

Harlan closed his eyes.

"If you don't tell me, I'm just going to call one at random." Pax went to the wall and squatted to plug in the phone. "There've been people in the house, too. You know that, right?"

"Of course I know it. Now help me up." He raised his arms like a child.

"Was it Vonda?" *She wants to milk me like a cow.* "Vonda or her grandson?"

"Up," he said.

Pax stepped in front of him. His father was just so damn *big*. Pulling him upright, Pax realized, would be an engineering problem, an exercise in mechanics and leverage. He straddled one of his father's legs and got a hand under each arm. "Ready?" he said.

Pax braced his feet and leaned back. His father held onto him, then with a lurch rose from the couch. For a moment they held each others' arms like dance partners: London Bridge is Falling Down. He was shorter than Pax remembered. Or maybe his spine was compressing, fat and gravity conspiring to mold him into a sphere.

His father looked up at him and laughed. "He arose!" Like that his mood had lightened. He moved slowly toward the bathroom, planting each huge foot a few inches in front of the other.

Pax made them a supper of canned spaghetti and afterward they sat together on the couch, watching TV, the way they had after Mom died—until the fighting started and it became impossible for them to be in the same room, the same town, and finally, the same state. They talked only during the commercials and said nothing of consequence. Pax did not bring up the way his father had beat him for any infraction. Harlan did not bring up how Paxton had run around, drinking and smoking dope and getting girls pregnant, bringing shame to the preacher's house.

Neither of them brought up Mom.

His father favored the Discovery Channel. Animals killing animals, raising animal babies. Funny, Pax thought, how they showed so much of the killing but so little of the screwing. Pax was bored and anxious, irritated by the smell of his father that covered them like a tent, and growing impatient because he knew the next fight would be coming—or rather, the old one would resume. But he sat there until the end of the fucking program, so he could check off another point in his Dutiful Son column. When I leave, he thought, Harlan won't be able to say I didn't help him. He won't be able to say I didn't try.

"I know you're going home in the morning," his father said. His voice was slow, as if he were falling asleep.

"I've got to work," Pax said. At a shitty job that he would have been happy to quit. But a job.

His father nodded. "Do you have a girlfriend?" When Pax didn't immediately answer he said, "You're not *married*, are you? You don't have children?"

"God no. No children. I'm not exactly husband material," Pax said. "Or boyfriend material. Actually, I'm not sure I'm material."

His father grunted. Was that a laugh?

They watched the screen until another commercial break, and his father said, "Twice a week."

Pax looked over and said, "Dad!"

Harlan's face had flushed. Liquid gleamed on the backs of his hands. "Twice a week she comes, sometimes three," he said. "But with you—with you here it's different. You have to leave, Paxton. You're just making it worse."

"That's it, I'm calling the doctor. We can—"

Harlan grabbed Paxton's bare arm. "Don't." His father's hand was damp with sweat. "Don't have any sons. Even if she begs you. Don't do it."

Pax scrambled off the couch. His skin tingled where his father had touched him.

Harlan's robe lay open. The blisters had erupted again. They were everywhere on his skin, all sizes, weeping and glistening. His father reached for him again and Paxton stepped back. He remembered that electric rush of emotion that had struck him last night, left him lying stupid on the floor. Love, or something like it. Connection. The eggshell had cracked open and for a moment everything had run together; he'd forgotten who was Paxton and who was Harlan. The feeling had been exhilarating and suffocating at once. A child's emotion: Love indistinguishable from total immersion.

*Watch yourself*, he thought.

His father's eyes were wide, roaming the room. "Every good tree," he said. "Every good tree brings forth good fruit. And every corrupt tree . . ."

Pax went into the kitchen and brought back a plastic garbage bag and a roll of paper towels. A blister near his father's neck had already split, weeping liquid. Pax put the bag over his hand and crouched beside his father. He touched a corner of a paper towel to the spot, and the substance soaked into it. He held it away from himself like a lit match and dropped it to the floor.

But the serum kept flowing. Pax tore off more towels, pressed them into the blisters, made a pile of damp paper on the floor. He worked for fifteen, twenty minutes—an eternity—until finally the flow subsided. His father had fallen asleep, his breaths coming deep and easy now.

Pax stood up, dizzy and sweating. He retrieved another garbage bag, shoveled the crumpled and damp paper into it, then finished by pushing the first bag into it as well. He carried the sack outside to the back yard.

It was evening but not yet fully dark. He held the bag in his hand, letting it twist, and stared up at the tops of the pines, dark against the bruised sky. Despite the heat and the thick humidity, he felt an antici-patory chill, as if he were thirteen again steeling himself to jump off the high rocks into the ice cold water of the Little River.

He opened the bag and reached in.

### 3.

Vonda and her grandsons showed up three days later. They climbed out of a beat up Ford Explorer and walked across the yard, Vonda in front, Travis and another huge boy—had to be his brother, Clete, they looked so much alike—clumping behind her. Vonda was a small, bony woman, angular as a voodoo fetish, her tank top and frayed cutoff jeans hanging off her like laundry.

Paxton stepped back from the door's tiny window. He knew they'd come, sooner or later. He'd been listening for the slam of car doors, waiting for the hard knock. She said, "I know you're in there, Paxton. Open the damn door."

"I have a gun," Pax said. His father didn't keep any firearms in the house, not even a .22 squirrel rifle. It was probably the only weap-onless household in East Tennessee.

"Well good for you," Vonda said. "Now open the door so Travis can apologize. He told me he was kind of rude to you the other day."

He stepped back from the door and listened. His father still snored in the back bedroom. He spent a lot of his time sleeping these days. So did Paxton.

He opened the door halfway. Vonda stood on the step with her hands on her hips—bones on bones—brown skin baked and cracked by sixty years of sun and cigarettes. A heavy smoker who'd been heavily smoked.

"You don't look so good," she said.

Pax gripped the edge of the door. "What do you want, Vonda?"

"Don't be that way," she said. "I changed your diaper more than once. You used to run around my house naked."

Uncle Lem's house, Pax thought.

Vonda said, "Say what you came for, Travis." The boy stared at Paxton with half-lidded eyes. She backhanded him across the bicep. "Travis!"

"I'm sorry," he said. "For *scaring* you." Clete snorted a laugh.

Jesus, Pax thought. He really did want to shoot both these kids. "I know what you're here for," Pax said.

"Do you, now?" Vonda said.

He'd thrown away the needle and syringe, but now he wished he'd left them on the porch. A smoking gun. "That's over," Pax said. "All of that. You won't be touching him again."

Clete said, "Looks like you've been touching him yourself. How you liking the vintage, cuz?"

Vonda raised a hand to silence the boy. She said to Paxton, "So you're staying, then? Years without a word, then you just move back in?"

"Pretty much." He'd missed work, hadn't even called his manager. If he wasn't fired by now he would be soon. He was playing it day be day.

Vonda said, "You don't know what you're getting into, Paxton. Your father has needs—special needs. Are you prepared to take care of him, every day, for the rest of his life?"

"I'll get help. I'll call his doctor."

Clete and Travis laughed, and even Vonda smiled. Clete said, "Listen, cuz, if you haven't called yet, you ain't never going to."

"I'll call the cops, though," Pax said. "Just stick around."

"I'm here to help you," Vonda said. "And help Harlan. He used to be a self-righteous son of a bitch, and lord knows he can get mean. But he needs help. He's hallucinating sometimes, isn't he? Calling you names? And then there's the weekly sweats—"

"Weekly? Try every night," Paxton said. "Eight-fifteen, like clockwork."

Travis and Clete exchanged a look. After a moment Vonda said, "So you know what we're talking about. It's even more important we help you out, Paxton. If you don't get the vintage out of them they go a little crazy. It's not pretty, but you have to do it."

The phone began to ring. Pax said, "Get the hell out of here." He started to close the door.

Vonda put out a hand to stop him. "I'll give you another week,

Paxton. You'll see you're in over your head, and then you'll call me. And you know what? I'll come back, with no hurt feelings. Because that's what family's for."

He closed the door, locked it. Then he hurried to the living room and picked it up on the sixth or seventh ring. He knew who it would be. The labored breathing on the other end of the line confirmed it.

"They're coming for you," a voice said. A voice drowning in phlegm. "You and the vintage."

That word again. "They came and went, Uncle Lem," Pax said. Or rather, they were leaving now. He watched Vonda and the boys climb into the Ford.

"Already? No. I have to go, I have to—"

"Wait! They just pulled out this second. You've got time. Are you all right? Are they hurting you?"

"Past hurting," he said. "Your father, though—" He coughed wetly. "It's the age. They'll be after him."

"You have to tell me how to handle them, Uncle Lem. How to handle *him*. You have to tell me what to do."

"Do? You do your job." He coughed again. "Do what your father did for his father."

A loud clatter as Lem clumsily hung up the phone. From the back bedroom, his father shouted a question.

"Nobody, Harlan," Pax called back. "Go back to sleep."


The vintage rolled in and receded like a tide, the flow growing stronger each night. The longer Pax stayed, the longer they talked and sat together and ate together, the more Harlan produced. It usually came on in the evenings. His father would look down at himself, and say, "Ah," as if he'd spilled something on his clothes. Then Pax would run to get the extraction kit.

He'd gotten the supplies in Lambert, ten miles away, where nobody was likely to recognize him and nobody had. In a drug store he'd picked up antiseptic wipes, a box of vinyl gloves, skin lotion. Syringes and needles, though, weren't on any of the shelves, and when he finally asked for them the clerk looked at him like he was a junkie. Did he have a prescription? He went to a couple hardware stores and kitchen stores, inspecting caulk guns, bicycle pumps, turkey basters, frosting sprayers, looking for anything he could rig. Then in the JC Penny's housewares department he found a nickel-plated monster called a marinate infuser. Eight inches long, with loop handles, a plunger, and a 30-cc needle. The tool Dr. Frankenstein would reach for to inject a couple quarts of spinal fluid. Pax used it in reverse, drawing the fluid out of his father, pressing it into tiny rubber-capped containers he'd found on the Tupperware aisle, each one holding a few ounces. After attending to his father he'd stack them in the freezer. Then, later in the evening, he'd remove one. One or two.

Hours later he'd wake up, not sure if he was in bed, on the couch, inside or outside. His first sensation was of his own mass, the vast bulk of his body stretched out across the dark like an unsteerable barge. And at the same time, he felt the brittle angles of wrists and ankles, the knobs of his knees like two river stones, the blades of his hip bones, the shallow pit of stomach. He stared at the walls of his bedroom, and up at the trees that lined the yard. He breathed and heard himself breathing.

The split, when it came, left him not just alone, not just half of what he'd been, but some smaller fraction. A shard. Near dawn he'd fall into a more fitful sleep, and by ten or eleven a.m. the cycle would begin again. He fed his father, moved laundry through the washer and dryer, cleaning the rooms. Each day he picked out something to do outside—mowing the lawn, clearing brush, washing the cars—just to get him into the fresh air.

"You don't have to prove anything," his father said. It was Thursday or Friday morning, and Pax was making his third attempt at scrubbing the kitchen floor. There seemed to be nothing he could do about the smell of the vintage. It was permanent now, baked into the walls and floorboards.

Pax had started the projects with a vague notion that he was preparing the house so that his father could get by alone, though Pax no longer had a clear idea of when he was leaving.

"You need to eat," his father said to him. He was standing up in the doorway, holding himself erect.

"I'm fine," Pax said.

"You're not fine. I know what's happening, Paxton. All this. It's not the first time."

Paxton stood up. "Really. When were you going to tell me?"

"Not 'til you needed to. Maybe never."

"Shit, Harlan! What about when it happens to me? You'd be dead and I wouldn't know what the hell was going on."

"Mostly it skips. There's only one or two every generation—"

"Every generation? How long has this been going on?"

Harlan pulled out one of the metal chairs and sat down. After a while he said, "Your grandfather begged me to end it. End the line. I couldn't do it. And later, your mom . . ." He shook his head. "I was weak. I knew what she was doing—what she *wasn't* doing." He looked up. "I shouldn't tell you this, but your mom—"

"Don't worry, I know I was a mistake." He walked to the back door and yanked it open. The room was hot, and it wasn't even noon. He had to get a couple more air conditioners into this house or he'd never make it through the summer. "Vonda's coming back, Harlan. I need to know what she's doing with this stuff. Is she selling it?"

His father frowned. "To who?"

"I don't know—anybody. You have to understand, this . . ." He couldn't say *vintage*; that was Vonda's word. "This stuff is stronger than anything I've ever heard of."

"It's no good outside the family, Paxton. There's no one to sell it *to*."

"What?"

"Sons and grandsons, yes. Daughters too, I suppose. But it does nothing for outsiders."

"Maybe she's selling it to cousins, then."

"She wouldn't do that," Harlan said. He didn't sound sure. "It doesn't matter if she is. Let her do what she wants. Go back to Phoenix or Chicago or wherever it is you're living now. I have my own plan."

Pax didn't believe him for a minute. "I'm not leaving you to her."

Harlan tilted his head. "Why not?"

He didn't have an answer for that yet.


There were only two checkout lanes open at Bigler's, but he picked hers. "That should make quite a few meals," Jo said. The cart was piled high.

"I'm stocking up," Pax said.

"Good. You look like you could use it." It was true, he'd dropped weight, and he hadn't started with much to spare. She said, "How is your father doing?"

"Good. I mean, okay."

She nodded, and Pax couldn't bring himself to say what he came to say. She worked quickly, scanning and bagging the items with practiced speed.

"You're staring at me," she said.

He felt heat in his cheeks. "I'm sorry," he said. "It's just—" He glanced behind him. There was no one else in line. "Were we in love, Jo? Or was it all just teenage hormones? Just chemicals?"

She tucked the last item, a box of cereal, into the bag. "I loved you," she said.

"But we were just kids."

"Old enough."

Old enough to make a baby. Old enough to lose one.

Her parents hadn't wanted him at the hospital—hadn't wanted him anywhere near their daughter ever again. His father washed his hands of him. Within two weeks of that night Pax was gone to Arizona to live with his mom's sister.

Jo finished ringing him up, and didn't object when he signed Harlan's name to one of his father's checks. She said, "I held a service, you know." Her voice was light, matter-of-fact. "They didn't want a public one, so I held my own. Out by the church. I only carried it for six weeks, but to me it was already our baby. I could feel it."

Maybe that was the difference. Jo had chemicals running through her system telling her the child existed, that there was someone there to love. He had nothing to hold on to but a concept. An abstract idea.

He touched her arm. "Jo, if we could start over—"

"Start *over?*" She drew back. Her smile was some mix of disbelief and pity. "Paxton, I'm married. I'm happy now. I have two beautiful children."

"That's . . . good. I'm glad you got over me."

"Of course I did. It's been twelve years. What did you think I would do?"

He pushed his groceries out to the parking lot. As he finished loading, Jo came out of the store holding a plate covered by a clear plastic lid.

"For your dad," she said. "He always liked coconut cream pie."

"Uh, okay," he said, and took it from her.

"Tell him I'm sorry for his loss." He stared at her blankly and she said, "His uncle. Lem?"

"What are you talking about?"

"I thought that's why you were buying all that food. We got the news this morning when Travis came in. What's the matter?"

"When did he die?"

"Last night, I think. Travis said it was going to be a quick funeral."

"I have to get home." He set the pie on the passenger seat, then climbed in. He looked up at her through the open side window. "Jo, I'm sorry. For everything. I was a coward."

She didn't contradict him.


He'd braced himself for the sight of Vonda's Ford, but the driveway was empty except for his father's Crown Vic. Pax left the groceries in the car and went inside. His father sat on the couch, a folded towel on his lap, watching the television.

"Uncle Lem is dead," Paxton said.

Harlan nodded. "I figured. The phone's been ringing off the hook."

"You didn't pick up?"

"They'll say their condolences, but I know what they really want. Where's the food? I'm starving."

Pax ferried the groceries into the house, checking half a dozen times for cars coming down the lane. He quickly made his father a sandwich and a tall glass of sweet tea, then stood where he could keep watch out the picture window.

"You're making me nervous," his father said.

"We have to leave, Harlan. I'm taking you back to Chicago."

His father looked at him. "In *what?*"

Good point. His Tempo was too small by half, and the Crown Vic probably didn't even run. "I'll borrow a truck."

"I'm not going anywhere," Harlan said. "This is my damn house. You're the one who needs to leave."

"You really want me out of here?"

"Of course I do. I never wanted you here in the first place."

"Liar." His body had been telling a different story since Paxton had arrived.

"You're throwing me off balance, son. Before you came, they couldn't get anything out of me but dribs and drabs once a week."

"You told me it was two or three times a week."

"They see me like this, they find out how much I'm producing, they'll get ideas. And now that Lem's gone—"

"I'm not going to let them take you," Pax said. He'd never told Harlan that Vonda and the boys had come to the house, or that he'd let slip how often the vintage was flowing. "I'll call the police. I don't care who finds out, I'm not going to let them kidnap you."

"No! No police," his father said. "When Vonda comes, let me handle it. Do you hear me?"

"Handle it how?"

"Never mind how." He handed him the empty glass. "Just fill this up."

For hours Paxton paced the little room, and then made random paths through the front yard. The phone rang a dozen times an hour. He'd decided to adopt Harlan's policy, and let it ring.

Near 8:00 the sun began to drop behind the trees. Pax didn't want to turn on the living room lights because the glare would make it impossible to see the driveway. His father refused to turn off the TV, though. Pax began to think that Vonda wouldn't show up tonight. And what if she didn't, what then? Stand watch every day?

Pax was at the window again when his father said, "Ah." Pax turned. Harlan's eyes had drooped. His face had begun to glisten.

Shit. The last thing he needed was the vintage coming in with Vonda here. And then he realized that that was exactly what she was counting on. Roll in on the high tide like a pirate and take what she wanted with Harlan too disoriented to fight her.

"Hold on, Dad. Stay awake."

"'New wine in old bottles,'" he said.

"Matthew, uh, nine?"

His father grunted. "Good boy. Nine-seventeen: 'The bottles break, and the wine runneth out.'"

Behind him, a pair of headlights swung down through the trees.

"I'll do it," his father said. "I'll break it wide open. Stop it all." His hand fumbled for the towel that lay over his lap.

Paxton pulled it out of his grasp and opened the towel. Inside was a black revolver. A .38? .32? "Jesus Christ, Dad, where the hell did you get a pistol?"

Outside, the lights of the big SUV were aimed at the front window.

Pax took the gun, then went into the kitchen. He opened the freezer and pulled out the white kitchen bag he'd put there. He looked at the five remaining capsules and thought about popping one open. But no, he couldn't afford to be in two places at once.

He walked out the front door, the pistol in his right hand, the bag in his left.

Vonda and the boys were waiting for him, the headlights making them into silhouettes. Vonda wore some kind of dark, sack-like dress.

"I really thought you were lying about the gun," she said.

Clete reached behind him to his waistband. "Look, we've got 'em, too." Both boys drew out silver automatics. Rap video weapons.

Pax felt his knees go loose. He'd never pointed a gun at another person, or had one pointed at him.

"Here," he said. He tossed the bag toward them. The frozen plastic containers clattered inside as it hit the ground. "There are twenty capsules, a few ounces each," he said, struggling to keep his voice level. "That's from one week."

Travis palmed his gun and picked up the bag. He tugged open the mouth and tilted it to catch the glare of the headlights. "Shee-it," he said.

"Harlan only does that when I'm around," Pax said. "Even if you took him, you couldn't get him to produce like that. I'm betting that's a lot more than Lem ever put out."

"And I'm betting there's more of that in your freezer," Vonda said.

"A little bit," he admitted.

"Or I could just take the cow."

"*Or*, Harlan shoots himself," Pax said.

"The preacher? I don't think so."

"Vonda, where do you think I got the gun? I pulled it out of his fucking hand." Pax stepped forward. "That's Harlan Martin in there,

Vonda, not some ninety-year-old man too terrified to cross you. You should know the difference between Lem and my father. He'll find a way."

She eyed the bag. "Every week you'll do this?" Vonda said. "Week in, week out."

"I told him I wouldn't leave him."

"You're fooling yourself," she said. She was silent for half a minute, then finally she shook her head. "All right," she said, and nodded at the boys. Travis took the bag back to the SUV. "You too, Clete." He followed his brother back to the vehicle.

Vonda nodded toward the house. "You want Harlan to think you're doing this because you love him, Paxton? That you're just being a good son? Fine. But you and I both know that this is because you've gotten a taste of the vintage." She laughed. "That's not love, Paxton. That's addiction."

"Explain the difference."

Harlan was waiting for him, still holding onto consciousness. Pax went to the kitchen and came back with the cloth towel that had held the gun. He sat next to him and gently patted the sweat from his face.

"You're still here," his father said.

"Still here, Dad."

"I couldn't do it," Harlan said. "I could have stopped all of this. But I couldn't—"

"Shh." Pax said. He pushed his father's hair from his eyes. "Go to sleep now. We'll talk in the morning."

# PETIT MAL #2: DIGITAL

Sometime after the accident, Franklin woke up to realize that his consciousness had relocated to his left hand—specifically, the index finger of his left hand.

Before the accident, which is to say, his entire life until then, his conscious self seemed to reside just behind his eyes, a tiny man gazing out at the world through a pair of wide windows. He'd never considered how odd this was, and how arbitrary that location. Was it because humans were predominantly visual? He supposed so, but that didn't explain why his *self* had been lodged there. Why not behind the nose? His sense of smell was quite keen, especially when it came to beer: he could tell a Belgian Abbey ale from an American microbrew knockoff with a single sniff. His taste buds were highly trained. If he had become a professional taste-tester, he wondered, would his consciousness have migrated down to his tongue?

His wife, Judith, could not seem to understand what had happened to him, even though he tried repeatedly to explain. "I'm down here," he told her, waggling himself to get her attention. He could not move his arm because of the cast that covered him from palm to shoulder. He'd broken his wrist, sent a hairline fracture along his ulna, and torn his rotator cuff.

Judith looked distraught. "It's the stroke, Franklin. I told you you were working too hard. Now you've suffered a stroke."

Perhaps that was the case. He'd been standing at the top of the stairs, reaching out to the banister, when suddenly he felt dizzy. Sometime later he awoke, face down on the parquet landing, his arm trapped beneath him. He felt suffocated, as if he were buried in an avalanche. When the EMTs rolled him onto his back, he moaned in pain, but at the same time experienced a profound sense of relief when his hand came free. Daylight! Air! Though of course he'd been breathing perfectly well the entire time, and he could see fine. What he could not decide, even now, was this: had the accident caused the shift in consciousness, or had he become dizzy because his self was on the move down his arm?

"Don't tell the doctors," he said. "They'll think I'm crazy."

She patted the back of his hand and he flinched. "I won't if you don't want me to," she said. Her fingers were stubby, which she tried to disguise with long, brightly painted nails. Liar's hands.

That afternoon, the doctors stormed his room to interrogate him. They shone pen lights into his eyes, wheeled him off to MRIs and CAT scans, tested his vision, speech, and cognition. Except for some awkwardness rearranging wooden blocks during the motor coordination exam, the fact that his self was now nestled 30 inches southeast from its old location seemed to make no measurable difference. He was perfectly capable of performing from his new mental home.

"Let's see if the feeling persists," the most senior doctor said, and handed Judith a dozen prescriptions to fill. "Call us if you experience anything odd, such as—" And here he rattled off a list of alarming neurological and physiological symptoms.

"The important thing," he said to Franklin, "is to avoid stress."

After eight weeks, Franklin returned to the hospital to have the cast removed, and then returned again a few days later for the first of a several physical therapy sessions to restore motion to his shoulder. His therapist's name was Olivia. She had lovely hands. She kept her nails trimmed, but they were painted with a clear gloss with white tips—a French manicure. Her long, delicate-looking fingers were quite strong; when she dug into the knotted tissue of his shoulder she could make him cry out. Whenever she touched his left hand, however, she was exceedingly gentle, which convinced him she'd been told about his mental condition. But on the third visit, when he worked up the courage to mention, casually, that his consciousness had migrated to the peninsula of his index finger, she seemed genuinely surprised.

"You feel like you are . . ." She nodded toward his hand. "There?"

"The funny thing is, I'm not even left handed."

She frowned, not disapprovingly, but in a curious, scientific way. "What's that like for you? If you don't mind talking about it."

There was nothing he wanted to talk about more. Judith found the topic distasteful. "Close your eyes," he told Olivia. "Imagine yourself as one great finger. Picture a long arm extending from your back that stretches up to a gargantuan body."

She closed her eyes and he watched her, moving his gaze from her white-tipped fingernails, to her face, and back again. The image was transferred from his retina to his brain, and there down his arm to his pulsing index finger. He curled against his palm, suddenly embarrassed by his thoughts.

"And up there," he said, "at the top of the body, is a huge, remote head like a planetoid. A bony house for the computer of your brain. It tells you things, but it's not you."

She concentrated for a few moments, and then opened her eyes. "I wondered why you kept looking at my hands."

"Sorry about that."

"It's all right." She lifted one finger, flexed it, and laughed. "Hi there."

He raised himself up and waved back.

She said, "Does it feel . . . odd in there? Cramped?"

"It feels like the most natural thing in the world," he said. "I'd always been a person who lived in my head, who kept his feelings contained. Now I can't imagine living any other way. I feel free."

He was worried that his confession might alienate her, but at the next session there was no strangeness between them. As they worked on his muscles he talked easily of his new life, the new insights he'd gained. "Have you ever noticed how careless people are with their hands?" he said during one visit. "The other day my wife grabbed a pan from the oven, burned herself, and then she stuck her finger in her *mouth*. She didn't even wash afterward." And: "I wonder if Helen Keller was hand conscious?"

He wanted the visits to go on and on, but his insurance ran out after only three weeks. At the end of the last appointment, he said, "You've helped me so much, I'd like to thank you somehow. Can I buy you lunch? You said you liked Thai food." Ever since she'd mentioned her love of pad Thai he'd been thinking of chopsticks moving in her fingers.

"I don't think that's a good idea," she said, not unkindly. She glanced down at his hand. "You're wearing a ring."

"But she doesn't—" He wanted to say, She doesn't understand me like you do. But that was going too far, extending himself in a way that would only lead to embarrassment for both of them. "She doesn't like Thai food."

*

His wife entered his study without knocking. On his computer screen was an ad for a ladies Rolex. Judith looked disgusted. The hand modeling the watch was beautiful, though a little too perfect for his tastes: the wrist was improbably narrow, the fingers obviously air-brushed. Fortunately, a few months ago he'd found an internet forum where people exchanged pictures of the best hand models.

"I've made an appointment," Judith said. "With a specialist." He told her he wasn't interested, but she would not be refused.

They drove to a clinic only a few blocks from the hospital where Olivia worked. The doctor wasn't a psychiatrist, as he'd feared, or a neurologist, but a family practice MD who'd written a book about alternate states of consciousness. He was bald except for a gray po-nytail, as if his hair had given up on general coverage and decided to specialize. The doctor seemed inordinately excited by Franklin's condition. "We must nudge the mind out of its cul-de-sac," he said emphatically, "and return it to its former home." He rambled on for some time before Franklin realized that his proposed solution was to amputate.

"It's the only way," the man said. "Sudden Egotic eviction."

"Are you insane?" Franklin said. "You could kill me!"

"Your hand is up in the air again," Judith said. And then to the doctor she said, "He does that whenever he feels defensive."

"Marvelous," Dr. Ponytail said. "May I see your hand? Your finger looks inflamed."

"Get the hell away from me!" He curled into a fist and charged out of the office. He did indeed feel hot, like a lawn mower engine revved beyond its specs. Outside he uncurled and saw that he'd turned red as a thermometer, his self-finger seeming to pulse like a rubber bladder. He cried out.

"Franklin? Are you all right?" It was Olivia's voice—Olivia! He spun his arm to reach out to her, and then the world continued to spin, and he collapsed to the sidewalk.

*

When he awoke, he was alone in another hospital room, and the feeling of suffocation he'd experienced on the stairs months ago had returned. He looked down, and saw that his left hand was encased in white bandages, from wrist to fingertips. His other arm was restrained by IV tubes, but he bit and chewed at the bandages until his fingers were free.

The index finger was still there. It had turned pale and shriveled, as if it had spent too long in the bathtub, but it was whole.

Something was wrong, however. The finger looked utterly unfamiliar to him. Had he really thought that he'd been *in there*, in that *pointer?* More alarmingly, the suffocating feeling had not dissipated.

At that moment, Olivia and Judith came into the room. They were holding paper cups of coffee, and it looked as if they'd been having a heart to heart discussion.

"It's all right," Olivia said, "You're safe now. You just passed out."

"Try to calm down," Judith said. And then she saw the scraps of bandages and frowned. "I suppose you're still . . ."

"No!" he said. "That's over! I'm—" Where was he? He was drowning, and he could feel his giant body above him, his voice thundering from far away.

"What do you need?" Olivia asked.

He closed his eyes, concentrating. This little piggy went to market, he said to himself. This little piggy stayed home. And *this* little piggy . . .

"Here!" he said, kicking up at the sheet. "For God's sake, get this sheet off of me!"

The women pulled up the linens, and at his pleading, removed his socks. He lifted his right foot into the air.

There he was. Third toe from the right. He was slender, with a thick, healthy nail. A single hair sprouted from his knuckle in a Superman curl. Yes, just a middle toe, but at last he felt completely at home: surrounded, supported, unstubbable.

# MESSAGE FROM THE
# BUBBLEGUM FACTORY

The guards, Dear Reader, are kicking the shit out of me.

The first few steps of my plan for breaking into the Ant Hill were simple: Drive through the outer gate in my rented Land Rover, brake to a halt well short of the second gate, and then step out of the car. I thought that once I'd assumed the posture of absolute surrender—prone, hands on the back of my head, stillness personified—that they wouldn't feel the need to stomp me like a bug.

Unfortunately, no.

The subsequent intake process, however, is everything you'd expect of the world's only Ultra-Super-Max prison. They carry me under a half-lowered blast shield that looks nuke-proof, then through a vault door, and finally into a series of cold, concrete rooms where I am fingerprinted and photographed, palpitated and probed, swabbed, scanned, and scrubbed, deloused and depilated. They keep me naked. My head throbs from the pounding I took at the gate, and my stomach feels like it's been turned inside out.

The paperwork is stunning. They even make me sign for the lime green jumper they throw at me.

The warden comes in as I step into it. Judging by the demeanor of the guards and the way one of them cracks me in the ribs when I don't zip up fast enough, this is an honor of some kind. One millionth customer, maybe.

The warden looks like a . . . does it matter? He is the warden. Supply your own visual.

He frowns at me. "You're the mascot."

"That's kind of offensive."

"The sidekick, then. The nut job who went crazy on TV last year."

"Now you're just being mean."

He looks me up and down, taking in my skinny arms, my puffy eye, my pot belly. He shakes his head in bewilderment. "How the hell did you think you would get in here, much less out again? Look at you. You're out of shape, you have no weapons, no powers—" He gives me a hard look. "Do you?"

"Not really," I say. "Well, one."

The four guards in the room suddenly tense. I hear a subtle but bracing sound: The double creak of a leather gloves pulling back metal triggers.

"I can't be killed," I say.

I smile. "I mean, not because of anything I can do. It's just—look. When I was hanging out with Soliton and the Protectors, I must have been kidnapped once a month. Held hostage, used as bait, snared in death traps. They especially liked to dangle me."

"What?"

"Over tubs of acid, piranhas, lava pits, you name it—villains are very big on dangling. Twenty years of this, ever since I was a kid. You wouldn't believe the number of times I've been shot at, blown up, tossed into rivers, knifed, pummeled, thrown off buildings and bridges—"

"You don't say."

"Oh yeah, half a dozen times at least. My right ear drum's still perforated from being chucked out of a plane." I lean forward, and the guard puts a hand on my chest. I ignore him. "See, here's the thing. I should be dead a hundred times over. But the rules of the universe don't allow it. I'm not bragging—that just seems to be the way it works."

The warden smiles coldly. "Cold" is the only form available to him, the sole version taught in Sadistic Warden School. "That's not a super power, Mr. King. That's a delusion. One shared by every teenager who doesn't wear a seatbelt."

The guards' guns are still aimed at me, but I no longer seem to be in imminent danger. The warden opens a manila folder. "You went missing from St. Adolphus Psychiatric Hospital in Modesto, California six months ago. No one's seen you since."

I shrug.

He flips through more papers. "Where have you been, Mr. King?"

"Does it matter?" I say. I wait for him to look up. "Really. Are you at all interested? Will it make a difference?"

He considers this. "No, as a matter of fact." He closes the folder. "I've already called for a helicopter to take you out of here and back to your doctors in California. This is not a hospital."

"I've heard that."

"People like you, even famous people, are not in my remit. You are not what this institution is for."

"But what about my crime? Don't you want to punish me?"

"What crime is that?"

"Assaulting a federal officer." And then I kick him in the nuts.

I'll give the warden this: He doesn't go down. He staggers back, red-faced and wincing. He gets his breath back while the guards whack me like a piñata until the candy comes out. And by candy, I mean, not candy.

After a while the warden kneels and lifts my head off the floor. "You win, Mr. King. You get an overnight stay." He taps my forehead. "You're going to talk to my men, and you're going to tell them everything—your deepest fear, your favorite color, your grandmother's social security number. You're going to tell us where you've been for six months, why you're here now, and what you thought you would accomplish. Everything."

I make a sound that ends in a question mark.

"Yes," he says. "Everything."


Picture it from above, Dear Reader, say from a huge, invisible eyeball floating above the plains. From 10,000 feet, the Ant Hill is a gray dot in the middle of a huge blank square on the North Dakota map, a cement speck surrounded by half a million acres of treeless prairie. Drop a few thousand feet. You make out a single road heading toward the heart of the Ant Hill. And then you make out concentric rings that the road pierces: the outermost ring is just a chain-link fence, easy enough to drive through, but the next two inner rings are taller, reinforced, with sturdy gates. The road ends at the innermost ring, a cement wall twenty feet tall. Inside the ring is an oval of cobalt blue, a manmade lake. Beside the lake is a gray cooling tower like a funeral urn, then the cement dome of the reactor building, and half a dozen smaller buildings huddling close. The familiar shapes of the tower and dome, repeated in nuclear power plants across the globe, have always put me in mind of mosques.

The Antioch Federal Nuclear Facility was built in the '80s, designed to manufacture weapons-grade plutonium for the hungry guts of America's ICBMs. A few months after Soliton's arrival, however, a freak accident shut the plant down. (Freak accidents became a lot more common after the Big S touched down, and we would have had to stop referring to them by that name if they hadn't created so many freaks.) Before the plant could reopen, Soliton's adventures had (a) ended the cold war, and (b) provided a need for a new kind of jail.

So they renovated. You couldn't see much of the work on the surface. But that's the thing about ant hills.

The guards drag me through approximately 3,000 miles of tunnels. I could be wrong—they'd smacked me around quite a bit. I'm just happy that I haven't blacked out or thrown up.

They toss me into the cell. I'm expecting a sarcastic line from the guards—"Welcome to the Ant Hill," perhaps—but they disappoint me by merely slamming the door.

I pull myself up onto the bunk and lay there for awhile. There's a toilet, a sink, and a cardboard box holding a roll of toilet paper. There don't seem to be any cameras in the cement ceiling—I'm too low a threat for the expensive rooms.

My stomach rumbles.

"Jesus, hold on a minute," I say.

I pull myself into a sitting position, put my hands on my knees, and take a deep breath. "Okay," I say. "One, two—"

My stomach lurches, and a ball of peach-colored goo flies out of my mouth and splats against the floor. It looks like Silly Putty, but it gleams with silvery veins like snail tracks. It's still connected to my gullet by a long, shiny tail, and I can feel the stuff shifting in my belly. "Gahh!" I say. Which means, roughly, Hurry the hell up.

The long stream of putty reels out of my stomach and out my throat like a magician's scarf trick. The glob on the floor grows as it absorbs mass, becoming a sphere about ten inches in diameter. With a final, discomfiting *fwip!* the last of it snaps free from my throat. The sphere starts to quiver like a wet dog, flinging silvery flecks in all directions.

I fall back against the cot.

A tiny, warbling voice says, "Just for the record? I am never doing that again."

A tiny hand appears beside my head, and then a doll-size thing climbs onto the cot. It looks like a miniature Michelin Man, all peachy beige, including round white eyes and a Kermit the Frog mouth. "What the hell took you so long?" he says. "The gel was starting to burn off I was in there so long. You know what it smells like in there? Exactly what you think it smells like."

"I wasn't enjoying it either, Plex."

He squints at my face. "You provoked them, didn't you? I couldn't make out what the hell you did to the warden."

I sit up. "He was going to send me back to the hospital. Now at least we get to stay the night." I nod toward the door. "You think you can get through it?"

"Please," he says, and rolls his ping pong ball eyes. "Take this." He holds up a three-fingered hand. The middle finger bulges, becomes a sphere, and then falls off with a wet pop.

I pick up the blob, mush it a bit between thumb and index finger, and press it into my ear. It's uncomfortably warm, like fresh-chewed gum. "Match the skin tone, okay?" I tell him. "I don't need to look like I've got a wad of white boy in my ear. Okay, give me a test."

*Check one, check two. Sibilance. Sibilance.* The voice is loud in my ear. The vibration tickles.

"Don't scream or you'll blow out another ear drum," I say.

*You know*, he says in a confidential voice. *If I go up any more of your orifices, we're registering for place settings.*

"Just get going. I'll wait here for you." I fall back against the cot. No pillow, but I don't think it's going to interrupt my sleep.

Guards come for me hours later. I assume it's morning. They put shackles on my wrists and legs, then frog march me to an elevator. According to my research there are 15 levels in the Ant Hill. We start on level 5 and then go up to level one. The administration offices are just a short walk from there.

The warden looks upset. He tells the guards to secure me to the guest chair and then get out. Then he picks up a sheaf of papers, glances at them, and looks at me with an expression of fresh disgust. "What's the matter with you?"

"You're going to have to be more specific."

"This nonsense about wanting to tell me Soliton's true identity."

*You told them that?* Plex says in my ear.

"I didn't think you'd want me to tell your employees."

"You're lying."

"Warden, I was a member of the Protectors—sorry, 'Soliton and the Protectors.'" The big guy always insisted we say it that way: He Gladys, we Pips.

"You weren't one of them. You just followed them around."

"Again with the demeaning statements. Just because I wasn't one of the people in capes didn't mean I wasn't part of the team. I was the first member, if you want to know. I was there on Day One. If you look at the first pictures of when he landed—"

"I've seen them. You're the boy dressed up in the baseball suit."

"I wasn't *dressed up*, I was the bat boy. That was an official Cubs uniform."

I loved that suit. Loved everything about that job, but especially hanging out with the players, chewing gum in the dugout while they chewed tobacco. A guy in my small group at the hospital said it proved I had an early tendency toward hero worship. Another patient said I had a costume fetish. I'm not saying they're wrong.

I was standing in the bullpen when somebody shouted and there he was, a man in T-shirt and jeans tumbling out of the empty sky like a shot bird. At first I thought a drunk had jumped from the upper deck. But no, the angle was all wrong, he was directly over center field and falling at tremendous speed. He hit and the turf exploded and the stadium went silent. Everyone just stood there. I don't know why I moved first.

"I was the first one to help him out of the crater," I tell the warden. "The first person he spoke to on the planet. He took off his glasses, shook my hand and said, 'Thanks, Eddie.'"

"He knew your name?"

"Spooky, huh? I didn't think much of it at the time. But later—twenty years later, embarrassingly enough—I realized that was the first clue. The first bit of evidence telling me what he was. Have you have ever read the Gnostic Gospels, warden? No, of course not. But maybe you've heard of them. *National Geographic* ran a translation of the Gospel of Judas a few years ago that suggested that the man had no choice but to—"

"Stop babbling. You're not making any sense."

"Fine, let me bring it down to your level. How about Bazooka Joe comics?"

"What do you *want*, Mr. King?"

Well, I tried. "I want to talk to Ray Wisnewski," I say.

He pauses half a second too long. "Who?"

*Eddie, is it part of the plan to tell them the plan?*

"Come on," I say to the warden. "Ray Wisnewski—WarHead? The man who killed two million people in Chicago?"

"I don't know what—"

"The glowing guy in your basement. I know he's here. All I need is a half hour conversation. See, I'm doing a kind of informal deposition. I'm putting together a case against Soliton."

"You really are insane."

"No, you're supposed to say, Case against Soliton? He's a hero, what did he ever do? And then I tell you that he's responsible for the deaths of millions, not to mention everyone on the planet who's been injured, widowed, made into an orphan, generally had their lives destroyed every time Soliton and the Protectors went toe to toe with some—"

"You're blaming *him* for Chicago? He didn't set off WarHead— that was the Headhunter."

"Ah. Let's talk about the late Dr. Hunter. Did you know that Soliton captured him not two months before Chicago? And then he was sent here, to your prison. Even though he'd escaped from the Ant Hill four times before."

"You think *I'm* responsible?"

"I think you're incompetent, but no, not responsible. You're just a cog—a malfunctioning cog, maybe, with a couple teeth missing, whose very flaws may be necessary to the continued running of the system—but not the prime mover. Not by a long shot. Soliton is the one responsible. Not just for Chicago—for *everything*." I can see he's too angry to listen properly. "So how about it. You walk me down to wherever you're keeping WarHead—"

"Absolutely not! You can't come in here trying to sell a hero's secrets to get some—

"Warden, I'm not selling secrets, I'm selling silence." He still doesn't understand. "If you let me talk to Ray," I say slowly, "I promise *not* to tell the world Soliton's real name."

"You're bluffing."

"That I know his name? Sure I do, it's D—"

"Don't say it!"

"Why not? You afraid he'll hear you?"

It's not an unreasonable fear. As far as anyone knows, Soliton doesn't possess super hearing, but he has a tendency to develop new powers whenever he gets bored.

"You can't do that." He grimaces. "You can't just—give away a hero's secret identity."

Funny, they didn't have a problem outing Teresa at her trial. "How about this." I lean forward. "I'll just whisper a clue."

"You'll do no such—"

"*He's my dad.*"

That shuts him up.

"Well, not biologically," I say. "You may have noticed that Soliton's white. Though I guess that could be one of his superpowers." I lean back in my chair. "Anyway, I was twelve years old the day he fell—that kind of rules out paternity at the chronological level. No, I mean, legally. He became my guardian after my parents were killed when I was fifteen—by two different supervillains, by the way. My back story's a little complicated. But basically, he's my father."

*He said he wanted everything*, Plex says.

The warden stares at me. It's too late for him now; the idea is in his head and he can't get it out. He knows he can look up my record, find out who my guardian used to be. He doesn't know Soliton's name yet, but forever after he will know that he *can* know it. Every day he'll have to decide whether or not to act on that knowledge.

Also, now he can't get rid of me. "So. Do we have a deal?"


The trip down to my new cell in the ultra max wing—an upgrade which I consider quite the compliment for a person with no powers—is a brisk affair. We ride the elevator down many floors below my original cell, and then the four guards hoist me by each limb and carry me like a battering ram, stomach-side down, at trotting speed through the corridors. I don't have much opportunity to look around, but the cell doors have small windows, some of them with familiar faces pressed close to the glass. Reptilian faces, deathly pale faces, faces with elaborate tattoos. If my mouth wasn't taped shut, I would point out to the guards which of these residents I helped put in here.

My new cell is identical to the old one, except for the lenses set into the ceiling. For the next several hours I lie still on the bed, breathing through my nose. I know I'm on Prison TV, but I'm intent on becoming the most boring channel imaginable, the C-SPAN of inmates.

I should have explained myself better to the warden. Dear Reader, do they have Bazooka Bubblegum in your world? Every piece has a tiny Bazooka Joe comic strip wrapped around the pink gum, and at the bottom of every strip is a fortune. The summer Dad fell to Earth, I opened one while I was in the dugout and the fortune said, "Help, I'm trapped in a bubblegum factory." I thought that was hilarious. I was too young to recognize an old joke.

The older I get, the more I realize that there are no new jokes. There are only minor variations, endlessly repeated.

I wake up when the door makes a sound like a shotgun racking a shell. My stomach thinks of lunch. Then the door swings open and a guard stumbles in holding his face. Except he has no face, only a blank patch of skin covering his eyes and nose and mouth. He stumbles blindly, then abruptly kneels down.

*I told him I'd open an air hole if he cooperated,* Plex says in my ear. *Could you knock him out, please?*

I glance up at the lenses in the ceiling. There's no way to tell if they've been blinded, but I have to trust Plex.

There's a truncheon strapped to the guard's belt. They don't carry guns on the floor, for good reason, but I know from recent personal experience that these guys *love* to use their truncheons. I pull it free, step behind the man, and take a batter's stance, aiming carefully at the back of his head.

I know how it must sound to you, Dear Reader. You're thinking, a blow like that could kill the man. Paralyze him, perhaps. Would it reassure you to know that I've been hit from behind like this more times than I can count? In any reasonable world, my brain should be hamburger by now. I should be dead or gibbering in the corner of a state hospital.

Yet I live on. I persist. And this man will live on, not because of who he is, but because of what he is. Yes, he is a minion whose real face is as blank as the Plexo-covered one, but he is a minion working for the U.S. of A, a good-hearted law man trying to do his part in the war on crime. At this moment, in this circumstance, he is as invulnerable to permanent harm as I am. And when he wakes up in the morning, perhaps with a headache and a nasty bruise, he will not even wonder at his good fortune. For men like him, the rules of this world prevent even the self-reflection that would expose its ir-rationality.

I swing, and the baton makes a sickening sound against the back of his skull. He pitches forward.

"Eddie? Hey Eddie?" I get the impression Plex has been calling my name for a while. He's slipped free of the man's face and formed into a thin little figure, a doughboy after a fight with the rolling pin. "You okay?" he asks.

"I'm fine." I toss the truncheon onto the bed and start stripping the guard of his clothes. "I take it you found the control room."

"I'm in about twenty pieces, crawling through the electrical pan-els. So far they haven't figured out why the cameras are out on this cell, but they're sending a couple guys to investigate. They'll be here in about two minutes, Naked Man."

I toss the jumper across the room.

"By the way," he says, "do you know they have Icer in here?" He's trying to sound casual.

"We don't have time for vendettas, Plex."

"What? I thought that was the whole point."

"Just tell me if you found out where they're keeping Teresa."

"Same floor as this one. They've got her knocked out, hooked up to some kinda I.V."

Not good news. My main plan, such as it is, depends on her being awake, mobile, and pissed off. "Okay, you go try to wake her up."

"Where are you—? Wait, not Ray."

"How many floors down is he from here?"

"You told me Ray was optional."

"He's still our best chance of getting out of here." I button my new black Ant Hill security shirt. As for the pants, the legs are too short and the waist too wide. At least the shoes fit. "Plus, I owe it to him."

"He's a crybaby! A boy scout crybaby, which is the worse kind." Several of him sigh. "Okay, fine. Though I have to tell you, he's half-way to China. Take the elevator down until you smell magma."

In the hallway we split up: I go right, and Plex goes left and up the wall to the ceiling. We haven't really separated, however—Plex is in my ear whispering directions like a GPS. I tuck in the back of my shirt and hustle toward the elevators, head down. Unfortunately, the staff dress code doesn't include face-covering helmets, so my disguise will be useless if I come face to face with anyone; I just hope it fools the people behind the cameras.

The elevator is waiting for me, the door thoughtfully held open by whatever chip off the ol' Plexo has gained access to the Hill's control systems. I step in just as the two guards come around the corner. The door slides shut.

"Thanks, man," I say.

*De nada.*

The ride seems to take forever, though mostly that's nerves. The LED numbers go up as I go down, and at level 13 Plex directs me down another hallway to a huge freight elevator. That one is supposed to take me the rest of the way down, though the gap between 14 and 15 is half a minute long. Finally the carriage jolts to a stop and the door opens on a cool, dimly lit room. Opposite is a huge door like a submarine hatch. It's pasted with yellow and black radiation warnings.

Two Demron radiation suits hang on hooks next to a rack of oxygen bottles. I pull one on one of the suits even though I know it'll be useless at the kind of levels Ray is capable of putting out. I decide to skip the SCBA and just go with the hood. Before I zip up I scoop Plex out of my ear and paste him to the wall. He squeaks in protest.

"You don't need to pick up any more REMs," I say. "Look what happened last time."

I walk stiffly up to the door. There's no doorbell. I knock, and when there's no answer, I start cranking. I immediately break into a sweat and the mask fogs.

After two minutes of work the hatch opens and I step into a cavern.

Sodium vapor lights hang from the high ceiling. The space is huge, but crowded: Yellow and blue barrels stretch into the dark, around piles of rusted scaffolding, stacks of construction equipment, even vehicles—all the irradiated garbage of Antioch. I may be imagining it, but my fillings seem to tingle.

There's a path through the barrels. As I walk I become aware of the thump of music coming from distant speakers. I circle around a yellow backhoe on deflated tires and see an open space decorated like the set for a high school play: A couch, several chairs, a kitchen table, bookshelves. Huge black rectangles are set up along the back of the space on makeshift easels. Ray stands in front of one with a paint brush, layering more black onto black.

He's a big man, almost seven feet tall, but he's hard to see clearly through the yellow haze surrounding him.

I don't want to get close when he's throwing off MeVs like this. I shout, but he doesn't hear me over the huge stereo. I find a length of rebar, bang it against a steel drum: nothing. Finally I cock my arm and heave it into his living room.

He turns, looks at the bar on the floor, then looks around until he sees me. He squints. I can almost feel the x-rays through my hood. He says, "Ed?!"

He starts toward me, arms open, then pauses when I take a step back. "Oh, sorry," he says. He concentrates, and the lightshow around his skin fades.

I take off my hood. "Just keep sucking in those neutrinos, okay?"

He grabs me in a bear hug. "I can't believe it! I heard you were in the hospital! What are you doing here?"

"Breaking you out, of course." He frowns and releases me. "Unless you don't want to."

He decides I'm joking. "Come on and sit down," he says, and leads me to the couch. "You want a beer? No, second thought, better not. You should keep the suit on, too." He walks to a stereo sitting on a bookshelf and silences it.

"So Ray. What's up with the paintings?"

"I dunno. Just something I've always wanted to do." He nods at the canvas in front of me. Another black triangle. "That one's called 'Girls at the Circus.'"

"They're very, uh . . ."

He looks at me expectantly.

". . . dark?"

He laughs. "To you, maybe."

I shake my head. "Listen, I came to ask you something, and I don't have much time."

He sits down on the couch. "You really did break in here. Just to see me."

"You, and Teresa."

"She's *here?*"

"Where else would they keep her? They've got her drugged up and locked down. I thought I would . . ." I smile, feeling embarrassed. I've only shared the plan with Plexo before now, and he's not quite a critical audience. "I'm putting the band back together, Ray."

He laughs. "I thought you were just the roadie." I give him my wounded look and he laughs harder. "Besides, Soliton and Gazelle already did that, didn't they?"

"Fuck the New Protectors. I'm talking about the real Protectors: You, me, Lady Justice, the Dead Detective, Plexo—"

"Flexo? He's alive?"

"He goes by Plexo now—the Multiplex Man. He's not just rubber anymore. After Chicago he became sort of . . . it's hard to explain."

Ray shakes his head. "He was always such a pain in the ass. But I'm glad he's alive. That makes me . . ." He purses his lips, controlling some emotion. "I'm glad."

"Chicago wasn't your fault, Ray."

He doesn't bother to answer.

"Ray, you know whose fault it is."

"I know what you're trying to do, Eddie, but when the Headhunter did that to me, it's because there was something in me that—"

"That's bullshit. It wasn't you, it wasn't even the fucking Headhunter! We have to go back to first causes, Ray. Before Soliton, we didn't have telepathic masterminds trying to turn you into a bomb. Yes, there were problems before Dad landed—wars, disease, regular crime. But we didn't have *supervillains*. When somebody got dropped into a vat of chemicals, they *died*, they didn't turn into fucking Johann the Lizard Man."

"Or me," Ray says.

"Or you." He was just a janitor, a poor schmuck caught in the tunnels when 3,000 degrees of radioactive steam hit him. In any sane universe he would have been instantly transformed into broiled corpse. "Sometimes one of the good guys gets lucky," I say. "But the point is, we wouldn't *need* heroes like you if our world hadn't taken a left turn. Chicago was . . . unspeakable. But it wasn't the start of it and it sure ain't the end. How many innocent bystanders are still getting killed each year from all this brawling?"

"Soliton saves people every day."

"Mostly from other super freaks! Think about all those city blocks destroyed, governments toppled—"

"Evil governments."

"Do you think America is *supposed* to be occupying all those countries he overthrew? Iraq, Iran, Afghanistan, Trovenia, Ukraine—what the fuck are we doing there? Our soldiers are getting blown up, because he can't be everywhere at once. Thanks to him, the entire world *hates* us."

"Eddie, is this about Jackie?"

"What? No. This has nothing to do with her.'"

"She didn't just join the team, she married him. That makes her your step-mom, kind of."

"You can shut up now."

"It's just, you seem to hate him so much, Eddie, and you two used to be so close. When you talk like this . . . It's like that night on the TV. You sound crazy."

"Someone had to speak up," I say. "Teresa didn't deserve to go to jail, not when it wasn't her fault."

"Eddie, she cut off Hunter's head."

"So, extra points for irony. She only corrected the problem Soliton refused to solve."

Ray looks sad. "You can talk that way in front of me, maybe. You can say that to other people in the Protectors. But not in front of the public, Eddie. They look up to us."

"They shouldn't be looking up to superheroes, Ray. They should be looking up to themselves. Okay, that didn't come out right, but you know what I mean." I stand up. "I just came to tell you, I'm getting Teresa out of here, and you're welcome to come with me."

Escape Plan A: Ray realizes that Yes, Eddie was right all along, and leads us through the very steam tunnels that created him, absorbing deadly residual radiation, until we reach the coolant tower and our magic carriage swoops down to take us away.

Ray stares at his feet.

"Don't worry about it," I say. "Really. But you should know that in the next few months, well, people will probably be saying lots of bad things about us. They're going to call us criminals. I just wanted you to hear from me first, so you'd know why I was doing it."

He looks up. "Doing what? What are you planning?"

"What we should have been doing all along. Saving the world."

*

After I've stripped off the Demron suit and mopped the sweat from my ears, I pop Plexo back in.

*Plan B?* he says. I can hear the eagerness in his voice. Plan B is chaos. And I don't have a Plan C.

"Call the television stations," I say. "And release the cyber-yetis."

He whoops in joy. Probably several of him do.

They aren't real yetis, of course, just genetically engineered gibbon/human/Linux hybrids, but they're eight feet tall, quick, and bitey. It would take pages to detail their origin and complicated history. Suffice it to say that Dad's fought them half a dozen times and had a hell of a good time on each occasion, because they kept coming back with upgrades and novel tweaks. Also, he likes monkeys.

I contracted anonymously with their creator to have a score of the Version 8.0's released in an abandoned amusement park in Newark, New Jersey, booted up in Rage Mode. All we had to do was make sure that Dad knew they were on the loose—the equivalent of showing a toddler a shiny object. That's always been his Achilles heel: Super A.D.D. Anything interesting, he has to chase after it, then punch it.

*Dialing now*, Plex says. Most of his mass is hovering high above the Dakota plains, surrounded by bizarro-tech equipment. *Oh, wait, almost forgot. There's a problem with Teresa. I've unplugged her, but she won't wake up.*

"Heading your way," I say.

I'm out of the elevator and hustling down the hallway when I see guards crowding around my most recent cell; they've found the man we knocked out. I turn and start back the way I'd come. "Plex, I need an alternate route, pronto."

*Go right at the next hallway, then right again. It's a big square.*

I turn the corner, and nearly slam into the warden himself, leading a trio of guards toting scatter guns. I duck my head and step aside. He glances at me, then shouts, "King!"

I've spent a lot of my career running, and I used to be pretty good at it. I knock aside the nearest guard and sprint for the next corner. I swing around that, into a long straight corridor.

"You're supposed to be guiding me!" I yell.

*Don't get snappy. I'm spread a little thin, you know. WNET has me on hold, plus, Teresa just threw up on me.*

That seems like a good sign. At least she's awake. "Go to phase four!"

*I love it when you talk all mastermind-y.*

The patch of wall next to my head explodes; shrapnel peppers the side of my face. I slow to a stop and put up my hands. Before I can turn around a guard crashes into me and pins me to the floor. Two other guards pile on. It's all very reminiscent of my first hour in the Ant Hill.

They roll me over. We're next to a cell door, and a long pale face looks down at me through the door's thick glass. It's Frank McCandless, or as he likes to refer to himself, The Hemo-Goblin. (Not even his friends could talk him out of it.) He smiles, showing his fangs.

The warden gets my attention with a poke of a gun. The double barrels are aimed at my nostrils. "I have half a mind to test that superpower of yours," he says.

He won't pull the trigger, of course. It would be cold-blooded murder, and he's not that type. But even if he was Lord Grimm himself, he wouldn't do it. They never do. They all want to talk first. Then move on to the dangling.

"Did you enjoy your conversation with Mr. Wisnewski?"

"I did, actually."

"But you didn't come here just to talk to him, did you? You're here for her."

I smile my aw-shucks smile. "You got me there."

He presses the barrels to my forehead. "She's a convicted murderer, Mr. King. You're not leaving with her. I've already—"

The lights snap off, throwing us into pitch darkness. "What the hell?" the warden says. A few seconds later the yellow emergency lights come on. Alarms blare.

I haven't moved a muscle—not with a gun to my head. While I have complete confidence that the universe is bound by the rules I've outlined, I don't believe in *taunting* it.

"What did you do, King?" the warden asks. Plaintively, it seems to me.

The cell door next to me makes a familiar shotgun-loading noise. The warden frowns. The next door clacks, and the next one. Up and down and across the Ant Hill, 305 cells unlock.

The phrase, "And then all hell broke loose" is probably as over-used in your world as mine. But basically, yes.

*

By the time I make it to Teresa Panagakos's cell, she's sitting upright on a hospital bed, eyelids at half mast—though with her that could mean anything. Plex stands on the pillow beside her, a hand patting her cheek. He's stretched himself into a stick figure with a lollipop head. He sees me come in and does a double-take, corkscrewing his neck.

I guess I look pretty bad. I shut the door on the zot and screech and roar of supercriminals having their way with their oppressors and sit down on a corner of the bed. Plex hands me a corner of the sheet and I wipe the blood out of my eyes. I'm not sure whose blood it is.

"How's she doing?" I ask.

Teresa mumbles something in reply. She doesn't look much like Lady Justice. Her face has no color, and her gray hair is long and straggly. The arms and legs poking out of the hospital gown are almost as thin as Plexo's.

"Teresa, it's me, Eddie. Eddie King. We've come to take you out of here, okay?"

"Stop," she says.

"Stop what, hon?"

"Talking to me. Like a baby." Her milk-white eyes fasten on mine. "Blindfold," she says.

"Oh please," Plexo says. "We're pausing to put on *uniforms?*" But he makes a spike of his hand, pokes through the sheet, and tears off a clean strip. Teresa leans into me as I knot it behind her head.

"I'm going to pick you up now, Teresa. Ready?" I put one of her arms over my shoulders and hold tight to her waist. "Here we go."

She's light as foam, but her legs barely take her weight. It takes us half a minute to cross the room. We're not going to get anywhere at this rate. Plexo's at the door, tapping his stick foot.

"I'm going to have to carry you," I tell Teresa. She makes a disgusted noise, but she doesn't fight me when I scoop her up.

At the cell door we pause for a moment to allow a huge armored form to charge past, then step into the hallway.

"Which way?" I ask Plex.

"How should I know? I fried every camera I could get my hands on."

"Plex . . ."

"Go right—that'll take us to the central stairwells and the elevators."

I shake my head. "That's where metal guy and everybody else will be going. I think there's another stairwell to our left."

"Why did you even ask me then?"

The corridor is surprisingly clear; the fighting has already moved past us to the floors above. With Teresa in my arms I can't manage more than a trot. Plex scampers ahead, and by the time I reach the end of the hallway he's holding open the stairwell door.

We start up. Shouts echo down from the floors above, but the way immediately ahead seems clear. After two flights I'm drenched in sweat and my back is killing me. I lower Teresa to the floor.

"You run like a chain-smoking baby," Plex says.

"Shut," I say to Plex, and take a breath. "Up."

He sighs, a neat trick in a body that seems to have no lungs. "I'm going to go scout ahead," he says. "You two take your time."

Plex bounces up the stairs. I try to get my breath back.

Teresa looks up at me through the blindfold. "I always knew you'd turn to a life of crime," she says. I can't tell if she's joking. I never could tell with her. We've known each other for 20 years, but I was just a kid when I met her, and I've never completely shaken off that first dose of hero worship.

"Do you wear your bow tie anymore?" she says.

That used to be my signature look: suit jacket, good shoes, and bow tie. "I gave it up," I say. "Everybody thought I was in the Nation of Islam. You think you can hold onto my back?"

I hoist her up and she fastens her arms around my neck. I walk bent over, pulling myself up the rails with both hands. "Why are you doing this?" she says into my ear. My non-Plex-filled ear, as it turns out.

"Guilt?" I say. "Sense of duty?"

"I don't think so."

But that *is* why I'm rescuing her. At least partly. "It's complicated," I say. "I need your help with something."

"You want to kill him."

I miss a step and grip the rail harder to keep my balance. "It's not like it sounds," I say. "Soliton has—"

"I'm in."

I stop. I can't see her face, but I can hear her breathing. "Really?"

"Really. Keep moving, please."

"I never could hide anything from you," I say, and then I stop talking because Plexo has just said, *Uh oh.*

"What?"

*It's your super ex-girlfriend.*

"Can't be. She's in New Jersey. They're all supposed to be in New Jersey."

"Are you talking to Flexo?" Teresa says.

I tap my ear and nod.

*Well, there's a plume of dust coming at the Ant Hill at, like, eight-hundred miles per hour.*

"But the alarm just went off!" I say. "Even at her top speed she couldn't have—"

Oh. The warden. He must have called them. Maybe even before I went down to see Ray.

Teresa says, "You have a radio?"

"Kind of. Any sign of the big guy?"

*Not yet.*

I lock my arms under Teresa's butt and start double-timing up the stairs. Teresa's a bag of bones jouncing on my back. "They're coming for us," she says.

"So far just the Gazelle." But we both know that anywhere the Gazelle goes, hubby and the New Protectors won't be far behind.

"I can't hurt him, you know," she says. "The sword can't even touch him."

"Yeah," I say. Meaning, Yeah, I noticed that when you tried to chop him in half—but I don't have the breath for that. I was with Soliton when he went after Teresa a few weeks after Chicago. I was still on his side, then. Still a believer. We'd just discovered what she'd done to Dr. Hunter, and I went along to try to get her to surrender peacefully.

Yes, I was an idiot.

She was waiting for us in the Utah desert, a hundred miles from the nearest town, so that they wouldn't kill anyone when they went at it. Until that day I'd thought that Lady Justice was Soliton's match—

the check to his nearly unlimited power—but no. That's not the way this world works. Soliton will have no other heroes before him.

We reach the landing at Level 1 and Plexo's yelling in my ear: *She just ran past me. And me! Down the central stairs. She's checking the stairwells, man. Move!* Somewhere below, a sound like the roll of thunder: titanium boots hammering concrete, fast as machine gun fire.

I yank open the door and stumble through into a long hallway hazed with smoke: the row of intake rooms where they processed me. The old woman on my back feels like a cast iron stove. I drop to my knees, and Teresa slides off and thumps to the ground. I manage a "Sorry."

Dim figures wrestle in the distance. Voices shout. I get to my feet, turn toward the stairs, braced for her.

I'm wrong again. She comes at me from behind, through the smoke.

The Gazelle, fastest animal on any number of feet, skids to a stop with a scrape and shriek. I wheel to face her.

God, she's beautiful. The costume looks like it's been redesigned by Jean-Paul Gaultier, but she's kept the thigh-high golden boots. They still knock me out.

"Hey, Jackie."

Her voice comes out in a squeal—she does that when she's revved up—but then she concentrates and brings down the speed. "—combing this place for you, Eddie. No, I've been looking for you for months. What the hell are you up to? What are you doing with *her?*"

I think it's pretty obvious, but I want to be helpful. "I'm kind of . . ." I take a breath, and then cough in the smoke. "I'm in the middle of a jail break."

"Oh, Ed. You were doing so well." I frown. I don't think I was doing well *at all*. She says, "Listen to me. I'm going to round up the escapees, so why don't you get out of the crossfire, and afterward—"

"You're using that mom voice again."

"Dammit, I don't have time to argue you with you. Take Teresa into a cell and wait for me to come back."

I glance back. Teresa's on the ground behind me, propped up on her elbows. I say to Jackie, "If you're trying to talk me into turning myself in, that only works once." I cough again. "I will say this, though, you were right about the quality of that hospital. Great doctors, professional staff, decent food. Except for the forced meds, it was—duck."

She becomes a blur, and a big green arm swings down through the space where she'd been standing. Her leg comes up in a roundhouse—two loud *thwacks* as she spins and connects twice before the man can even recoil—and Johann the Lizard Man hits the floor.

"You still trust me," I say.

"I heard him coming." But there's a smile in her voice.

"You know what diagnosis they gave me?" I say. "*Adjustment disorder.* I'm not much for psychological mumbo jumbo, but I had to admit that that one was dead on."

"Eddie . . ."

"You ever read the Gnostic gospels, Jackie?"

She stares at me.

"It's like they're talking about Dad. An insane, capricious god messing with us for his own amusement. That's when I realized, if God is insane, how can there possibly be a cure for an adjustment disorder?"

"Ed, your jailbreak is over. The only question is—"

"Over? Before Dad gets here? He'll hate that. He loves chasing down bad guys—he's like a fucking Labrador retriever shagging Frisbees." I take a step forward. "Jackie, you know how bored he gets when there's no one to fight. He hates it. And the past few years, he's been getting bored more and more easily. The usual shit isn't doing it for him anymore. You can see it in his eyes."

"What? I see no such thing."

"We're not *real* to him. Not like the people back on his home Earth."

"Don't start this again," she says.

"Listen to his voice when he talks about the people he used to work with at that lab. Or Jesus, that fucking Mustang he used to drive. *That's* the real world to him. This is just . . ." I stop, see how still she's gotten. "He's never talked about his home world with you?"

"We talk about everything."

She's lying. "Then he told you how he didn't have powers there? No one did. It's like our world used to be. Like it's supposed to be."

Her hips shift in a familiar way. At any moment she'll put the left side of one golden hoof across the right side of my head, and there's not a damn thing I can do about it.

"Jackie, wait. He doesn't love you. And you don't love him, not really. See, he's got to have a girlfriend—that's in the script. That's what he wanted, and so that's what happened. He's *making* you love him, just like he made those supervillains hate him. But you can fight this, Jackie. You can join us."

"This conversation's over, Eddie."

And then, heat. A jet of flame whooshes between my legs. Jackie becomes a human torch, whirling around in circles. She doesn't scream, but I do. I jump sideways.

A few feet behind where I'd just been standing, Teresa's on her stomach, aiming a sword of flame where my crotch used to be. I'd forgotten she was back there. "Take her down!" she yells.

I step up to Jackie, clench a fist. "Hit her!" Teresa yells. "Hit her!"

Then Jackie's gone, disappeared into the smoke—probably to find a fire extinguisher. Or the lake.

She'll be okay, I tell myself. She's a fast healer.

"Are you kidding me?" Teresa says. The sword disappears and her hand unclenches. "*Join* us?"

I don't want to talk about it. I extend a hand, figuring Teresa's has cooled off by now. "Can you walk?"

She can, sort of. She looks stronger than she did five minutes ago. I put an arm around her and we limp through the smoke. Prisoners come up from behind, push past us. Some are winged or clawed or bulging with muscles, but most of them look like ordinary men and women in cheap coveralls, unremarkable and indistinguishable without their costumes. In their mad rush for the exit, they don't seem to recognize us.

The vault door has been torn from its hinges. Teresa and I shuffle through, and then we're in the no-man's-land between the vault door and the blast shield. The shield has been stopped just a few feet above the floor; prisoners slide and skitter under it like roaches.

I manage to direct Teresa through the gap, and when I scramble after her I'm blinded by golden light. I shade my eyes and squint, heart hammering. But it's not Soliton—it's just the afternoon sunlight streaming through shattered windows. The floor is a glittering beach of broken glass.

Outside, the guards are taking their last stand. They're firing down into the yard from towers and administration buildings. A few of the prisoners, the berserkers with more testosterone than sense, are throwing themselves against the buildings and crawling up the towers, but most are running for the fences. The flyers and other fast movers are already gone.

"Plex," I say. "Where the hell are you?"

*Little busy!* he yells in my ear.

"Please tell me you've got a way out of here," Teresa says.

And then I see Plexo. A dozen pint-size blobs are swarming a red-haired prisoner, tearing into him like a gang of ninja gingerbread men. I don't recognize the man he's attacking until I see that one of his hands is made of crystal. He grabs the neck of one of the little Plexos, and the miniature turns white and shatters into a puff of flakes.

Plex screams, *You want a piece of me? Huh? You want a piece of me?*

I yelp and grab my ear. The bit of Plex I've been carrying has launched itself from my ear canal toward the fight.

"Jesus, Plex, leave the Icer alone, we've got to—"

I hear a distinctive, whooshing hum. The air above the yard shimmers like a heat mirage on a desert highway, and a huge black sphere, 50 feet in diameter, abruptly appears, dropping fast.

"That sound," Teresa says. "I know that sound." She looks in my direction. "It's that piece of crap the Magician used to ride around in."

"Please don't call it names when we're inside," I say. "It's sensitive."

Painted on its side is a black 8 in a white circle. Before the sphere can touch down, the circle irises open and a six-by-six slab of Plexo leaps out, flattened like a flying squirrel. The Icer has time to scream before he's enveloped by a blanket of flesh.

I grab Teresa's hand but she shakes me off. We need to run but she can only move at a walk. A few of the other prisoners are looking at the sphere, dimly realizing that their most likely means of escape has just landed. A steel ramp extends from the base of the door with a rusty shriek but stops a foot short of the ground. I take Teresa's hand again and before she can pull free I tell her to step up.

She scowls at me and says, "They're here."

"Who?"

She points over my shoulder at the eastern sky.

From a mile away, the group of flyers are no bigger than specks. The lead figure, however, is unmistakable: that golden glow, that speed, those impossible, inertia-less changes of direction, like the beam of a flashlight flicking across a wall. The laws of physics do not apply to him. He is not in the world, Dear Reader, but projected upon it like a cartoon.

I would like to say that the sight of him doesn't faze me. But Jesus, I've seen the man shrug off an atomic explosion. I'm not ready for him yet.

I shove Teresa's bony butt up and through the door, then scramble in after her. "Eight-Ball!" I yell. "How're the batteries holding up?"

On the main video screen, white text swims to the surface: "Reply hazy, try again."

Shit. I lean out the door. "Plex! Dad's here!"

Below, Plex unwraps himself from the Icer, and the man falls unconscious to the ground. "Now would be good," I yell.

I scan the sky. The flyers are closer, and I can count them. Only three with Soliton. Half the team is probably on the east coast, fighting yetis. Not that it matters. Soliton alone can mop us up.

But then the group dives toward the ground, disappearing from my line of sight. They're rounding up the faster escapees first.

Plex pogos up and through the hatch. I slam a button and the door begins to cinch closed. "Make with the disappearing," I tell the 8-Ball. "And get us to five thousand feet right n—"

Talking becomes impossible as the G's throw me to the floor. Half a minute later I push myself upright and stumble to a screen and toggle to one of the cameras aimed at the ground. The heroes are in the yard now. I make out a couple of blurred forms careening between lime green dots—Gazelle and Dad, the only two capable of those speeds, having their high-velocity way with the prisoners.

Such fun they must be having.

"Eddie." It's Teresa. "Eddie, look at me."

"When he gets like that you just got to poke him," Plex says.

"Eight-Ball, get us higher," I say. "But not so fast this time. Then head east."

Teresa's gotten to her feet. She says, "Did you really believe what you said to Jackie back there? You think he's a god?" She's adopted the tone of a cop talking down a junkie.

"Don't get him started," Plex says.

"Then you're already screwed, Eddie. If he's scripted Jackie, if he's scripted everything, then the story already includes us. What we're doing now. Everything you're planning."

"Pretty much," I say. I thought this through months ago. "Head-hunter's dead. Dad's got to have a nemesis—he wouldn't know what to do without one. Might as well be me. Besides, there's plenty of precedent for sons wanting to kill their fathers—it's not exactly an original plot line." I smile. "The difference is, I believe in my job."

She doesn't say it, but I know what she's thinking. "You don't have to believe me for us to work together, Teresa."

"I don't," Plex says.

"We all want the same thing," I say. "We need each other."

"If the sword can't touch him," Teresa says, "Nothing can."

"Nothing in this world," I say.

"So you're going to hurt him how? Harsh words?"

"The sidekick has a plan," Plex says.

She tilts her head. She seems to be staring at me through the blindfold. "No. Now he's the criminal mastermind."

"Excuse me?" I say. "*Insane* criminal mastermind."

Even at this speed it's a long trip to the ruins of Chicago. Plenty of time to explain what I have in mind.

This is my message to you, Dear Reader: We're tired of being trapped in here with your madman, your psychopath playing out his power fantasies with us. Two million people were erased from my city. I lost every relative, every childhood friend, every neighbor and teacher and shop clerk I grew up with. Why? Because it was *interesting*.

No more. We're sending him back to you.

Watch your skies for a man tumbling to earth like a shot bird.

# FREE, AND CLEAR

**W**arily, Edward told Margaret his fantasy.

It's Joe Louis Arena in late August, peak allergy season. He's in the ring with Joe Louis himself, and as Edward dances around the canvas his sinuses feel like impacted masonry. Pollen floats in the air, his eyes are watering, and everything beyond the ring is a blur. Joe Louis is looking *strong*: smooth glistening chest, fierce gaze, arms pumping like oil rigs. Edward wipes his nose on his glove and shuffles forward. Joe studies him, waiting, drops his guard a few inches. Edward sees his opening and swings, a sweeping roundhouse. Joe sidesteps easily and the blow misses completely. Edward is stumbling forward, off balance and wide open. He looks up as Joe Louis' fist crashes into his face—but it's not Joe's normal fist, it's the giant Joe Louis Fist sculpture that hangs from chains in downtown Detroit, and it's swinging down, down. Two tons of metal slam into Edward's skull and shatter his zygomatic lobe like a nut. Sinus fluid runs like hot syrup down his chest and over his silk boxing shorts.

"That's what I like to think about the most," Edward told her. "That hot liquid draining."

His wife stared at him. "I don't think I can take this much longer," she said.

The address led them to an austere brick building in an aging industrial park.

"It doesn't look like a massage parlor," Edward said.

"It's a *clinic*," Margaret said. "For massage *therapy*."

Edward could feel a sneeze gearing up behind the bridge of his nose. He pulled a few tissues from the Kleenex box on the dash, reconsidered, and took the whole box. "I don't think this is going to help," he said. It was the first line in an argument they'd performed several times in the past week. Margaret only looked at him. He sneezed. In the back seat his four-year-old son laughed.

Edward lightly kissed Margaret on the cheek, then reached over the seat to shake hands with Michael. "Be a soldier," Edward said, and Michael nodded. The boy's nose was running and Edward handed him a tissue.

Margaret put the car in gear. "I'll pick you up in an hour. Good luck."

"Good luck!" Michael yelled. Edward wished they didn't sound so desperate.

The waiting room was cedar-paneled and heavy with cinnamon incense (heavy, he knew, because he could smell it). There was a reception desk, but no receptionist, so he sat on the edge of a wicker couch in the position he assumed when waiting—for allergists; endocrinologists; eye, ear, nose and throat specialists—his left hand holding the wad of Kleenex, his right thumb pressed up against the ridge of bone above his right eye, as if he were working up the courage to blind himself. Periodically he separated a tissue from the wad, blew into it, switched the moist clump to his other hand, and wedged his other thumb against the left eye. It was all very tedious.

A chubby white woman in a sari skittered up to him and held out her hand. "You're Ed!" she said in a perky whisper. "How are you?"

He smoothly tucked the Kleenex under his thigh, and as he lifted his hand he ran his palm against the side of his pants, a combination hide-and-clean move he'd perfected over the years. "Just fine, thanks."

"Would you like some tea?" she asked. "There are some cups over there you can use."

She gestured toward the reception desk where a mahogany tree of ceramic mugs sat next to an electric teapot. What he wanted, he thought, was a syringe to force a pint of steaming Earl Grey up his nose; what he wanted was a nasal enema. He said no thanks, his voice gravelly from phlegm, and she told him that the therapist would be available in a moment, would he like to walk this way please? He followed her down a cedar-paneled hallway, tinny sitar music hovering overhead, and she left him in a dim room with a massage table, wicker chair, and a row of cabinets. A dozen plants hung darkly along the edges of the room, suspended by macramé chains.

He looked around, wondering if he should take off his clothes. His wife had read him articles about reflexology but he couldn't remember if nakedness were one of the requirements. Once she'd shown him a diagram in *Cosmopolitan*: "Everything corresponds to something else, like in voodoo," Margaret had said. "You press one spot in the middle of your foot, and that's your kidney. Or you press here, and those are your lungs. And look, Hon." She pointed at the toes in the illustration. "The tops of the four little toes are all for sinuses." He asked about people with extra toes, what would those correspond to, but something interrupted—tea kettle or telephone—and she never answered.

He sat on the table rather than the chair because it was what he did in most examination rooms. When the door opened he was in the middle of blowing his nose. The masseuse was short, with frizzy brown hair. She waited politely until he was finished, and then said, "Hello, Edward. I'm Annit." Annit? Her accent was British or Australian, which somehow reassured him; foreigners always seemed more knowledgeable than Americans.

"Hi," he said. Her hand was very warm when they shook.

"You have a cold?" she asked sympathetically.

"No, no." He touched the bridge of his nose. "Allergies."

"Ah." She stared at the place where he'd touched. The pupils of her eyes were wet black, like beach pebbles.

"Can't seem to get rid of them," he said finally.

She nodded. "Have you seen a doctor?" Obvious questions normally annoyed him, but her sincerity was disarming. The accent, probably.

"I've seen everyone," he said. "Every specialist my insurance would cover, and a few that I paid for myself. I've taken every kind of pill that I'm not allergic to." He chuckled to show he was a good sport.

"What *are* you allergic to?"

He paused a moment to blow into a tissue. "They don't know, really. So far I seem to be allergic to nothing in specific and everything in general." She stared at his nose. "Allergies are cumulative, see? Some people are allergic to cats and, say, carpet mites. But if there's carpet mites but no cat around, they aren't bothered. Cat plus carpet mites, they sneeze. Or six cats, they sneeze. They haven't come up with a serum that blocks everything I'm allergic to, so I sneeze at everything."

"For you," she said, "it's like there are six cats around all the time?"

"Six hundred cats."

"Oh!" She looked genuinely concerned. She jotted something on the clipboard in her hand. "I have to ask a few other questions. Do you have any back injuries?" He shook his head. "Arthritis? Toothaches, diabetes, emphysema, heart disease? Ulcers, tumors, or other growths? Migraines?"

"Yes! Well, headaches, anyway. Sinus-related."

She made a mark on the clipboard. "Anything else you think you should tell me?"

He paused. Should he tell her about the toe? "No," he said.

"Okay, then. I think I can help you." She set down the clipboard and took his hand. In the poor light her eyes seemed coal black. "Edward, we are going to do some intense body work today. Do you know what the key is to therapeutic success?" She pronounced it "sucsase."

He shook his head. She was hard to follow, but he loved listening to her.

"*Trust*, Edward." She squeezed his hand. "The client-therapist relationship is based on trust. We'll have to work together if we're going to affect change. Do you want to change, Edward?"

He cleared his throat and nodded. "Yes. Of course."

"Then you *can*. But. Only if we trust each other. Do you understand?" All that eye contact.

"I understand."

"Okay, Edward," she said briskly. "Get undressed and get under the sheet. I'll be back in a few minutes."

He quickly removed his clothes and left them folded on the floor. Should he lie face up or down? Did she tell him? Down seemed the safer choice.

He struggled with the sheet and finally got it to cover him. Then he set his face into the padded doughnut and exhaled.

Okay now, he thought. Just relax.

Almost immediately, the tip of his nose began to itch and burn. A hot dollop of snot eased out of his left nostril.

He'd left his Kleenex with his clothes.

He scrambled out of the bed, grabbed the box, and got back under the sheet. Ah, facial tissue, his addiction. Like a good junkie, he always knew exactly how much product was in the room and where it was located. While making love he kept a box near the bed. He preferred entering Margaret from behind because it kept his sinuses upright and let him sneak tissues unseen.

Edward propped himself on his elbows and blew, squeezed the other nostril shut, and blew again. He looked around for a place to toss the tissue. At work he had two plastic trash bins: a public one out in the open, and a small one hidden in the well of his desk to hold the used Kleenex. But he didn't see a trash can anywhere in the room. Was it hidden in the cabinets?

A knock at the door. Edward pitched the tissue toward his clothes and put his head back in the doughnut. "Okay!" he called casually. He tried to arrange his arms into what he hoped looked like a natural position.

The door opened behind him and he felt her warm hand on his shoulder. "Feel free to grunt and make noises," she said.

"What's that?"

She peeled back half of the sheet and cool air rippled across his skin. "Make noises," she said. "I like feedback." He heard a liquid fart as she squirted something from a bottle, and then felt her oiled hands press into the muscles around his neck.

Well, *that* felt good. Should he tell her now, or wait until it got even better? And what feedback noises were appropriate?

Ropes began to unkink in his back. She used long, deep strokes for a time, then focused on smaller areas. She pressed an elbow into the muscle that run along his spine; at first it felt like she was using a steel rod, but after thirty seconds of constant pressure something un-clenched inside him and the whole muscle expanded, softened. "You work at a computer?" she asked.

It took him a moment to realize it was a question, a moment more to remember how to answer. "Uh-huh," he said. His mind had gone liquid. Grunt to give feedback, he thought.

Annit was strong for being so small. She finished his back, then rearranged the sheet to do his legs. The top half of him was loose as a fish, but from his lower back to his feet he was aching with tight-ness. How could he not have noticed this before now? When a long stroke reached to his buttock he felt the first twinge of an erection, but then she pressed her thumbs between the muscles of his legs and he could think of nothing but the cold fire of cinched muscles stretching apart.

Time became slippery. He might have fallen asleep if it weren't for the persistent tightness in his forehead and eyes. Still blocked. It's what Margaret would ask as she watched him honk into a Kleenex: Still blocked? Still. Always. Margaret would circulate the house, emitting little disgusted sounds as she plucked hardened clumps of tissue from the kitchen table, from between the cushions of the couch, from inside his forgotten coffee cups. "Why don't you take another pill?" she would ask, irritated. But Margaret was a free-breather and could not understand. Antihistamines clamped down on his nasal passages, setting up killer headaches. Pseudoephedrine only made his nose drip incessantly without ever coming close to draining his constantly re-filling reservoirs of snot. "Here, Daddy," Michael would say, and hand him a tissue.

Annit touched his neck. "Okay, Edward," she said very quietly. "Let's turn over."

She held up the sheet between them and cool air hit his skin. He rolled onto his side and had to stop himself from rolling right off the table. He shuffled his body over and Annit let the sheet settle over him like a parachute.

His nose was full and a sneeze was growing. "Could I . . ." He looked for the Kleenex box. "Do you have a . . .?"

She opened a cabinet door and steam drifted out. She handed him a warm, moist, cotton hand-towel.

"Oh no," he said, appalled. "I couldn't." He talked from the back of his throat, trying to hold back the sneeze.

"This is part of the therapy, Edward. You must use the towel. No harsh paper." She smiled and touched the back of his wrist, prompting him to lift the towel to his face. He couldn't hold back any longer: he sneezed explosively. And again. And again.

Weakly he wiped the tip of his nose, his upper lip, and the delicate frenulum. He was ashamed, but the warm cloth felt wonderful.

Annit whisked it away from him and he leaned back into the table and closed his eyes. His nasal passages re-filled like ballast tanks, but at least the sneezing fit was over.

Long moments later Annit lifted his ankles and set them onto a pillow. She oiled his feet, working the surface tissue with firm strokes. A groan of pleasure escaped him. She had a gift. She understood his body. She knew its hidden pockets of tension, and one by one she'd burst them all.

She seemed to change her grip, and he felt a sharp prick, obviously accomplished with a metal instrument. He tensed his body, but said nothing. She stabbed him again and he nearly yelped.

With some effort he lifted his head and looked down the land-scape of his body. Annit's hands were empty. "What's that you're doing?" he asked. Trying to sound mildly curious.

"Reflexology," she said, and smiled. "The note from your wife said you wanted to try this."

"Oh." The voodoo thing. He let his head fall back against the table and thought, maybe she won't notice the toe.

With thumb and forefinger she held his right foot just below his ankle in a delicate grip that burned like sharpened forceps. He sucked air and waited for her to release.

"So," he said casually, his voice tight. "What points do those cor-respond to?"

"The penis and the prostate."

"Ah," he said, as if he'd guessed as much. She continued to hold the foot. My God, he thought, my balls are on fire. After a time she shifted to his other foot, and in the three-second gap between feet a chill coursed up his spine.

"You have six toes on your left foot," she said. "That's wonderful."

The words made him flush. He knew he should make a joke, ask about correspondences, but was too embarrassed to speak. Mar-garet disliked the extra toe, barely acknowledged its existence. She only mentioned it in public once, obliquely, in the delivery room; she looked down at Michael's perfectly numbered digits and said, "Thank goodness he has my feet."

Annit worked the tips of his toes, the areas the *Cosmo* article had linked to sinuses. Her fingers were like needles but he began to anticipate the pain and move into it. Grunt for feedback.

Annit's voice drifted up from the other end of the table. "Do you trust me, Edward?"

Her finger punctured his small toe like a fondue fork.

"Ugh."

Time slipped away again. He thought about Annit's carbon-black eyes, her earnest, non-American voice: *The key to therapeutic suc-sase is trust.* He should have told her about his daydream, about Joe Louis.

Grunt to give feedback.

Sometime later she moved to his face and massaged his cheek

bones. "Urrm," he said, a little hesitantly. She hooked her fingers into the ridges above his eye sockets, three fingers to each socket, and pulled back. Bones creaked and he sighed. She pressed her palms to each temple and squeezed; he hissed. She wedged her thumbs against his nose and pushed east, south, west, north.

"Okay, Edward," Annit said, a little out of breath. "How are those sinuses?"

He tried to inhale through his nose: A wall. He tried to exhale and the air was forced out his mouth. "Still blocked," he said. Despair almost choked him. He could not move.

Annit cursed softly in another language. She touched his face and he closed his eyes again. "Trust me, Edward. Trust me. Lie here for a second."

Still blocked. Always. And the sins of the father would be passed on to the son. He could see the signs already. In the woods Michael's eyes would water. Dusty rooms made him sneeze like his old man. "Why couldn't he get my genes?" Margaret would say. It would have been better for the boy if he had. But a part of Edward felt . . . not proud, not satisfied . . . *validated* perhaps. Here was proof of lineage, distinctive as a hideous birthmark. There was something comforting in the fact that no matter how much their lives diverged—no matter if Michael grew up to be an astronaut or a drag queen—they would always share this. They would always have something to talk about.

The smell of incense was stronger. Edward opened one eye. Annit was lighting a candle on the floor a few feet beyond the table. Other candles were lit; little flames lined the walls.

"Isn't this a bit—" He swallowed. His mouth was dry. "A bit dangerous?"

Annit looked at him. Her face was painted in thick bands of yellow and red. It took him a moment to realize that she was also naked. She held up what looked like a celery stick. "Put this in your mouth," she said.

He opened his mouth and she wedged it in crosswise. He carefully touched it with his tongue; it tasted like bark. Annit stepped behind him. She began to chant in what sounded like B-movie American Indian: lots of vowels and grunts. Moments later her voice was joined by a loud moaning sound; when she danced into his peripheral vision he could see a stick on a rope whirling above her head. He'd seen that thing on the Discovery Channel. A . . .

*bullroarer*—that's it. Remembering the name reassured him. He closed his eyes again.

The chanting and roaring went on for some time. It was soothing, actually, in the way that a chorus of washing machines made him sleepy in Laundromats. Grunt for feedback, she'd said. Edward hummed along with the bullroarer.

There was a knock at the door. Annit's voice broke off and the bullroarer wound down until it clattered suddenly against the floor. He heard the chubby girl's voice, and Annit answering in a whisper, "I need more time."

"But his wife—"

"To hell with the wife. I've got a class-five chakra imbalance here." The door closed. There was the distinctive *clack* of a safety bolt sliding home.

He felt Annit's hand under his chin, and then she pulled the celery from his mouth.

He blinked up at her. "What was that you were doing?"

"Maori action dance. Very cleansing. Any luck?"

With an effort he brought his hand to his face and checked. Left nostril. Right nostril. Blocked as collapsed mine shafts. He sighed.

"Shit," Annit said. Edward let his head fall back against the mat. He listened to her move around the room, rustling papers and muttering. The ceiling was stucco, troweled on in overlapping circular grooves. Theoretically there should be a final circle that did not overlap any of the others, but he couldn't find it.

A sound like a window shade springing up. Edward turned his head. Annit was consulting a life-size chart of the human body that had unrolled from the ceiling. She cradled a heavy book in her left arm. "Okay," she said. The book dropped to the floor, loud as a cannon shot. The chart snapped upward. "Turn over again, Edward."

"I don't think this is going to help," he said, half to himself. He did as he was told. Annit removed the sheet completely and applied fresh oil, rubbing him deeply until he forgot his plugged nostrils and his mind began to slide sideways into the half-dreaming trance he'd attained earlier. She worked especially on his arms and legs, pressing her fingers deep into every joint from elbow to wrist, knee to ankle, and finished by wrapping each extremity in something thick and smooth. His limbs were numb. He drifted, dreaming, drowning happily. For a long time Annit didn't touch him, leaving him alone with the squeaks of ropes and pulleys. Edward imagined elephants from the circuses of old movies, lumbering beasts dragging poles into place, hauling on ropes to pull the tents erect. Out there in the desert, in the shadow of Ayers Rock, there was a special tent going up, the arena where he and Michael were kept as freaks. Bright posters screamed SEE! SIX-TOED SINUS MAN! AND! NASAL BOY! The crowd roared as the tattooed warriors attached block and tackle to their cage and hauled it up above the audience.

Annit touched his neck. "Not that dream, Edward," she said. "Not the false dream-time." He heard a loud crack and suddenly he was hanging in space. He opened his eyes and found himself swinging above the floor, the massage table on its side against the wall. Several still-lit candles rolled in arcs across the floor. He tried to scream but his position made it difficult to take in air.

Annit's voice was warm and commanding. "Edward. Edward."

He was splayed apart, macramé ropes at each limb suspending him from the metal planter hooks. Annit, still naked, caught his shoulders and stopped his swaying. She bent down and held his face in both hands. Her eyes were even with his. "So what's it going to be, Edward?"

His arms were easing out of their sockets. His groin muscles were taut. "Huh?"

"Don't play stupid, Edward. What's it going to be? Back to your miserable world? Dripping and sneezing your way through life, never three feet away from a box of Kleenex?"

He shook his head, trying to assemble his thoughts. Far away, a pounding and the sound of Margaret's voice, calling to him.

Annit slapped him across one cheek, then gripped his jaw and tilted his face toward her. "Come on, Edward! Are you moving forward, or going back? What's it going to BE?"

His cheek burned. He could pull out now and walk into the lobby, shaking his head and thinking, *Crazy woman.* Margaret would run up to him, all expectant eyebrows: Still? His son would hand him a tissue.

Edward drew a breath. "Unngah."

Annit kissed him hard on the lips. "Okay, then." She put her hands on his shoulders and pushed him back like a child in a swing—slowly, slowly—then back-pedaled to catch him and shove again. He closed his eyes as she worked the rhythm, feeling his arc grow by degrees heavier and steeper, his speed becoming tremendous. At the top of the arc, sinus fluid pressed to the front of his skull. As he swooped down lights crackled under his eyelids.

The pounding on the door deepened and stretched and buzzed, becoming the bass throb of the bullroarer.

"Edward!" Annit shouted, and he opened his eyes. He was at the zenith of his swing. The room was a fishbowl, walls curving out and back. Annit stood at the other end, naked except for her right arm, which was sheathed from elbow to fist in gleaming chrome. The gauntlet was medieval in design, covered with overlapping plates and studded with inch-long spikes, and seemed to end in too many fingers.

Annit stood waiting for him, legs apart and arm cocked, her eyes locked fiercely on his own.

She was braced for him. She could take him, if he trusted her.

He nodded—in agreement, in surrender, in benediction—and fell into her, swinging down, down, like two tons of metal.


Something furry brushed his cheek. He breathed deep, taking in a dense wave of unfamiliar scents, and opened his eyes.

He lay on his stomach, arms and legs spread, sunk deep in the grasses of a sunlit field. He turned his head. The cat, a white Persian with blue eyes, rubbed its forehead along his brow, marking him with its scent glands. He stroked the cat's back, and it arched into him, purring. A second cat butted against him, and a third, and a dozen more.

He got to his feet, careful not to tread on tails and paws. The prairie stretched for miles in all directions, a green ocean of Bermuda grass and Kentucky bluegrass and brilliant ragweed, swirling with rust and orange eddies of redtop and sagebrush. The plain stirred with the movements of furred animals: long-haired cats, thick-ruffed dogs, sleek-coated mammals he couldn't name.

In the distance was a massive slump of naked rock, glowing pink in the sunlight. It was the flat-topped mountain he'd seen in his dream.

Annit walked to him through a stand of towering pigweed, her hair wild, her skin still vividly painted. Michael held her hand, talking excitedly, and when she gestured to Edward the boy shouted happily and ran to him. Edward scooped him up and swung him around. The boy's eyes were clear and dry. His nasal drip had disappeared.

Annit stood a small way off, smiling.

"Where are we?" Edward said.

A breeze touched his face and he inhaled deeply through wide-open nasal passages. The air was heavy with dense floral bouquets, earthy molds, and the pungent musk of thousands and thousands of cats.

# DEAD HORSE POINT

**T**wenty-three years of silence and all it takes is one call. Not even a conversation, just a thirty-second message on her voicemail. Come now, Julia's voice says. Come now before it's too late. From anyone else it would have sounded melodramatic, but Julia never exaggerates; she's always careful with her words. Venya books a flight to Utah the next morning.

Later she'll think, wasn't it just like Julia to say it like a command. As if Venya had no choice but to come.

The park ranger tells her where to find their campsite but the RV is locked, nobody home. She sits in the rental car for an hour with the engine on and air conditioning blasting, reading park maps and informational pamphlets and squinting out at the hard sunlight, until she sees the two figures walking down the campground road toward her. They look like they've been on a long hike. Kyle's shirt is tied around his waist and his chest shines with sweat. Julia, following in his wake, wears hiking shorts and a webbed belt, plastic water bottles at her hips like six-guns. Both of them walk head down, lost in thought.

Venya steps out of the car but it's another minute before Kyle looks up and sees her. At first the only expression on his face is exhaustion, but then he recognizes her and puts on a smile, becoming the winning boy she met decades ago.

"Oh my God," he says, loud enough for her to hear, and laughs. He glances behind him at his sister but she doesn't look up.

Kyle reaches Venya and holds up his hands. "I can't hug you, I'm too sweaty!" he says, but Venya steps in and hugs him anyway. The last time she saw him he was a pale, hyper kid of 20. He's in his mid-forties now, but still tanned and fit, hair grown to messiah-length and sun-streaked. Only his face hints at his age, and that is masked by his wild smile.

"I can't believe it," he says. "How on earth did you find us?" He steps out of the way. "Julia, it's Venya."

Julia doesn't raise her head. She frowns in concentration at a point somewhere past Venya's right hip. Her hair is gray shot with black, a negative of two decades ago. Kyle must have decided to have it cut into something short and easy to maintain; Julia wouldn't have had an opinion.

"How you doing, Jay?" Venya says to her.

Her eyes remain fixed on empty air.

"The same," Kyle says.

He pulls a key from his shorts pocket and unlocks the RV. Julia follows him inside automatically. It's cooler inside, but not by much, and the air smells of ripening fruit. Kyle starts the RV's engine to boost the air conditioning.

The vehicle looks new—probably a rental—but Kyle and Julia seem to have been living in it for several weeks. The counters are crowded with food wrappers, unopened groceries, and stacks of paper plates. Books and papers cover the little table and most of the seats.

Julia sits at the kitchen table. Kyle fills a plastic cup with ice from the small fridge, pours in some water from a collapsible jug, and sets it down in front of her. She lifts it to her lips without blinking.

"How about you?" Kyle says. "I've got beer, bourbon, juice—"

"Some of that water would be good." Venya restacks some books that have spilled across the bench seat and sits down opposite Julia.

Kyle fills a cup for Venya, then opens a bag of dried apricots and sets it down on the table facing his sister. Without shifting her gaze from the tabletop, Julia reaches into the bag and puts an apricot in her mouth.

"I was driving out here from the airport," Venya says. Kyle gulps down a cup of water and starts refilling it. "I'd forgotten how empty the highways are. I'd look down at the dash and realize I'd covered forty miles without realizing it. I thought, this must be what it's like for Julia. Autopilot."

"Julia's driving a lot these days," he says. "And I'm still the road she follows." He finishes the second cup-full. "I'm going to get a clean shirt on. You okay with her?" Before she can answer he says, "What am I talking about, you did it for seven years."

What he doesn't say: seven years, not twenty-three.

Watching Julia eat is still an unnerving experience. She chews methodically, swallows, and reaches for another piece of fruit, automatic as eating movie popcorn in the dark. The entire time her eyes are focused on some inner landscape.

"How long has it been since the last time she was awake?" Venya calls back.

"Three weeks?" A note of embarrassment in his voice. "Maybe three and a half."

"That can't be," Venya says.

Kyle comes back into the main cabin wearing a faded blue T-shirt. "It's gotten a lot worse since you were with her, Venya. At Stanford she was never gone longer than what, a couple of days?"

"Julia called me two nights ago," Venya says. "A voicemail message. She said she was calling from the Dead Horse parking lot."

"That's impossible." But he's looking at Julia. "She must have come awake at night. I don't leave her alone—" He shakes his head. "I don't. She must have come awake in the middle of the night and snuck out."

Julia lifts her plastic cup and sets it down without sipping; it's empty. Kyle takes it from her and refills it.

"What did she say?" he asks. "On the phone." From the middle of the mess on the counter he picks up a glass—a real glass, not plastic—and blows into it.

"Not much. She said you two were staying here at the park. She's working on a hard problem. Something important."

He unscrews the cap from a half-full bottle of Canadian Mist and pours a couple of inches. "That's true. Then again . . ." He smiles.

Then again, Julia is always working on a hard problem. Even in undergrad, when she resurfaced from one of her "away" times, she'd start writing furiously, page after page, as if she'd memorized a book she'd written in her head and had to get it down before it evaporated. She'd talk as she wrote—explaining, elaborating, answering Venya's questions—making Venya feel that she was part of the solution, some necessary element in the equation.

Kyle holds up the bottle but Venya shakes her head. He shrugs and sips from his glass.

Venya says, "She said she needed me to come down, before it was too late."

Kyle's grin falters, and for a moment he looks a decade older.

"How bad is it?" Venya asks. "How much is she gone?"

"Ah." He turns the glass in his fingers. He takes a big sip, then presses his lips together. "The past couple of years she's been away more than she's been awake," he says finally. "The trend line's pretty clear. We always knew lock-in was the probable end point." He says it matter-of-factly, as if he's practiced saying it out loud.

"This had to be tough on you," Venya says.

He shrugs, and the smile is back. "She's my sister. And her work is important. She really does need someone to help her organize it and get it out there."

"I read your book," Venya says. "The cover had her name on it, but I knew those sentences were yours."

He laughs, nods. "Julia's much too addicted to passive voice for pop science." He lifts his glass. "Thank you, and congratulations— you're the only one of our thirteen readers to have seen through the charade." He tosses back his drink, sets down the glass, and claps his hands. "But enough about us imposters! Let me get you settled in, and we'll do some barbecue."

Julia stares at the table top as if it holds an equation about to unravel.

The cement shower stalls of the campground washhouse remind Venya of the first semester in college, the year she met Julia. Venya stands in the cold stall for a long while with her head bowed, letting the hot water drum the crown of her skull and pool around her veined feet. She thinks, this is exactly how she found Julia that day.

They'd only been roommates for a few weeks, two first-year women assigned to each other by the University of Illinois mainframe. Julia came from money, her clothes made that clear. She was pale and beautiful and solemn, like one of those medieval portraits of a saint. She rarely spoke, and only an occasional, fragile smile betrayed her nervousness.

Venya was a little put out by the girl's reserve. She'd come to school with the idea, picked up from God knows where, that college roommates were automatically *best friends*. They'd decide on posters together, share clothes and shots of Southern Comfort, hold back each other's hair when they puked. But after a few days of trying to

get the skinny, quiet girl to open up, Venya had almost gotten used
to the idea that Julia was going to be little more than a silent reading
machine that lived on the other side of the room.

One morning during the third week, Venya woke up late, dashed
into the big bathroom they shared with the other girls on the floor,
and quickly brushed her teeth to get rid of the dead-shoe taste of
stale beer in her mouth. As usual, Julia had gotten up before her, and
Venya saw the girl's green robe hanging outside one of the stalls, the
shower running. Venya went off to her back-to-back morning classes,
then to lunch. It was 12:30 or 1:00 before she went back up to her
floor to drop off her books and take a pee.

Julia's green robe still hung on the hook, and the shower was still
running.

Venya must have called Julia's name—that would have been the
natural thing—but she only remembered running to the rubber curtain and yanking it aside. Julia stood under the spray, looking down at
her feet. The water was still running hot, thanks to the industrial-sized
boilers in the building, but the woman still shivered. When Venya
grabbed her arm, Julia immediately stepped out of the stall to stand
beside her.

Venya couldn't get her to speak, make eye contact, or even
change expression. But Julia obligingly allowed herself to be dried
off, led back to the room, and tucked into bed. She lay there with her
eyes open, staring past the ceiling.

Venya's first thought was that someone had dropped LSD into
Julia's breakfast. But the symptoms were all wrong—no acid trip,
good or bad, was this calm—and in fact the symptoms didn't match
any drug she had experience with (and she'd experienced more than
her share). She didn't want to get Julia in trouble, but she finally decided to call the R.A., who called the paramedics, who took Julia to
the ER.

Julia snapped out of it sometime during the night. She suddenly
sat up in the hospital bed, looked over at Venya, and asked for pen and
paper. The doctor on duty shook his head disbelievingly; he made it
clear to Venya that he thought Julia had been faking the whole thing.
Julia apologized, but kept scribbling.

At four a.m. her family arrived. A thirteen-year-old boy bound-
ed into the room and jumped onto the bed next to Julia. Her father
and mother came next. Professor Dad, as Venya instantly decided

to call him, shook her hand, thanked her for staying with his daughter. Professor Mom sat down in the chair next to the window, holding a silver pen in her fingers like a cigarette she was dying to light. Julia said hello to each of them, and immediately returned to her writing. The boy kept up a running comedic monologue: about Julia's gown, the age of the hospital, the fat nurse by the front desk. Even then Kyle was the entertainer, the performer, the distracter. So it took Venya some time to figure out that the parents were arguing. It took her even longer to realize that the argument had been going on for years.

Professor Dad made oblique references to Julia's room at home; Professor Mom scowled and shook her head. "She needs help," she said at one point. "Professional help." There were no questions, no talk about what had happened in the shower: Julia had "disappeared" before, evidently, and would disappear again.

Later Venya would hear the whole medical history, how when Julia was a child they diagnosed her mental absences as petit mal seizures. After CAT scans turned up nothing, they called it mild autism. As she grew older and the gaps grew longer, they started calling it Dissociative Identity Disorder, which was just a fancy name for multiple personalities. One psychiatrist thought there was a "monitor" personality who could perform daily tasks while the Julia personality went somewhere else. But Julia never bought the Sybil explanation. When she "woke up" she remembered most of what had happened while she was out. It didn't feel like there was another personality in her. And she knew the difference between the two states—she knew when she'd been out.

The way Julia described it, her condition was the opposite of Attention Deficit Disorder: she couldn't *stop* paying attention. An idea would occur to her, and then she'd hop on that train of thought and follow it right out of Dodge. She was missing some neurochemical switchman who could move her attention from reverie to awareness of the outside world.

But in the hospital, Venya understood only that Dad wanted Julia to come home, and Mom wanted her to stay in a hospital, any hospital.

And Julia?

The girl stopped writing. She put down the pen, folded the papers in half, then in half again. Her expression was tight, and her eyes shone with unshed tears. "I can do this," she said finally.

They didn't seem to hear her. Her father and mother continued to argue in their cool, knife-edged voices.

Kyle turned to Venya and silently mouthed: *Do Something.*

Venya looked away, but the idea had been planted. A terrible, awful, stupid idea.

She raised her hand, and the professors dutifully stopped talking. "How often?" Venya asked. They turned their attention to her, as if regarding her from podiums at the far end of a great lecture hall. "How often does this happen?"

Professor Dad shrugged. "Hardly ever, anymore. She made it through senior year without—"

"That's not true," Julia said quietly. She caught Venya's eye and held her gaze. "Three or four times a week, a couple hours at a time. But they're getting longer."

Venya nodded, as if this made perfect sense. She stared at the shiny hospital floor so she wouldn't have to see the entire family looking at her.

Keep your mouth shut, she told herself. This is not your problem.

"Okay," she said. "I'll do it." She offered to watch over Julia for the rest of that semester. Only a semester.

Venya still doesn't know why she did it.

There was nothing in their relationship to that point that obligated her to help. The offer made sense only in terms of what came after, as if the next seven years—in which she led Julia through undergrad and grad school, and along the way became Julia's best friend and then, eventually, her lover—caused her to speak at that moment.

Julia accepted Venya's offer without comment.


They eat their dinner at the picnic table, in the shadow cast by the bulk of the RV. Six p.m. in September and it's still in the nineties, but the lack of humidity makes for a 20-degree difference between sun and shade. All around the campground, people fire up grills and pull open bags of chips. At the campsite next to them a van full of twenty-something Germans laugh and argue. The sky hangs over them, huge and blue and cloudless.

"It's beautiful out here," Venya says. "I can see why you came."

"I figured Julia could work anywhere, and if she came awake

maybe she'd like seeing this place again." He dabs mustard from Julia's cheek and she continues to chew her chicken breast obliviously. "This was the last vacation our family took together before Mom died."

Professor Mom killed herself when Julia was in grad school; Venya went with Julia to the funeral. Professor Dad checked out in a completely different way. He took a position in Spain, and soon after found a new wife. Everyone in the family, Venya thinks, has a talent for absence. Everyone except Kyle.

"What about you?" Kyle says. "Did you ever make a family? Two kids, cocker spaniel, house in the suburbs?"

"I have a son," she says. "He started college last year. His mom and I broke up a few years ago, but we all get along. He's a good kid."

"A son? That's great!" he says, meaning it. "It sounds like you've had a good life."

"Good enough. And what about you? Ever find someone?"

"Julia's the only woman in my life." He laughs, forcing it a little. "Well, I've had a few relationships. I'm just not very good at keeping them going, and with Julia . . . I stay pretty busy. Here, I want to show you something."

He went into the RV and came out with a fresh bottle of Canadian Mist and two glasses in the fingers of one hand, and a big three-ring binder under his arm. "You remember this?" He sets down the bottle and glasses and shows her the binder cover: "HOW TO DO IT."

"My God," Venya says, and takes it from him.

"It's not the same cover, had to change that a couple times. But some of the original stuff you put in is still there. Still accurate."

When Venya decided she had to leave, she gave Kyle a binder like this. Operating instructions for Julia. Names of doctors, prescription dosages, favorite foods, sleeping schedule, shoe and clothing sizes . . . everything, down to the kind of toothpaste Julia liked. The binder is much thicker now.

"It's all there," he says. "The trust fund accounts, computer passwords, insurance papers."

Venya isn't sure what to say. "You're a good brother."

"Yeah, well. I am my sister's keeper." He sets the binder at the end of the table.

They lapse into silence. Venya pushes the last of the baked beans around on her paper plate. Kyle drinks.

"You have something you want to say," Kyle says.

Venya exhales. "True." She takes the remaining glass and splashes a bit of the whiskey into it. She swirls it around, inhaling the sharp scent, watching the liquid ride the sides of the glass. She's never particularly liked hard liquor.

"When she comes out of it," Venya begins. "Do you talk about how she's feeling?" He waits for her to explain. "You said the absences were growing longer. Eventually . . . You called it lock-in. She's got to think about that. Does she feel trapped?"

He smiles, tight-lipped. "I don't think so."

"Kyle, you can tell me."

"I would know," he says. "We've always understood each other. We don't have to talk about it." He sips from his glass. "When Julia comes back, all she wants to talk about is her work. Non-stop Q.M. She just starts scribbling, because she doesn't have much time before she goes away again. Even before she resigned from New Mexico I was helping her write up her papers—not just the layman stuff, the journal articles." He gestured toward the RV. "I should show you the stuff she's turning out now. She's dismantling Everett-Wheeler and the other interpretations. I can't follow the math anymore, but that's not important. The job now is to organize the notes and get it into the hands of people who can understand her. This is her chance to get into the history books, Venya. She *wants* to follow it."

"What if she follows it so far she can't find her way back?" she says. "What if she can't stop from disappearing for good?"

"I don't think she'd mind," he says. "In there, that's where her real life is. Everything out here is just . . . distraction."

"You don't know that," Venya says. "When we were together, she was afraid of getting lost. We talked about it. We didn't call it 'lock-in' then, but that's what she was afraid of."

"So?"

"So, I made her a promise."

He stares at her.

"I think that's why she called me, Kyle. Because she's getting close." Because she's afraid you won't be able to do what she needs.

He puts up his hands. His laugh is brittle. "Don't take my word for it, then. Ask her yourself."

Venya smoothes back a stray hair blowing across Julia's eyes. "I'll need some matches," she says.

\*

Venya clears a length of the RV counter and sets out the baggie of grass and the rolling papers. A bong would be better—cooled smoke is best—but Venya didn't want to put one through airport security. It was nerve-wracking enough just to pack the marijuana, rolled up and hidden in her tampon box.

She shakes out a little of the grass onto the paper. She hasn't rolled a joint in years, but motor memory guides her hands. In the end she spills only a little of the pot.

"This is your plan?" Kyle says. "Get my sister high."

"It worked in college." Twenty-five, thirty years ago. Marijuana screwed with Julia's focus, derailed the train—if the concentration of THC was high enough. Venya's co-worker assured her that the pot was near-medical-grade, but there was no way to know if it would be enough.

Venya sits cross-legged on the floor of the vehicle, almost under the table. Kyle guides Julia until she's lying face up on the floor with her head on Venya's lap, staring at the ceiling. Kyle lights the joint for her, and Venya breathes with it to get it going.

"Pinch her nose," she says, then takes a long drag and holds the smoke in her mouth. She lifts Julia's head, and holding the glowing joint away from their bodies, bends to place her lips against Julia's. Venya exhales, a long sigh. Smoke eddies above Julia's mouth, then slowly drifts across her eyes. Julia blinks, but doesn't shift her focus from the ceiling.

"It may take awhile," Venya says. She draws on the joint again, thinking about the first time they kissed. Julia seemed so afraid, as if she didn't know how to live in her own body.

After a few minutes Venya's lower back and shoulders begin to ache from the awkward position. Even though she's trying not to inhale she feels light-headed. The pot is indeed strong, or else Venya is indeed old. She suspects both.

Julia never liked marijuana. Or any of the prescription drugs the doctors tried on her in the early days. None of them worked for very long once she developed a tolerance, most of them had uncomfortable side effects, and all of them, Julia said, made her stupid. She couldn't bear stupid.

The smoke alarm goes off. Venya jerks, and Kyle, laughing, reaches up to the RV's low ceiling. He pulls off the alarm's plastic cover and yanks out the battery.

Julia hasn't moved.

"I don't think this is working," Kyle says. The joint's already burned down half its length.

"Look, her eyes are closed," Venya says. She tugs one of Julia's ear lobes. "Come on now, Sleeping Beauty."

Julia opens her eyes. She looks up at Kyle, then turns her gaze to Venya. Her hand lifts and touches Venya's cheek.

Julia smiles. "My Princess Charming."

Kyle helps the two women to their feet. Julia laughs, coughs, then recovers, smiling. "We're both old women!"

"Fifty is the new seventy, Jay." But Julia's wrong, Venya thinks. Or half wrong. Julia awake seems as beautiful to her as when they first met.

Julia looks around at the cabin, at the stacks of paper in the slanting light. "I need to write some things down," she says quietly, then catches herself. "But not now. What time is it—seven? We can watch the sunset."

"If we leave now," Kyle says.

"Vee, you better roll another one of those before I go away again."

Kyle passes out flashlights for the way back, then leads them out of the campground. After a hundred yards or so they step off the park road and onto a well-traveled hiking trail. Julia smokes as they walk, putting the joint down by her side when they pass people coming back from the point to the campground. The trail runs across sandy ground, then over patches of slick rock where the trail is marked by small cairns.

Julia puts her arm in Venya's. "I'm so glad you came," she says.

"You called," Venya says simply. She doesn't know what she can say in Kyle's presence. Julia called her without telling her brother, without even telling him that she'd woken up while he slept. "Kyle says you're working on something important. Something about dismantling the many-worlds interpretation."

"You remember Everett?"

"A little. I proof-read a lot of your papers, Jay."

"You kept correcting my semi-colons," Julia says. She takes a hit from the joint and grimaces. "It's not just Everett, and the Deutschian spin-offs of that. I'm also taking down Zurek's many-histories, and Albert's many-minds, and Bohm's pilot waves. The Copenhagen Interpretation already died with the failure of complementarity."

"You don't say," Venya says. In two seconds Julia's zoomed years beyond her reading. "And your idea is . . .?"

"Wheeler-Feynman's absorber theory, but fully extended into QED." QED is quantum electrodynamics—Venya remembers that much—but she's never heard of the absorber theory. "With a few of my own twists," Julia adds.

She's animated, waving the lit joint like a sparkler. Venya takes it from her and squeezes it out. There are matches in her pocket if they need to relight it.

"There's no need for an observer to collapse the wave," Julia says. "No need for parallel universes sprouting out of control. The universe is not a growing thing, it's already complete. From the moment of the big bang, all the work has already been done. It's whole and seamless, going backward and forward in time. There's no 'now' and 'then.' *Everything's* now. Everything's happening at once. Look—"

Julia stoops to pick up a small rock, and scrapes an upside down V on the sandy ground. "A particle going forward in time meets an anti-particle going forward in time." She scratches a minus sign on the left-hand segment and a plus sign on the other segment.

"Oh God, more Feynman diagrams," Kyle says.

Julia digs into the intersection of the two lines. "That's an electron colliding with a positron. They're destroyed, and emit two photons that fly off in opposite directions." She draws two lines extending from the intersection, making an X. "It doesn't matter which way time's arrow is pointing. We can read the diagram from any perspective and it's equally true. Read it from left to right and you can say that electron meets a photon and emits a photon and a positron. Or from the top, two photons collide and emit an electron and a positron. All are correct. All *happen*."

"Okay . . ." Venya says. She looks at Kyle, her expression saying, How do you put up with this stuff? She has no idea where Julia is going with this, but after hours with the absent version of the woman, it's a pleasure to be with a Julia so *present*.

"But it's equally true," Julia says, "to say that an electron strikes two photons and emits a positron that travels backward in time." Julia looks Venya in the eye to see if she's following. "Time's arrow doesn't matter. If the map is true, it's true for any point in time. It's a map of the world, for all space-time. The future is as set as the past, for everyone. The territory doesn't change."

"For particles, not people."

"What do you mean, not people? Schrödinger's Cat, Venya. The EPR paradox. People, and their choices, are already factored into the equation."

"But people have free will."

"That reminds me of a joke," Kyle says.

Julia tosses the rock away. "Free will just means that you don't know what's on the map. You don't create the future, it's already there, waiting for you like a Christmas present. All you have to do on Christmas morning is see what's inside."

"A Calvinist dies and goes to heaven," Kyle says.

"What?" Venya says.

"Ignore him," Julia says. "I do."

The trail runs through a narrow neck, perhaps thirty yards wide, with sky on either side of them. The park pamphlet said that cowboys would fence the narrows and corral wild horses out on the lookout. The legend is that one winter the cowboys left for home and forgot to take down the fence. Naming the point came easy after that.

The land widens again, but then the trail ends in sheer cliff. Julia gestures toward a nose of rock jutting into the air. "My favorite spot," she says. She walks onto it like a veteran high diver. Venya's stomach tightens to see her standing on that slender platform, sky above and below.

*Suicide runs in the family*, Venya thinks. Maybe she isn't here to help Julia kill herself, but witness it. Or help Kyle cope with it.

But then Julia sits down, and slides forward so that her legs hang over the edge. Venya cautiously follows Kyle onto the shelf. They sit down on either side of Julia with their flashlights between their thighs, letting their feet dangle over a thousand feet of empty air.

They face south, looking out toward hazy mountains 50 or 60 miles away. Between Dead Horse and the mountains are 5,000 square miles of canyon country the park maps call Islands in the Sky. A good name. Venya looks down on an ocean of air, a stone basin walled by raked cliffs over 2,000 feet high. The bottom of the basin is a vast labyrinth of stone: mile-deep chasms; sharp reefs and table-flat mesas; crenellated buttes like castles surrounded by invisible moats.

At the very bottom flows the only water visible in this stone country, the olive green coil of the Colorado. The river winds out of the south, aiming lazily for Dead Horse Point. Two miles before it reaches the point, the river abruptly goosenecks, bending 180 degrees around a butte shaped like the prow of a ship, and disappears again into the southern maze of canyons.

Venya thinks of those horses, dying of thirst within sight of the river.

"Wow," she says.

"Mmm hmm," Julia answers.

They sit in companionable silence. In the fading light the land seems to flex and shift. The cliffs to their right are already in twilight, but the eastern faces glow with deep reds and smoldering oranges. Shadows run down the cracks and seams, pooling two thousand feet below at the darkened feet of the cliffs.

"This Calvinist goes to heaven," Kyle says.

Julia sighs, and then starts chuckling to herself.

"But instead of the pearly gates, there's a fork in the road, and a sign pointing down each path. One sign says 'Believers in Predestination' and the other says 'Believers in Free Will.'" Julia shakes her head, and Venya wonders how many times she's heard this joke—and whether she heard it while awake, or as background chatter while she was thinking of something else.

"The guy's always believed in predestination, so he goes down that road, and eventually he comes to a huge wall and a big door with the word 'PREDESTINATION' written over the top. He knocks, and an angel opens the door and says, 'What brings you to my door, mortal?' And the guy says, 'Well, there were these two signs, and I chose the one that said predestination.' The angel says, 'You *chose* it? You can't come in here, Bub,' and slams the door. The guy's heartbroken. Finally he trudges back to the crossroads and goes down the other road. Eventually he comes to another giant wall and a door that says 'FREE WILL.' He knocks and another angel opens the door and says, 'Why did you come this way, mortal?' And the guy says, 'I had no choice!'"

"Slam," Julia says, and laughs.

Venya laughs with them, but she wonders at these two odd, grown children. Orphans, really. Maybe they like the joke because they share the certainty that the universe will screw them over. No—that it already has.

Venya scootches forward and leans out over her knees, staring down. A thousand feet below is a pink shelf perhaps two miles wide and perhaps another thousand feet above the river.

"That's the White Rim Trail," Kyle says. He means the pale thin track that runs along the shelf like an old surgical scar. "Jeep road from the uranium-fever days. I always meant to drive that. I've never even gotten down to the rim."

"There's always the quick way down," Venya says, and Kyle laughs. "One gust of wind."

"Stop it," Julia says.

Kyle says, "When we were here when I was a kid I used to scare myself by thinking of the rock snapping off under my feet, like in a Roadrunner cartoon. I'd hang there in the air for minute, then *thwip!* A little puff of dust where I hit."

"Bury you right there in your silhouette-shaped hole," Venya says.

"With a gravestone that says, 'Ouch!'"

"Stop it, both of you!" Julia says. She pushes back from the edge and her flashlight topples and starts to roll. Kyle snags it before it reaches the edge.

"Careful," he says.

Venya says, "Jay, what's the matter?"

"We should head back now," she says evenly.

Kyle doesn't answer.

"It's getting cold," Julia says.

"I'm fine," Kyle says. "I'd like to stay out here a while longer."

"Let me take her," Venya says to him, and realizes she's slipped back into talking about Julia as if she isn't there. She quickly adds, "Jay and I need to talk some more physics, right Jay?"

Kyle laughs. "Liar." He squeezes Venya's arm, a silent thanks. The man's been on duty for more than twenty years, Venya thinks. Walking Julia home is the least she can do. And she and Julia do need to talk: The light is fading, and the pot probably won't last much longer.

"Are you sure?" Julia says to Kyle.

"Of course. Here, take my jacket." He starts to untie the gray fleece from around his waist.

Julia walks behind him and squeezes his neck. "Always the good little brother." She bends and kisses the crown of his head.

Venya's forgotten how quickly darkness falls in the desert. The sun drops behind some far ridge and suddenly Venya can barely see Julia beside her.

Venya clicks on her flashlight and plays it over the trail. After a few minutes of walking she says, "You sounded scared when you called me, Jay."

Julia doesn't answer. For a moment Venya thinks she's disappeared again, but then she makes a sound like a sob. "I'm so sorry, Vee. It wasn't fair to call you."

Venya wants to see her face, but resists the urge to lift the flashlight. "I promised to come back," Venya says. "If you ever got lost." So lost in her head that she'd never be able to tell anyone when she wanted out, when she wanted to end it. "You said you were afraid of not having a choice."

"That's not what I'm afraid of anymore," Julia says.

"What, then?"

Julia walks on in silence. She still hasn't turned on her flashlight. Venya feels for the lump of the joint in her jeans pocket. "You want me to light up?" she asks.

After a few seconds Julia says, "Sorry, I . . . When I woke up and saw we were at Dead Horse, I knew what he was thinking about. The last good time we had."

"He told me about that," Venya says. "The vacation before your mom died."

Another long silence. Venya thinks they're passing through the narrows, but it's hard to judge in the twilight. She thinks of the mustangs, made stupid by a simple barrier of crossed logs, unable to escape without someone to guide them.

Venya touches her arm, and Julia says, "The path out is the same as the path back. It's laid out like a map . . ."

"Stay with me, Hon. No math now. Tell me why you called me."

"He's so tired," Julia says. "You can't see it—he's being Kyle for you. But you can't see him like I do. It's like time travel. Every time I come back, he seems to be aging so much faster."

"Julia?"

Julia stumbles against something on the trail and rights herself. "He couldn't tell me, of course. He knows how important the work is to me. But I was so afraid he'd leave me before you got here, and without him . . . I'm very close, Venya."

Venya stops but Julia keeps walking automatically, her voice growing softer. "The math is . . . the math is laid out like . . ."

Venya seizes her arm, jerks her to a halt. "Julia!"

She says nothing.

"Julia, I need you to snap out of it. *Listen* to me." She shines the flashlight in her face, but Julia's staring into nothing. No, not nothing. The map of the world.

Venya pushes down on her shoulders. "Sit here. Don't follow me. I'll be right back." Julia lowers to the ground, her knees up by her chin. "Good girl. I'll be right back."

Soon, Venya will find his flashlight on the shelf of rock, turned on and pointing into empty air. Sometime after that, when the park rangers and police have finished with their questions and she's signed the papers that Julia cannot, she'll find the binder that Kyle set out for her. She'll turn to the pages about meals, and make Julia her breakfast.

Now Venya turns and begins to jog back the way they came, the flashlight beam jumping from rock to bush to gnarled juniper. Behind her, Julia rises and begins to follow.

# IN THE WHEELS

*And I looked, and, behold, a whirlwind came out of the north, a
great cloud, and a fire infolding itself, and a brightness was about
it, and out of the midst thereof as the colour of the amber, out of the
midst of the fire . . . and this was their appearance; they had the likeness of a man . . . Whithersoever the spirit was to go, they went, thith-
er was their spirit to go; and the wheels were lifted up over against
them: for the spirit of the living creature was in the wheels.*
—Ezekiel 1:4-5, 20

It was just a car.

"No!" said Zeke from underneath it, "it's more than that, Joey.
It's fucking perfect."

We were fifteen. Zeke had found a huge underground vault, a
crypt of old cars in the City, and he had dragged me out there to hold
the lantern while he checked it out. I was supposed to be on the way
to my Uncle Peter's farm to help bring in the hay.

"Zeke, don't be crazy. Let's get out of here." The City was death,
everybody knew that. I could feel the germs and the rads crawling
across my skin. We were going to be dead in three days with huge
welts all over our skin. Superstitious, I know.

Zeke could always get me to do stuff I never would have done on
my own. He would say something like, why don't we go up and sit
on the white highways; and even though I thought it was a completely
stupid idea, I would go. Or he would say, let's go into Dead City and
look for a car, and even though nobody'd lived in The City since before the Cold, I would say all right, and we'd go.

And here I was.

The car looked to me like a crumbling wreck. It was a big Chevy,
which Zeke pronounced "Shev-ee" like his father Frank. The tires
were flat and rotted out, the paint job was webbed with cracks, and
the stuff on the inside was all split and pitted.

Zeke rolled out from beneath the car and grinned. "Don't be such a little girl. The block's intact. It'll work."

"You're crazy," I said. The car looked nothing like the chariots they raced on the white highways, and I told him so. "Besides, how are you going to get it out of here?" We'd had to dig our way through rubble ourselves, and I saw no way to get this heap up to the surface.

"Leave that to me," he said. I should have known then that he was serious. There was no natural way to move that much rock out of the way, much less carry the car up.

Two weeks later Zeke caught me as I was walking home from the schoolhouse. The palms of his hands were wrapped in rags. "Joey, boy. Tonight we should take a little trip."

"What did you do to your hands?"

"Nothing. Hurt 'em working on the car. Will you be there?"

"I can't sneak out again without getting caught. Why can't we wait til Saturday?"

My sisters raced past us. "We're gonna tell Firstmother you're talking to Zeke!"

"Oh Lord Jesus," I said. I would catch heck later.

"Don't worry about it. Tonight, all right? And bring paint."

"Paint? Where am I going to get paint?"

"Check your barn, stupid."

Zeke was right, as usual. There was paint in the barn, some old cans of red that Grampa had mixed years ago. But I couldn't take off with it until nightfall.

The fire is always the center of the home. Father had built the chimney first, stone by stone, and the kitchen around it. As the children were born he had added small rooms that sprang off from the kitchen at odd angles, and after I'd gotten big enough to help him we built the porch around the front door.

Firstmother started her prayer that evening with the usual, "Thank you Jesus for the Summer Sun," while Sara, my pop's new young wife (barely older than me), passed potatoes and a little mashed corn around the table. Pop took a potato and bit into it. Firstmother went through the entire list of crops we were hoping for, plus all of the sins me, my sisters, Pop, and most of all Sara had committed that week. She kept going until she saw that Sara was almost finished setting the table, and then Firstmother finished off the whole thing by saying, "and especially watch over our young Joseph, and protect him from the temptations that so beset a young man." My sisters giggled; then we all said "Amen." Sara sat down gratefully.

Firstmother eyed the table. "I don't see no salt here."

Sara jumped up and vanished into the kitchen, and Firstmother said, "I been hearing that you were running around with Zeke again after Schoolhouse." My sisters giggled again.

"No ma'am, I wasn't 'running around,' I just . . ."

"Don't talk back to me, boy." Sara came back into the room carrying the salt bowl. My father was chewing intently, silently, as always. And Sara was worse than no help, a liability.

It was time. I either had to stand up for Zeke or listen forever to everything Firstmother said. I looked her in the eye. "What's the matter with Zeke, anyways?"

She stared back. "You know what's the matter with Zeke. His father's a drunk, a black magician, a road racer, a no-good consorter with demons—"

"Enough, Rachel."

Firstmother stopped in mid sentence. Sara and us kids dropped our eyes instantly to our plates. Pop *never* spoke at the dinner table.

"What did you say, Samuel?" Firstmother said icily.

Pop looked up. He kept chewing as he talked, red potatoes mashing between his teeth. His voice was quiet, like when he was explaining why he was going to hit you for not feeding the horses on time. "I said, Rachel, that enough was enough. Frank Landers has had his troubles. I don't want any wife of mine continuing to add to them."

Firstmother was almost sputtering. "I will not have my son hanging around with the son of a demoner!" She picked up her plate and stalked to the kitchen.

Pop picked up another potato. My sisters stared moodily at their food. And even with her head bowed and her hair falling across her eyes, I could see the barest beginnings of a smile on Sara's face.

*

Just after ten that night I was banging around in the dark with two cans of red paint. I'd stuffed my blankets with pillows and climbed out the window, hoping that Firstmother wouldn't think to check on me—she did that sometimes.

I was circling Zeke's house to knock on his bedroom window when I saw lamplight seeping through the cracks of the old shed set away from the house. The door, usually chained shut, was busted open. Zeke was there, his back to me as he rummaged through some cabinets at the back of the shed. And there was something else.

It was a Pontiac—one of the big cars they race down in Mexicana. It was painted almost all black, but in the flicker I could make out a spiderweb of silver lines. The tires were low, and there was some rust along the bottom of the driver's side door, but overall it looked real good.

"You're late," Zeke said when he turned around. "Here. Grab these." He was holding up three dusty books, two cans of paint and a bucket of brushes in his bandaged hands.

"Lord Jesus, Zeke! Where did this thing come from?"

"Nowhere." He dropped the paint at my feet and circled the room, blowing out lanterns.

"C'mon, whose car is this? Is this your dad's?" There'd been rumors about Zeke's dad, Frank, ever since I was a kid. Everybody knew he was a drunk now, but every once in a while you'd hear an adult say something about the magic, or a pro driver.

Zeke pushed me and the buckets outside. He wound the chain up around the door handle and said, "Forget it. That car ain't there, you understand?" He turned to me, and in the moonlight I could barely make out a smile. The smile was always the end of the argument with Zeke. "Ready for a little hike?"

We took the short-cuts and made it into the city in under two hours. For the entire trip, Zeke wouldn't talk about the Pontiac, but the subject was still cars.

"Joey," he said, "I'm gonna race on the white highways. I'm gonna win. Then I'm going to Mexicana and I'm gonna race the Brujo."

"The Brujo? Phil Mendez? You're crazy, Zeke."

"You know I'm crazy. That's why I'm gonna win."

"That's why you're going to die. Messing with the demons and magic is serious stuff. I don't even know why I'm helping you."

He nudged me. "You haven't figured that out, Joey? Because you *love* this shit. You love being bad, breaking the rules, messing with magic. And if anything goes wrong, you can blame it on mean old Zeke."

"You're full of it," I said. But I knew he was right.

The Chevy was sitting in an alley that had been cleared of rubble.

"Christ in the tomb," I whispered.

Zeke started lighting lamps that had been placed in a circle around the car. I was conscious of Dead City surrounding us on all sides. I set my buckets on the ground and walked forward.

"Christ in the tomb," I said again, louder. "How did you get it up here?"

"An angel pushed the boulders out of the way. What do you think?" Zeke opened one of the books and began flipping through its pages.

"Zeke! You already did it? What happened?"

"Nothing happened." He studied a diagram on one page of the book. "Now get those cans of red over here. I want to prime it in red."

"Jesus Lord, I should have known it when I saw your hands." I followed him around the circle. "What was it like? Did it have wings? Did it look like the Devil?"

"How the hell would I know what the Devil looks like?" Zeke snapped the book shut and handed me a big brush. "Smooth, slow strokes, all over the hood. Don't mess it up." He set the books off to the side carefully.

"Zeke, why do we have to work on it out here, in the City?"

"Can't you feel it?" His voice sounded like he was speaking from under the ground. "There's a lot of death here. A lot of power." Death. Power. I was out of my depth.

I didn't ask any more questions. We worked silently for almost three hours. Two hours before dawn we put the cans and brushes beneath the car, doused the lamps, and walked home. Zeke whistled the whole way.

\*

One or two days a week for almost two months I made the trek out to the city with or for Zeke. He had stopped going to schoolhouse. He would stay awake for days, working on the car, talking about how he was going to take it on the circuit and blow everybody else away. I'd bring him some food from home and he'd barely look at it.

Looking back, I know I could have done something to stop him. I could have hid the tools, or sabotaged the paint, or told my folks what we were doing. But Zeke was Zeke. And I couldn't imagine any situation that Zeke couldn't handle.

Me, I was a different story. I was petrified Firstmother or Father would find out what I was up to. I would tell Zeke that I was absolutely never coming back out to the City. But Zeke would tell me he needed me to bring something out; and, sure enough, that night I would climb out my window and head toward Dead City. Considering my nervousness and lack of confidence, I had amazing luck. Of all the times I sneaked out of the house to go help him, I was only caught once.

It was mid-June and I was late coming back from the City. The sun was just starting to come up behind me. I was about to boost myself over the window ledge and start pretending to be asleep when Sara walked around the corner. What was she doing up this early? She stared at me and I slowly dropped back to the ground. If she told Firstmother (which she wouldn't) or Father (which she probably would) I was in big trouble.

"Sara, listen . . ." I began. She shushed me with a finger to her lips. She grinned like a little kid.

"I'm pregnant," she said. "I'm Secondmother now."

"That's great," I said. We stood there in silence for a while, me nervously watching the sun get bigger and brighter every minute. Finally she reached up and touched the top of my head.

"You'd better get inside now, Joseph." She turned her back to me and walked around the corner again. I scrambled up the wall and dove into bed. A few minutes later Father came in to wake me up for the morning chores.

\*

The night we were to call the Engine, I walked into the City early, just before dusk. I wanted to look at the car alone, in daylight.

I took almost as much pride in it as Zeke did.

At that time I'd only seen one race on the white highways, between two cars on the pro circuit from Nevada. I'd thought the cars were the most beautiful, terrible things in the world. But Zeke's car, our car, surpassed them.

Not in beauty. Even by lamplight, the lines on the Chevy did not look delicate; the interior did not look padded and luxurious; the wheels were not trimmed in gold like the circuit cars were. But for sheer terribleness, you couldn't match Zeke's Chevy.

It was red, but a red shot through with yellow and white lines that, by lamplight, flickered and burned. I'd asked Zeke how he did it. How did he know what design was needed, what pattern of lines and circles and rectangles was called for. Zeke said that every pattern on every car was exactly the same, but I said that was horse-hockey—I'd seen the pro cars, and each design was as different from the other as strangers.

As I entered the alley I could see that the Chevy was no less terrible by daylight. I could make out each line and shape, and as I looked I began to grasp the logic of their relationships. Each line bound one shape to another; each shape froze the line in its path. There was no way to look past that design to the base red, and there was no path from the red out.

The pattern was bars to a cage, and the cage was the car.

Suddenly I realized that there was someone in the car behind the wheel; nearly as quick I knew it was Frank. The door opened and he heaved himself out. He stumbled forward, then leaned against the hood. As I walked toward him he drew a flask and swallowed hard.

"Who are you?"

"Joseph Peterson," I said. I was ready to break and run if he got crazy. I'd seen Frank drunk, but I'd always stayed out of his way. So did Zeke.

His eyes narrowed. "Sam's boy?"

"That's right." He shook his head as if to clear it. He looked at the car beneath his hand.

"What the hell are you boys trying to do out here?"

"Nothing, sir."

"Nothing? C'mere, boy. Look at this." Cautiously I walked over. He traced one of the lines with his finger. The finger, and now I noticed the entire hand as well, was covered with pink scars. I looked at where he pointed. There was a small break in the paint. "That's sloppy, boy, sloppy that could get you killed. That line's useless, and if your Engine finds that break it's gonna try to pop right out of there." He pulled me around to the open driver's door. "Look at that steerin' wheel."

I looked. "I don't see anything wrong."

Frank made a sound like a man trying to push a mule uphill, and he shoved me into the seat. "Put your hands on the wheel."

I did as I was told, but I was also trying to see if I could scoot over to the other door and get out before he could grab me again. "No no no. Look where your hands are. Put 'em at two o'clock and ten. Now, see where the pattern stops to either sides of your hands? Those are your channels, and if your hand's not *completely* covering those blank spots when the blood's flowing, the Engine's gonna climb up into your lap and bite your head off. Then you go zombi."

"Zeke's hands are bigger," I said defensively.

"Nobody races with channels that big. Don't you understand, boy? It's a two way street. *You* reach *in*, and *it* reaches *you*."

"But Zeke says with bigger channels you get more speed, more fuel out of the Engine . . ."

"Boy, speed's not everything."

Suddenly a big bandaged hand reached in and hauled Frank out of the door. Zeke held him by the shirt collar and shouted at him. "What are doing here, old man? What are you doing here!" Zeke pushed Frank away from him. Frank stumbled backwards and fell to the ground.

Zeke stalked off to the other side of the car. I was left looking at Frank. He wasn't getting up. After half a minute I got out of the car and went to see if he was all right.

His eyes were open, but he wasn't seeing me. It was like he was caught up in a memory, or a dream that he couldn't shake.

"Can I give you a hand?" I asked. His eyes focused on me. He shook his head and slowly levered himself up into a sitting position. After a while he eased himself up and walked stiff-leggedly out of the alley.

"That was kind of rough, don't you think?" I told Zeke.

He didn't answer, or even look at me. He was flipping through one of his books again. And if I hadn't known Zeke as well as I did, I would have sworn he looked like a boy about to cry. He slammed the book shut, picked up a brush, and began filling in the breaks in the lines of the pattern with quick, angry strokes. He left the channels on the steering wheel untouched.

An hour or so later Zeke began to talk again as he worked, but it was only about the Circuit, and how fast this car was going to be, and taking on Brujo Mendez in Mexicana.

"What's the big deal with Mendez?" I asked.

"He's the best," Zeke said. "No one's ever beaten him."

By eleven, Zeke was almost finished.

If the car was a cage, the Gateway pattern was the carrot to lure the Engine in. Zeke had drawn three blue circles on the ground, lined up in a row, each circle edge touching the edge of another circle. The biggest circle was around the car. The middle circle was smaller and laced with intersecting diagonal lines. The last circle was the smallest. Zeke was sitting in the center of that circle and painting in a complex double row of shapes and lines around the inside of the border.

"I don't get it," I said.

Zeke smiled. "I sit here," he said, "and the demon pops up there." The middle circle. "Then it becomes a test. Can I push it into the car or not."

"What if you can't?"

"Then either of two things is going to happen. It's going to force its way into my circle, or it's going to go back where it came from."

"And if it gets in?"

"Then you'd better run like hell, Joey. I'll already be gone."

"Shit."

Zeke laughed. "I never heard you swear before! You're hanging out with the wrong guy, Joseph."

"I know it. When do you start?"

"Midnight."

We waited out the hour (Zeke inside his circle, me outside the whole pattern) listening to the silence of Dead City. I still feared the City, but it was a familiar fear.

I tried to imagine thousands of people living in these buildings, but I couldn't do it. Where would all the food come from? What did they do for a living, besides drive cars?

Zeke said, "All right. It's time." Zeke told me to douse the lanterns around the alley. Before the last of the lights went out, though, I saw Zeke take off his bandages. The scabs on his palms that looked like black holes in his skin. I turned away and doused the last lamp.

Moonlight glinted off something metallic in Zeke's hands. I heard him gasp, and then I saw blotches of phosphorescent blood appear in the middle circle. Then the entire pattern flared into blue fire.

After a minute the fire subsided to a glow that lit up the alley. Zeke sat in the center of his circle, hugging his knees, staring at the middle circle. The blotches were burning brighter now. I gazed from Zeke to the middle circle to the car. For the longest time nothing happened at all.

I can't tell you how the thing appeared, because I was looking at Zeke's face when I heard it. It sounded like a huge downpour, or the center of a waterfall. Zeke gritted his teeth and grunted like he'd been stabbed in the gut, and I flicked my eyes to the middle circle again. It was already there . . .

. . . the most beautiful thing I've ever seen. It swirled like a dust-devil, but a dust-devil made of light. It was not green, or red, or any other color, really. It simply was. I know that's crazy.

It spun toward Zeke, moaning like a tornado, and as it moved I saw the bright blotches rise up and become part of the whirlwind. It battered at Zeke's circle, sparks flying as flakes of paint chipped off the ground and joined the spinning air. Zeke clenched his fist. Blood poured down his arms. The thing spun backwards; then Zeke was on his feet, shouting at the top of his lungs. I couldn't make out the words over the roar.

After that it was over almost instantly. The whirlwind broke through the circle surrounding the car, then vanished. The circles and rectangles on the Chevy flared a moment and went dark. The blue circles on the ground faded.

We were in darkness.

That's when I realized Zeke was calling for help. I ran to him, picked the bandages off the ground, and began to wrap up his hands. There was so much blood I couldn't tell where the wound was: but I cinched both bandages tight. Zeke's hair was matted to his head with sweat. A smile was playing around his face. He stood up, holding me. Then he looked at the car and whooped for joy.

When Zeke got in and started her up, I whooped too.

August was race season. Any kid who could escape his family snuck off at night to the white highways.

The highways have always been here. They are cracked, and full of holes, and some whole sections of bridges have collapsed, You can still ride the white highways from one ocean to another, from Canuck to Mexicana. And if you're a driver, you can race on them.

The pro driver that first Saturday in August was a blond-haired guy from Appalachia who called himself the Bobcat and drove a blue and gold Ford. The local girls who'd ditched their folks were pooling in the glow of his headlights like moths, jockeying to get closer to him. The boys were standing around in tight bunches outside the light, looking at the car. Everyone was very careful not to lean on the Bobcat's car.

We watched him from a ridge above the highways. Zeke had said he wanted to size up the competition. He snorted. "I'm gonna bury this guy."

I wasn't so sure. The Bobcat wasn't famous on the circuit, but he was still a pro driver, and Zeke had never raced before. But Zeke was Zeke. And he was confident as hell. "Let's go," he said. I climbed in from the passenger side and Zeke slid in the other door. He planted his big hands on the steering wheel—completely covering the channels, I saw—and his face contorted into an angry sneer like he was wrestling the Engine for control. Finally he smiled.

We shot down the ridge, the Engine growling like a caged bear, and popped through a hole in the railing. Zeke slid to a stop just behind Bobcat, his lights focusing on the blue Ford. The blond-haired driver looked at us for a moment. I thought I saw a little doubt in his face, but then he shrugged and turned back to the girls.

Zeke eased the Chevy up to the line. "Hey, piss-head," Zeke said. The Bobcat ignored us.

"I said, 'Hey, piss-head.'"

Bobcat thumbed one gloved hand at us and asked one of the girls, "Who is this yokel?"

It was Lydia Mitchum, the Preacher's daughter, who answered. "That's Zeke Landers."

The Bobcat turned to us and leaned down to look into the car. "That's it? Just 'Zeke?'"

Zeke was ready to jump out of the car and punch this guy. I looked at his wild red hair falling like a mane down his back and I said, "Don't you know who this is, little Bobcat? This the King of the Beasts, Zeke the Lion!"

Zeke gave me a look that told me to shut up, but the word was already out among the watchers.

Bobcat looked annoyed. "Okay, 'Lion.' What stakes are you willing to put up?"

Zeke didn't hesitate a second. "Pink slips."

"Are you crazy, yokel? You're going to go zombi for sure."

"I win, I take your Ford."

"And if I win, I take your ugly Chevy and drive it off a cliff!"

"Do what you want," Zeke said. "Down to Busted Bridge, two miles." He grinned. End of argument.

"Two miles. You're on." Bobcat pushed the girls out of the way and climbed into his Ford. Zeke and I watched him pull the inserts out of the palms of his gloves, prick the exposed skin with a small knife, and then fit his hands over the channels. He called Lydia over to tie the thongs of his gloves to the steering wheel.

Zeke snorted. "Wimp." Zeke's hands were bare as always. I pushed the handle to get out.

"Hey! Where you going?"

"I'm going to watch," I said.

"Like hell. Don't you know you're my lucky piece? You ride with me!" I got back in, scared but excited as all hell. The Bobcat started his Engine and the crowd backed away to the railings. Zeke tightened his grip on the wheel. Our Engine growled to life.

Lydia Mitchum stripped off her green t-shirt and stood between our headlights. I couldn't take my eyes off her breasts. "On my mark!" she yelled, raising the shirt above her head. Zeke snarled under his breath. Lydia brought the green cloth down. "Go!"

We went.

I think I screamed most of the way down the track. And then I looked over at Zeke and saw that he was smiling. Maybe I should have realized then that I had no part in this, but with Zeke so confident and in control, I started to smile too. We beat the Ford to Busted Bridge by a quarter mile.

The Bobcat was furious. "Who the hell are you!? What kind of Engine is that?" He kept yelling. Zeke told him to keep his shitty car and go home.

Zeke grabbed me by the shoulders. "So what do you say? Do we hit the circuit or what?"

I was young. I had just won my first race with Zeke. I said yes.

I left a note for my Father telling him I would be back for the harvest in October. Then I hopped out my window, a sack of clothes in my hand, and headed out across the fields to Zeke's house. When I got there, Zeke was taking an axe to a tin contraption behind the shed. "What is that?" I said.

"His still." He broke up the last of the tubing, dumped a big barrel of mash on the ground, and then tossed the axe into the field. "Maybe this will keep him alive 'til I get back," he said.

We drove the white highways, only getting off when the road was too ridden with holes or the bridges were out. Zeke the Lion became the new name on the circuit. "I refuse to lose," he'd say to me before each race. And he didn't. We drove through Kintucky, Appalachia, Texas, Misery, taking on all challenges. We would sleep outside, or in the Chevy if it was raining.

There were always girls at the races. A lot of times I would have to walk around for a couple of hours while Zeke was using the car. Or he would gather a bunch of kids around, slowly strip off his bandages, and tell them what it was like to drive one of the Engines. Zeke loved every minute of it. I spent every minute horny as hell, but the Driver magic didn't seem to rub off on me.

And Zeke was changing. By late August he was staying out later and later before each race. He'd get roaring drunk and then shake me awake. He always wanted to talk. Most of the time it was racing: about the cars he'd beaten, or was going to beat in the next town, and especially how he was going to take on the Brujo in Mexicana.

But sometimes it was weirder stuff. "Joey," he said to me one night in Texas, "the voice is getting louder. When I start a race, I can hear it screaming at me. It's getting *in*, Joey." I asked what he meant but he only stared at his hands and mumbled again, "It's getting in, I can feel it." Then he took another slug of corn-gin. After a while he shambled off into the darkness.

By September we were in Mexicana.

The Brujo was nothing like I expected. I first saw him standing near his big white Caddy, surrounded by a group of racers. He was talking in a loud high voice and when he laughed he sounded like an old woman. His face was fat, and he beamed at everyone around him like an idiot.

When he saw Zeke and me step out of the Chevy he walked over. His body was as fat as his face, much too soft for an Engine driver's. He held out a big gloved hand to me and smiled. Long leather thongs hung from the gloves. "I am Phil Mendez! You must be Lucky Joe!" That had gotten to be my name on the Circuit. We shook hands but his eyes were already on Zeke. Those eyes were flat, professional.

His smile faded. "This is the Lion?" Zeke was in bad shape. His skin was pale from blood loss, his hands were shaky, and his eyes were bloodshot. He hadn't eaten well in days. And he was still drunk from a binge last night.

"I want to race," Zeke said. His voice was raspy.

"My friend, Zeke," the Brujo said, "you aren't well enough to shit on a rock." The Brujo's gaze swiveled back to me. "No race. Get him out of here."

"No!" screamed Zeke, and he grabbed Mendez by the shirt. "You can't chicken out on me, sucker." Mendez looked at him coldly. I suddenly realized that the Brujo was an old man, maybe older than Frank.

There was a few seconds of silence. Then the Brujo smiled. "Okay, little man. What kind of car you want to put up?" Zeke let go of his shirt and Mendez looked over at the Chevy. He studied it for a moment and then looked at me.

"Who painted that car?" he snapped.

"Zeke did."

"Bullshit." He walked up to the car and circled it once. "I know this pattern."

Zeke shouted at him. "So what's the deal? We race?"

"You're from up around Illini, aren't you?" I nodded. The Brujo shook his head sadly. "I thought so. I thought so." He turned back to the circle of drivers waiting for him by the Caddy. "Okay, little man. You get your race."

We watched the Brujo take on three challengers that day, which was almost unheard of on the Circuit. Every time the Brujo's big caddy beat someone to the two-mile marker Zeke would say, "I can take that. I can take it."

We were scheduled for the next morning. Racers and girls and local kids stopped by our car to wish Zeke luck tomorrow. Bottles were passed. Zeke wasn't drinking that night, but for the first time I was. It tasted horrible.

"I need an edge," Zeke said to me after everyone had left. He passed me a bottle. "He's got a bigger Engine in that Caddy."

"Forget it," I said. My voice was too loud. "There's no way for you to get a bigger Engine."

Zeke leaned against the hood. "Not a bigger Engine, Joey. More fuel, that's all that matters. Bigger channels."

I drained the last of the bottle. The world was spinning a little crazily and I just wanted to lie flat on the ground. I pulled my blankets out of the car. "Sleep on it, Zeke," was the last thing I remember saying.

The next morning I woke up and Zeke and the Chevy were gone.

From the direction of the white highways I heard the Chevy's roar, and in a second I was up and running toward the sound.

As I climbed the embankment I could hear the Brujo's Caddy starting up. Zeke was right, it was a much bigger Engine. I hopped over the rail in time to see Zeke easing the Chevy up to the line.

I ran up to him, my bare feet smarting from the rubble on the highway. I looked at his hands. The bandages were off and blood was already running down his arms. The Channels in the steering wheel were nearly twice as big as they had been. His hands couldn't cover the gaps.

Zeke turned to me and smiled. "I'm gonna bury this sucker," he said. "Hop in, Joe. You're my lucky piece."

"Are you crazy?" I screamed. "Don't do this Zeke!"

I heard the Brujo's voice. "Get out of the way, Joe. Tell Frank the Crank that I beat his son."

"What?" I turned around. I was between the Caddy and the Chevy. A big driver reached me and pulled me out of the way. The start girl raised the green flag.

The two cars took off. The exhaust smelled like sulphur.

Since I was at the starting end of the track I didn't see how it happened. Spectators at the far end said they saw the Brujo's Caddy was ahead the whole way, until the ¾ mile marker. There the Chevy suddenly put on a burst of speed and passed the Caddy. Everyone agrees that the Chevy crossed the finish line first.

Only a couple people said that they actually saw the Pattern blow, or that they saw a whirlwind of light spin into the cabin with Zeke. Even the Brujo, driving right behind him, said that he couldn't be sure what happened. But everyone could hear that Engine roaring like the wind in their ears and screaming like a calf at the slaughter.

The Chevy never slowed down. It left tracks of blood on white cement.


I hitched my way across Mexicana, California, and Arizona. Some drivers wouldn't stop for me, but the ones that did knew who I was and wanted to talk about Zeke's race. Except for my last ride, Naomi.

Somewhere in the middle of Texas she looked at me through the rear view mirror, blew air through her lips like a baby, and then laughed uproariously.

"You scared of a woman driver, Lucky Joe?" she yelled over the roar of the wind.

Was I? Naomi was one of the few female drivers on the Circuit; she was in her mid-thirties. They made fun of her off the highways. On the highways they tried their damnedest to beat her.

I shook my head no, for safety's sake.

"You should be, Lucky, you should be. I think women are going to dominate racing soon." She must have seen my disbelief. "Oh no? Tell me, Joey. What's an Engine?"

"Everybody knows what an Engine is," I said. "A demon."

"A demon? An angry, vengeful spirit trapped in the pattern of a car." She shut her eyes to consider this. We stayed perfectly on course.

Her eyes sprang open. She smiled. "Exactly right. A demon. But what is an Engine before you trap it?"

"That's stupid . . ." I began, but then stopped. I remembered the beauty of the whirlwind spinning inside blue circles. "I give up. What is it?"

"An angel."

I snorted.

"Think about it, Joey. If you trapped a creature, made it do what you wanted, whenever you wanted, and then destroyed it, wouldn't you feel more comfortable calling the thing evil? Torturing an 'angel' would bring so much *guilt* to our manly drivers."

I remembered Zeke, the tracks of blood. "You don't know what you're talking about lady. I've seen my friend . . . a guy, go zombi. That was no 'angel'."

"Even an angel might go insane." She gestured dismissively with one hand. "And you're right, the name 'angel' is meaningless. All names are meaningless."

Naomi shut up suddenly. She was looking at me strangely. "Are you okay?"

I looked out the window and let the hot Texas wind blow tears off my face. Naomi drove on in silence. A long while later, when it was dark and we were half way into Kentucky, I only asked, "So why do women make better drivers?"

She chuckled. "Revenge."

It was a late afternoon three days after she'd picked me up when Naomi stopped the car and let me out near my father's farm. She had driven the whole way without sleeping. The cold October wind whipped at my clothes, tugged at my bedroll. She smiled up at me.

"Here you are, Lucky Joe."

"Thanks, Naomi. I appreciate the lift."

"Any time. Take care of yourself, now. And do me a favor; stay away from the Engines. Fall in love, settle down and be a farmer."

"Okay, I promise." Then I said: "What about you?"

She patted my hand with one scarred palm. "Good," was all she said. Her eyes sparkled like no color at all. I watched her disappear before I turned my face to the wind and started down the embankment.

I walked the two miles from the highway breathing in the familiar smells of harvest. The corn was only half cut, though, and we were only weeks away from snow. A knot of fear cinched tight in my stomach.

I stepped up to the porch and pushed through the door. It was supper time. The family sat at the table, my Father at one end, First-mother at the other, my two sisters and Sara in the middle. My place was empty.

My sisters swiveled in their chairs as I walked in, then quickly turned back to the table and dropped their eyes. Sarah looked up, smiled slightly, and started to get up. Her belly was hugely round beneath her dress.

Firstmother quietly said, "No." Sara sat down awkwardly.

Father chewed slowly, his eyes on his plate.

I pulled out my chair. The scrape sounded deafening. I sat down. There was not much food on the table.

I wanted a confrontation. I wanted screaming, yelling. I wanted punishment, hard labor in the fields. They gave me silence.

When they had finished eating, each person drifted away from the table and went to their rooms.

Much later I heard a timid knock at my door. Just as I covered myself Sara stepped in. She was holding a plate of beans and corn-bread.

"I thought you might want some," she said.

"Thank you." I tore of hunks off cornbread and sopped them in the beans. It was delicious. Sara watched me eat.

"When is it coming?" I said after awhile.

"December twenty-third," she said. "His name will be Elijah."

"You seem pretty sure."

"I am sure. A mother knows these things."

When I finished she took the empty plate from me and touched the back of my neck. "You'd better get some sleep."


I woke up just before dawn feeling warm and comfortable be-neath the blanket. I could hear my Father moving around in the kitch-en. It was time for chores, then school, and then maybe a walk with Zeke out to the City . . . .

No.

It suddenly felt very cold in the room. I pulled on my clothes and stepped out into the kitchen. The first light glowed through the frosted windows. First frost, and the crops not even half in. I heard the front door bang shut. I followed Father out into the yard.

He was gazing at the husks glistening like a glassblower's interpretation of corn. His back was stiff, straight. I stood next to him and stared into the fields.

"I know it's too late," I said, "but I would like to help."

He was silent for a long while. "What happened to Zeke?"

"He . . . died. In a wreck."

Father looked at me, his eyes squinted tight. "Ain't there something you should be doing?" He jerked his head toward the Lander's place. "Get back here before noon or don't come back."

"Father, I'm . . ."

"Go." I took off at a jog.

In the daylight the house looked like a wreck. I stepped up onto the porch, boards creaking beneath my feet, and knocked on the door. It swung open. There was no answer. I knocked again, taking a step inside. "Mr. Landers?" I said quietly. "Frank? It's me, Sam's boy, Joseph."

I walked further into the house. The rooms were strewn with garbage, and there was a terrible stink from the kitchen. I found him in the back bedroom. At first I though he was dead.

"Frank?"

One eye slid open, then slowly closed. I waited a minute, and then said again, "Mr. Landers?"

Without opening his eyes, he said, "I know, boy. I know. I've known for a week." His voice was hoarse.

He was drunk. I pressed on. "Mr. Landers, Zeke was in an accident." I told him what some of the spectators had said. I did not mention the tracks of blood.

Finally Frank's eyes opened again. "I *know* what happened. I felt it the minute he went. I guess you ain't so lucky after all, huh? Now get the hell out of my house."

His eyes closed again. I left.

The harvest came in, most of it. The snows came a week later, and on December 24th Sara gave birth to Elijah.

On Christmas Eve Firstmother killed one of the chickens and wrapped it up. She handed it to me and told me to take it over to the Landers' place.

"Even sinners must eat on Christmas," she told me. I headed out into the cold, the chicken heavy under my arm.

I had been visiting Frank about once a week. We had talked about everything except Zeke, and racing. So in a way we'd been talking about nothing at all.

The snow was drifted up onto the porch. There were no lights on in the house. I went in, half expecting in each room to see Frank's frozen body curled up in a corner. The house was nearly as cold as outside. He was not home. I thought he might be in the outhouse, so I went out the back door.

There was a light on in the shed.

I stepped into the warmth of the place. Every lantern was lit and a fire burned in a shallow stone pit to one side of the room.

Frank was working on the Pontiac. He was moving quickly, scrubbing the old black and silver paint off the car. He had already cleared most of the hood.

When the frigid wind blasted in he turned to me with eyes that were clear and stone-cold sober. "Shut the damn door," he said. "We've got to talk, Lucky Joe."


It was only June, but already corn crowded the embankments. Ahead of us, heat shimmered on the white highway.

The Engine roared like the wind in your ears and screamed like a calf at the slaughter. It was a mean, rage-filled sound.

It sounded like Zeke.

Frank turned at the noise. He slammed the hood of the car down with a bang. He frowned. He looked completely calm, like the Brujo, or Naomi.

Frank the Crank was a pro.

I was scared shitless.

"Do you think we can take him?" I said.

I could make out the shiny grillwork, the headlights reflecting like cat's eyes in the sun, the silver rectangle of windshield. The engine grew louder. The familiar patterns of the car were just becoming clear. Frank's voice was rough. "We will." He looked me in the eye. "How are *you* doing?"

"Fine," I lied.

"Bullshit, Joseph. But it doesn't matter. Just remember to concentrate."

"Frank, you—"

He looked away.

"—you should be the driver. Let me—"

"Shut up, son." The car was suddenly there, bearing down on us. For a moment I thought it was going to run us down. At the last moment the car braked hard, went into a skid, and sprayed gravel at me and Frank. The car slid to a stop with the driver's side door facing us.

The engine wound down from a howl to a rumbling growl, and then was silenced. An ugly knot of fear tightened in my stomach. "Father, Son, Spirit, Lord . . ." I heard myself saying, and then shut my mouth. It was too late for prayers now, and I was certainly in no position to ask.

The door cracked open.

The overpowering smell of shit and blood nearly made me puke.

The door swung wide, and I saw first one booted leg, then another touch the ground. The thing stood up to full height and stretched its arms toward us. It cocked its head sideways and leered at us with a mouth of rotted teeth. "Joey! Poppa! Good . . . to see you!"

The thing had Zeke's voice, Zeke's wild red hair, and Zeke's broad shoulders and height.

But the shell was empty. The body was starved, the clothes ripped and soiled, the skin a sickly white.

Only the eyes—Zeke's narrow eyes—seemed animate. They flashed in the sunlight, like coals left burning during the day for the night fires.

The thing laughed.

"Aren't you . . . glad to see me?" It stepped forward and Frank picked up a rock.

"Stay the hell away from me."

"Poppa!" The thing shut the car door, leaned against the hood. I almost gasped, the gesture was so like Zeke. The creature's gaze swung toward me. "So, Joey. What do you and this . . . piece of *shit* . . . want?"

I fought down my anger. "I want a race."

It laughed again, a dry chuckle. "A race. Joey wants to race. We haven't . . . raced together . . . in a long time."

"From here to Busted Bridge. Two miles. One shot."

The thing grinned, shambled forward. "But what are the . . . stakes. What are the stakes?"

"Pink slips," I said.

"Pink slips?" It cocked his head. "But I have no . . . *need* for a car." Then the thing smiled. "No. Not . . . a car." It touched its chest in mock depreciation. "I need another . . . vehicle." It pointed one long finger at me. Zeke's finger. "This one wears thin. You are pink . . . and *fresh*."

A thrill of terror ran down my spine. "Exactly," I said. "I want him back."

It laughed. "You want my faithful Engine?"

For the first time its gaze fell on our car, parked behind us. It moved forward, its smell rushing before it. I felt bile burning at the back of my throat as it stepped past me. It looked cautiously at the blue circle painted around the car, then stepped over it. It held out one pale hand.

"Get away from it," Frank growled.

Its hand hovered over the car. The thing stared intently at the patterns from hood to trunk. Then it hissed: "Who is it?"

Frank and me said nothing.

"Who . . . is it?"

Frank shrugged elaborately. "Maybe nobody you know."

"I know . . . *everyone*." It slowly touched one finger to the silver pattern painted on the hood. The grotesque face curled into an expression of surprise when the lines did not burn. "It's empty!"

"So? Do we have a deal?"

It nodded, laughing again. "It is just . . . a car!" It walked back to its car, shaking its head.

I felt Frank's hand on my shoulder. "I want you to thank your folks, Joe, for all the help they've done me."

He held out his hand. We shook, his scars feeling rough against my palm.

"Now remember. Let me do the work. It's between me and Zeke now." He smiled. Like Zeke. End of argument.

I walked to our car. A silver ox was painted on the driver's side door. Symbol of the farmer, Frank had said. On the other door, where the creature could see it clearly, was a silver lion.

I sat down in the Pontiac, pulled the door shut, and placed my hands over the channels. A part of me wanted to cut my hands and shed some of my own blood in this race. I stared ahead through the windshield so as not to see the thing that wasn't Zeke in the Chevy next to me.

The Pontiac was surrounded by a pattern of blue paint drawn on white cement. Diagonal lines shot off from that pattern on the side opposite the Chevy and joined to another, smaller circle. Frank sat in that circle, holding a knife. He looked at me and nodded.

I slowly turned my head to face the Chevy. I yelled, "Ready?" The thing grinned and the Chevy Engine screamed to life.

"Start your . . . Engine!" it rasped, then threw back its head and howled.

I nodded to Frank. For a moment he looked at me. There was hope and fear in his eyes. He stared at the knife in his hand. With a quick movement he plunged it into his chest.

The Pontiac engine roared. A wave of heat rolled up my arms.

On the pavement where Frank had been sitting there was only an empty corpse.

I looked over at the Chevy. "Now, you fucker!"

The Pontiac bucked and flew forward. I did not scream. I could feel a steady heat, like a murderous calm, flowing up my arms from the channels.

The white highways stretched like a snake before us. There were two miles between us and Busted Bridge, and I had never really driven before. My Engine was untested, untamed.

But it was effortless. The wheel would jerk in my hands and suddenly we'd be skirting a pothole that I hadn't even seen. Frank's spirit gave itself up willingly, threw its entire being in the Pontiac's engine. There was not even any need to conserve anything for a second race.

The highway made a slow curve, and then the columns of Dead City were rising before us like a mountain range. After a mile and a half the Pontiac and the Chevy were still even.

Then a searing pain in my arms nearly made me jerk my hands from the wheel. I held on. I heard the creature scream as we passed it.

We were almost to the edge of the City when the Chevy's pattern blew. In my rear view mirror I could see blue flames explode from the pattern on the hood. The Chevy skewed sideways across the road. The car ground against the railing, spewing sparks, and then swerved back onto the lane.

But it was not under control. The car began to spin, almost gracefully, creating bright red ovals on the white cement. The car crashed through the opposite railing.

I yelled and slammed on the Pontiac's brakes. I nearly lost control myself before I could turn the car around. As we approached the split railing of Busted Bridge I felt my arms go cold, and the Pontiac choked to a halt. I jumped out.

Zeke was on fire. He fled from the Chevy in a stumbling half-run, and then dropped to his knees. He looked up with pain-filled eyes and saw me.

Behind him, the car exploded with a light that was no color at all. Zeke smiled.


Father died a year later. Firstmother crumpled up with grief and followed him into the grave in six months. Sara's still a young woman, and she makes a good wife. My brothers and sisters that were her children have become my sons and daughters. Sara's pregnant with the first of mine, and it looks like I won't need a secondmother for many years.

Unless Lydia Mitchum ever shows up here again. She ran off about six months back from the Preacher and the rumors have been coming by about her and some woman driver. I think of her—and her green shirt and her breasts—sometimes. But not too much.

Father's land is mine now. You can make a good living off it if you're not afraid to work, and I know there will always be food on the table for the kids. I don't race anymore. The farthest I want to travel is to the edge of my acres, and only as fast as the horse pulling the plow ahead of me.

The other night I couldn't sleep, so I eased out of bed quiet enough to not wake Sara. I walked over to the Landers' place in the cool night air, and I stood on the porch of the dilapidated house. I could see the two gravestones on the hill, spaced just a few feet apart.

I went around to the shed behind the house and unchained the doors. Moonlight spilled across the silver and black car. I rummaged around in the shed a while, looking at wrenches and brushes and rusted car parts. At one point I climbed behind the wheel and looked out through the windshield. I lightly touched the channels. The car was empty, completely empty.

When I was all done remembering, I unscrewed the caps from the kerosene lamps and sloshed liquid up and down the walls and across the car.

I stood near the back of the house. The shed burned for a long while. There must have been a big can of kerosene somewhere inside, because suddenly a whole side of the shed exploded out and the roof tumbled down.

It was dawn before I got home. My house looked solid and clean in the growing light. Sara stepped out onto the porch as I walked up. She had a worried look on her face.

"What is it?" she asked.

I shook my head and touched her rounded belly beneath her gown. Sara said we would name him Joseph. "Nothing." It was time for the morning chores, and from inside the house one of the children started crying.

It was a happy sound.

*As for the likeness of their faces, they four had the face of a man, and the face of a lion on the right side: and they four had the face of an ox on the left side . . . .*
—Ezekiel 1:10

# PETIT MAL #3: PERSISTENCE

*I see your face in every flower,*
*Your eyes in stars above.*
*It's just the thought of you.*
— Billie Holiday, "The Very Thought of You"

I wake up to see my daughter's face. Her lips are pulled back in disgust, an expression of furious condescension that is one of the primary weapons of the American fourteen-year-old. Her skin is pale in this winter light, washed in the glow of frost-hazed glass, her brown eyes almost black. Dark hair, the same shade as her father's when I first met him, falls over one cheek. Oh, Franny is so angry. Yet even outraged, worn out from too little sleep, she is beautiful.

Her face, frozen in this moment, is the first thing I see when I awake, the last thing I see before I fall asleep, and at every moment in between.

The tumor had been growing for some time. The warning signs, the physiological notices advertising the tumor's acquisition of new territory, were apparent only in retrospect: a few more headaches than usual, an occasional flutter in the right corner of my vision that I chalked up to too many hours at the computer screen. There was no reason why this was the moment that my vision froze. It just so happened that on that day, in that second, one more cell divided, one more neuron fired in agitation or failed to fire, and the mental movie (but not a movie, it's more complicated than that) stopped on that final frame.

Franny: dark eyed, shouting.

My brain didn't know what to make of this cessation of activity. The retina continued to blast pixels into the visual cortex, but somewhere in the thalamus, that trillion-rail switchyard that routes sensation to the conscious mind, a track had been shut down. And so the thalamus delivered the only freight it had, the identical pattern of impulses it passed along a moment before. But the mind demanded more: What next? What next? The thalamus, empty handed, pushed the pattern again, and kept pushing, an infinite string of boxcars bearing the same image: Her angry, beautiful face.

What I see is not like a photograph, or a blurred still from a movie. The world has depth, as shimmering and fully three-dimensional as the world on the other side of anyone's eye. It seems to me not as if the world has stopped, but that I've become stuck in time. I'm staring at Franny, waiting to rejoin her.

I can't remember the exact words she yelled at me before that moment, or what new syllable was forming on her lips. Something like, It's my fucking phone! That morning, she'd lost her cell again, and for the second time that week we were running late because she'd spent ten minutes calling her own number, tossing bed clothes and checking pockets, to no avail. We got into the car without it, and I made my usual threat to cancel the phone if she couldn't keep track of it. A trivial, silly argument. In that moment, I wanted to strangle her, and I'm sure she wanted to do the same to me. But that moment only. These shouting matches weren't matches at all, merely flare-ups, as dangerous as a single firecracker. My husband never understood how we could be screaming at each other one moment and in the next deciding on lunch, signing a permission slip, kissing goodbye. I told him that Franny could yell at me because she knew she couldn't hurt me. I was her mother, and I could weather her blows. She knew, bone deep, that I wasn't going anywhere.

When I awoke in the hospital Franny was there, scowling, in mid-shout. Behind her, the voices of doctors described my condition. The neurologist—my first neurologist, like a first boyfriend, destined to be remembered only vaguely by a set of brief, awkward interactions—explained that when they brought me in, they ordered the MRI because of the threat of concussion, and were surprised to see the tumor there. So in a way, he said, the accident was lucky. (Lucky. Lucky for him I was too doped on painkillers to respond to the insult, too weak to slap him.)

The surgery to remove the tumor was a success, or rather, not a total failure. There were depths they feared to excavate, but with radiation and chemotherapy I had a very good chance of living through the year. As for the persistence of vision, it certainly was . . . persistent. (He chuckled at his own joke, but of course I couldn't see his face.) Unprecedented, really.

I didn't care about that. Tell me about my daughter, I said. Tell me about Franny.

More doctors arrived. They feared too much emotion would slow my recovery. They proceeded to itemize my other injuries, as if my body had not already delivered the news. I could feel the subsonic ache of deep bruises and fractured bones; every move of my limbs moaned the damage. My constant hallucination was a welcome distraction. I was not only in the hospital; I could look out at the bright winter day, the sun coming through the windshield, shining on the face of my daughter. Each morning I woke to her angry face, yelling silently at me: It's my fucking phone!

A psychologist suggested, in oblique terms, that perhaps guilt was preventing me from letting go of that moment. But he had his facts wrong. The tumor froze me before the accident. When I turned to look back at the road, my hands on the wheel, I could see nothing but Franny from a few seconds before. I blinked and shouted, not understanding what was happening. It was as if I had fallen asleep, and could not shake the dream from my head, or open my eyes. I mashed the brake in panic. As it turns out, this was the wrong thing to do. The road was icy, the traffic too thick around me.

I told the psychologist, in non-oblique terms, to fuck off.

My condition was neurological, and I became a student of how the tumor had sabotaged my vision. What we see, when we say that we are seeing, is not a snapshot of transmitted light, not a slideshow projected on the inside of the skull. The fovea, the most sensitive area of the eye, is only a millimeter in diameter, capable of capturing a cone of light only a few degrees wide. But the eye makes due. It flicks this tiny lens about a dozen times a second, jittery as a robin, snatching photons. The image is a composite, a patchwork of these snapshots, with the gaps (and there are many gaps) filled in with expectation, embroidered with biases, colored and shaped by experience. Edges and depth and motion are illusions manufactured by specialty neurons. The scene we picture in our heads, this model, is an act of imagination, like summoning a word from a string of letters. Franny, in the moment that I keep with me, is not just jumble of light in a Franny-like shape. She is everything I know about my daughter, everything I expect to see, complete in herself. Not a letter, or even a word. She is a poem.

\*

There are many old people in this facility. You cannot live very long on this planet without experiencing tragedy. Most have lost spouses. Many have lost children. My own story is nothing notable. But I wonder how many of them can still picture the faces of their loved ones? So many of my fellow residents have minds hollowed by Alzheimer's or rewired by dementia. Or perhaps they've merely forgotten. Age is a sneak thief, an untrustworthy orderly who pockets your spare change and takes only what won't be missed until you go looking for it. The thefts happen every day, day after day.

I am lucky. I have lived much longer than the year they gave me. And no matter how old I get, my condition has made it impossible to forget what my daughter looked like at fourteen, eyes rimmed by too much eye liner, pale and furious and vibrant.

I am also famous, in certain white-coated circles. Neurologists, some of them quite young, come to see me. Very rarely, someone proposes a new treatment. I tried many of these in years past, but I'm done with that now. I will not submit to surgery again. I don't want to lose what little I have left.

The doctors ask me how I cope. I tell them that there was a time (lasting for years, but I do not say that), that I wished the tumor had struck me truly blind. Or failing that, frozen my vision on something banal. Why couldn't my final sight have been of some boring landscape, or beige ceiling, or the red-black of the inside of my eyelid? Why not something I could ignore?

But now I am content. Every day is a sunny day, I tell them. Every moment it is morning. And I have my daughter.

She is a middle-aged woman now. Her wheelchair—the latest in a succession of wheelchairs, each more sophisticated than the last, this new one capable of climbing stairs—has been no impediment to her visits, or to her life. She has two grown children. A grandchild, my first great-grandchild, is on the way. Franny comes twice a week, without fail, to sit beside me, her warm hand on mine. I can tell her anything. I can tell her when I am afraid, or missing her father, or frustrated with the limitations of life in this place. And when I have nothing to say, she says, Tell me about when I was young.

# THE CONTINUING ADVENTURES
## OF ROCKET BOY

**W**hen I was sixteen, my best friend, Stevie, built his own space-ship. In a certain light, at a certain angle, it was beautiful: A rough cylinder over twenty feet tall, balanced on four thrusters, braced by stubby delta wings. The body and wings were warped plywood. The thrusters were four 50-gallon steel drums, painted black, rimmed in aluminum foil. Later, police determined that Stevie had packed one of the drums with plastic milk jugs full of hydrogen peroxide distilled down to hydrogen monoxide—homemade rocket fuel. People heard the explosion as far away as Boone, five miles west.

I was a lot closer. At the edge of the field, maybe fifty yards away, both arms resting on the rail of a chain link fence. The fence stopped some of the bigger shrapnel, and that's probably the only reason I'm alive. I carry my piss around in a bag now, and I stump around on crutches. But otherwise I'm fine. It's just a body, after all. It's not me.

That's what Stevie was always saying, anyway. I try to keep that in mind.

The block where Stevie and I grew up looked the same as it always did: parallel trains of ranch homes parked under old pines and mountainous weeping willows. Some houses had gotten new paint, and a few back porches had become glassed-in family rooms, but nothing essential had changed. They were still just Masonite boxcars with small windows and big shutters.

The real estate agent didn't want to sell me a house here. She kept trying to show me the new "developments," two-story houses on tiny, treeless lots on the north side of town where there used to be only cornfields. But I wanted to live here, on my block, preferably in the same house I grew up in. Stevie and I had grown up side by side, in houses so similar that our families could have swapped without having to buy new furniture.

My old home, however, wasn't for sale. My parents left it years ago, while I was at college, and moved to Arizona. The current owners had torn out the hedges and fenced the yard, but hadn't changed much else. They parked a tow truck in front of the house at night. Months ago I'd had the agent make inquiries, but they didn't want to move, even at 25% over market value.

My second choice opened up all on its own. It was on the other side of Stevie's house, well within the hundred-yard range I required for my project. The owners had been the Klingerman's, people I'd barely known. They didn't have children, but they did keep little yippy dogs, terriers or something.

Stevie's parents, the Spero's, still lived in the same house. My new bedroom window faced the window to Stevie's old room. The drapes were light blue now instead of Spider-Man red. My first night in the house, sleeping on the floor because the furniture hadn't arrived, I could hear their new baby squalling.

On summer nights, Stevie would shimmy out of his bedroom window, cut across the back yards, and hiss through my window screen to come sneak out with him. We were twelve, thirteen when he started doing this. If my parents were both asleep, and if I could work up the courage, I'd go with him.

He was the same age as me, but ten pounds lighter, a skinny kid with pale, lank hair, thin lips, and translucent skin. Even by moonlight you could make out the blue vein that ran from his temple to his jaw.

The park was five blocks away, the quarry less than a mile. We'd dodge headlights the whole way, pretending every car was a cop out to bring us in. We'd dive into a ditch, and then he'd look at me and say, Oh man oh man that was *so* close. We were scared of getting caught, especially by Stevie's dad. Mr. Spero scared me more than anyone else I knew.

But we went anyway. We built a fort in the trees beside the quarry. We talked about aliens and spaceships, but we didn't know anything about real rockets, or real stars and planets. It was all *Star Wars* and *Battlestar Galactica*.

The summer after seventh grade, we started making movies; really, one long movie with dozens of unconnected scenes. My dad had gotten a video camera for Christmas. It was a big, bulky thing, though we didn't think so at the time. Since it was my dad's camera, I was the Cameraman and Director. Stevie was in charge of Story and Special Effects.

Most of the effects required fishing tackle. We strung ten-pound test line between the trees and glued hooks to the tops of the models. Stevie would pull the ships from twenty feet away, reeling them in with a fishing rod. I would lie on my back, a cassette deck held up close to the mike to provide background music, and videotape the ships as they jerked overhead. We wanted to get the stars behind them, like the opening scene in *Star Wars*. The stars never came out on the tape.

We staged improbable space battles: a two-foot wide Millennium Falcon versus an eight-inch U.S.S. Enterprise, a couple of T.I.E. fighters vs. a Japanese Zero and an Apollo 11 rocket. We stuffed firecrackers into exhaust ports and turrets and blew them apart. We doused the models with gasoline, lit them (ignorant of the impossibility of fire in space), then yanked off the escape pods with fishing line.

After Stevie died, the papers made a lot of this obsession with spaceships and explosives and fire. The Signs Were There, if someone had Only Paid Attention. Bullshit. *Of course* we were obsessed with spaceships and things that go bang. We were American boys in Bumblefuck, Iowa.

"Timmy?"

"Hi, Mrs. Spero. It's just Tim, now." She stood on her front porch, holding something that looked like a toy walkie-talkie—a baby monitor. The baby was somewhere inside; I didn't hear it crying.

"You're moving in?" She sounded surprised and happy. I'd seen her look out her front window a half dozen times since the Atlas truck pulled up an hour ago. Time enough to prepare that happily-surprised voice. To remind herself not to look at the aluminum crutches.

I nodded toward the two guys carrying a dresser into the house and managed a smile. "Sort of. Most of the furniture's going into the back bedroom until I can get the carpets taken out and the floors refinished."

She stepped off the porch and walked toward the driveway, moving slowly, as if unspooling a safety line behind her. The baby monitor's red LED pulsed every few seconds.

Mrs. Spero had been one of the young moms, the hot moms, a fit-looking woman who pulled her hair into a ponytail when she worked and wore sleeveless shirts in the summer. Even before I hit thirteen I started watching whenever she reached to a high shelf, waiting for a glimpse of white bra and curve of skin.

She was in her late forties now, and though still attractive she looked worn out. Her face was puffy, and she'd gained weight in her hips. Her eyes seemed to have sunk a fraction further into her skull. Had the new baby done this, or had the transformation started earlier?

I told her my folks had gotten the Christmas card with the birth announcement inside. "William Ray. That's nice. He's what, eight months old?"

She smiled, surprised. "Next Tuesday. We call him Will. You have a good memory."

She asked about my family. I told her my parents were looking forward to retiring in a few years. My older brother was still in grad school. My sister was in Maine, with a kid of her own.

The monitor's read-out rose and fell. I couldn't help looking at it.

She told me about my house and the neighborhood. Mr. Klingerman had died of a stroke, and Mrs. Klingerman moved into a home. She didn't know what happened to their dogs. We talked about the new people on the street, and the few changes in town.

"So, where are you working?" she asked.

"Right here. In the house. I'll be telecommuting."

"Oh. Right at home. Working on a computer, I guess?"

"I analyze quality control data for a parts manufacturer." Nine times out of ten, this is as far as I have to go to explain my job.

"Well, that sounds . . . " She searched for a word. "You were always a smart one, Tim." She glanced at the monitor, then back at her house. "I better get back."

"Can I listen?"

She looked blank for a moment, then smiled. "Sure."

I held the monitor to my ear. The baby seemed to be sound asleep, each deep breath loud and fuzzed by static.

"I can hear the ocean," I said, and she laughed. I looked at the back of the device and noted the brand name. "This thing's amazing. You can hear everything."

"Almost too much. Every little breath."

"I bet. Well, tell Mr. Spero that I'll be here all the time," I said. "If he ever needs anything."

Stevie made bigger and bigger models out of painted plywood and pieces from other models. He blew them apart with M-80s that could rip open a mailbox. I wouldn't give him my dad's video camera anymore, but he stole a Super-8 camera and a projector from the school A-V room and switched to film. He couldn't do sound anymore, but he didn't mind. Video is a cold medium, he told me.

One night the summer after freshman year, we were coming back through the yards at 3 AM. Stevie had the camera, and I was pulling a wagon full of props and models. We came around the corner of the house and saw Mr. Spero. He was sitting in a lawn chair under Stevie's window, a plastic tumbler in his hand. I dropped the wagon handle, but before I could take off he told me to stand there, and I was too afraid to move. He made Stevie drop his pants, right there in front of me. Told him to put his hands against the side of the house. Stevie was already crying. Mr. Spero stood up, unlooped his belt, and folded it in half. He held it by the buckle, and slapped it against Stevie's thighs. The boy yelped, and started bawling.

I'll give you something to cry about, Mr. Spero said.

Sometime during the beating I ran to the back door of my house, not even bothering to sneak, and ran into my bedroom. My mom tried to get me to tell her what was going on, and I blubbered something about Stevie and his dad.

A few minutes later, Mr. Spero was at our front door. My dad went to the door barefoot in his robe, and then he called me in to the living room.

Did you sneak out? he asked me.

I nodded.

Don't do it again, he said.

And that was it.

I stood there for a moment, stunned, and then ran out of the room.

But I didn't go far. I ducked into the bathroom and put my ear to the wall above the sink. Mr. Spero kept talking, in a low, spiteful voice. My dad didn't say much.

When Mr. Spero finally left I heard Dad say to Mom, That man's the southbound end of a northbound horse. I was fourteen, and thought that was the wittiest thing my father had ever said.

And then I started wondering. How long had Mr. Spero been sitting there in the dark, waiting for us?



The baby monitor Mrs. Spero used broadcast at 43 kilohertz. I bought a scanner in Des Moines and tuned in to Radio William. I listened to him whenever he was on. The format was pretty regular: he cried, he breathed, he jabbered in his private language. I learned to differentiate the various cries, from hunger to anger. He had a special kind of yelp when he wanted to be picked up after his nap. Mrs. Spero would come to retrieve him, speaking to him in her calm way, and when she leaned into his crib it was like she was speaking into my ear. At night I would lie in bed and try to time my breaths to his, but he was too fast, like a rabbit.

Mr. Spero was a background noise, a distant rumbling that occasionally resolved into words. I listened for any change of tone, waiting for the flat contempt he'd used with Stevie. That first week I watched him leave for work in the morning, and come home in the afternoon. He looked the same: pale skin and thin lips, hair combed back on his forehead in a mini-pompadour. Only the hair color had changed, from sandy brown to white.

I unpacked, and shopped on the Internet. Most of the sites encouraged homeowners to be paranoid: about their babysitters, their housecleaners, or anyone coming within twenty feet of their front door. I was amazed at the range of equipment available. I put together a complete package for less than two thousand dollars: cameras, digital switcher, software, antennas, cables, everything.

UPS delivered it in pieces over the next couple of weeks. I played with my new toys, and I listened to Radio William.

*

All Stevie's movies—our movies—were part of a long saga
called The NovaWeapon Chronicles. The plot was impossible to explain, even to ourselves, and changed depending on whatever special
effects were available. We shot parts of the story over and over when
we changed our minds or got better models. There were large gaps in
the story that we never filled in.

Most of the "chapters" had to do with Rocket Boy, played by
Stevie in black snow pants and a mesh shirt. Rocket Boy was the
only kid our age (twelve, fourteen, sixteen) who could pilot his own
starfighter in the Counter-Revolutionary StarForce, which we'd called
the "Rebel Alliance" until some kids said we just copied from *Star
Wars*. In the later chapters Rocket Boy became the strong silent type;
once we'd switched to film we couldn't record dialogue anymore.
Stevie would act out Rocket Boy working on his warp engines, or at
the controls reacting to unseen laser shots, or gazing meaningfully
into the distance. I appeared in various roles, from Flight Commander
to Alien Overlord. My younger brother was drafted into playing en-
signs, lackey aliens, and especially corpses. Stevie said Hitchcock
used Bosco for the shower scene in *Psycho*, but we found out that
Karo Syrup was cheaper, and looked just as good. On black and white
film, Karo looked more realistic than real blood.

For the action shots, Stevie's stunt double was a G.I. Joe with
life-like hair and Kung Fu grip. We dressed up the action figure (*never* a *doll*), inserted him into scale models, and then punished him in
various ways. One day during summer vacation—this was the year
before Stevie died, in 1991—we threw the Joe off the side of the
quarry about fifty times. It was ninety-degrees and ninety-percent
humidity, and I was losing interest in the Chronicles. But there was
nothing else to do, and Stevie swore it was a critical scene that he
needed me to film. Rocket Boy's starfighter had been hit, and his
escape pod had burned up in reentry (or something), and Rocket Boy
was supposed to parachute the rest of the way down. So Stevie stood
at the top of the cliff with a handkerchief bunched around Joe, and
I was at the bottom of the pit with the Super-8 shooting up into the
sun. There was no wind down there and no shade and sweat was
pouring off me.

And the fucking handkerchief would *not* come open. Joe just
crashed into the rocks, over and over. And every time he hit, Stevie

yelled down, Did you get it? Did you get it? Like there was anything to get.

After two hours Joe's face was looking like he'd been in a knife fight. I climbed out of the hole with the camera hanging from a strap around my neck, yelling that it was his turn to sit in the pit and broil.

Stevie was pulling on his shirt. His pale skin had turned bright pink, but before he tugged down the shirt I saw a dark stripe on his chest.

What the hell is that? I said.

This? He lifted his shirt. A long, thin welt, like a snake wending its way from his collarbone to his navel. That's nothing.

What did he use on you?

Stevie shrugged. One of my cables.

Holy shit, I said. That had to kill.

He shrugged. Not really. Pain's just a signal from the equipment. Like a telephone ring. It only has to hurt if you decide it should hurt.

He'd been talking like this all summer. The body is a machine, the mind is a pilot.

Yeah, I said, you're a regular man of steel.

I'll prove it to you, he said. Punch me.

Oh you don't want me to punch you, I said.

This is an ugly thing that Stevie brought out in me. I was bigger than him, stronger than him. I could put him in unbreakable head-locks, manhandle him into closets, make him cry if I wanted. I didn't do it often, but I liked knowing I could.

So he tried to slap me and I knocked his hand away. Come on, come on, he said, and kept slapping. I fended him off, and flicked a few shots at his chin. He started swinging wildly, and I pushed his arms away, and then his fist connected with my lip. That pissed me off. So I socked him in the side of the head.

He spun away from me, a hand over his ear. See? he said. His eyes were welling with tears, but he made himself laugh. Okay, good, he said.

He charged at me again, throwing crazy punches, a tantrum, going for velocity and damage and not even trying to protect himself. You could only fight like this with your brother, or your best friend.

We went on like that for a while, until I was straddled on top of him, my fist raised. But I couldn't hit him while he was flat on the ground, bleeding, and smiling at me.

He dabbed at his nose, and held up his red hand. Sprung a leak, he said.

Sure, I said, and it doesn't hurt a bit.

Nope.

Why'd you start crying then?

He shoved me off him. Nobody has *total control*, he said condescendingly. Too many systems are on automatic. But I'm working on it.

I don't remember what I said at that point. Some crack.

Stevie shook his head and pulled up his shirt. You think this is me. *This*, he said, running a finger down the bruise, is hull damage.

He grinned. The pilot, he said, is intact. He pointed at his eye. Behind there. Can you see me? Hey man, I'm waving at you.


"It must be hard to do this again," I said. We were in her back yard, sitting on the same green wrought-iron patio furniture they'd always had.

"You mean, at my age." She was breastfeeding William, holding him close with a blanket draped over her shoulder and covering her breast, but he was a big guy, and kept yanking off the blanket. I kept looking away.

"No! Well—"

"It's all right. You know, I didn't breastfeed Steven. Back then, formula was supposed to be better. You were a formula baby, too." She glanced up at me. "I never would have planned on this. But it happened, and I wouldn't trade him back."

"Of course not."

"Still, it'll be good to get away." Mr. Spero was going to a convention over the weekend, and she was taking William to her sister's house in Cedar Falls. "Thank you for watching the house, by the way."

"Not a problem. That's what neighbors are for."

The baby's head lolled sideways, eyes half closed. He looked drunk. She dabbed the thin milk from the corner of his lips, and he smiled. Then she did something to her bra, and deftly buttoned her shirt. All with one hand.

"Do you still have any of Stevie's movies?" I asked. She didn't look up. "You know, the videos, or the film cans?"

She shook her head slightly, still not looking at me. "I don't think so. I'm sure they're gone."

"Gone where?"

"We gave a lot of stuff away, after. Boxes and boxes."

The car pulled up behind me, the engine loud against the side of the house. I turned around, putting a smile on my face.

Mr. Spero stepped out of the car, his suit coat over one arm. "Well look what the cat dragged in." He said it lightly, a little chuckle behind it.

"Hello, Mr. Spero."

"Claire told me you'd moved in. I couldn't believe it." He draped his jacket over the back of one of the patio chairs. His shoes were still shiny, his bright yellow tie still cinched, as if important clients might ring the bell at any moment. "Now where's my boy?"

He took the child from Mrs. Spero and turned to me. "He's a big one, isn't he? What a monster!"

It was true. He looked like he'd be much bigger than Stevie, more solid.

"Careful, I just fed him," Mrs. Spero said. "I need to go turn on the oven." She disappeared into the house, and Mr. Spero jiggled the boy in his arms.

"So what brings you back to our little town, Timmy? It can't be the job prospects."

"I work over the Internet," I said. "My office can be anywhere."

"The Internet? I thought you guys all went out of business." The baby started to fuss, and Mr. Spero sat down where Claire had been. "There we go, there we go." He patted his back, and the baby twisted his head back and forth, knuckles crammed into a slobbering mouth.

"So why come back here?" Mr. Spero said. "I'd think that someone in your situation would want to be near family."

"Situation?" I kept my face blank. I waited for him to glance at the crutches leaning against my chair, or the bulge under my shirt from the flange and colostomy bag. Just glance.

He stared at me over the top of the baby, and huffed. "Never mind. No one could ever tell you what to do. Or your dad, either." The baby pushed up on his legs and grabbed one of his father's ears, and Mr. Spero shook his head back and forth playfully.

"I like this town," I lied. "And somebody has to come back. To watch over the neighborhood. Make sure it stays a nice place to raise kids."

"So you sit in your room and type on your computer. That's a hell of a job."

"I analyze quality control data for a parts manufacturer."

The baby grabbed an eyebrow, and Mr. Spero said "Ouch!" and pulled his face away. He held the baby's hands, and the boy stood shakily. Mr. Spero bounced his legs, and the baby went up and down, grunting: *hyuh-hyuh-hyuh*.

"I try to explain catastrophic failure," I said. "Like when a tire blows out, or an O-ring disintegrates on lift-off."

"Really," Mr. Spero said. The baby grinned madly. Mr. Spero chuckled and bounced him higher.

"Estimating catastrophe time is a different problem, statistically, than estimating gradual wear—you get a Weibull distribution rather than a normal curve. We do test-to-failure runs, and just try to grind a part into dust. Everything fails eventually. My job is to figure out why some things fall apart too soon. I sort through all the variables and find out which ones contributed to failure."

He ignored me. William looked ecstatic.

"A lot of the time, it's because of some flaw from early in the manufacturing process, like a hairline crack in the seal, say."

The baby's head dropped forward, and a mouthful of gray fluid dumped onto Mr. Spero's shirt. William grinned, ready to play.

"Damn it! Claire! *Claire!*" He thrust the baby away from him, dangling it in the air. The child spit up again, spattering the floor, and started to howl.

Claire rushed out of the house, a towel already in her hand. "Were you throwing him around? You know what he's like after—"

"Christ, Claire, can you just get him off me?"

She took the baby from him and Mr. Spero grabbed the towel from her. He dabbed at his chest. "I'm too fucking old for this," he said.

I held up my arms. "Here, let me take him."

Mr. Spero threw down the towel and stomped into the house, already unbuttoning his shirt.

She shook her head. "I need to clean him up," she said. "Maybe you could come back after . . ."

"Naw, I've got to get going anyway," I said. "And you've got to pack. Enjoy your trip. I'll take care of things here."

*

I said that he was my best friend. That's a lie. Sophomore year, I stopped making night runs with him, I stopped helping with the movies. I barely talked to him at school. I'd gotten onto the soccer team, and I had a group of good friends, some of them seniors. I had a girlfriend. What the hell did I need Stevie for?

He never stopped pestering me. I remember when he stopped me in the hall to tell me he'd spent spring break building a full-size starfighter out of silver-painted plywood.

See? He flipped open his notebook to his storyboards. He showed me a cartoon of a stick figure climbing into the hatch of a starfighter. The ship was maybe three times taller than the pilot, and drawn in much more detail.

You built this?

It's almost done, he said. He flipped pages. Now, he said, we switch from live-action to the models.

The panels showed the launch, then a far shot of the starfighter rising through the clouds, then a closer shot of the ship outlined against black space.

Look, he said. It's all there. It's a two-stage rocket.

God, he could be so pathetic. I don't remember any bruises on him that day, though at some point I'd stopped looking. It was easier to stop worrying about Stevie in the winter. With our windows closed we couldn't hear Mr. Spero shouting at him.

I took the book from him. Jagged pen strokes showed the starfighter exploding. What's this? Lasers or something?

The NovaWeapon, he said. It hits his ship.

In the next panel, Rocket Boy ejects. The last picture showed him in close-up—the stick figure filled up most of the frame, any-way—floating in space.

He can't eject into space, I said. He doesn't have a space suit. He'd die in ten seconds.

We'll make a suit, Stevie said.

I tossed the notebook back to him. Don't be a fucking retard, I said.

*

Even in the dark, I could tell that there was nothing left of Stevie's old bedroom. The shelves crammed full of plastic models were gone. The paneling and wallpaper had been pulled down, the walls painted glossy white and trimmed in pastel blue. The bed was gone too, replaced by a crib. The bed frame had been blond wood, with panels in the headboard where Stevie kept his paperbacks, videotapes, Super-8 cassettes, and cans of developed film. Had they really given everything away?

I toured the rest of the house in the dark, not wanting to turn on the lights and alert the neighbors. The basement had been divided into rooms and partially finished, but the other rooms looked pretty much as I remembered. The main difference was that every trace of Stevie, except for a few pictures, had been removed.

It took me most of Friday night and part of Saturday to install the cameras and mikes and routers. I needed spots that were high up, with wide angles. The finished rooms in the basement were easy, because the drop ceiling tiles could be pushed out of the way. The upstairs rooms were harder. These ranches didn't have much of an attic, just crawl spaces above the house and garage that you accessed through little square holes. The work was draining: hours balanced on the beams trying not to put a leg through the insulation and plaster. I was used to working one-legged, but after a half hour I was sweating and trembling from exertion, and itching like mad from the insulation. I had to take a lot of breaks.

I ran power from the light fixtures, drilled down through the plaster ceiling, and popped the little fish-eyes into them. Each camera was about as big as a fifty-cent piece, and most of that was above the ceiling. The lenses themselves were smaller than a dime. I wired the circuit boards on the backs of the cameras to the digital switcher, which was broadcasting at 2.4 gigahertz. I put the antenna next to the wall facing my house. According to the specs I didn't need the antenna—I should have been able to pick up the cam signals from 700 feet away. But if there's anything my day job has taught me, it's that spec-writers lie.

Only three cameras came on without a hitch. The others had cabling problems of one type or another, and I had to spend another two hours crawling around in the attic. Last, I had to vacuum all the plaster that had dropped onto the floors. The house would be cleaner than they'd left it.

By Saturday night I had everything working. I could sit at my desk and tab through most of the rooms in the house from my PC.

I went in again Sunday morning, and this time I actually watered the plants. Then I went room by room and searched every closet, trunk, and suitcase, looking for anything of Stevie's. I spent a lot of time in the storage room, going through Rubbermaid containers filled with Christmas decorations, photo albums, and old clothes. Under the basement workbench, hidden behind a toolbox, I found two new Jim Beam bottles, one empty, the other down to a couple brown inches, with a plastic cup over the neck. I put them back exactly as I'd found them.

Except for one box of grade school papers, there was nothing of Stevie's in the house.

It wasn't until nearly noon that I remembered the attic space above the garage. I had no idea when the Spero's were coming back. But I had to check it out.

I left my crutches on the floor of the garage and hauled and hopped my way up the stepladder to the square hole. I pushed aside the lid and groped above my head until I found the string for the light.

The junk was half-familiar, stuff that could have come from my own family. A box for a plastic Christmas tree, a rotary fan, a set of kitchen chairs I remembered, taped together boxes with pictures of toaster ovens and car stereos and power tools. I stumped deeper into darkness, toward a stack of cardboard boxes. The seams were thickly taped.

I used my keys to poke and saw through the tape. The first box I opened contained a metal box, like a typewriter case. "Ames H.S. Library" was stenciled on the side. I flipped the metal clasps and pulled off the top.

It was the Super-8 film projector. There was even a spool of film on the arm.

I knew it. I knew they hadn't thrown it away.

I worked my way through the other boxes, unfolding the cardboard flaps and hauling things into the light. It was all there: the notebooks, the videotapes, the film cans. Even the models—two boxes filled with nothing but plastic spaceships and props.

\*

I'll pay you, he said.

He was standing under my window, in broad daylight. He wore black cargo pants, shiny black combat boots. He even had on dark eye shadow. He looked like a dork.

Why don't you come to the front door like everybody else, I said to him. And then: How much?

Ten bucks. It's the last scene. The last time I'll ever ask you. All you have to do is hold the camera.

I'm not going to sneak out of my window for ten bucks.

Twenty bucks. Come on, you know you have to see this.

It was a Saturday afternoon, and I didn't have anything else to do. I went out through the back door, though I made sure nobody saw me.

First, give me the twenty, I said.

He looked annoyed. You're going to take the money?

I held out my hand. I didn't want it—I just wanted to see if he had it. And if he'd really pay me.

He handed me two tens, and I stuffed them in my pocket. All right, I said. You've hired a camera man.


My house became a studio. The bedroom office was already wired to receive the video broadcasts from my cameras. In the living room I moved the couch to face the large blank wall, and set up the projector on the end table. I pushed the TV and VCR into the corner, so I could watch the videos without leaving the couch. I spent my nights moving between the two rooms, watching whatever I was in the mood for.

That first Sunday, before the Spero's had even returned, I watched the first tape. Stevie had numbered the videotapes and film cans, so I was able to place them in order. Chapter One of the NovaWeapon Chronicles featured a twelve-year-old Stevie and Timmy, and interminable scenes of plastic models being jerked along on fishing line.

I expected it to be worse than I remembered. But it was worse even than that.

I started watching with the idea that I would capture the interesting or well-done bits and edit them into something coherent. But the videos were almost unwatchable. Often the screen was so dark I couldn't tell what was happening, and most of the time I couldn't remember what we'd intended. I was the only person on the planet who could possibly appreciate the NovaWeapon Chronicles, and I was fast-forwarding through hours of it.

The stream of images from next door, however, never stopped flowing, and those never bored me. Even when I was working, I kept a window open on my desktop that I could maximize whenever something caught my eye: Mrs. Spero mopping the kitchen, barefoot. Mr. Spero slipping into the basement and back in less than a minute, like a magic trick. I'd never been that interested in webcams, or reality shows, but this was riveting.

I could follow them from room to room, with a few exceptions. I hadn't put cameras outside, or in the garage. And I hadn't put any in the master bedroom or bathroom. I didn't want to be able to see the Spero's naked, or having sex, because I knew I'd watch. Still, it was a small house. I'd like to say that I shut down the window the first time I saw Mrs. Spero walk from the bathroom to the bedroom with a towel around her waist. I never even reached for the mouse.

I found the televised William even more fascinating than the audio-only version. When he slept, he abandoned himself totally: jaw slack, arms thrown to the side. When he cried, he threw his entire body into it. I admired his focus. Sometimes when he was crawling toward a certain toy, or reaching toward the airplanes that dangled above his bed, I could *see* him thinking.

I was surprised that when he cried in the middle of the night, it was mostly Mr. Spero who got up to hold him. He picked up William without a word, and walked around the house like a sleepwalker, letting the boy cry himself out. After work, he threw William around like he had on the patio that day. He rarely changed diapers or bathed the child, but he did get on the floor and play with him.

Had he been like this with Stevie, at first? Before Stevie crossed him for the first time, at the wrong time? Perhaps he liked his children better when they were small and helpless and compliant.

I waited for that moment when Mr. or Mrs. Spero would look up at the ceiling, squint at the discolored plaster, and go get the stepladder. But no one looked at the ceilings except William. Sometimes he'd be on his back, staring straight up at the camera, and I'd pretend that he knew. That some baby instinct told him I was up there, looking down on him. I'd wave at the screen. Hiya, Will. What are you thinking about, down there?

We walked out to the quarry, Stevie lugging the camera and a gym bag. The starfighter was set up on the field on the other side of the pit. It was twenty-two feet tall, sitting nose up like the shuttle before launch. The body was primer gray, with the red and black Counter-Revolutionary StarForce logos on each stubby wing. The foil rims around the thrusters glinted like hammered metal.

Holy cow, I said. You really did it.

It was only when we moved around the side that I could see that the back was unfinished. The cylindrical body was hollow, the two ends held together with crosshatched strips of unpainted wood.

The back doesn't matter, he said. We'll only film it from the front.

On the grass behind the ship were paint cans and stacks of cloth and empty milk jugs. One huge cardboard box overflowed with crumpled brown plastic containers. Stevie had been out here a lot.

I helped him lift his dad's extension ladder out of the grass, and we propped it up against the side of the ship. The structure shuddered and swayed.

I climbed up, excited despite myself. Stevie had managed to make a curved clear hatch out of two sheets of Plexiglas. It fastened to a wooden crossbar with big hinges, so you could swing it open and closed. There was a little platform in there, with a metal folding chair on its back, so Stevie could sit with his face to the sky. The flight stick was a black broom handle, the instrument panel a slab of wood with painted-on controls labeled in the alien alphabet we'd made up in eighth grade.

A car battery sat next to the chair, close to where Stevie's head would be. The red and black clamps of jumper cables lay next to the battery, unattached. The cable disappeared through a hole in the platform.

What's the battery for?

Special effects, he said.

*

Even with work and hours spent watching William, I skimmed through the dozens of taped chapters in a week. I promised myself I'd take more time with the Super-8 footage.

The films required more of a ritual. Before viewing each reel I spooled through it by hand, reconnecting the sections where the splices had broken. Stevie had sometimes used real splicing tape, but more often he'd used Scotch tape that had yellowed and split. The Bell and Howell projector was touchy. I learned how to thread the film with a loop of slack to stop it from stuttering. I learned how to replace the lamps, ordered over the Internet from a warehouse in Oregon.

The filmed chapters were much better than the tapes. Shorter, for one. The film cost money to develop, so we couldn't let things just run on and on. And Stevie had edited down even the short scenes. His technique matured from reel to reel: he paid attention to time of day and the location of props, he showed exterior shots before jumping to the interior, and he cut cleanly between characters. Scenes had rhythm.

And I realized that Stevie was right: Video *was* a cold medium. It's too *specific*: all harsh colors and wind noise and tinny dialogue. Better to reduce to shades of gray and silence, and develop slowly in darkness. I don't know where the warmth comes from. Maybe something in the act of projection: the lamp blasting each frame onto the screen, suffusing it with light, reconstituting each tree and person and building in photons.

I took my time. I watched only one reel a night, though I allowed myself to watch it multiple times. After all, there was no reason to hurry. There was no final reel. Once there'd been a Super-8 cassette, undeveloped, pulled from the wreckage of the camera. Maybe it still existed. Maybe the police still had it, or the Spero's, hidden in some niche I hadn't found. Or maybe they'd burned it, and no one would ever see it.

It didn't matter. I knew how the story ended.

Perhaps that was part of the attraction of my little cameras. Channel William, his ongoing saga broadcast live to my PC, was never in re-runs. Some nights I slept on the futon in the office, so I could check on him just by opening my eyes. I'd long since stopped feeling like a voyeur. I felt like I was in the house with them, intangible and invisible. The family ghost.

\*

I climbed down the ladder, shaking my head at how much work he'd put in. The whole structure swayed with my weight.

Is that thing going to hold you? I asked.

It doesn't have to stay up long, he said. This is the last scene I need to film.

How can this be the last scene? What about ejecting into space, the whole space suit thing? How can you have him ejecting before you even launch?

Don't be a fucking retard, he said, in the same snotty tone I'd used. This is the last scene I need to *film*. I already finished the other stuff. Nobody films in sequence. I'll put it all back together in the editing room.

You mean your basement.

He rolled his eyes.

So what did you make the space suit out of? I asked.

There is no space suit.

And when he ejects, what? Suffocates? Explodes in the vacuum?

Stevie didn't answer.

Really? Rocket Boy dies?

What do you care? he said finally.

I started laughing. Come on, five years of the NovaWeapon Chronicles and they just shoot him out of the sky and he *dies?* That's like killing off Luke Skywalker.

Obi-Wan died, he said, and came back in the sequels.

Only as a ghost. Ghosts don't count.

Stevie ignored me. He pulled off his T-shirt and squatted to open the gym bag. His back was covered with bruises so blue they were almost black.

Holy shit, I said.

He pulled the black mesh shirt out of the bag. Don't worry about it, he said. Just hull damage, right? He pulled on the shirt, and he was Rocket Boy again.

There were any number of things I could have said or done. New ones still occur to me.

Listen, Stevie said. I want a long shot—an establishing shot. He handed me the notebook, page open to the storyboards.

Just like that, he said. Stand over there by the fence. Film me getting into the rocket, and closing the hatch. Make sure you get me moving inside the cockpit, so they know it's not a model. Just keep filming until I tell you to stop, got it? Don't turn off the camera.

Obi-Wan was only a supporting character, I said, and started walking across the field.

The night I should have been paying the most attention, I was in bed, in the next room. I didn't even have the scanner on. The screams came through the computer speakers in the office.

I don't know how long they'd been going on before they woke me. Maybe only seconds. Maybe minutes. I bolted out of bed and stumble-hopped down the hall without my crutches. I swiveled the monitor to face me.

The baby was on the floor, shrieking. Mr. Spero stood over him, dressed only in pajama bottoms, his fists on his hips.

William had never made a sound like this before. It was a *screech*, as if he'd been cut or burnt.

Mr. Spero abruptly squatted, grabbed the baby under the armpits, and carried him out of the room. William was still screaming. I switched to the hall camera, but Mr. Spero walked straight into the master bedroom and I lost him again.

Fuck. I clicked through the camera views, but I couldn't see a thing. But I could still hear William. That piercing cry was being picked up by all the microphones.

I rushed back to the bedroom and pulled on a pair of sweats and a T-shirt that pulled down over flange and bag. I grabbed my crutches and lurched outside, bare toes scuffing the pavement as I crossed the two driveways.

I mashed the doorbell, then without waiting for an answer, banged on the wooden door and yelled. "Open the door! Now! Open the door!"

No one answered. I could still hear William screaming. I twisted the doorknob, but it was locked. "Mr. Spero! Where are you? Where's the baby?"

The door flew open. Mr. Spero's skin under his robe was fish white. "What the hell do you want?" he said, shocked.

I pushed forward, and got inside the frame of the door. "Show me the baby."

"Get the hell out of my house!"

"Show me William."

He started to close the door, but I lunged forward, got another leg inside. Mr. Spero raised his right fist.

"What are you going to do, Mr. Spero. Hit me?"

I wanted it. Local Man Hits Crippled Neighbor. I wasn't worried about being hurt—this body's only a vehicle, after all.

He slammed the door back against the wall. "Get out of my fucking house."

"Not until you show me the baby."

Mrs. Spero came into the room, wearing a green nightgown, holding William on her shoulder. He was quiet now.

She frowned at me. "Tim? It's two A.M."

"I know, I just—"

I couldn't say, what was he doing on the floor? Did Mr. Spero drop him? Throw him on the ground?

"I heard him screaming."

"Babies do that," Mr. Spero said.

I ignored him, and looked only at Mrs. Spero. "He's all right? Are you sure?"

She turned slightly, so I could see William's face. His eyes were screwed up tight, and he was sobbing, but he didn't look bruised or hurt.

"Is he all right?"

"He had a stomach cramp," she said. "He's fine."

My memory is a series of still images, squared off by the viewfinder.

Stevie on the first rung of the ladder, knee raised, hands gripping the rails.

Higher, a dark look over his shoulder—not toward me, but toward some point in the distance, perhaps the enemy troops flying in.

At the top, the lid of the cockpit open like a beetle's wing, and Stevie gazing into the crowded compartment.

\*

From my desk I watched her place the baby in his crib. He had fallen asleep in her arms, and barely stirred as she laid him on the mattress. Mr. and Mrs. Spero exchanged only a few words, then disappeared into their bedroom.

I sat in front of the PC for an hour, watching and listening. William's face was dimly lit from his nightlight. The house was absolutely still except for the sound of his breathing.

I went into the living room, too wired to sleep myself. I picked up the can of film I'd set aside for tomorrow night's viewing. It was the last can from Stevie's boxes, the last reel before the never-developed Last Reel.

I checked the film, going slow because it was heavily edited, spliced every dozen frames. He'd worked hard on this one. Eventually I threaded it into the projector and flicked on the lamp.

No sound except the clack of sprockets in the brittle film. The titles came up: a hand-stenciled sign. "The NovaWeapon Chronicles." Flick, and the sign changed. "Final Chapter."

I frowned. So far, Stevie had never made a chapter that spanned two reels. The movie couldn't be complete without the scene I'd filmed.

The screen flashed—sun glare on the lens—and out of the white a tiny silhouette plummeted out of the sky. The camera cut to another angle: the same figure, still far away, falling and tumbling, arms and legs outstretched. Then another cut, and another, each shot from a slightly different angle, and the figure fell closer and closer.

I saw a flash of rocks in the background. It was the quarry. I remembered filming it, shooting up from the bottom of the pit, staring into the sun.

And then there were new images, things that Stevie had filmed himself.

I finished the reel, rewound it, watched it again.

A dark shape in the Plexiglas bubble like the pupil of an eye, his hand lifted in a StarForce salute.

\*

I answered the door still wearing the sweats and T-shirt I'd pulled on the night before.

She held a squirming William on one hip. She turned toward the door as it opened, and smiled in a way that seemed rehearsed.

"Tim, I wanted—are you all right?"

"I'm fine." My eyes felt raw. I probably looked like hell.

She paused, and then nodded. William pulled at her shoulders. "I'd like to talk about last night."

"Sure."

She smiled again, nervous. "Let's not do this on the front step. This boy is heavy."

William bent backwards over her arm, sure that it was impossible for his mother to drop him. He looked fine. Absolutely fine.

Mrs. Spero had never come into my yard before, much less my house. I glanced behind me. The drapes were pulled, and the room was dim. The box full of films and tapes sat in plain sight on the floor. The projector was next to the couch, aimed at the wall.

"It's kind of a mess."

"I promise not to tell your mom," she said. A thin smile.

I didn't open the door. "I'm sorry if I upset you," I said.

"I know what you're doing, Tim."

My face went hot, and I smiled automatically. "Yeah?"

"You're looking out for me. For the baby. But you don't have to do that."

"I don't? That's what neighbors do for each other."

"John's different now. He's good with William."

"Hey, that's great," I said. "That's really good."

"You don't believe me."

"I'd like to believe you. Does it matter? I hope you're right."

William squawked at me, excited but serious, frowning like Alfred Hitchcock. I held my hands out to him, and he grabbed my fingers, hard. I laughed.

"He stopped drinking, Tim." She waited until I looked at her. "You know he used to drink?"

I shrugged, still holding William's hands. I'd only figured this out later, after college, after I'd met a few people who were in recovery. When I was a kid, I'd noticed Mr. Spero always had a drink in his hand. But he wasn't a *drunk*. That was Otis on the *Andy Griffith Show*. "I guess that's a pretty good excuse," I said lightly.

"It's not an *excuse!*"

I dropped William's hands, and he leaned toward me. Mrs. Spero shifted him higher on her hip.

"That's not what I'm saying," she said, her calm voice back again. "But you have to understand, he was a different person then. He shouldn't have been so hard on Stevie, but—"

I stared at her. *Hard on him?* Did she not know? Hadn't she seen the bruises?

No, of course not. She hadn't seen a thing. None of us had.

"Tim, people can change. There are second chances. I know you may not want to believe this, but after Steven's suicide—"

"It wasn't suicide." I struggled to keep my voice level.

"What?"

"He showed me the storyboards. It wasn't a suicide. It was a plan, in two stages, like—"

"Tim, stop . . ."

"It was a *launch*. The starfighter is destroyed, but Rocket Boy ejects. The pilot is intact."

Mrs. Spero shook her head, her eyes wet. "Oh, Tim." Her voice was full of pity. For me.

"There's something you need to see," I said.

The ship, splintered with light. In the middle distance, the hint of bright metal and wooden shards, blurred by speed and spin, slicing toward the lens.

We sat on the couch like a little family, William between us, sitting up by himself and obviously pleased. Mrs. Spero regarded the blank wall, her face composed. She hadn't commented on the projector, or the box full of videotapes and film cans. She must have recognized them.

I turned on the projector lamp and the light hit the white wall, askew. I adjusted one of the legs and the image straightened. The machine chattered through the blank leader tape.

William ignored the light and sound. He abruptly threw himself forward, making for the floor, and Mrs. Spero automatically put out a hand.

"Could I hold him?" I asked.

She nodded, her attention already on the flickering wall, and I moved my hands under his arms. I was surprised how heavy he was. I sat him on my lap, facing me. He was unimpressed.

The opening titles appeared. The final chapter. If she was surprised, she didn't show it. I might have been showing her the dense data tables I worked with.

In silence we watched the tiny figure falling out of the sky, falling out of the light. Reentry. The figure drew closer, until finally the rock walls flashed up and Rocket Boy hit the ground.

The camera switched to a point just above the pit floor, tilted slightly down. The sheet—the parachute—settled over the ground and covered a man-shaped lump. Touch down.

Mrs. Spero looked at me.

"Just watch," I said. "He filmed this himself." Before the explosion, before the Death of Rocket Boy.

*Nobody films in sequence.*

William twisted around, looking for his mother. "Don't worry," I said. "She's right there. I got you." I jiggled him on my good knee, wondering at what frequency and duration his stomach became unstable.

The screen darkened. It was night, and the camera looked down from the top of the quarry. At the bottom, the sheet reflected the moonlight. It was too big to be our handkerchief, and the lump it covered too long to be G.I. Joe.

The camera switched to the floor of the pit, tripod level. The "parachute" glowed prettily, but it was obviously just an ordinary cotton sheet, with none of the sheen of silk.

The sheet moved, and a naked arm reached out, fingers twitching. I had to smile, imagining the melodramatic background music Stevie would have wanted. The arm was streaked with fake-looking blood. Too pale, too shiny. He should have used Karo.

William pulled at my T-shirt, trying to get his feet under him. On screen, Rocket Boy tossed back the sheet.

"Oh God," Mrs. Spero said.

Stevie was curled into a fetal position, naked. The blood described rivulets across his arms and neck. His back was covered with dark blotches—bruises. On film, they were too flat, too black, like holes through his pale skin, as unconvincing as the blood.

Stevie slowly got to his feet, facing the camera. Naked, pale skin shining. He looked up to the stars.

"The Return of Rocket Boy," I said to her.

Rocket Boy raised his arms in triumph, held them there. The screen went black.

Mrs. Spero sobbed almost silently, her shoulders jerking with ragged breaths.

The last of the film ejected. The reel continued to spin, the tail of film slapping the body of the projector. Mrs. Spero stared at the square of empty light.

William yanked at the collar of my shirt. I lifted him in the air, and his face cracked open into a wild grin. His eyes were bright.

I recognized that look.

I tilted him left, right, flying him in my arms, and he cackled. Hey there, little man. Can you see me in there? I'm waving at you.

# STORY NOTES

This section of the book is for my friend Gary Delafield, who buys short story collections based almost solely on whether they include author introductions, front notes, end notes, or anecdotes about the writing life. Sometimes he even reads the stories.

I have to admit that I love story notes, too. Maybe it's because when I was first trying to learn how to write, I thought these tidbits and asides would contain clues, the secrets to telling a story, or offer me some glimpse of the fabulous life of an author that awaited me. I was almost always disappointed—and if that's what you're looking for, you will be, too.

These remarks are tucked away at the back of the book because I hope you read the story before reading its corresponding note. I've not policed myself for spoilers, and I may very well ruin the story for you. But then again, if you're like Gary, you may not be planning on reading the story unless the note gets you interested. In that case, have at it!

## "Second Person, Present Tense"

This story is about a weird neurological fact that has bothered me for years: experiments since the '70s have proved that "consciousness" is in some cases a post-decision phenomena. Before you decide to, say, lift a finger, your unconscious brain has not only already decided to move that finger, but sent the command to the muscle, up to a half second before "you" decide to move it. Weird, eh? So, if consciousness is an add-on, what would a brain and body look like without consciousness? This is a thought experiment that philosophy of consciousness guys call the zombie problem—what, exactly, do we need consciousness for?

On my website I go into a lot more detail about the science behind the story, and list some of the books and articles I found helpful. But here I'd like to talk about two other things that went into the story. First is the family background. Like Theresa in the story,

I grew up Southern Baptist. I even sang in a Gospel quartet through high school and into college. But at the same time I was reading a lot of science fiction, and raising questions that the kind folks in my church didn't know how to handle. SF's main message is, It could be different. The church's message is, This is the one true way. The cognitive dissonance was extreme, and I often felt like two people, a teenage experience probably not unique to me.

But I was not interested in demonizing the parents. I once may have been an estranged teenager, but now I'm a parent, and I know what it's like to fear for your children.

Another thing that guided the writing of this story was "The Runaway Bunny" by Margaret Wise Brown. When I was writing "Second Person . . ." we were reading Brown's book to our kids. It chokes me up every time. Because no matter what the child becomes—a fish, a crocus in a hidden garden—the mother changes too and goes after him. Finally, the bunny is exhausted by his mother's persistence, and says, I might as well stay home and be your little bunny. And the mother says, Have a carrot.

## "UNPOSSIBLE"

The first two fantasy books I ever read, not counting *Herbie the Love Bug*, were *The Phantom Tollbooth* and *The Last of the Really Great Whangdoodles*. If I read other fantasies first, I can't remember them, but these two books planted the virus that made me want to tell stories. They lit up my brain from the inside.

Fast forward a couple of decades, and my wife and I are reading those books aloud to our kids, along with *Where the Wild Things Are* and *My Father's Dragon* and eventually the Harry Potter books. As an adult I was struck by all the similarities in the tales, as well as to stories like *The Wizard of Oz* and *The Lion, the Witch and the Wardrobe*: the plucky young heroes, the magical vehicles and doorways, and the inevitable return home, which always seemed kind of sad. Reading them again with my children, I felt grateful to be able to re-enter those worlds (though only halfway; I would never again be pulled all the way up to my eyeballs as I was when I was ten). But I couldn't help wondering about the heroes themselves, who (with certain notable exceptions) were never able to return, and certainly not as an adult.

Around the same time, I started thinking about writing a story about Mr. Rogers. I'd watched him growing up, and he was still on the air when my kids were born. He was a kind of hero, a man who from all accounts was as kind and thoughtful in real life as he was on TV, and who genuinely cared about children. When he died, I thought about writing some kind of an homage, a story in which the children come to lift the old man onto the Magic Trolley, and bear him off to the Land of Make Believe. "Unpossible" was as close as I got.

## "Damascus"

This story came from the intersection of three ideas.

First, Temporal Lobe Epilepsy: After "Second Person, Present Tense," I'd built up a small library of books on consciousness and neurology, and I became interested in temporal lobe epilepsy—TLE. In V.S. Ramachandran's book, *Phantoms in the Brain*, he talks about TLE, and I later saw a television documentary in which we meet one of Ramachandran's patients (search on YouTube for Ramachandran and temporal lobe epilepsy and you should find it). What struck me is that the patient's hallucinations were accompanied by the certainty that he really was in contact with God. Certainty itself was a symptom.

Any talk of TLE eventually gets around to Michael Persinger, the Canadian researcher mentioned in the story. His "God Helmet," which he used to induce a feeling of "a presence" in his patients has failed to be replicated consistently (Richard Dawkins tried it, and said he felt only a sensation of relaxation), and may be a scientific dead end, but it was too good a detail not to use.

Second, "Your Own Personal Jesus": I knew the Depeche Mode original, but it was Johnny Cash's cover of the song that I listened to over and over while I wrote this story. From the Persinger experiments I'd decided that everyone's Jesus would appear differently, but I think it was because of this song that I decided that Paula's savior would take the form of a rock star beloved by her husband.

Third: Prions. In high school I read *Dream Park*, by Larry Niven and Steven Barnes, which mentioned Kuru, the laughing disease. Then along came Mad Cow disease, and the discovery that it and Kuru were both prion diseases, and I had my vector for a neurological disorder that could be passed on—and passed on through ritual. There must be plenty of horror stories that link holy communion with cannibalism—body of Christ for dinner, anyone?—but when I read about the sacramental aspect of cannibalism in Papua New Guinea tribes, I had found the foundation of my religion.

I wanted to tell the entire story of a religion, from its ecstatic, revelatory beginning, to the secret sharing among a small core of believers, to evangelization and mass conversion. The most difficult part of the story was working out the structure. I wanted to cover several years, so that meant flashbacks, but I wanted each track to have its own momentum and tension. I beat that outline like a dog until I had the shape I needed, and then I regularly broke the outline whenever I thought of something new I wanted to add, forcing me to start over again. I no longer remember how long it took me to write the story, and I don't think I want to know.

## "THE ILLUSTRATED BIOGRAPHY OF LORD GRIMM"

This is probably my angriest, most political story. I know, I know, it seems odd that a story about supervillains and superheroes could be so angry, but the war in Iraq was pissing me off. Remember "shock and awe"? The arrogance of the phrase, a marketing tagline for bombing the living shit out of human beings. During the early stages of the Iraq war, we were told that we "had to fight the terrorists over there, so we didn't have to fight them here." That strategy, unfortunately, depended on there being a finite number of terrorists, who were either buying plane tickets for the USA or staying home, depending on where the action was. We'd somehow lost track of the fact that the quickest way to turn a moderate into a radical was to kill their friends and relatives.

I wanted to tell the story of someone caught at ground level during one of these wars, watching a superpower flex its muscles. As a comic book geek, the metaphor was obvious. And I took as inspiration books like *Marvels*, by Kurt Busiek and Alex Ross, who told stories from the point of view of mere mortals caught in the crossfire.

I love comic books. I now write comics. But in Iraq, our government tried to turn a real war into a superhero tale, complete with swaggering good guys blithely leveling city blocks, irredeemable bad guys cowering in their palaces, and all but invisible bystanders.

Mission fucking accomplished.

See? I told you I was angry.

## "GARDENING AT NIGHT"

Here's a tip for you beginning writers out there: If you want to write a short story, don't start by writing a 400-page novel first. However, if you find yourself with a 400-page novel that just doesn't work, there are worse things to do than cutting it up for parts and selling what you can.

This is one of two stories in this collection (the other is "Dead Horse Point") that had its genesis in my first, unsold novel, *The Rust Jungle*. The novel had multiple point of view characters and alternating storylines that only gradually converged. One of those plotlines was about a down-on-his-luck temp worker named Reg, who fell in with a crazy homeless ex-scientist growing his own autonomous robots. I'd gotten interested in artificial life back in the '90s when I stumbled across a collection of science and technology articles called *The Reality Club*, and one of those articles was on artificial evolution. I soon hunted up everything I could find on the latest research, digging up terms like cellular automata, emergent behaviors, and "fast, cheap, and out of control." Some researchers were demonstrating evolutionary principles in virtual environments, and other folks were building modular robots. I think I was one of the first people to combine the two ideas. And as a boy who was raised up Southern Baptist, the link between software and hardware sounded a lot like those opening verses in John: "In the beginning was the Word . . . and the Word was made flesh." (Notice that in the story, Reg, that benighted atheist, attributes the verse to Genesis. This is not at all because the author forgot that the verses were in John. Nope.)

While I was writing the novel, New York and a few other cities were experiencing an outbreak of multi-drug resistant tuberculosis. As I read about the mechanisms of TB, I began to see all kinds of links between bacteria and robots, and how intelligent-seeming behavior—downright trickiness and what looked like *strategy*—could evolve from simple initial conditions.

But while the tech and the TB and some of the character names survived the transformation from novel to short story, most of the plot did not. In short stories, you have to streamline. So Reg the temp became Reg the roboticist, and the crazy homeless scientist of the novel became Eli the mentor, and Reg's son doesn't contract TB, the old man does . . . and so on. But I kept the setting of Salt Lake City, where

I'd lived for a year, and I kept the dinner with Cora, which is entirely based on my wife's recipes for lasagna and killer garlic bread.

## "PETIT MAL #1: GLASS"

I got an email from *Technology Review* magazine asking me to write a story, and the page rate was so wonderful I couldn't say no. But the conditions were strict: the story had to be 2000 words or less, it had to be hard SF, and it had to be about prisons and incarceration? Why? Because they already had a story about prisons and they thought it could be a theme.

I began frantically trolling for ideas. Luckily, my wife is a psychologist, and you can imagine the kinds of books that turn up in our house. Two of them were about psychopaths, AKA sociopaths (the terms are nearly interchangeable). I'd also been reading some reports in the popular press about mirror neurons as a possible explanation for why we feel empathy. The trick, then, was to tell a coherent story, including an explanation of the science, in so few words. The nods to *Alice's Adventures Through the Looking Glass* were added for my own amusement.

By the time I turned in my story, they'd dropped the theme. Algis Budrys had died, so they'd decided to run my story next to his. I didn't mind, though. Sometimes being told the exact size and shape of the box you have to fill makes you more creative, not less.

## "WHAT WE TAKE WHEN WE TAKE WHAT WE NEED"

This story had a complicated birth. In 1988, while at Clarion East, the science fiction and fantasy writing workshop, I wrote a story about a man who manufactured drugs in sacs and blisters on his skin, and about his son, who had inherited the ability. It was set in a non-specific far future, and it didn't arrive at any kind of ending. I tried to rewrite it several times over the years, setting it in the present day or the near future, rearranging the plot. I could never make it work, but the images stuck with me.

Years later I was writing a novel called *The Devil's Alphabet*, about a small Tennessee town named Switchcreek that had been struck by a gene-altering disease. The disease created three clades—three distinct strains of humanity—each with different physical characteristics. I gave the drug-oozing disease to one of the clades, a member of which was the main character's father.

But I still wanted to see if I could make the story of this father and son work as a short standalone piece, an (almost) two-character drawing room drama, albeit one with syringes and pus and addiction. Out went the clades, the background information on quantum evolution, and most of the other characters. Some of the remaining characters shared names with characters in the novel, but they were not those characters. And why not? *The Devil's Alphabet* was a novel that talked about parallel universes, so a story about an alternate Switchcreek seemed well within the rules of the game.

## "PETIT MAL #2: DIGITAL"

In some ways this is a companion piece to "The Continuing Adventures of Rocket Boy," which is all about the illusion that there is a self sitting behind your eyes. I wrote it to read aloud at Fractal 2010, a conference about science, technology, and the arts in Medellín, Colombia. I wanted something short and amusing that would be fun to perform, and liked the idea of reading most of the story with my left index finger in the air. I'd like to say it was a hit, but a good portion of the audience didn't speak English.

## "MESSAGE FROM THE BUBBLEGUM FACTORY"

Here's another story written on assignment. Chris Roberson had handed Lou Anders a copy of "The Illustrated Biography of Lord Grimm," and based on that, Lou invited me to write a story for *Masked*, an anthology of stories about superheroes and supervillains, written by both prose and comics writers. Lou's instructions were to avoid camp and metafiction—just write stories about living in a superheroic universe. I am chagrined to report that I immediately set about disobeying him.

I love comics, and now write them. But the big shared universes of DC and Marvel are messy, irrational places. *Everything* is true: magic, science, demons, mutations. Laws of physics are violated at random. Industrial accidents don't kill you, they give you powers. And everybody rises from the dead.

I wanted to write a science fiction story that would explain how such a universe could come to be. The secret mechanism of that shared universe would be the main problem of the story, and the solution. It would also circle back to my bugaboos about free will.

Some people have called this story metafictional, and rightly so. It has a protagonist who directly addresses the reader, and the story itself is what's under interrogation. But it is also a hard science fiction story, in which, unfortunately, there is space only to hint at the underlying science. (I plan at least two more episodes in this story, so explanations will be forthcoming.) But it is also a straight-ahead superhero story, featuring a supervillain prison breakout, something I've always wanted to write. My thanks to my college roommate, J.R. Jenks, the best gamemaster a guy ever had, who convinced me to keep the CyberYeti.

## "FREE, AND CLEAR"

Some stories are based on personal experience. Perhaps a little too personal.

At the time I wrote this, I suffered from terrible allergies. (These days, after burying the cat and moving into a house with almost no carpeting, I suffer from merely annoying allergies.) I did indeed go to a very New Agey massage therapist, told her about my allergies, and tried to relax as she went to work on my skull and back. She was no help whatsoever, except that she helped me get this story.

## "DEAD HORSE POINT"

As you may be able to guess from the story, Dead Horse Point is my favorite state park. When my wife and I lived in Utah we camped there several times, and a couple years ago we introduced our kids to its epic vistas and vertigo-inducing ledges. As a writer, the park was a ready made metaphor, if I could only find a story to fit.

The idea for Julia's condition—call it Attention Surplus Disorder—came years earlier. A friend of mine was a genuine mathematical prodigy and very likely a genius. When he was working on a tough problem, he could go into a trance-like state for *days*, barely talking to anyone, rarely making eye contact, and eating whatever was put in front of him. One day he told me that he very much wanted to have children. I told him, Dude, those kids would be *dead*.

Julia, Venya, and Kyle first showed up as characters in an unsold novel called *The Rust Jungle*. I kept coming back to the characters, and their strange relationship: the former helper, the current helper, and the genius they were supposed to support because, well, she was the genius. Science fiction stories are always about the genius who saves the world, with the loyal helpmeets in the background, where the little people are supposed to stand. It wasn't until I realized that the story wasn't about Julia that I figured out how to write the story.

Oh, and my genius friend? He's a wonderful father. Doesn't get as much math done these days, but he's happy.

### "IN THE WHEELS"

Ah, the first sale. Is there anything sweeter to a writer, or more likely to cause future embarrassment? I wrote the first draft of the story in the first weeks of Clarion. It ended with Zeke possessed, and Joey gazing off into the distance. A week later, Samuel Delany arrived as our new teacher, and he told me the story wasn't over until Joey went home. I rewrote the story, because when Chip Delany tells you to do something, you do it, damn it. I mean, the guy looks like God, and not the friendly New Testament version. After I showed him the new draft, he said, Congratulations, this will be your first sale. It was a pronouncement. Of course I believed him; He was God.

I can't read the story too closely without wanting to edit it. I've refrained from doing so, however, because it would be unfair to that kid at Clarion who wrote it, and unfair to the story. But if I squint, I can see some of the themes and tropes that I'd keep coming back to in stories and novels: the Bible verses, the rural setting, the demons that aren't quite demons, the point of view character who is the guy *next to* the coolest guy in the room. So, here is the story as it is, the first thing I ever wrote that was worth a damn. It turns out that I'm not too embarrassed about this story.

### "PETIT MAL #3: PERSISTENCE"

Another story about vision, and another response to "The Continuing Adventures of Rocket Boy." A lot of the lab work on consciousness starts with experimenting with vision, or talking to people with visual disturbances, and it's become clear that the eye is no camera, simply relaying what's "out there." Vision is instead the brain telling stories to itself, composing a meaningful scene—with actors, mood, intentions, and dramatic revelations—out of sometimes minimal sensory information. Oliver Sacks has written about patients with visual disturbances before, but in his latest book, *The Mind's Eye*, one of the patients is Oliver Sacks. I listened to an interview with him in which he described being treated for eye cancer in his right eye. He was washing his hands, then closed his eyes, and was startled to see the room still there in front of him. The illusion lasted for several seconds. I thought that was very interesting. But only a few seconds? That's no place to end a science fiction story.

## "The Continuing Adventures of Rocket Boy"

This is my second First Sale. For ten years I hadn't written any short stories, instead knitting away on a sprawling novel that would never see the light of day. But short story ideas kept percolating in the back of my brain. For years I'd been thinking about the illusion that we exist behind our eyes, each of us a homunculus steering the ungainly ship of a body. It seemed to me that that illusion would be particularly attractive to someone whose body was being abused—someone who wanted out of it.

I often find myself writing about the kind of intense friendships that boys can make—and later break. This was going to be one of those stories, so I set about borrowing details from my own childhood, and from the lives of my friends, including days making Super-8 horror films in my friend Ted's house.

But for the longest time I couldn't figure out how the story ended. And then I thought about those lunar capsules, returning to Earth after the rest of the rocket had burned out and fallen away, and I knew where Stevie had gone, he was coming back, and how I would return to science fiction.

# ABOUT YOU

You are born in 1965, in a suburb of Chicago. Sometime around third grade you read your first chapter book, the novelization of the movie *Herbie the Love Bug*, and you keep reading, so much so that your Southern relatives don't know what to make of you, though every birthday they buy you more books. You are an only son, the middle child between two sisters. You go to church three times a week, which renders you incapable of reading a page of any book, even a Hardy Boys mystery, without seeing a Christ metaphor. You write a few proto stories that make little sense. You go to college and double major in English and theatre, which makes you twice as unemployable as the usual liberal arts major, and write a few more stories that make little sense. You get married and find a job teaching high school.

Then in 1988 your wife says, have you heard about this Clarion thing? You attend the Clarion Writer's Workshop in East Lansing, Michigan, and suddenly the idea of writing fiction that might be published seems a little less like a pipe dream. You write a story about demons and drag racing, you send it to *F&SF*, and when you open that envelope to find a check you experience one of the top five moments in your life. You sell a couple more stories. You're on your way!

Or maybe not. Life gets busier. You move around the country as your wife finishes her Ph.D., and you switch jobs a couple times. You have a daughter, then a son. Your wife is trying to get tenure. You decide to write a novel, and you promise yourself that, no matter what, you will work on it at least two hours every . . . week. The results are predictable.

Ten years later you start over. Your children are older, your wife has tenure, and now you can carve out more time for writing. You throw out the novel (keeping some of the best bits for later). You write a story you've been thinking about, on and off, for ten years, and when Gordon van Gelder publishes it you think, okay, don't blow this. Keep writing.

And you do. You keep writing every day (or almost every day). Then, a few years later, when Patrick Swenson asks you to write an author bio for the short story collection, you write it in second person, present tense—you know, as an homage to your own story?—but in the end it starts to feel so *precious* and courage fails you and you deliver the standard third-person summary, a form that from the dawn of publishing has allowed authors to brag about themselves from behind a veil of faux-objectivity:

*In 2004 Daryl Gregory began to publish a string of stories that prompted Gary K. Wolfe to call him "amongst the most interesting of the newer writers to emerge in the past decade, and rapidly becoming one of the most unpredictable." The stories in this first collection, most of which originally appeared in* F&SF *and* Asimov's, *have been reprinted in ten year's best anthologies and have been translated into multiple languages. "Second Person, Present Tense" won the* Asimov's *Reader's Choice Award and was a finalist for the Sturgeon and Speculative Literature Foundation awards.*

*In 2008 his first novel,* Pandemonium, *won the Crawford award for best fantasy by a new writer and was a finalist for the World Fantasy Award. His second novel,* The Devil's Alphabet, *was named one of the five best SF books of the year by* Publisher's Weekly, *and was a finalist for the Philip K. Dick Award. His third novel,* Raising Stony Mayhall, *appeared from Del Rey Books in 2011. He lives in State College, Pennsylvania where he writes programming code, prose, and comics.*

You fool no one.

# ACKNOWLEDGEMENTS

I'm deeply indebted to the editors who not only first published these stories, but made them better. My thanks (in chronological order) to Ed Ferman, Gordon Van Gelder, Sheila Williams, Jonathan Strahan, Kristina Grifantini, and Lou Anders. My special thanks to Gordon and Sheila, who were so kind to this newcomer, and offered friendship and advice to a guy who was pretty clueless about the whole business.

My thanks as well to the editors who republished the stories in "best of" editions and foreign language anthologies, and brought my stories to a wider audience. David Hartwell and Kathryn Cramer in particular were early champions of these stories.

Before these stories saw print, however, there were many, many drafts, and many people who took the time to point out the flaws in the stories, or kept me from throwing out what worked. My thanks to my writing teachers, Damon Knight, Kate Wilhelm, Tim Powers, Lisa Goldstein, Samuel R. Delany, Kim Stanley Robinson, and Francois Camoin. I am especially grateful to the many friends and colleagues—Clarion classmates, fellow writers in workshops, patient relatives, guys with improbable names like Jack Skillingstead—who critiqued one or more of these stories. Three of these people have read nearly every page I've written for the past twenty years, and given me invaluable feedback and encouragement; Gary Delafield, Andrew Tisbert, and Kathy Bieschke, I love you folks.

Finally, my thanks to several professionals who made this book happen. Martha Millard worked her usual agent magic. Antonello Silverini, the artist behind the cover of the Italian version of *Pandemonium*, created the beautiful cover you see. Nancy Kress offered to write the introduction to the book, and her kind words have stunned this self-effacing Midwesterner. Last, but certainly not least, Patrick Swenson gave these stories a permanent home. Thank you all so much.

CPSIA information can be obtained at www.ICGtesting.com
Printed in the USA
BVOW08*1734151015

422625BV00002B/6/P